I0823267

PRAISE FOR *LOVE & OTHER MONSTERS*

"*Love & Other Monsters* is the reason to read historical fiction: a completely immersive voice and experience, transporting you out of your own time and place, landing you somewhere else entirely—where candlelight, the sublime Alpine landscape, and after-dinner debates of poetry and human nature all live beside the all-too-familiar feelings of longing, fear, and struggling to find one's place in life. Every time I picked up this book I felt like I was knocking on a door to another world."

—BEN SHATTUCK, AUTHOR OF *THE HISTORY OF SOUND*

"With perfect tone and remarkable skill, Emily Franklin brings to life the core writers of the Romantic literary movement while revealing the travails of one young woman who was at the center of it all but whose presence was erased. While others bore the fruits of fame, Claire Clairmont had no choice but to fall into the role so common for women of her time and ours: that of being pleasing, amiable, and invisible. With Franklin's gorgeous narrative full of wisdom about womanhood and art, the talents and hopes of Clairmont finally get the attention they deserve."

—MARJAN KAMALI, AUTHOR OF *THE LION WOMEN OF TEHRAN*

"Emily Franklin's novel is as thrilling and tempestuous as the storm-battered summer that inspired *Frankenstein*. With prose that is both elegant and urgent, she illuminates the tangled desires, rivalries, and creative fervor of these legendary figures—not as icons, but as flawed, yearning humans. Like my favorite Chekhov plays, *Love & Other Monsters* gives us a collision of restless artists, unrequited loves, and the longing for purpose that both fuels and frustrates creation. Franklin writes with a piercing compassion for her characters, revealing the comedy, tragedy and absurdity in their compulsive drive to connect. In Claire Clairmont's searching voice, we feel the pull between love and delusion, duty and independence, art and survival. This is a rich, haunting novel about the monsters among us, the ones we create, and the ones we harbor within ourselves."

—DAVID LINDSAY-ABAIRE, PULITZER PRIZE AND TONY AWARD–WINNING PLAYWRIGHT

"A rare literary achievement with prose as beautiful as a painting and a story that is propulsively page-turning. Claire Clairmont (stepsister to Mary Shelley) must forage for her sense of self in the summer of 1816, as she is beset and baffled by love and betrayal, genius and cruelty, passion and creativity, while living at the shores of Lake Geneva with writers as brilliant and moody as the descending storms. What was her role (whether forgotten or erased) in the lives and artistic development of Lord Byron, Percy Shelley, and her stepsister Mary's creation of *Frankenstein*? I could not put down this thought-provoking, poignant, well-researched yet wholly original novel."

—JENNIFER ROSNER, AUTHOR OF *ONCE WE WERE HOME*

"A gorgeous tour de force. Magnificent and fiercely told, *Love & Other Monsters* is at once a literary page-turner and a spellbinding coming-of-age novel. With her masterful gift for storytelling, Emily Franklin breathes life into an untold history that feels entirely relevant to our world today. With electric insight, she maps the shifting tensions between creativity and passion, artistic ambition, familial betrayal, and the risks of desire."

—DAWN TRIPP, AUTHOR OF *JACKIE*

"Emily Franklin brings the summer of 1816 to life through Claire Clairmont's vivid voice. Claire's initial pursuit of Lord Byron, the 'mad, bad, and dangerous to know' celebrity poet, is thrilling to read, and the unusual family unit of Claire, Mary, and Percy Shelley is nuanced and compelling. Franklin has written a book about a girl on a precipice, and the reader tumbles over it with her."

—KAREN E. BENDER, AUTHOR OF *THE WORDS OF DR. L*

"Emily Franklin's *Love & Other Monsters* is a gorgeous work of historical fiction that breathes life into the literary circle that shaped an era, yet widens its lens to reveal the story of Mary Shelley's sister Claire Clairmont, a woman too long left in the shadows. Told with meticulous and immersive historical detail, Franklin delivers a narrative that is both sweeping and intimate, with themes that are all too relevant today."

—JANE HEALEY, AUTHOR OF *THE WOMEN OF ARLINGTON HALL*

"*Love & Other Monsters* is an intricate and moving story about power dynamics, sisters, celebrity, lust, and the importance of art and storytelling. Claire Clairmont is a vibrant heroine, and I'm so glad Emily Franklin brought her into my life. I loved this book."

—ANNIE HARTNETT, AUTHOR OF *THE ROAD TO TENDER HEARTS*

"Let us each write a ghost story, Byron commands in the early pages of Emily Franklin's *Love & Other Monsters*, a thoroughly researched and intimately written story of sisterhood, celebrity, and obsession. While her more famous stepsister pens *Frankenstein*, writing alongside her already-married fiancé Percy Shelley, Claire Clairmont records the events of their wintery and wild summer on the shores of Lake Geneva. She explores the monstrous drive toward creativity in writers who may themselves be monsters, and the real life ghosts of those we quietly love, children we lose, and parts of ourselves that never get to bloom."

—MEG WAITE CLAYTON, AUTHOR OF *TYPEWRITER BEACH*

"*Love & Other Monsters* is at once a portrait of a passionate woman hemmed in by her time and place and an encounter with perennial questions: How is the self formed in relationship to others? What must we sacrifice for love? For art? Emily Franklin has written a moving and fascinating book."

—ELIZABETH GRAVER, AUTHOR OF *KANTIKA*

"In *Love & Other Monsters*, Emily Franklin masterfully reveals how everyday decisions can morph into monsters. Claire Clairmont's turning points are skillfully woven by Franklin from the textures of the quotidian—the baby's wail, the unseasonably chill air, the soreness after passion, the giddy pleasure of a secret, the sting of a sibling's insufficient love, even the grit of homemade toothpaste. I was hooked from the first witticism on the first page, and readers will find much to cheer, groan, rage, weep, and laugh about in this captivating story of lust, betrayal, celebrity, and silences only broken centuries later."

—MARIA PINTO, AUTHOR OF *FEARLESS, SLEEPLESS, DEATHLESS*

LOVE & OTHER MONSTERS

ALSO BY EMILY FRANKLIN

ADULT FICTION, NONFICTION, MEMOIR, POETRY

The Lioness of Boston

Tell Me How You Got Here

Too Many Cooks: Kitchen Adventures with 4 kids, 1 Mom, and 102 New Recipes

How to Spell Chanukah: 18 Writers Celebrate 8 Nights of Lights

It's a Wonderful Lie: 26 Truths about Life in Your Twenties

The Girls' Almanac: Linked Stories

BEFORE: Short Stories about Pregnancy from Our Top Writers
(CO-EDITED WITH HEATHER SWAIN)

Liner Notes

YOUNG ADULT FICTION

Last Night at the Circle Cinema

Tessa Masterson Will Go to Prom
(CO-WRITTEN WITH BRENDAN HALPIN)

Jenna and Jonah's Fauxmance
(CO-WRITTEN WITH BRENDAN HALPIN)

The Half-Life of Planets
(CO-WRITTEN WITH BRENDAN HALPIN)

At Face Value

The Principles of Love, Books 1-7

Chalet Girl, Books 1-3

The Other Half of Me

LOVE & OTHER MONSTERS

A NOVEL

Emily Franklin

GODINE / BOSTON

Published in 2026 by
GODINE
Boston, Massachusetts
godine.com

LIBRARY OF CONGRESS CATALOGING-IN-PUBLICATION DATA

Names: Franklin, Emily author
Title: Love & other monsters : a novel / Emily Franklin.
Other titles: Love and other monsters
Description: Boston : Godine, 2025.
Identifiers: LCCN 2025025326 (print) | LCCN 2025025327 (ebook) | ISBN 9781567928556 hardcover | ISBN 9781567928563 epub
Subjects: LCSH: Shelley, Mary Wollstonecraft, 1797-1851—Fiction | Shelley, Percy Bysshe, 1792-1822—Fiction | Byron, George Gordon Byron, Baron, 1788-1824—Fiction | Clairmont, Claire, 1798-1879—Fiction | LCGFT: Fiction | Biographical fiction | Novels
Classification: LCC PS3606.R396 L67 2025 (print) | LCC PS3606.R396 (ebook) | DDC 813/.6--dc23/eng/20250625
LC record available at https://lccn.loc.gov/2025025326
LC ebook record available at https://lccn.loc.gov/2025025327

First Printing, 2026
Printed in the United States of America

For Dad,
with all of the Moons and Junes

"But what a weak barrier is truth when it stands in the way of a hypothesis!"

—MARY WOLLSTONECRAFT,
A Vindication of the Rights of Woman

"Nothing is so painful to the human mind as a great and sudden change."

—MARY GODWIN SHELLEY,
Frankenstein

"Even while I write, my burning cheeks are wet. Alas, that the torn heart can bleed, but not forget."

—PERCY BYSSHE SHELLEY
(FOR CLAIRE CLAIRMONT)

". . . this is the truth, and truth is best at all times."

—CLAIRE CLAIRMONT,
LETTER FROM MAY 1815

PROLOGUE

MARCH 1879
FLORENCE

All love stories are ghost stories waiting to happen.

When the parcel arrives, delivered in the second post of the day—thick brown paper secured with plain cordage, no gift ribbon, no note—I hold the mystery of it in my hands. The item is a surprise at first. But the heft and shape are familiar. Underneath the wrapping, I know instantly what I hold: my journal lost so many years before and within it, the ghost of the girl I was.

We leave behind our younger selves and imagine them far off at sea—a quick goodbye wave through a salt-crusted porthole—never to be seen again. Yet like all dead, we carry those shadow selves with us. Who sent the journal back to me? Who kept it all this time, holding in their hands the eighteen-year-old me of 1816? Who shoved that girl underneath the waves and tried to make her disappear?

Inside the blue linen-wrapped cover are loose pages I wrote prior to purchasing the journal, back in the murky March before I made a decision that changed everything.

No matter progress in the form of newly fashioned fabrics for warm clothing, germ theory for tuberculosis and cholera, discoveries made which protect us from the elements or from disease, there have been no inventions to protect us from emotional hurt or pain. Why might that be? Perhaps we humans are not as clever as we believe.

Ought I close the journal now, sit in the shadow hour, and forgo the suffering that comes with looking back? I was always curious—there is no denying my wish to dive into the pages and somehow solve the puzzle of my previous self.

Of course you've heard of one of us.

Probably some of us. Unlikely that you would know of all of us.

There were five in our group that summer at Villa Diodati. If one were to read in *The Times* about us—an article that would leave out the most important parts of our sojourn—we would be mentioned by name, a headline luring the reader in: *A Most Scandalous Group!* Lord Byron, who had rented the mansion, my stepsister, Mary Godwin—for she had not yet married Percy Shelley, who was also there—Byron's new personal physician, John Polidori, and myself, Claire Clairmont.

I am the one you have never heard mentioned. There is nothing that deflates the soul quite like being irrelevant. We all like to think of ourselves as having mattered. I always wanted to mean something—but to whom?

What a group we were: beautiful, filled with desire, young, though we did not feel it at the time. In sunlight, we were a basket bouquet: colourful, unpredictable, artistic in our emotional arrangements. But in foul weather—of which there was too much—we were a ragtag group: disheveled and wild, connected in a complicated stitching, each with our own needs, our own secrets.

Eighteen-year-old Mary had not yet written *Frankenstein*, almost twenty-four, Shelley had not yet been lauded as one of the major poets of our time, celebrity Byron had yet to live through the storm during his twenty-eighth year which would inspire him to write "Darkness," Polidori—only twenty—had not yet penned "The Vampyre," that modern elegant bloodsucker modeled after his louche employer. At seventeen, I had not yet become myself.

And still the gossip papers could not get enough of us that summer.

So obsessed with our group were journalists and the general public because of Byron's celebrity that the hotel across the lake installed a special telescope for better viewing of our lawn games, our trysts. An excursion company charged an extra fee for boat rides with binoculars, all the better to catch a glimpse of us dashing from lake edge to villa.

Though there is no photograph in the journal—Joseph Nicéphore Niépce's invention would not happen for another decade—I can see myself that summer: eyes the colour of dirt, crow-wing hair, significant thighs, strong hands, shoulders I always felt were too wide, especially next to my smaller, blonder, older sister. True, Mary was stepsister only, yet I felt she was more blood to me than my own limbs at times.

Impossible to be eighty now, and yet it is a blessing, too. We age, we age—the hands show this. Yet the inside of us remains the same. No one explained this to me when I was young. I am a paper doll—me with my former selves, each of us holding hands with the one behind, only there is no one in front of me now save for the journal which will lead me back.

I close my eyes today and I can repack my trunk from memory: journal, lightweight muslin dresses, bonnets the colours of a sweet shop window's display, white and plum calf leather boots Shelley had given me in private. They would never see daylight—I was too ashamed of the gift, but also because there wasn't any sunlight to be had. We did not pack properly for 1816, the time that would come to be known as The Year Without Summer.

SUMMER IS meant to be mist-spun early light stretching itself from first tea through midday, a cold joint of beef set on white plates, marrow toasts in hand as the picnic demands shielding one's eyes from the glowering sun. Yet in that Year Without Summer, I redefined the word. *Summer, summer, summer* as though that one particular summer became all summers. I started those months one way—gentle and unformed, I suppose—and ended as quite another.

We are all stories of before and after. That was the last summer of my first life.

Saint Augustine wrote *the dead are invisible but they are not absent.* In this way, I think, we come to the earth already haunted. Everyone from that summer has lived in me all these years. And now in the pages before me.

Looking back, it seems I ought to have better predicted what would happen to me, to our group. I was always thinking, always writing onto bits of paper, slipping those papers between book pages, into my journal. I had been told a story of myself, and I believed it. Now I understand we are terrible predictors of our own good fortune, our own miseries.

BEFORE WE set out for Lake Geneva, we knew nothing of Mount Tambora's eruption in the Dutch East Indies. It had wreaked havoc—miles of rocks spewed into the air, typhoons, thick-set ash that blocked sunlight and covered the ground, ruining crops and driving up the price of food, as so little grew in such darkness. A worldwide climate disaster whose devastation we did not fully understand—frost and snow in July, rain torrents where there ought only to be sun, a typhoon which forced us to seek shelter in unlikely pairs.

When we set out for the easy shores of Lake Geneva, Switzerland's largest body of water, I wanted to be wholly filled with excitement. Yet, like the lake with its French side, Lac Léman, and its Swiss side, Lake Geneva, I was divided. I wished to be with my sister Mary—to prove our connection deep and abiding—yet this was not the entire reason for our trip.

I wanted love. Desired desire. I wanted so much at seventeen I felt I wanted to consume the world—possibly to avoid being consumed by it. Am I responsible for what happened? Mary said I brought everything on myself, and yet how can this be so—I was young and vain and poor and—the years have shown me—lonely, too.

I admit I wanted to be a part of the group. Yet there was a small part of me—the divided part—that wanted to go off alone. Or perhaps I state only a partial truth, which Byron loathed. *Say the thing, Claire,* he'd told me. Perhaps what I mean is I wished only to be with my older sister—older only by eight months in fact, yet in practice, by years. And I longed to have our sisterly bond strengthened.

I thought of Mary as my protector, but she could not save me. Perhaps I asked too much of a girl who had no mother. No, that is incorrect. For we all grow up in the shadows of our parents. Mary and I were no exception, though perhaps hers loomed larger than most. The world knew her mother, the famous Mary Wollstonecraft, who had died just after Mary had been born, and my stepsister was raised in her late mother's feminist philosophy, her lingering unconventionality. And when Mary's political father, William Godwin, married my mother, I, too, had no choice but to shelter under those ideas.

WHAT DID I know of love? Of sex? Of my own self in the twisted bedclothes and sweat-damp nights, of the vulnerability hope brings with it? Not enough. We think ourselves formed already at seventeen, at eighteen, yet we are not fully armoured enough for the world. What did I know of making something that would last beyond that summer, beyond however many years we are granted? I wish to ask Mary: What of those summer girls remains, what will be revealed in these pages in front of me?

I miss Mary more in my mind—a great ache that fills me—than I do in the day-to-day. I miss not so much the girl she was, but what might have been had she not both demanded I entwine with her and punished me for it.

EVERY RETELLING becomes a fiction.

We are all unreliable in our narration, having been in the midst too long or off to the side too often. I remember the violet-blue star, edelweiss pushing out of the craggy stone as I found—and lost—the great love of my life. But who was it? All of this preserved in the journal splayed open now—the way youth makes living experiments of us all. Cut me open, I wish to demand now, find the shape and irregularities of my heart.

Some days I feel like the young woman I was—until I pass the looking glass.

Here is the journal in which I never age. I am fixed in those pages.

That summer I began wanting one thing but by August found I wanted something quite different. Yet I could not walk backwards to find myself at April again. And one finds little choice in the memories that rush and flood from youth. All along, I have accepted those monsters of memory. Who knows why we recall one moment with such perspicuity and another is fog-filled with swampy conversation barely pieced together. So much of what we live we will not hold onto.

This is sad. Necessary, too. We forget so we might be able to be fully alive the next day. Sometimes forgetting saves us.

As I sit, ready to read my journal, I am aware of my mind's drawers, satchels, all overstuffed with memories of those months. For decades I lived without the book. My mind became the pages. Now, the rush-back of written memories will swirl with everything, layer upon layer, the way an oil painting builds from canvas out.

What troubles me most—as I cannot correct it—was my own mindset. I pity the young woman waiting for her life to begin. At seventeen, eighteen, I felt that waiting in each morning. What I wish I could say to my younger self—to be sure I would grab her shoulders and shake ever so gently but enough to wake her from such waiting—is to tell her to stop.

As young people, we wait so long for real life to begin, not realising it already has.

MIDWAY THROUGH that summer I copied radical Mary Wollstonecraft's words in my journal: *I do not wish women to have power over men; but over themselves.*

I swear I wrote those words. I wrote of so much that year: of the tiny house I shared with Mary and Shelley in London, that city's busy spring streets as I chased love, my heart crammed full of secrets. I detailed everything on the page: spring slamming into summer when we arrived at Lake Geneva, only to disappear with no warning. I wrote of foraging for food, which became scarce, of love, which—like the typhoon—came on with gentle wind and then threatened to kill us. I wrote of sex, of nature, of my sister, of ruin.

Yet until now I have had no proof.

For though I kept a journal always and those other diaries are stacked next to me now in a careful tower of the past, this journal I kept so diligently in 1816 was gone as though it had never been written.

For decades I had crafted possible stories: The journal—bound in a shade of blue I had never seen before I purchased it on a daring shopping outing in London before everything changed—was simply left behind at summer's end. Or it drowned, somehow left lakeside, words and binding swallowed. Still another idea was that the journal was misplaced—I retraced steps, had I left it on my makeshift desk, on the lawn, near the coppice of trees I frequented? Yet I knew these scenarios unlikely, for I kept the journal carefully, and—especially after a few pairs of prying eyes fell upon its pages—made sure I hid it well.

No, the journal delivered today in which I detailed everything did not disappear. Yet it did not survive in my possession. Someone in that group was responsible for its vanishing. It could have been Polidori, with his interest in salacious gossip. Or Byron, who wished only to leave those months in an icy mist long ago forgotten. Or perhaps Mary—who worried I would publish the journal. Or Shelley, who saw himself so differently than I did. Or Elise, the ever-present nursemaid Shelley hired to help Mary with baby William.

And now, with the cover opened—no matter who took it—evidence. Here are the days I lost, the hours I have wanted back for so long, the voice long muffled now clear on the pages as I relive and remember it all. Some forget their pasts in order to move forward. Others keep their letters, old tickets, recall dates, and what was said and by whom in order to make sense of their lives.

We all become archivists or arsonists.

PART ONE

MARCH & APRIL 1816

LONDON

1

It is a commonly held belief that siblings—especially those close in age—have between them an unbreakable bond.

Yet as I stood in the arched doorway of our rental house, watching my sister nurse her new baby in the sitting room, I wondered if such closeness required siblings—and sisters perhaps especially—to be similar in order to remain close. For we are born immediately into comparison: who is fairer, who sleeps more soundly, who is more amiable, or more prone to crying, who is most thoughtful, who survives.

Our siblings are our first friends, first classmates, first tutors. How they see us is also how we come to see ourselves. And how lost we would be without siblings to anchor us. Yet my sister could also be my greatest adversary.

Mary had been in residence at Arabella Row in Pimlico since giving birth in January. I joined shortly after. When first she greeted me at the door, she had the look of a doll loved too fiercely—worn and frayed—and she was too many nights without sleep either to welcome me warmly or to turn me away. She could not say she needed me, yet I had felt there was little doubt.

I cared for her with milky tea, with a stone I placed in the oven and set in her sheets each night so she would find the bed already warm. I rose each morning with baby William while Mary slept fitfully, plagued by gloom. She'd relied on me these past months, which I relished; yet I felt closed off from the world because of her, and now I wished to venture outside.

Mary was the serious one, at eighteen years of age, and I, seventeen, her lighthearted opposite. This is what we had been told growing up and so had settled into those roles. If Mary was quiet, I laughed. If she said no, I, in reaction, said yes. Mary knew how to construct a sentence, how to listen and later rephrase her father's words, her mother's. And this garnered her praise. Yet I had practical skills. I could iron a shirt, the cuffs so stiff they might chafe a wrist. Mary might ponder why girls wore bows in their hair, where I could tie a ribbon so the bow lay flat. And, in the past few years, since being out of her father and my mother's house, Mary had indeed wanted the bows. For she had a clever brain yet a quite conventional affect. She wished for bows and clean hems, which I provided, for my arms were scrub-strong and I had no fear of dolly sticks and tubs, as laundry often gave me a reprieve from any household tensions. I cared far less than she about my dresses, about my hair, which I wore long and uneven and often down, as I could not be bothered with curls and ties. Mary—feminist home scholar though she was—told me I was wasting natural appeal. Perhaps I did so in order to annoy her, which I quite enjoyed. Or perhaps she only pointed out my heedlessness to poke me, which she quite enjoyed.

More likely, I had come to realise that how I acted, or dressed, or spoke was still somehow in relation to how Mary acted or dressed or spoke.

When Mary had shown me into the house for the first time with barely a whisper a month before, I had set about overly loud and cheerful, cleaning, propping up my sister and the pillows behind her.

Everything about Mary shone yellow—hair long and prone to curl without setting, hazel eyes that gave a golden glow, cheeks that radiated the gold-pink yolk of a fresh egg. Her shiny locks distracted from her stern nose, her eyes perfectly even-set and her brow shaped so well she appeared timeless, inclined towards stateliness, though she had a small frame and tiny mouth prone to disdain, especially with the grief that radiated from her being. Above all else, she appeared—even in front of me with a nursing infant latched to her breast—impenetrable, and it was only this quality that caused me to be envious.

I knew her well, noticed the slope that had taken over her shoulders, the downward mellow grimness that had gripped her since her first pregnancy and lost child—an understanding of not being in possession of, but rather possessed by, her own body.

The house we lived in had the shape of a poorly baked cake, one room stacked wobbly on the next, each a more defeated colour than the last. The entryway where I stood had once been rosy but appeared grimy, despite my scrubbing the walls only the day before. I stood leaning on one of those walls as I gazed upon Mary.

Always appearing more favourable in deeper colours, she wore a dress the colour of beetroot. I could see the sleeplessness under her eyes. She sat in the front room in a tufted chair, looking out the window, with William in the crook of her arm. He had nursed long enough that drowsiness took over, and both the baby and Mary seemed at peace.

I knew this would not last.

The baby was prone to wailing when not attached to her breast or completely full, belly rounded.

"He is like a miniature drunkard," I told her.

She gave me a quiet smile, which filled me with joy—she found life rather humourless and so gave out smiles infrequently, and even less often because of her low mood after giving birth to William. Her first baby, born too soon last year, survived only days. Mary had fallen pregnant with William quickly after that. Afterwards, she could not mention the first baby's name. In my mind I did it for her—*Clara*, though she said the choice had nothing to do with my own name. Mary's dire grief splayed itself over her face. I worried about her well-being constantly.

Her smile faded. "Do you think you might take over, Claire? My arm is tingled, and I can barely sit upright from fatigue."

I nodded and went to help.

DUCKING IN from the doorway in a strange crouch that silenced my skirts, I toe-stepped over to Mary and held my sister's gaze. Moments such as these I knew we were truly sisters, despite having no shared blood, raised nearly as twins in a highly unconventional household. Of course, when one is in the midst one does not understand the true lack of convention. It was only at school I came to understand that not everyone was raised with beliefs about free love, open dialogue at the table:

politics, money, power, of being born a bastard, which I was, though my mother sought to cover it up, dousing me with the scent of shame.

Mary beckoned me closer to begin the elaborate process of transferring her baby to my arms. We had our sibling shorthand and had created between us numerous jokes and systems, including swapping places. If we could move William without waking him, he would keep quiet. If we jostled him, there would be noisy hell to pay, his wails filling the small house, both of our days ruined.

Mary kept her steady focus on me as I reached my hands under William's weight just as she pulled back. He moved slightly. Mary and I both grimaced as our fingers touched under the baby. Still hunched over, my back began to ache, yet I did not move. Keeping my stance, I backed away as Mary rose from the chair, stretching her small form. She shifted past me and beckoned me to sit in the chair. I did so. It was warm, which felt nice in the chilled room, and also uncomfortable, as the arms were wood in need of smoothing and the stuffing needed plumping and I was an altogether bigger person than Mary and so could not sit entirely in the chair while propping my arms for the baby. His head lolled against my forearm, a slim line of milky drool escaping the small blossom of his mouth.

Mary patted my head as I gazed at her child.

The light had shifted from sighing late morning sun to the bright, hopeful light which meant spring and narcissus nosing up from the earth in the small cracked pots on our front steps. I wanted to be out in the air. By the time I looked up, Mary regarded me from the doorway, ready to turn on her heel.

"You don't mind being with Willmouse, do you, Claire?" she asked. William did not stir with voices, only jostling.

"Of course not," I said.

"Only so I might work," she said. I went along with her lie. She had not worked in months. I knew full well she would read and then fall asleep with a book clutched to her chest. The skin around her cheekbones was puffy. I wanted us to be the sort of siblings who knew the other's needs, who filled in the gaps without much explanation. Yet while I could see she was weary, she did not seem to know my mind.

I looked again to the outside world. I knew not what I might find there, only that at seventeen I felt increasingly frustrated at being trapped inside. Something was waiting for me in that city, and I would find it. "I would like to take a walk, though, so perhaps, you might limit your work to an hour? Or two? Only so the light remains."

Mary nodded, and when William stirred in my arms, she whispered, "Two hours. Surely I could not write for more than that. Unless I am required elsewhere."

She did not mean required by me, nor required by William, nor required by the faulty fireplace with coals that would need lighting, nor any of the other quirks that came with the rental house. For while we had an unspoken domestic understanding—she had a child, I did not and needed to help her at all times—we were not alone.

Mary, her fiancé, Percy Shelley, and I all lived together. While I was grateful for parts of the arrangement, other parts could be trying. Still, I counted myself lucky to have them house me and tried not to complain, especially as both had their own frustrations. Shelley because despite earlier success with writing, he'd had trouble securing a publishing contract, and Mary because her dreams of writing were larger than her actuality.

"Shelley is due back soon," I said.

Mary nodded. "You know more of his schedule than I."

She did not say this with any spite. Only fact. For while Mary had taken Shelley's name and signed notes as Mary Shelley, they were not yet married, and it was true I was the one who knew his whereabouts at any given time. When I was not relieving Mary or cleaning, I was—at Mary's urging—accompanying Shelley all around London. Publishing houses to secure possible book deals, banking meetings to secure possible loans to keep our household afloat. Anywhere Shelley went, I went with him, struggling to keep pace with his long stride while Mary stayed home with the curtains drawn. It was Mary who had made her bed, but I was the one who had to lie in it.

Mary often forced herself to be different when Shelley was

present—wilted flower reinvigourated, gaping sail puffed taut when he entered the room. I had yet to feel that amorous energy so still felt rumpled in a house that was not ours. None of the houses we lived in were.

"Oh, little Willmouse." Mary yawned at her baby. "I might never recover from lack of sleep."

"Go," I told her. "But first." I opened and closed my hands from a prayer position to that of handout, asking her silently to bring me a book whilst I sat trapped.

Early March sunshine touched her dress through the window as Mary went to the shelf and offered *Mémoires pour servir à l'histoire du Jacobinisme* by l'abbé Augustin Barruel, which, though I was fluent in French, seemed liable to force me to eat my own hand out of tedium. I shook my head.

"Mary," I said, in a particular tone which, in our lifelong connection, conveyed an entire sentence. I shifted so the baby's heft was on my chest. Mary frowned as she brought me the book she knew I wanted.

"I fear you know more of the characters in novels than you do of the world." Mary sighed. "You expect too much from love, Claire."

"I do not," I said. This was a lie. Surely it was not wrong to want witty rapport, desirous looks, and a chase resulting in a man who found me brave or brilliant or beautiful. Or ideally, all three. "Besides, are you not the example of love for all to follow?"

Mary gave me her grateful gaze. She and I had such closeness that I had followed her on her elopement nearly two years before—*too young, too soon*, her father had written, *too scandalous*, my mother had screamed to our faces. Still, I went with my sister, even though she and Shelley had not actually married. Bearing witness to their intense connection, I had pushed away our parents' worries. Had the five years' age difference between Mary and Shelley concerned me? It had not. The fact that he had already his own also-young wife and she was again pregnant? Well, a little. Yet we'd been raised in chaos, and I thought Mary the soundest of mind of anyone I had ever encountered. So when she had asked me—pleaded with me—to come with her across Europe with Shelley, I had not a moment's hesitation. "Does love disappoint you, Mary?"

She held her hand to her chest as though instructing me where her heart lay. "No, of course not. Shelley and I are—you of all people bear witness to the kind of love we share. Yet, it is not always . . . simple." She looked at me and at the floor and then the ceiling. I was not kind enough to appreciate this as humility. "It is wonderful. Yet it is not everything."

I pretended to take notes. "Not everything, noted. Lower expectations, also noted."

"No." She pinched her mouth and wagged a finger at me. "Never did I say lower expectations, for that is devaluing oneself. You mustn't do that, Claire."

"You vex me, Mary."

She pointed to the novel. "What I wish to say is—it is all very well, important, I think, to have high expectations."

"I do." I looked at the books on the shelf, willing her to bring me one. "I enjoy the story. The characters. The way—"

"Life is not in the pages of some popular fiction by an *unnamed authoress*," Mary said, pointing out what she perceived as cowardice, the novel being written only "by a Lady" and bearing no name. "Reading drivel only furthers your unhealthy fantasies."

Had my hands not been filled with her baby, I would have pressed my palms to my cheek to stop the blushing. I felt caught in an awkward state of in-betweenness. "I harbour no fantasies," I said, lying. "I am only watching your baby and simply wish to read—"

"Reread, for the pages of this and the others are nearly in tatters."

True, the volumes of *Sense and Sensibility* were stained on the cover from countless cups of coffee—we could not have afforded so many cups of tea—with pages flapped and marked. She handed me the first volume of *Pride and Prejudice*, equally battered, though it had been in my possession for a shorter time; I had purchased a copy when I lived in Lynmouth the previous year, when Mary had all but banished me.

I had lived by myself, after Mary had decided Shelley had turned too much attention towards me. Yet when I was confused by this, Mary would not elaborate. And after more than a year living with my sister and her betrothed, living alone had been a great shock. Though I missed

Mary, I had nature for company: full trees and honeysuckle vines. Mary had written, of course, saying she merely wished space for herself with Shelley free from—as she had put it—my incessant influence as his sister-in-law.

Mary sighed. She did not wish to be associated with my lowbrow choice of text. And the more she judged my reading to be dim-witted, the smarter she appeared. Conversely, if I showed immunity to her baby crying, she appeared short on patience.

Sisters and brothers were always in a dance of amplification or suppression. Every preference, each conversation, every interaction with others forced us to declare ourselves: If I preferred the bustle of a shopping street, Mary proclaimed the quiet in an empty theatre preferable. If she became vocal about politics to match Shelley and his diatribes, I hushed. If she hurried, I slowed. If I expressed myself clearly and with love, and accepted not knowing my own rake of a father, having a mother with a disheveled past, Mary held back and held back, desperate to prove her own father's well-regarded righteousness, her own famous mother's sainthood. Her mother, Mary Wollstonecraft, had so staunchly defended the rights of all women yet had not survived to defend the rights of her daughter.

Mary put her hand to her forehead as though checking for fever.

"Will you please rest?" I asked.

"I will," she said. "After I work. I must work, Claire." I nodded to tell her I understood.

Mary could not help herself. "Still, those are silly books. Army camps and men in peril ought not be the subject of romantic speculation and admiration," she said, and sounded part herself and part like Shelley. She took particular pleasure in having opinions about lip varnish she had never worn, pages she had never read, countries whose people she had never met, all of this especially as her judgement related to me.

With William's downy head nestled, I gripped the novel in my hand and knew I would begin right at the beginning, the best place for a reread when that shining anticipation clutched the stomach. I would find that kind of love. That kind of escape.

Mary crossed her arms. "I feel compelled to say to you, Claire, do not be horribly shocked if some disappointment finds you eventually."

Oh, siblings, how quick we could be to proclaim and to judge. Caretakers and adversaries both. I wanted to hug her and tell her I worried for her, for she was already wearied by life. I wanted to push her away and scold her for making me feel foolish. Another reason I admired the fictional Bennet sisters: They were close and chatty, flouncing onto a bed or settee with great flair to confide or pinch one another's cheeks for perfect blush before the ball, yet their relationships were not based on need. They harboured the duty of the coincidence of their births and also seemed genuinely to enjoy each other.

I needed Mary. And ever more each day, Mary needed me.

"I shall only be disappointed if I am not allowed out in the fresh spring air today," I said, louder than I ought to have. And with that that baby cried and Mary gave a frustrated growl, surprisingly deep for someone of her size, and whisked herself away, leaving me to contend with a soiled, screeching, tiny but wild thing. No reading about Elizabeth Bennet for me.

I wanted a relationship that would elevate me not from the social order, necessarily, but that would transform me as though transformation was something that happened to you as opposed to happening within and from you. I took this process seriously because I wanted to be held in high regard, which was almost impossible for a woman: impossible until—and if—one reached a very old age and still had teeth and wisdom. I wanted to find love, to be wanted, to be taken seriously, and, on any given day, I wished for one more than the others. Mary thought I wanted what she had. I did not.

Mine would be a marriage of minds without papers and with more time behind a closed bedroom door—for we were raised to believe less in law than free love—though I had no idea how to find such. Certainly, love was unlikely to find me under the small pile of smelly human on my lap.

2

In the morning I woke early, not because of noise but because of quiet.

My room was downstairs in what was formerly used as a repository. One small rectangle with a long transom window at the top let in a dull, milky sort of light, either from sun or from streetlamps. I stood on the bed and peered out the window to find a world covered in white. Snow blanketed everything so much so that I could not make out anything other than humps and blobs. Only the streetlamp poked through like some lost, thin giant.

This felt at once exhilarating—for it was sudden and unusual—yet also disappointing, for I had not managed to leave the house the day before and thought today would bring that opportunity.

I used the commode—the house was old and had no water closet—pushed it under my bed, reached for my dressing gown, and paused in front of the filmy looking glass. Despite dreams in which I readied for a ball or ran through a field with surefooted abandon whilst my hair cascaded and gleamed, I had not changed overnight.

I was pretty in a not startling yet appealing way, a bit plump, also in a way I rather liked as I was not—like Mary—in danger of being blown over in a heavy wind. I was in possession of one well-behaved eyebrow and another that erred and eyes that were no colour other than brown. I could carry things in my strong hands, careful with my belongings both because I had not very many and also due to moving place to place.

I was in possession of a few books. I owned a silver cannister in which I kept a gallimaufry of objects: a smooth beach rock from Lynmouth, a ribbon that I believed still smelt like my mother's neck, my few shillings, a lovely small wooden horse, an ugly small clay bird, a cobalt pottery marble Shelley had given me from his own childhood, and a hairpin I had taken from Mary back when we lived on Skinner Street with her father, my mother, and our various other half- and stepsiblings, five offspring in total. Mary's hairpin had a black bauble on the end, and because I had dark hair, lots of it, the pin was as good as lost on me when I wore it.

The silver cannister was not true silver. When I had gone with Mary on her elopement—caught up in secondhand passion though annoyed at Mary taking Shelley's surname without a marriage—she and Shelley and I had walked through Europe. With Napoleon abdicated and gone to Elba, English were allowed to travel to Europe. With no more Continental Blockade, our days were spent amidst the destruction of post-Napoleonic Wars, the Battle of Paris still fresh.

To say the walking was arduous was to sprinkle mildness on the word and douse it with castor sugar. My feet became bloodied, shoved into boots regardless, the blood pooling at my heel and coming through the thin leather. I knew not ever where we were walking, and if I had asked, Mary would not have heard me over the din—for destruction leaves in its wake the noise of pilfering, cleaning, removing rubble, only to rebuild with the same stones something new that would in all likelihood be razed by another war. It was in one of these piles that, when Mary fussed over Shelley, who had grown woozy with heat, I found the cannister and the lovely horse, though not together. I held it in my hand, and a man nearby saw and asked for money. *Unique en son genre*, he'd said. *One of a kind.* He'd held out his hand. I gave him the small bit of money I had. Mary and Shelley pulled me on. I turned back and saw the man take from his pocket a replica of the horse I had bought. To the next passerby he said, *Unique en son genre.*

My bedroom was just large enough for a narrow bed and next to it a chair upon which I stacked books and a candle. In the hallway outside my room were two small steps that led to a cramped nook where former tenants had kitchen storage: pots of jam, racks of eggs, plums packed in sugar syrup which I had found when I moved in and which I had consumed in secret one night to the next until they were gone. I felt bereft at finishing them, but saved the containers and in them kept my quills, for the nook itself held a very small writing desk Shelley had installed for me.

Without slippers, I went to the front room for a better look out the window. I spotted a soft brown mouse in the corner, its tail curved in a backwards shape like a question that had already been asked. Perhaps the snow would stop. The sun would come up strong and buttery and melt the crusted ice and drifts of snow mounded on the steps, covering the pots of flowers that only yesterday had beckoned spring.

I had grown accustomed to daily outings. Since letting the scullery maid go to save those wages, Shelley had asked me to do the shopping. So Thursday mornings I found pleasure in Pimlico with the remnants of old cobble and grazing land, the Thames Bank Distillery with its heady malt and barley smell. I walked and walked, joining the throngs at the weekly pedlar-meet, clamoring for sacks of flour or sugar, desperate for decent cuts of meat—the last in line got mostly gristle—jars of ginger, hawkers with their wares, parcels of taper candles wrapped in newsprint, good deals on seconds, ones with nicks in the wax from being dropped. Sometimes the sellers came to us, street vendors calling out or going door-to-door offering oysters or cherries, rabbits and rhubarb. Normally the crates and carts were chockablock full, but there were slim pickings as of late. I had managed to secure a giant cabbage, and boiled the outer leaves for Mary, who pressed them to her engorged breasts until the swelling had gone down.

No vendors shouting today. No carts. I hoped I would still be able to leave.

BY AFTERNOON we still could not venture outside. I felt ill at ease, desperate to do the household shopping as an excuse to explore London. Instead, we settled by the fire, the popping and hissing from the coals the only sounds until Shelley coughed.

At twenty-three years of age, Shelley commanded a room. This was half because of his size—tall and lean, as though he had once been a smaller man but had been stretched to fit his trousers—and half because, like many men of great stature, he had an air of confidence that belied his insecurity.

And it was this self-doubt, the kind which also seems to plague thin men, men of the mind rather than the body, that when mixed with his great passion, formed a potent cocktail that drew us in. Mary especially, for she liked his soft manners and elongated face. Everything about Shelley was exaggerated—his build, his hair, length of limbs, and lanky walk. After our travels, time had softened him, faded the edges. His clothing au courant without the effort required to be fashionable. Cuffs lightly frayed from writing, heels of his shoes worn. This, too, was part of his appeal. For whilst Mary had been drawn to his fiery politics, his radical passion, what drew others to him was his scruffy elegance, which accentuated his perpetual depth of thought.

This was partly the grace of being born a man—for men might show less care towards their appearance and exist somehow in the intellectual realm. If I had worn clothing in tatters, had I not mended my seams, I would be slovenly, and no one would pay heed to my brain.

Near Shelley, Mary appeared to be even smaller than she already was, and—though she protested this on the one occasion I asked—I believe she enjoyed being a doll compared to Shelley's life-sized human.

I did not find his physical form appealing, but he was kind in a stooped and apologetic way, which endeared him to everyone. He stood, still in his nightclothes, the simplicity of the off-white flannel longcloth making him appear more jimberjawed than usual, lower jaw projection upon which his significant face rested.

"Claire, I have a little something for you," Shelley said. He was always giving me trinkets—a new pen nib, the cast-off ugly bird, words of praise. He handed me a paper-wrapped parcel.

Mary, near the fire, kept one finger on the book in her hand, which rested on William's head, and an eye trained on me. Upon unwrapping, I found a set of books. *Emma* by A Lady.

My smile widened as a frown of equal size crept upon Mary's face. I beamed and thanked him. "What a perfect snow day treat. I shall read and reread as I have the others."

"I bought it right at Christmas—but with everything . . ." He gave a sweep of his hands that meant the baby, Mary's health, the finances.

He had an aristocrat's ability to refuse to pay his debts, even when legal action followed. His allowance from his father was barely enough to hold him, but he had the safety of knowing he was heir to a wealthy baronetcy. Though this was in the future, he used expectation of inheritance to convince banks to lend him funds, but even they had grown wary of his debts with the downturn in the economy.

"How thrilling," I said. I turned the books this way and that, noting John Murray as the publisher.

"Why do you indulge her so?" Mary asked Shelley. Her voice was not unkind, but thin.

"Thank you," I said to Shelley, who put his chin on his knuckles, bemused. Mary fiddled with William's hands. His arms had come unswaddled, and he flailed as though he were a musical conductor gone mad until she tucked him back in, at which point her breast came out of his mouth and let go a spray of milk across his face.

All night I would stay awake, dawn duties with William be damned. I would take my time. I glanced at a page from *Emma. She was one of those who, having once begun, would be always in love.* Yes and yes, please! I kept reading, racing ahead only to turn back and reread.

"I am famished," Shelley said after a while. "Claire, you must have one of your good dishes in mind for our meal." He was always polite, grateful for feeding.

"Indeed," I said, though I had no such thing in mind, as all of my mental energies had gone to imagining myself striding alongside Emma. Of course to say this aloud would have been ridiculous, so instead I gave a curt nod and left to throw something in a pot. I hoped it would be edible.

"Are we not lucky to have Claire," I heard him say to Mary, who again nursed William.

He treated us equally, which cannot be said of many in his position.

IN KEEPING with the odd snow day stuck inside, we took early dinner on our laps.

"So much snow," Mary said, gripping her bowl for warmth. She was unable to keep up the pretense of being well any longer.

"That settles it," Shelley said. "No longer can I tolerate seeing you ache with cold, Mary. We must get away again. Spend the summer elsewhere. Perhaps longer—if we can afford it."

That we might find ourselves again exploring Europe did not lift my sister's depression. And of course I had not been consulted in the slightest; yet I could not argue. I would go with them to France. Or Bath. Or the Turkish Empire. I had no other place in the world but with them. Our parents had made it clear: choose to leave, stay gone. I sacrificed my security to keep her company. Still, the three of us were stuck in Shelley's financial waiting game. If funds did not come through, we could not go anywhere.

Shelley wrote a list as he ignored his food—I could see the names of publishers. I could also see that he waited for Mary to ask him about the list and, moreover, waited for her pallor to shift. When it seemed unlikely to budge despite the dangle-hope of going abroad, Shelley grew annoyed, which he displayed by sucking air through his teeth, which in turn annoyed my sister. I felt pleased that neither her mood nor his twitches rubbed me the wrong way—I was far too used to both.

"Would you spare Claire tomorrow?" he asked Mary. "Part for your lovely penmanship, Claire, and part so you might accompany me to John Murray."

"Again?" I asked, for we had gone the month before to that publisher's office. I blushed. For John Murray was not only the publisher of *Emma*, but also Lord Byron. The more I pictured the famous Lord Byron in Murray's office where I had also been, the more I blushed.

During my stay in Lynmouth I'd been besotted with *Pride and Prejudice* but had not much else to keep me company, so Shelley had suggested I use my time there to better myself by participating in the common practice of writing to the famous, those impossibly glamourous people always out of reach yet who felt somehow known. Shelley had once written to Wordsworth, and to Godwin. I could have written a novel. Instead, I'd written a letter to Lord George Gordon Noel Byron—whose full name was a public affair though he was far out of reach—which Shelley thought a fine idea, though the two men had never met.

I was sorry I'd listened to him. My fawning letter to that celebrity was something I regretted, though I had the small mercy of not having signed the letter. I coughed on a carrot. Mary came to pat my back. I shrugged her off. Oh, the embarrassment of my own insipid words to Lord Byron. (*You probably think me a stupid girl for driveling on about your many talents!* How I wished I had at least not placed the exclamatory *!*.)

"I should think you know Murray's answer already," I said to Shelley. I did not wish to revisit the office at 50 Albemarle Street for fear I might, in fact, see evidence of Byron's work and fall into a pit of lust on the floor from mere mention of his name.

Besides, though Shelley had modest success with *Queen Mab*—which he had published himself—Murray had rejected Shelley's "Alastor" only recently. I had read "Alastor" when Shelley brought it to Lynmouth from Bishopsgate, where he lived with Mary the autumn last. It was then untitled and remained so until Thomas Love Peacock, a friend of Shelley's whom my brother Charles called Best Named & Most Idyll-Inclined Man, thought to give it a haunting title. Still, even with its poetic start, the collection had been rejected by Murray, and the thought of returning there yet again made me feel humiliated for Shelley.

Yet Shelley did not share my discomfort. "It cannot hurt to go to Mayfair once more—perhaps Murray's mind has changed now that Hamilton has published me. Competition amongst publishers is generally a good move. I shall give Murray the opportunity to consider my newer works."

I looked at him and thought how nice it must be to live in the world of men, thinking oneself always deserving and thus that Murray had made a mistake and missed an opportunity rather than that Shelley's work did not merit publication.

"Though of course I wish you best efforts in securing publication, I should prefer not to go there, especially when . . ." I tried out the words to see how they felt aloud, "when he publishes also George Gordon, Lord Byron."

"Whyever would you use his full name," Mary said, eyebrows raised, shaking her head.

I gave up on not blushing. "I do not know him!"

"Well, it is embarrassing, all the same," she said.

"Fine," I said. "I shall call him Lord B!"

"Claire!" Mary dropped her spoon.

Everything I did and said seemed to embarrass her. Shelley looked at us both, amused and annoyed at the same time, and said, "Byron will not be there, surely. It is merely his publishing house. Claire?" He employed the quiet, forceful look he gave his biggest desires.

"Of course I shall go with you," I said and then regretted it as I always did.

I did not wish to trot along behind him—and it always was behind. Not only because his stride was so long but because—and this I had said to Mary—because Shelley liked it when I was a pace or two back. At sixteen years old during their elopement, I had made it a game, but at nearly eighteen, I felt odd doing so. I did not know the words for the oddness, however, so still I said nothing. I picked at my food.

"Claire, must you eat each pea individually?"

"Mary, must you comment on how another person chooses to consume nourishment?"

"I shall have to leave the table if you cannot be civil," Shelley said.

Mary corrected herself, brightening for Shelley. "I read Homer today. What is gripping is his specificity. Each line is relatable. His ability to engage the reader with a plight and such clear emotions." Perhaps my own writing would benefit from her advice. "I read while Claire took on the rather Herculean task of looking after Willmouse again."

I softened. Mary searched her bowl for a chunk of swede, her favourite vegetable. I tried always to put them in dishes for her, but the crop had been scarce this winter.

"Taking care of a baby is hardly on the list of the Twelve Labours of Hercules," I said.

"It ought to be," Mary said. "For I should rather slay a dragon—"

"No dragons," I said. "Only birds. Lion. Hydra. Bull. Boar. Mare."

"You forget Geryon." Mary pointed her fork at me. At once, she and I both dropped our cutlery in our bowls and made our hands into claws and held them near our faces. Shelley joined.

"Now we are the Geryon," I said. "For it is a monster with three bodies and three heads."

Mary nodded. "Or one with one body and three heads."

"Or," Shelley said, "I believe it might also have three bodies and one head."

"That sounds uncomfortable," I said, and they both laughed—Mary's small and Shelley's hearty. This was what I loved most: the easy flow of conversation, our shared knowledge, the ways we understood and helped each other despite some discomfort in doing so.

Shelley's laugh was followed by a cough, which broke our moment as he often did.

"I might be unwell," he said, and Mary paled. She rose and touched his cheek in exactly the way a woman was meant to tend to her beloved. Everything Mary did was with precision and care, whether turning the pages of book, licking a finger to smooth down an eyebrow, or touching her pale, cool knuckles to Shelley's face. I felt beastly beside her.

She pushed her bowl towards him. "Perhaps you need more food."

"You know I won't touch the meat." He was a boastful vegetarian, but did accept a forkful of her potatoes. He saw himself as being without judgement of difference, but when I lifted a piece of lamb to my lips, I noticed he looked disappointed.

I ate all of my food. I was not a glutton—I only appeared and felt so next to Mary, who pecked at her peas, each a regretful shade of defeated grey. Shelley ate the rest of Mary's potatoes, setting the fork down on the bowl's edge without it making a sound. He had been raised too well to ever have it make a sound.

"Please stay home tomorrow, Shelley. I should think you need to mind your lungs. Let Claire run out if we should require anything."

Mary had twice succeeded with her words: She had set me free from the outing to John Murray's office, and also kept Shelley at her side.

AFTER WILLIAM'S cry caused Mary to abandon the rest of her meal and after Shelley had written to another bank requesting funds in advance of money he assumed he would inherit and after I had fetched water from the cistern and scrubbed the dinner dishes, I made a decision.

I would, after everyone had gone to bed, try to write. Not a book. A letter. A better letter than I had managed from my quiet solitude in Lynmouth.

Surely part of love is bravery. I had witnessed this with Mary running away with Shelley. Yet hand in hand with bravery was foolishness. And part of writing was revising. I wanted to be the version of myself I saw in my mind.

Writing a letter—specific, filled with emotion—to the most famous man in the country, a man far out of my league in looks, glamour, and class, felt like the first step.

~~*I beg your pardon.*~~

~~*I am a stranger unknown to you*~~. Of course I was unknown to him. That was the very definition of stranger. No.

An utter stranger takes the liberty of addressing you. I seek to know not the public idea of your personage but of the You. Please pardon the intrusion & ~~*know this is not sent on impulse nor is receipt based on pride for I know pride often destroys our own happiness & that of others.*~~

I should not mention pride, for his wife, Lady Byron, had called *Pride and Prejudice* "the fashionable novel," and her words had been all over London and I knew not if they were favourable (good fashion) or disparaging (fashion was but a fleeting fancy).

I tremble at your reaction to this letter. I find myself on the verge—but of what, I cannot say. The result of which hastens my decision to write to you. I did not say *again* in the hope he had forgotten or never read the first letter.

Ought I include reference to his infamy? There are those obsessed with fame. Or more accurately with the famous. Names printed time and again on newspaper and in gossip strips. I liked to look at fashion pictures—for who does not want to look nice in a new shade of jonquil? I could not afford anything in the sketches yet enjoyed them nonetheless. I had seen one entitled "Dandies & Monstrosities of Hyde Park"—waists cinched far too tight, feathers far too tall gawking from hats, hunched young women and buff-chested men uniformed as though going to battle when they were only flaneurs, everyone ridiculous and alluring nonetheless, which I supposed was the point. Byron was not named amongst the costumed crew, yet I could imagine his face on any of the bodies.

Still, he likely received missives such as mine by the bushel; he had shot to fame, selling ten thousand copies of *The Corsair* in a single day. Byromania had swept London, then Europe, then the world. How I relished *The Corsair*'s pirate story, a man risking love to save a Turkish slave. Still, Byron needed no reminder of his fame. For people most often know who and what they are—the fat know of their bodies, the rich of their wealth, the desperate of their situation.

I am young and vain and poor. Perhaps I brought all of this on myself and yet how can this be so? For is it my fault that I am half girl, half woman and—I admit—lonely?

What else might I add to comply with Mary's literary notes? My doglike loyalty and enthusiasm. Was being doglike a winning quality? Perhaps we describe our fine qualities as those in which we personally find value and I ought to seek out dogs rather than be one. Alas. Perhaps I called myself doglike only before someone else used the word and inflicted its other meanings.

I could nearly feel Mary reading over my shoulder. If criticism were a sport, Mary surely would have won the Scorton Silver Arrow. In this way, she was far more like my mother than I; all of her comments which she believed were only comments settled on me like critical doves. I ought not include too much of myself in the letter. Only just enough to pique curiosity. I began again.

I am young and vain and poor. The result of which hastens my decision to write to you. Perhaps I brought all of this on myself and yet how can this be so? For is it my fault that I am young and—I admit—lonely? I want so much to be loved to have love to be wrapped in love . . .

I felt this so heartily that I turned away from any notion I might be distorting myself to have it. This is a lesson girls learn early—finding and holding love requires a certain amount of muzzling one's own mouth.

> *I am married to language yet in truth unattached and unafraid of this unattachment. My greatest wish is not to intrude upon your day—or night should you be one who reads by candlelight when the city sleeps as some literary men do—yet I wish to be known to you. I attempt here to use laconic sentences to save you time and thought. I do so hope I have succeeded.*

I thought of the novels I read and reread.

> *Do not let pride keep you from responding to me—for pride can keep us from happiness.*

I thought of Mary reading Homer. Specificity. Relatability.

> *We are all stories of before and after. Will this letter be my After? This, my Lord, is a choice for you. Will you not find it in your own large heart to visit with my lonely one?*

In Lynmouth last summer, I had written without my name attached. This was not so much hiding—for I did not feel cowardly, at least not completely—but rather, I felt I was somehow ducking down behind a stronger version of myself, one who might speak up. Thinking about

Mary, about Shelley, about the houses we lived in, none of them ours, the rather rented life I felt I was living, I dashed out my initials.

Or I tried to. My nerves overtook me, so rather than a simple *CC* or *CJC*, what I scratched on the page read,

> *Yours in spirit,*
> *CGB*

Who was *CGB*? I blushed with fury at myself yet did not have the strength to redo the letter. I folded it in quarters and then again in half, burnt my sealing wax, closing it—and my heart—up for the night.

3

FROM UPSTAIRS, WILLIAM'S WAILING startled us all, and my breakfast toast paused before my mouth, hovering in a strangely suspended fashion. Mary gave me a pleading look as the baby cried again. My letter to Byron rustled in my skirt pocket. I hoped it did not draw attention.

"Claire, would you—" Mary said.

I stood up. I was raised to be agreeable and similar—that is, similar to those in good standing. I ought to be a looking glass reflection to them rather than my own person, for the trait most prized in a girl is being altogether amiable.

It was only with Mary I felt I could let my true self leak out. When we were alone, she seemed to relish this, and give back to me the small privacies of her mind. Yet when others were there—first our parents and siblings, then any visitors, this waned. Especially as Shelley became a fixture and then tried to pair Mary—unsuccessfully—with his best friend, Thomas Jefferson Hogg, whom Shelley had known since first term Oxford. Shelley posed it as an example of the free love in which both Mary's father and Shelley believed. Hogg had pursued Mary with

Shelley's blessing; Mary pushed him off at first but then revealed she was quite taken with him yet more out of wanting to please Shelley. Mary's lackluster attraction dwindled—she did not want to share or be shared—this she confessed to me when we were alone.

Even though we had been raised in the philosophy of free love, I believed Mary found the unrestraint distasteful—yet being with Shelley required subscribing to it. *Love is free*, Shelley had written, *to promise for ever to love the same woman, is not less than absurd.* I did not yet know what I believed. Still, I found myself so well trained in the art of being agreeable I often could not wriggle out of its heavy cloak. William wailed again. Mary pleaded with me.

Shelley said, "Mary, let Claire eat."

I set my toast down to say I did not mind, but Shelley touched Mary's hand, and she rose from the table to fetch William. Shelley had tried once or twice unsuccessfully to share a room with them, only to find the baby's cries, even William's peaceful snuffling, were enough to keep Shelley awake for hours, so Mary had moved to another room—permanently it seemed—and shared it with the baby.

I had offered to be the one to share with the baby, but Mary felt it ill-advised. For after Europe with Mary and Shelley—before my exile to Lynmouth in May of the year before—I had suffered night terrors. In truth they had started at the end of their elopement.

When I bolted upright, screaming, Mary would come to my aid. Or Shelley. A doctor was consulted—fifteen was too young to leave home, perhaps. I could barely stand to be away from my mother, though she pecked at me so. Then, before the matter could be resolved, we had settled in another rental in which Mary could rest, as she had fallen pregnant. She slept so much. When night came, Mary slept still, and that is when I would feel panic grip. First my ribs, as though I were caught in a joiner's vice. Then my breath shallow and fast. A chill line of sweat on my upper lip, though I did not feel cold. Try as I might to lull myself into slumber, I often woke mid-scream, arms flailing. Mary would send Shelley to wrestle me back into human form.

The episodes continued—neither doctors nor we knew why. Mary grew weary of them, of me, and pressed Shelley to help. He would sit and speak softly to me, stroking my hair, coaxing me out of darkness by reciting poetry or confiding stories from his youth during our nocturnal tête-à-têtes.

Back then, Mary grew concerned my issues weighed upon Shelley, yet time and again he reassured me he wanted only to make sure I did not—as he worried—despise him. We had read Ariosto's epic Italian poem *Orlando Furioso*, together which Shelley had selected for me because he felt I ought to devote time to bettering my mind, as I had not much in the way of proper schooling.

"*Orlando Furioso* is the basis for so much," I had told him, proving I had been paying attention to the story of a knight and a sorceress. "Handel, Vivaldi, Haydn, so many composers are swayed by this tale." He had beamed at my gratitude—and truly I was filled with it, for there are not many men who would have taken the time to give me such exposure.

Still, he had acquiesced when Mary pushed me out. I had nowhere to go, as neither Mary nor I were welcomed back to our childhood home, and no one took to hiring me as a governess, despite my language skills. A predicament: raised in the realm of free love yet this belief did not apply when it came to me or to Mary.

Away from Mary's terseness and slumber, I tried for contentment in the cottage rented by Shelley. He had rented the same one a few years before with his first wife and her sister. Knees tucked to my chin, I had spent summer afternoons staring at the green-black sea in Lynmouth, wondering about the adult life my sister had back in London. *A life of sixteen years is already too much to bear*, I wrote to her during my months of isolation.

Only once did I have a visit from Shelley, who made me swear not to ever—ever!—tell my sister, for fear she would grow angry again whence she, too, had regained a sense of calm. I had kept my word, despite my confusion at Shelley's visit, his familiarity that led to entering without knocking, the way he disregarded my feelings of abandonment from Mary.

Upon my return to living with them this winter, I promised Mary that the nighttime terror episodes would not return. And so far, they hadn't. Shelley told me he was sleeping better too, with all of us together again. Still, it was better I not share the room with the baby.

Shelley dotted his bread with butter and furrowed over bills. I listened as Mary cooed to William upstairs and wondered when I might make my escape to post my letter to Lord Byron. Safe in my pocket, it nuzzled my thigh.

While I did not any longer have terror-filled nights, I did find myself sometimes unable to fall—or to stay—asleep. My mind churned over a girl who had once wronged me, or I imagined setting myself inside a novel. What I would say. What I would feel. The dialogues appeared in my mind, and I often gave in to the night, went to my desk, and scribbled. Sometimes Shelley found me. The two of us would talk, blankets around each of our shoulders as he stood towering over me at my little desk. "You are very devoted," he'd told me on more than one occasion.

"You call it devotion, I might say routine," I had said, for I found difficulty in accepting kind words.

"A productive routine, then," he had said. "We are similar in that way—for you likely have learnt from me." I did not know why it was so difficult for men who could be nice to also keep from being smug.

"All I do is write the day's events, my feelings about them. That sort of thing."

"That sort of thing," he had said, "is how all writers start."

"I am not *only* starting," I had reminded him. I had written a novel during our European trip following their elopement. Likely he had forgotten due to being enraptured by Mary.

Now with his breakfast, Shelley studied my face, concerned. My mother used to insist he was an unlikely brother to me. Yet, as he also insisted, a brother all the same. Good thing he had not come down last night, for I had been writing my letter to Byron at that hour.

"Did I hear you awake again last night?"

"Yes." A small cough at the back of my throat. I did not permit its escape lest Shelley push a spoonful of Mother Bailey's Quieting Syrup on me. I did not wish to be quiet as that.

He studied me. "And what words appeared on your page last night?"

I shrugged, a movement he found distasteful and of the market class. I felt a small pinprick of pride at not changing my behaviour to suit him the way I had witnessed Mary tamping down her shrugs so as to better appeal.

"Were you at a loss for words, Claire?"

"Quite the contrary," I said, thinking of my cross-outs and add-ins to Byron. I willed my cheeks not to redden. "I had many words. Some useless. So I wrote, crossed out, and made a mess."

This seemed enough of an answer for him. When he could no longer tolerate the stack of bills in front of him, he rose and went to Mary. I left the dishes and, feeling hope folded into the letter, crept out to post it.

4

DID I WAKE DESPONDENT at the lack of last evening's post addressed to me? Was I an ever-growing fool to think a celebrity author would both receive and respond to my letter? Moreover, was I not the most ridiculous girl in all of London to expect anything to come of my midnight missive?

When the second morning mail delivery bell rang, I sprang up, hopeful. The post-boy stood waiting in the wet-slop of melted snow with expectant palm for his payment. My heart became a crow hell-bent on clutching something shiny. Yet when I saw the outside of a letter addressed to me had 'two sheets enclosed,' my birdness flew off, for more sheets meant double the cost to me. When I saw the neat curve of script, the back, which had no name, only the Mayfair address which I had committed to memory, I flew to my silver tin and paid.

With fingers barely remembering how to prove their use, I found the two pages. One blank. One requested my presence that evening at the

Drury Theatre. My first thought was, an entire page left blank—imagine!—and at my expense. This was followed very quickly by thrill.

Byron wished to meet me. Or wished *me* to meet *him* that very night at half past seven. I had pulled this future event out of thin air, conjured it out of my own wishes.

I put his letter in my pocket, keeping the secret of it there while I cleaned then helped Mary bathe William in a large bowl I mostly used to make bread. I could feel the letter's thick corner poke my skin but gave no sign of this on my face.

I could tolerate discomfort in the name of a secret. Mary thought she knew everything about me, yet she did not. And while she and her clean, downy baby tucked in early in their room and Shelley snored in his, all of them slumbering till morning, I readied myself for my meeting.

I LIVED in a world without much choice. I had accepted this my whole life without knowing I had accepted it because it was simply the way of everything. I chose not what I did with my days nor where I slept, not where I lived. The first choice I had ever made was to accompany Mary. My second was to slip out of the house to meet Byron on my own.

So as I left, I felt a surge of excitement.

I wore a mulberry-coloured dress I did not care for but which my mother had told me made me appear smaller and had the side benefit of being dark enough to hide stains. My hat was missing one of its plumes but its duckbill-shaped brim cast my face in shadow which made me feel mysterious.

I did not wish to be early for our meeting, for that would speak only to my lack of grace, my clumsy youth, so I did not hurry as I stopped before the looking glass. It was old and gave everything a smoky appearance. I studied my face and pinched my cheeks so hard I winced. The red would last a good while. I was meant to care very much about how I looked and yet was supposed to also pretend that I cared not at all about how I looked.

I made a horrible face at myself—what would the world think of me like that?—and then put myself back together, and smiled.

My boots scuffed the front steps. Barely could I contain my joy of knowing I would behold him in the flesh, perhaps in a crowd of others, perhaps at a distance, yet nonetheless closer than I had ever been to such celebrity. I would be near enough to touch a person I had seen only in papers, read about, heard of in the gossip of literary circles and fish-mongers. I would breathe the same air as this man.

And before I plunged from our address towards the theatre, I paused. The evening air was oddly warm, the snow a distant memory. I had the world to discover. Yet I could hear my mother's whisper—*what on earth do you think you're doing, Jane* (For surely she would not call me Claire, though I had been known as such for some time?) And I could hear Godwin, Mary's father: *What is the measured action at this moment?* So often the voice one heard in one's head was not one's own. I had to forget them to move into the golden hue wrought upon celebrity. How close I would stand to such gleam. How a simple girl such as myself might kick into action the whole next chapter of her life.

Perhaps this would be the best and most important move of my life thus far. I tried not to consider the opposite—that I would come to shelter it under the parasol of poor decisions for the rest of my life.

I journeyed to the West End in a hackney, its floor coated in oil and grit. Covent Garden hawkers mainly gone for the night, crushed hyacinths underfoot gave sweet, heady smells as I trod also on rotted vegetable remnants. Before the Theatre Royal Drury Lane, where I knew he was on the management subcommittee, I caught my breath and steadied myself.

I entered through the main doors, expecting a swarm of patrons, but the grand hall was empty; the show had started. He had told me to meet him but had not specified where. I stepped lightly towards the back halls with my frumpy dress swishing. Polished walls beset with inlayed pearl and lapis. Painted vines on the flooring pulling me towards a doorway marked *Private*, which was a word I ignored, for I believed that behind that door, on the other side of that word, was Lord Byron.

I did not have expectations, only a young person's heart. This was only a sentence I had constructed in case he accused me of forecasting. When I opened the door I saw a velvet chaise whose tattiness gave me comfort, a sideboard piled with small cakes, powder, rouge, wigs on their silent wooden heads.

No Lord Byron.

I moved towards the cakes with no intention of tasting one but found myself with icing sugar on my finger just as the door creaked open. I turned.

When he entered the room, I felt stricken. There is not another way I might say that, for when one has gazed upon a person in the papers, studied the way their lips curve, imagined saying words so witty those lips part in laughter and then finds that soul in truest form within grasp, well, one is struck.

That he was handsome was not opinion, only fact. Documented time and again from his youth to present, twenty-eight years of age and still youthful of face. His was a slippery sort of beauty, and that very transient quality only urged his appeal. Rather than further stain my less than pristine dress, I quickly licked the sugar from my finger. If this enticed or repulsed Byron he gave no sign.

"Have we had the pleasure?" he asked.

"Not before this day," I told him.

He gave my dress a slow once-over. "Interesting." He held off further comment and went to the cakes. "Mine is an irrepressible sweet tooth. I order them for the actors, yet I am the one who indulges." I watched him consider the treats. This was not a man who would lead me out of the rented house on Arabella Row in a gust of romance. This was a man who wanted sweets but—with a dramatic sigh—denied himself and instead took to doing up the buttons on his coat. He would leave if I did not try another tack.

"I wrote to you," I said. When he did not respond right away I rearranged my face to show no hurt.

"You did," he said, with no tone to assure me he knew or to query if this was actually the case. "You must understand I receive quite a great deal of correspondence, equally from admirers and loathers." He paused. "I can barely tell one from the next. I invite many people to the theatre, but to see a show—not to see me."

I blushed, for I had misunderstood. He had not granted me an audience with him, but offered a free ticket. And I had been too late for that.

Now tedium on his face told me he had been in this room, many rooms, with legions of worshippers and was nudging me into the crowd of the nameless fame-hoverers. I needed to separate myself from those crowds. When I had met Shelley I had not been impressed with him—this was, he had told me, what piqued his curiosity.

The route to infiltrating fame seemed to be adoration followed quickly by unintentional disrupting of the adoration cycle followed by slight dismissiveness.

"Your work is brilliant, of course, but truly I did not write to you because of you." I paused. "I wrote because of me." This proved successful. "Perhaps you remember my words?" I felt foolish quoting myself but dared to press on. "I am young and vain and—"

Byron fished in his pocket and brought my letter out. "Yes. This nearly went in the fire, but as I read I was taken in." He gave me a look which made me feel as though the sun shone only on my face, my feet, my hat, which perhaps did not quite carry off its missing plume. "It is rare to see a clever turn of phrase matched with truth of feeling. Are you a risk-taker by nature?" I did not know how to answer, for I had never considered myself one or not one. I said nothing. "Of course, anything on a page is a risk. Still, I admire your effort."

So what Shelley and Mary had advised with regards to Homer had charmed him. Byron moved closer to me, still holding my words in his hand. I understood that the girl I had been when I had written the letter and the one I was becoming in the readying room at the Drury were already far apart in experience.

Then, without warning, he appeared bored. He looked to the door.

Panic rose in my chest, for I could not bear the thought that this—our only meeting—would end so quickly. "I would be so obliged if you should refer me to any who might help me in my career."

Byron looked at the cakes again and sighed. "And what career would that be?"

What ought I to say? Writing—or no, too close to his profession. "Acting?"

"Are you querying me?"

I blushed, faltering. "Perhaps . . . I do not know. How might anyone choose anything—a cake? A profession?"

He looked less bored, drawn in by my doubt. I had a translation process by which my mouth took phrases and ideas I had and made them into language appropriate and acceptable for a girl such as myself. Mostly, I kept my strangeness where it belonged—folded into tiny parcels tied in meticulous bows and stacked in the imaginary library in my head. Only Mary sometimes read in that imaginary place. Yet in that dressing room with Byron, for the first time, I felt I was in the presence of someone who might also appreciate that oddness, but I would have to take another risk. "Perhaps I am meant to be on stage," I said. "Or on the page."

"Or earn a wage."

I laughed too hard, and he gave me a pitying look. "Rest assured, sir—my lord—I am not an imposter, despite being poorly versed in necessary instructions for one intending such a career."

"Well, one hopes you do not consider me an expert in all things, Miss—?"

I swallowed hard and met his glance. "Not in all things." I could not bear him not remembering my name. "Clairmont. Miss Claire Clairmont."

I reached for a cake and tore its prettiness in half, ate one and gave him the other. This he liked. And knowing he appreciated my candor and appetite only made him more appealing to me. I was sharing a cake with a celebrity. One whose mouth was flustered with crumbs. I wanted to kiss them off and have him praise me for it.

"I beg your pardon," he said. "For I am not quite myself today."

"Who is?" The words slipped out with no mind and fluttered in the air as he smiled. I had no chance at seeing him again, so I thought I might as well be myself, silly and serious, insistent and hungry. I had not read the gossip pages due to the snow day, so I knew not if he had a new scandal plaguing him. His old scandals were enough to stoke a bonfire—a penchant for drink and drug, philandering with all walks of life. I gazed at the flesh-and-blood man in front of me. He did not embody only charm. He managed to balance playfulness on his mouth, sadness in his gaze, and a laxness that made me—and, I assumed, anyone in his company—feel comfortable while still feeling it was a great honour to be near him. "I often know not who I am on any given day."

"So we are strangers to ourselves then," he said. I nodded. He considered my face. "Shall we have tea with them? With—"

"With the us and the not-us pairs?"

"My very thoughts exactly," he said. "When next we meet we shall all have tea."

We both grinned. Small smiles, the sort that suggest larger ones are to come. I admit he was beautiful. A gorgeous face, compelling the way a dark sea calls out when one is alone on a bridge too close to dusk. He was the sort of person who—right there, in front of me—became a sort of precipice.

5

LIFE IS GOING TO CHANGE. This I wrote down on a loose page and held in my lungs with each breath, in my belly as I made myself a butter and jam sandwich, taking care to get the preserves exactly to the edges of the bread.

I was built for change, raised to renovate. My mother raised me to find always, and often quite immediately, ways to improve—a room might be better suited with furniture arranged differently. I might be prettier if I wore a different shade, changed my hair. In my mother's eyes, no landscape was without possibilities for improvement. I felt she tried to renovate me.

Yet whilst I had gained skills necessary for home- or self-improvement, I gained also the large detriment of being unable to appreciate anything—meal, house, entryway, person—as they *were* rather than what I thought they could be.

I had met a man who required no betterment and yet—if one believed the gossip—still might benefit from a soothing, a touch of care from a regular person.

Without Mary to scold me, I ate my sandwich standing up, catching some crumbs in my hand while others fell on the pages of the journal she and Shelley and I shared as I read words in Shelley's hand:

She has a habit of touching her thumbnail to her lips,
following their outline as though trying to memorize. This
small act draws the eye the way one is drawn to the moon
no matter its present shape nor the colour of the sky.

As I read this I had my thumbnail to my lips—a habit Mary and I shared. I knew not who had done it first. Shelley had noticed Mary doing so and written about her with an attention anyone might crave. Mary had written in the margins, leaving little space.

I separated from my body long ago, she wrote. *I find we are always in conversation yet never truly one.*

I felt sorrow course through me on her behalf. She and her body were not one, and I knew my body was mine and yet also not mine, for that was part of growing up, it seemed. I wished we could talk, but instead I brought her a sandwich.

Mary's anguished face kept me near to her, kept me refreshing her coffee, a blanket on her lap as she refused to move from the chilly draft near the windowsill, where she looked at the world but did not venture out into it. She did not eat.

"You are so good to me, Claire," Mary said. "I do not wish to be a burden."

I took her hand. If only I could ease her suffering. If only I might share with her the excitement in my heart about Lord Byron. She would not approve, would discourage me—either because of her mood or because she did not think me worthy of one such as Byron. She was bright enough to enthrall someone like Shelley. But Claire? Or no, perhaps she'd be concerned for me.

If I had in my mind always pictured finding a great romance, it was with the full understanding that I would share each moment of it with my sister. I wanted her to read love notes, discuss the tone of any suggestive words said to me. I wanted her to follow along with the pitch and roll of my heart as I watched the sea storm of my feelings. Yet I knew if I told her anything of late she would pull me quickly back to shore and leave me there to dry alone.

"How could you be a burden to me, Mary? We are siblings and must always take care of each other."

6

THE NIGHT SOIL MEN were finished, daylight just edging up the sky in a promising shade of lemon curd as I rode to Byron's in time for his first tea, which he took before anyone sensible was awake. London smelt of old fat, sewage, peat fires, and coal, and in the carriage, of my sad attempt at homemade perfume. We could not afford real scent, and I'd read of Napoleon's desire for Joséphine when she wore tonka bean or patchouli—granted that marriage had ended, yet I imagined he felt wounded when he again smelt those things. I wanted to make someone swoon and then ache with remembering.

Mary had an ageing jar of sappy-smelling tragacanth picked up on our walk through Europe—she'd added citrus and carried it back, daily dabbing bits of paste on her neck to disguise our lack of baths. I smelt my wrist and frowned. This was not the allure of far-away ambergris or even something simple and cottagey—rosemary, perhaps. My stolen tragacanth smelt of its true name, goat's thorn.

The citrus had long since faded, and I worried I had made a mistake dabbing it on my wrists. I removed a glove, licked my thumb, and tried to remove the paste. All of this made me wish I had stayed home—far safer to be there with the fantasy of the man rather than in close proximity to the real one, smelling poorly. Though I had bathed not long ago and taken care with my hair, I was plagued with doubt.

I would return back before Mary had awoken if I went home. Yet before I could act, the carriage stopped. I had arrived. With a clutched chest, I reached out to bang the carriage door to say turn around.

I did not know how Lord Byron would see me. Shelley described me once to my own mother. *A tall fawn of a girl with black eyes,* he had said. *Her eyes are brown but never-you-mind,* my mother replied. Since then the words had come back often. When I walked up the imposing steps to Byron's double front door, I imagined my feet as hooves. A tall fawn. Too wide to be gangly but with the same wobble-kneed gait. This worked in my favour, too, for under my bland dress I had a shapely body, which I preferred not to trot out publicly, yet it went with me everywhere. The carriage pulled away. However I smelt, however I appeared, I had arrived at 139 Piccadilly. My heart was on the prowl, sniffing, looking this way and that before starting through the oversized gate up three wide stone steps.

Upon entering I met first his valet called Fletcher. I stood in the entryway with its Roquefort-coloured marbled floor, the matching interior staircase graceful and curved as Byron's side smile had been. Fletcher led the way into one of the many cavernous rooms off the entryway and requested I wait.

Which I did. First I stood in a natural position. Then I subtly arranged my features and shoulders in the best way possible, angled and with a fetching glance. This lasted awhile, but when the waiting went on, I managed no longer and slouched.

The ornate rosette on the ceiling felt like an eye looking at me as I explored the room. Carved fireplace, bookshelves filled to the heavens. I scanned them but did not see Shelley's *A Vindication of Natural Diet.* Byron seemed like a man who tore into meat. Rich rugs, a shadowy looking glass that took up half a wall, six lion head candelabras with candles stuck into the roaring mouths. A highback chair upholstered in mustard silk in front of a table. Pretending to fix my dress, I leaned to see what papers were on the table, but before I could, Fletcher announced his employer.

Byron did not apologise for his delay. I recalled my mother telling me the late person controlled the room.

We stood regarding each other in the quiet. The walls behind him were Prussian blue, which gave him the appearance of floating in water or sky. I told him this, and he laughed as a tea service was set in front of us.

"You said at the theatre you were not yourself. Was this mood or circumstances?" I asked.

"How forward you are," he said. I was glad Mary was not present. Still, Byron seemed charmed by me or at least not repulsed by my inquisitive nature. "To answer you, both. For one prompts the other. My wife left me—"

"Oh dear."

Surely there was not a person in all of London who did not know this, yet I kept the farce of surprise and concern. I knew what was reported: Annabella Milbanke had cast him out for reasons not mentioned in the papers nor clarified by him. I knew she had pushed him off and they had been separated since the birth of their daughter. I also knew that scandal followed him or he courted it.

"Does that concern you?" he asked. "Miss Clairmont?"

Pleased he had committed my name to his lips, I spoke freely. "I am not quite sure the meaning of your question. If you mean to suggest this is not my business, I understand. However, if the question is do I think that one woman's severing of a man entirely from her life ought to be a warning, then I must confess my response is that I am a different sort of person raised in a different sort of way and you—" I looked at him directly, "seem a very different sort of man."

I did not add that I harboured a wish that I was the sort of woman who might make him into a different sort of man. "May I ask after your current mood?"

He sipped his tea. "Foul on the brightest day. I breathe cloud and dust."

"Oh you poor, sad dragon," I said. This caused him to choke on his tea.

"Surprising." He set he tea down and rubbed his elegant hands together. "You are delightful." I pictured those hands writing *she walks in beauty, like the night.* I pictured him writing *Lara, A Tale* and wondered—for only a moment—if he might ever one day write of me.

He moved closer but did not touch my hand nor move his knee to press against mine. I wanted him to do this. Instead he stirred sugar into his tea so slowly I felt my stomach give. When he put his cup to his mouth I could not look away.

"How old are you, Miss Clairmont?"

"Soon to be eighteen."

"How soon?"

"Next month. Twenty-seventh of April, I believe."

"You believe?"

"Yes. That is the date I was told was my birthday, so I have always accepted it as such."

"You believe what people tell you, then."

"Should I not?"

"Is the date not proven? Your tone seemed to suggest it might be otherwise."

I set my tea down so I could steady my hands against my thighs. I knew he saw this, and I took the liberty of placing one of his own hands atop mine. Mary would have been appalled.

"There is not record of my birth," I said. "Truly. No church nor town evidence."

"And where, pray tell, was this magical appearance of you, the unicorn of maidens?"

"Switzerland?"

"That is a country, not a question."

"It is all I have, for my mother was filled more with hearsay and fantasy than anything practical."

Lord Byron nodded. He kept his hand pressed on my hand, which pressed into my thigh. I was being myself. And that was quite enough to entertain and engross him. I wanted to throw my arms around him, but I resisted. We sat in pleasant chatter alternating with pleasant quiet until the tea grew cold.

Once I had scrounged from my mother's sewing basket silk and velvet trimmings left over from mended dresses and jackets. I'd sewn a sampler of the softest kind, each wonky square more tender and brilliant than the next. Byron, too, seemed like he might be fashioned into something altogether even more wonderous.

I could not help but give him an encouraging smile.

"Miss Clairmont. Claire. I promise you two things: You will enjoy yourself in my company, much of the time anyway." He sipped his tea and slid an open palm over the top of my knuckles, which until that very moment I had not known were part of my body. "Also, I will never live up to any image of me you might have made."

He watched my face. I was caught between knuckle rapture and gazing at him, despite the misery of his words.

"I have no expectations," I said, and was glad Mary was not present to catch me out in the lie.

"Fear not, Claire," Byron said. "For meeting anyone requires engaging in a contract of assured mutual disappointment."

7

I SAT IN MY WRITING nook, which felt smaller and smaller the more time I spent away from it. I could hear the slosh of Shelley's hand in a bowl while shaving and the patter of Mary's steps above.

If Mary and Shelley wondered at my regular absences—for I had been to visit Byron daily the past couple of weeks—they said nothing. Perhaps they had not noticed, for I had still managed to go with Shelley to John Murray, who declined once more to publish anything on offer. Dejected but determined, he strode home, and I had followed to help Mary bathe. Even as the scalding water turned her pink skin pinker, she encircled her torso with her own arms, unable to undo her indelible sadness.

I tried to write in the journal Mary and Shelley shared—she wrote backwards and he forward in order to conserve paper. That Mary shared a journal with Shelley had been a point of contention between us, for when we were growing up she and I often wrote together, notes and stories, largely in a secret coded language in which only we were fluent so if our parents or siblings had found the notes they would have thought them rubbish. On our trip to Europe she had begun a journal and asked me to again write with her. I went to add my words to hers, only to find Shelley had gotten there first. They'd taken turns writing, passing it back and forth, each encouraging their desire to be similarly minded. They'd asked me to write with them, though I suspected this was Shelley's doing and Mary only went along with it as a form of appeasement.

Upon my return from Lynmouth a long nine months later, having been driven from all I loved, Mary and Shelley had urged me to share a journal with them. A confusion, for it only made us more entwined.

My words the past few days were simple, a bluff to hide my new feelings, champagne froth and icing sugar and all things lustful and Byron.

I had written:

> *At last, I found rhubarb—served Mary spring trifle today.*

Following mine, Mary had written:

> *Motherhood makes of us a before and after example. I thought this change in me—anxious, ill-tempered, aware of life's ills and shortcomings—would revert upon having a new, living child. Yet I am still not my old self. That girl is gone and no one—not a single person, though this is an*

event that has happened forever—thought to warn me. No one thought to tell me to grieve my loss of her, even whilst I carried her, for children will always leave us.

So painful were her words, so tight the space forward and back, that I vowed to be done sharing their pages. I would go and buy my own journal. Each day I would document the previous day. If I skipped a day, I would redouble my efforts in the journal. No more loose pages for me. Nothing would slip by unnoticed, unwritten. And I would shield it from view. It would be only mine.

Upon hearing I had written a novel—lost, sadly, I'd said, and he'd stretched his face into an exaggerated frown—Byron had suggested that perhaps I was a writer still. Oh, how I nestled his encouragement in my chest, let it wriggle into my underthings.

B—

You bid me write at whenever such mood strikes and so I am, knowing I will see you only hours from now. At our meeting last you said I surprised you, yet I find myself much surprised. Already I have been witness to your gentlemanly nature & your kindness, which is altogether different from the image portrayed in the lurid papers. This I know: Having met you one might never forget you and, perhaps equally of note, having been seen by you, one feels altogether different.

I wished I had not used the word *altogether* twice, but alas, I needed to go to the stationers for more paper so could not begin again.

I touched the tip of my quill pen to my tongue, an old habit Mary had chided me for as long as I had been able to write. *You will stain your tongue forever,* she had said. Mary's knowledge could make her overbearing and disagreeable, yet her slightness and blondness and sweet face tempered these qualities and made her altogether irresistible, even in her sadness. Perhaps more so. I did not begrudge her this. Yet my tendency towards sarcasm, cleverness, openness, surely came from this. Where she appeared tight-lipped and locked, I presented myself as an open door. I tried to show this open door each day to Lord Byron.

> *Should my folly in finding you bring you concern, keep in mind the Creator ought not to destroy his Creature.*

Was I saying I was the Creator for I had sought Byron out, or saying he was for he had called me to the theatre and then to his home? Or was Desire my great Creator and I under its control? I was the one who had created the letter but soon it would be away from me and become a creature of its own.

I scribbled more.

> *Worry not, for unlike those who feel they know you, I am convinced I <u>will</u> know you. That already I do. I am not prone to love, merely curious. And now, as you are bemused by me in ways I would not allow myself to imagine, I am so cheered by the hours ticking by and the long minute hand drawing me ever-closer to your door.*

I folded the page and with a nub of my best wax—the one which smelt of ambergris—sealed it by pressing the small fob I wore on a slim chain around my neck into the wax. Satisfied, I hoped he would not judge me for using wax rather than a wafer seal. I heard the letter carrier's bell in the street and started towards the door, only to realise I had not signed it.

What if he did not know the sender? The thought that he might confuse me with another admirer caused me to feel ill.

I reached for the letter opener my mother had kept on her table, slid it most carefully under the wax. In the chill of my quarters, the blob had already dried. Still, I finessed the unsealing, added *Cl___ Cl__* to the bottom, refolded, and—this was the trick I had learnt from only occasionally reading my mother's letters, which never failed to disappoint with their financial focus—burnt the tiniest of new wax on my pointer finger, and ignored the pain as I slicked it under the already made imprinted seal.

There. Done. Redone.

ONCE THE letter was out of hand and on its way to Byron, I hurried to the kitchen.

Boiled swede mashed and mixed with one old plum and an apple wrinkled as a school matron. This with cream I whipped by hand would serve as the main meal. Mary craved only sweets, and Shelley cared only that Mary be inspired to eat, given her pallor of mood. The slump of fruit would again suffice. As I mixed and stirred, I heard a row brewing: Mary's raised voice and Shelley saying *no, no* in his deep timbre.

I hastened with the food so I could stand by the doorway and eavesdrop.

"The issue is not only the baby, the baby, the baby," my sister said. "You cannot possibly understand!" Her shriek was unexpected, and I nearly dropped the bowl. "You have more words pouring from you in a day than I have managed in weeks. Months. I feel I have dropped bits of myself along a cobbled path."

Had I been in the room and not only eavesdropping I would have offered her a hand, a leg, the ear she dropped, and she would have laughed. If I went in she would accuse me of throwing an Apple of Discord. I leant on the doorframe and considered charging in to help them.

Shelley wished to solve the problem of Mary. The fact that he could not made him edgy. I knew his actions when he felt this way; he would wriggle his long pale fingers and fidget with his chin, though the hairs grew in light and sparingly.

I started to go to Mary and stopped myself. I could hear her voice crack as she told of her fatigue, her feeling of uselessness without writing yet how she could not write because of fatigue. Fighting my instinct to intervene—for this would delay me, annoy her, and only help Shelley—I went to my tiny room. I drew a long breath and looked at my four rather ragged dresses and willed one of them to transform into anything new.

All of them were appalling in their own way—dirty hem, sleeve cuff in need of mending, a colour not in fashion. How could I go to Byron in a dirty old dress? Perhaps it was petty on my part, but I registered a loss at not being able to swap clothes with my sister. Not least because it gave one the appearance of having a larger wardrobe, but more for the closeness girls shared when borrowing, temporarily putting on each other's skins.

I sat on my bed, miserable the two moments I allowed myself, for I had not been raised to admit disappointment, until I remembered something. From under my bed, I pulled a box. Inside were more books, an old half-filled journal, a poorly done sketch I had made in Lynmouth back when, having lost the novel I'd written in Europe, I thought I might become an artist. Under all of this, a flash of colour. A new dress.

It was not new, but new to me. In Lynmouth I had befriended a laundress, and when items were left behind—patrons short on funds or leaving town in haste—she let me pick through. She made money on the side wearing in uncomfortable new boots for wealthy women who did not need to suffer. My own feet proved the wrong size for this labour.

I pulled out the seaside bathing dress and held it on my lap. The silk was a drake's elegant blue-green. The laundress had found the *Morning Post* advertisement wrapped around the garment. I read the words aloud softly as though reciting poetry: *Made in the form so contrived that stays, petticoat, and pelisse are all put on quickly. A flounce of gauze edge ornaments the dress. It is a lady's advantage to be able to dress and undress so quickly; the most fastidious belle must confess that nothing can possibly be more becoming than this Sea Side Bathing Dress.*

Would anyone know it was a dress made for bathing? I stepped into it, looked down, and decided it was every bit as lovely as the description and no different from a non-bathing dress except in description. It would do.

I TOOK some of the week's egg and cheese money and used it at the Temple of Muses, the largest and cheapest bookseller in all of England, if not the world. Even Shelley could not fail to be impressed by them. It was he who had brought me there first so I might buy a few items before Lynmouth. Shelley had bought me Robert Southey's poems to push across the idea that Lynmouth was lovely—*Little Switzerland*, Southey had called it, and Shelley had presented the poems as an apology for cloistering me there.

A part of me worried about being caught: *Why have we no eggs?* Shelley would shout, though this was unlikely. He was not a shouter. He was a prodder, a man of quiet concern. So if he did notice the scrambled portions scant, he would likely attribute this to my needing money for something personal, and he would not wish to pry—not yet. And Mary was still too tired to notice much of anything, let alone a lump less Stilton. Still, I felt anxiety for being thought selfish.

At the Temple of Muses, I went through the cavernous main room with its floor-to-ceiling shelves, rolling ladders, and ducked upstairs to the shabbier rooms with their lounging couches and remainders of books long abandoned by the reading public. I found a slim volume of Coleridge to bring to Byron and purchased it from the massive circular island at the centre of the room. The interior stamp would read Lackington, Allen & Co., which would remind Byron of my finances. I did not carry shame for this. I used my last monies at the stationers next door: a clutch of new quills, a few new pages on which to continue my letter writing, and—finally—a journal of my own. Stunning blue. Heavy in cover, with pages thick enough to last a lifetime.

8

THROUGH THE STREETS OF London I walked and then rode to Byron. With growing unrest, some days the carriage had to take the long way round to avoid being stuck in a swarm of protesters. Papers told of possible riots planned—the cost of bread rose faster than the pay wages, and I knew the crowds we avoided were hungry ones.

Past the edges of the park, down Piccadilly's wide grandeur, I felt great guilt over the bread I had allowed myself while others I passed starved. Still, the thing I hungered for most was Byron's gaze.

My visits followed a similar pattern: tea and talk, pastry, his gaze on my face, a question in his eyes not required on his lips. And then, a change in pattern. I went to where he sat on an armless chair. Because of the furniture's structure, he could pull me to him. I stood between his knees.

"Claire."

"I do love when you say my name," I told him, "perhaps because it was not the name given to me at birth."

"Your birth of which there is no record."

"Yes." He gripped my legs, brought his hands round to my backside, never once breaking his glance.

"Why the change?"

"I started as Mary."

"Unfortunate but not horrific."

"Mary Jane."

"Ah."

I had planned on giving him the Coleridge volume but realised doing so would break the spell. I no longer wished to look down at him and—he had not asked for this—instead sat astride him so our faces were close, mouths closer.

"Clara Mary Jane Clairmont was my given name," I said. "Mary was my sister, so we could not use that in the house. So Mary Jane was the girl I'd been, which helped to distinguish me from Mary, my sister. Then when I followed my sister on her elopement—I shall tell you more about that later—the Mary fell off. I became just Jane." I recalled the pitying sighs. "Poor Jane." I shook my head and tried to look away from his lips. "Then Jane Clara. And then it was suggested I just use Clara."

I did not say that Shelley had chosen Clara. It felt immature or odd, as though I belonged to someone else. I went on. "And then I decided upon Claire. For the word is easy on the tongue without another syllable."

"Claire," Byron said. My name from his mouth created a frenzy in my chest that was in competition with the space between my legs. Heat pushed from there as he said my name again. I wished I had chosen Claire for myself, with none of the idea from Shelley.

Byron held my face in his hands, looking. Waiting. I looked at the scythe curve of his mouth.

"You are transparent," he said, as I focused on his mouth. I liked that he could read my face again and again the way I had reread my favourite books.

"Say my name again." My voice was lower, soft. The command made him grip my hips as he said it. Any words out of his mouth filled me with desire. He could say my name or recite a poem or describe emptying the ash can, which was not something he had likely ever done, yet I would swoon, keening towards him with my full body. I leaned down to take the words from his mouth with my own. His mouth on mine, his hands roamed my back as though it were a land only just discovered.

"Claire," he said again. Entirely clothed yet feeling otherwise, I felt my hips move forward and back, a great rustling of fabric mixing with his moans, which sent a chill the length of my arms, for I knew I was the one causing the sounds escaping from his mouth. And I felt, too, a warmth in my own body, a spreading of pleasure and good feeling building until—abruptly—he gripped my waist and bade me to stop.

In the rasping afterwards, he kissed my neck and pecked at me for family details.

"My mother met Mary's father, William Godwin." I check his face for recognition. "At this point he was already well known as a philosopher, political writer, widower of—"

"Mary Wollstonecraft, yes, I gathered as much," Byron said. "A hyena in petticoats, was how Horace Walpole described her."

"What might that politician have said if Wollstonecraft had been male?" I shook my head. "Anyway, Godwin believed my mother to also be a widow."

"Ah, a shared misery," Byron said. "Works like a charm. Was that not the case?"

I paused. There was a choice at hand—to create a diversion, to hold my fan to my chest (too late for that, Claire!), or to offer a slimmed-down version of the truth. Words tumbled out bare and true. "My mother was no such thing. She had another child, Charles—my older brother—yet his father and mine are not the same, I do not believe. They cannot be. For if Mother went to Switzerland as she said, and well, there is no proof, yet I did find papers once—"

"Are you and Charles alike in face?"

"No. And he is blond as I am dark." I shook my long hair over my face. Byron parted it as one might a stage curtain. Perhaps that was my purpose—entertainment. For here was my tale, not of woe, exactly, but of a bastard life in a crowded house. "Do you know we were eventually five children, none with the same parentage?"

Rather than horror, Byron clapped his hands. "Marvelous."

"Is it?" I asked, images of chaos—shared shoes, never enough heat. "Ours is a complicated family tree." I looked at the excitement in his eyes and understood desire was part physical and part the wish to absorb details to remember. I arranged the tiny pastry squares and began slicing them, pressing their halves together to demonstrate each pairing.

"Before Skinner Street we lived on the northern edges of London in Somers Town," I said. This seemed to mean nothing to him. "All of us lived together. My stepsister, Fanny Imlay, whom we call the kindest one, is by blood Mary's half sister—older, the product of Wollstonecraft and Fanny's American father." Byron plucked the Fanny-Mary plum and raspberry pastry and ate it. "Charles who is fairest, my older half brother, my mother and Who Knows as the father." He pinched the lemon-plum square between finger and thumb and put it in his mouth. "And Mary, of course, and our baby brother, darling William, is the only offspring from my mother and Mary's father. He is perfect and away at boarding school."

Byron cleaned his mouth with a pressed linen serviette which had his initials on the corner. "It does seem a rather mixed lot," he said. He did not say this disparagingly, which was a relief, for I was used to a certain degree of shame in regards to my upbringing.

"In any case," I said, "my mother invented the surname Clairmont."

"How aristocratic."

"Her point exactly."

Byron looked at the pastry-strewn mess, my lips, which I realised had raspberry on them, and kissed me. "And here you are."

"Here I am." I watched him watch me as I stood, trying to regain my composure. Perhaps I had shared too much. "Please do not think of me as unseemly entertainment."

"On the contrary, I think you quite seemly."

I felt for my hair ribbon, which had come loose. He watched me slip it in my pocket.

"Have you siblings?" I asked, though I knew the answer. I knew many things about him, yet purported to be naive in this regard because I could tell he found my lack of knowledge about him refreshing.

"Only one—though we were not raised together. A half-sister, Augusta. Same father."

"Whether one shares the same father and mother or not, no child is ever treated the same way in any household. This one has a clever mind that must be cultivated, and thus we shall send her away to Scotland—"

"One presumes this was not you."

"Quite so. That was Mary," I said. She had gone away small and come back small. I had changed quite rapidly, not understanding that how a girl looks determines how long she has the good fortune to remain a child. "Mary's was a delicate nature which needed shelter from the whirlwind of rubbish that was my mother's verbosity."

"Yet you withstood the lashings?"

"I suppose." I looked at him. "It is not only my hips that are sturdy."

He moved close to me again. "So it is your soul, too?"

"You jest, yet I believe I have soldered a shield of sorts."

"Ah, so you are a knight in a girl's body. How perfect," he said. I grinned. The look on his face then was that of a man before a great and ready table. I did not yet allow him a seat.

9

EVERYTHING I KNEW ABOUT my body I had first learnt through my sister.

It was she who had injured her wrist trying to stand upon her head, so when I tried I spread my fingers wider for balance. And it was Mary who showed me a dance she had learnt in Scotland—presented to me in a highly serious way, all scowls and careful-toed, also known as boring, and when she had waited for me to imitate her, I had turned a cartwheel, which Mary reacted to with annoyance, but eventually I won her over.

It was she who had practised kissing in Scotland with her friend Isabella Baxter and told me it was quite usual for girls to kiss or share affections, as this was good training for marriage. Mary herself preferred the gentleness of her friend's mouth to the chapped lips Shelley had when first they kissed.

Where Mary found horror in her own monthly process, I found it quite fascinating—an entire world was happening inside my own body, and yet it was a country I could never truly visit. And while Mary found illness quite grotesque, I admitted a bit of, if not enjoyment, for who wishes anyone ill, then at least curiosity about how the body became sick and why.

Bodies and their faults and inherent messiness bothered my sister. I knew some of this was likely due to the particulars of Mary's mother's death, which clung to her. And when Mary first fell pregnant, it ended rather suddenly and with more blood than one could imagine. I had cleaned her legs and the floor and soaked the sheets in lye and sour milk.

Yet, despite Mary's numerous attempts to sway me towards embarrassment—for being a woman contained this word from the outset it seemed—I refused. Truthfully, I found bodies both beautiful and disgusting—a baby could have placid eyes and a sweet-smelling cheek pressed to mine, and also shit itself down my dress-front, and I could have graceful hip curves and muscled thighs from so many walks, cascading locks down my back, and yet also have dark hair on my calves that seemed rather manly.

And Shelley could have his commanding height, which spoke to a certain regal form, and yet his shoulders were in perpetual slump, which, while not truly disgusting—for no pus nor growth protruded—I found revolting.

So when I had asked Mary years before about the physical nature of her relationship with Shelley, she'd told me only of their conversations, of his encouragement of her ideas to write, which is to say she whispered to me nothing useful. I continue to push her in this regard, suggesting she enlighten me about fornication.

"You say the word as though it is amusing," she'd said.

"Is it not?"

"Not for me."

"Oh, it is serious always, then?" I remember Mary had closed her eyes and sighed the way she did when she wished me to know she existed in a complicated intellectual realm that I might never comprehend.

"Do you know about playing the blanket pipe?" she'd asked. The words ridiculous, her voice pronged as an olive spear.

"Is that part of the Royal Philharmonic Society?" I'd asked. When I felt condescended to, I never took the time to think properly.

"Oh, Claire," she'd said. "Come back to me when you are better informed."

And now I wondered, How might I become better informed if Mary was not to be the one to inform me?

10

I CREPT FROM MY ROOM through the nook in the same hunched crouch I used near the baby—I did not wish to wake anyone. When I reached the door, footsteps behind me raised the hairs on my neck.

"Where are you off to, then?" Shelley asked, down the stairs too soon for me to get away.

I held my reticule in my hand. "Shopping," I said. He looked skeptical. It was not that he would forbid me going out, only I had nowhere in particular of my own to go. I could see him thinking about the date and day, and I added, "Though it is not market day, I believe I might find beetroot or fennel."

He reached for my arm, his grip strong but not forceful. He had never hurt me, nor said an unkind word. Still, he preferred when I was near. It was a sort of possessiveness he had and one I had grown accustomed to, as my mother said it was brotherly to watch over someone in this manner.

"It is safer for you at home," Shelley said. "With the food riots." Bread or Blood riots had taken hold of the city. Still, the distress outside did not seem threatening to me.

I needed to push on one of Shelley's weaker points. "Fennel is thought to aid in digestion."

Shelley brightened. "Oh, that is most thoughtful of you, Claire. For you know my stomach pains me at night."

I turned to leave, relieved, and then realised I would need to procure a fennel bulb before I returned. "If I do not find the fennel at my regular stops, I shall hunt high and low until I do."

Shelley nodded, satisfied. "Claire, you know you can tell me if there are . . ." he lowered his voice, "problems you need to air." He came closer. "For Mary has begun to wonder if you have some secret . . ." I tried not to let my nerves show as I wound and unwound the strap on my bag.

"I have kept nothing from you," I said, and felt my own stomach sour with the lie. Secrets were purported to be exciting, and I had experienced this. But I also understood that secret-keeping was a lonely and sometimes dangerous business.

"Mary saw you with the tawdry papers and thought perhaps your head was in the gossip pages and that produced some dissatisfaction in you. Or perhaps you worry about our trip to Europe this summer—which will benefit us all." He studied my face. "We both want only your well-being. I take your time away from the house as an attempt to give us privacy. Please do not feel you have to do this for us—we manage so well with you near."

"Never fear, Shelley. I am well!" I said, rather too brightly. "I only wish to see as much of London this season as possible before we depart for Europe." He accepted this with his eyes if not his mouth, which frowned.

Part of me wished to shout about how I, the younger and sillier sister, had not only read the gossip but managed to finesse my own meeting with their star feature. Yet I did not. I was learning that power came from keeping some things to myself.

11

I TOOK TO ARRIVING A few minutes before the agreed-upon time so I might pause at the front gate and gaze upon Byron's house without hurry. Curling around the base of the metal were new vines that a groundskeeper would likely pull up before they could wrap and twist, but I checked daily on their progress. Despite the unsettled weather—an earthquake only yesterday in the north of the country was all the news—new buds had appeared overnight. I knew not the name of the plant, but I knew there were flowers that bloomed at night, and I wished to be among them. One day, I vowed I would spend more than the day at the house. I would know the dark overnight hours, too.

Inside, Byron puttered around his desk.

I had in the past been criticised for looking too long or too hard at people. I'd learnt that people found this rude or did not care to be studied. Byron did not seem to mind. So while he read from a stack of post, I wandered the vast room where we had spent many hours day upon day.

I had trained myself to be subversive in my espionage tactics—side glances, a pretense of looking far off when in fact I focused on the small hairs on the back of his neck, the gold stitching on his brocade jacket. I did not mention the stitching needed redoing, as I had learnt well not to comment on everything I noticed. Someone might be in possession of the most unfortunate of hairstyling or might overuse the phrase *indeed!*, their profile might resemble a Roman numeral, and where I might have blurted this out before, I was now a skilled vault-keeper.

This made Mary's life simpler and mine easier, yet some aspects of my verbal guardedness offered a misrepresentation of myself. I appeared smiling, agreeable, and social to Byron, yet I worried my cheerfulness made me appear diminished. Mary's serious nature made her seem intelligent. I soured my expression in an attempt to mirror her.

Byron set his letter down, ready to give me full attention. He did not begin with kissing me, which I found confusing. For if one has already had the pleasure, did not one begin again right there? I wished there were a manual, a guide of some kind I might read and study the way I had done Italian, French, Latin. I knew how to cross my ankles yet not what to do with my heart, my desirous mouth.

Byron motioned for me to sit.

I moved with mild confidence to his side of the room. My grace was not based on my abilities, for I did not yet know what those were, exactly. Rather I moved with a guile my mother had told me was afforded only to the young, those who have yet to know the impossibility of preventing misfortune.

Again we started with tea. Today's delicate flavour was complemented by its colour: a shocking blue—true blue liquid sugared in the pot and served initially with no milk until Byron gave a barely perceptible flick and a pitcher appeared that made his tea turn a paled lilac.

I saw everywhere the discrepancies between our wealth: his multiple chimneys puffing smoke, though he could only be in one room at once. Cakes he tried but did not favour and so left them half eaten. Copious amounts of hot chocolate, rich and thick and pricey.

"I've come to enjoy tea," I said. "Though I am far more used to coffee."

I doubted he knew coffee was cheaper than tea, or that tea sometimes diluted with crushed leaves or detritus sold for even less as smouch. "Even as children we had coffee with scalded milk."

"I've succumbed to East India Company's propaganda, and now I must have it throughout the day. Slay me for falling prey, despite all evidence of colonial expansion and the heritage of cruelty."

"Is it not merely tea?" I asked.

"It is never merely tea, Claire."

The tray before us had narrow sandwich fingers stacked like logs. Butter and crisp green marrow, which again spoke to money: the staff sourcing such vegetables when there had been so little at the market of late. I understood finances. I did not understand money.

To cover feeling silly for not comprehending the depths of tea, I went to my reticule to fetch the Coleridge I'd bought him only the week before—it seemed much longer ago.

"What a thoughtful gift," Byron said. "Did you know he is a good friend?"

There seemed many small tests he put out for me—if I knew too many details about him I would appear a fame-sucker. If I knew nothing, I would be woefully uninformed. I prided myself on the delicate balance I'd achieved thus far. Byron had a tight literary circle, and I wanted him to know I existed if not inside it, then adjacent to it.

"Mr. Coleridge came frequently to our house growing up," I said. "Wordsworth, too." There were men at the table, smoke plumes and heated discussion, words like *revolution* and *rational perception*, *poetry is an overflow of feeling* that became our lullabies. "He and Godwin were close. I recall one night crouching behind the sofa so we might hear him recite 'The Rime of the Ancient Mariner,' and when Godwin tried to shoo us away, Coleridge intervened and insisted we stay. His son Hartley came to play sometimes, though I think he found us odd. Once he remarked upon 'the cadaverous silence of Godwin children,' which he meant as a comment of concern and which Mary and I took as a compliment."

This had the desired effect of setting him at ease—he was one in a long line of famous men I had encountered. He did not ask me to inscribe the book but walked directly to a section of the bookshelf and placed it there. I followed to see an entire section devoted to Coleridge, my gift barely noticeable. The volume I had given—*Dejection: An Ode*—now seemed a terrible choice. What did I mean to convey to Byron?

"*Christabel* will publish next month. A mix of brilliance and terror," he said. "Witches, ghosts, half humans."

"Do you like to be scared?" I asked.

"Most of all, I like to be pulled under, if not drowned then submerged," he said. "Fear can do that." He paused. "And other intense emotions."

I wished to tell him of the rush of feeling I fought against. I could hear Mary's voice in my head, see the pinch of her lips, the effect her terseness had on enticing Shelley. Even if Byron enjoyed intensity, I ought to keep mine to myself. Perhaps seeing my slight remove, Byron bade me to move a fraction closer to him, as though he were decrepit and needed me to speak close to his ear. "You have yet to regale me with the story of your elopement."

"Mine? Hardly." I was used to his humour already. "My sister's elopement." He looked at me, expectant. He chose a pastry the size of a thimble and waited for me to speak. "One hardly knows where to begin. So much happened before and has happened since."

He chewed, swallowed, sipped his tea, and offered this: "The beginning of a story is often not the start one first believes. For example, you have said that your sister asked you to accompany her. Yet that does not feel as though that moment is the actual beginning."

I thought of our shared bedroom, how Mary and I had held hands over the space between our small mattresses—a hand bridge, we had called it. I thought of her propensity towards rumination, often about her mother. Neither of those were the start of the story. What had I learnt from reading and rereading *Pride and Prejudice*?

A sympathy of character. "Percy Shelley was gentle-mannered yet not formal. He was introduced to Godwin by poet Leigh Hunt."

Here Byron had a look: the kind that men have when impressed by other men. That Shelley knew Hunt made Shelley somehow more worthy in Byron's view. Byron urged me on.

"So Shelley came to have dinner with Godwin, but we all hodgepodged round the table."

"A stranger arrives. That does seem a promising start." Byron allowed himself another cake. I knew he was settling in then, for he plied himself with sweets when he felt relaxed.

"Shelley and his then-wife Harriet used to visit nearly daily. They met when she was fifteen and married quite quickly." I paused to think what to say next. "Shelley had not yet met Mary because she had been away."

"In Scotland."

He remembered! Lord Byron took me seriously, for he registered all my life's information. "Shelley studied with Godwin in the morning, and then when the parents were occupied with the printing press—children's books mainly by then—Shelley and I had time together." Another pause. I had never told Mary just how much time I'd been left alone with Shelley. "When Mary returned and met Shelley and they—well, it was sweet to watch. Mary is often a bit . . . dour. Yet with Shelley she came alive."

"And your talks with Shelley?" Byron looked at me closely.

"Oh, those were less frequent." I paused. It had been a relief. "This did not sadden me—he was, as my mother oft pointed out, only like a brother to me." I took a pastry but realised I was not hungry and set it back down. "You might enjoy him—Shelley—for though he has not quite your quick wit and mind, he has so much to offer."

"One gathers." He sipped his tea and refilled my cup. As he did so he gave a quick glance to the door. I wondered if he might be expecting someone. Then, just as quickly as that thought occurred to me, I remembered what lay on the other side of that door. The entryway. And in that chamber, the grand curve of marble staircase that led upstairs. I took a long breath. "Mary and Shelley began sneaking off. I would cover for her."

"You are a good sister, then?"

"I am devoted," I said. "Mary and I have the sort of relationship that remains even-keeled so long as we remain fixed to our never written—yet agreed-upon—contract," I said, feeling at once adult in my opinions.

"Which is?"

I spoke carefully. "We either do not speak of consequential things or, if the subject is important, we ought to be in agreement." I paused. "So when Shelley—who was initially twenty to her fifteen—showed her attention, I had no objections. I could hardly speak ill of him—and why would I? His only flaw seemed to be he was already married."

Byron frowned. "A common hindrance."

"Then, one night, we made our hand bridge." I set my teacup down and showed him, explaining our tradition. "And Mary told me Shelley no longer loved Harriet. Their dramatic start—Shelley and Harriet had run off, taking Harriet's sister Eliza Westbrook with them—had flamed out." I drew a breath and saw Byron raise one eyebrow. "I did not say to Mary that I had heard our parents discussing Shelley's behaviour in shrill tones."

"Had he fallen out of their favour? I thought Shelley a sycophant who could do no wrong."

I rose to Shelley's defense—for Byron had never met the man.

"He is merely unconventional," I said. "Their concern was only because Harriet was then pregnant." I looked at Byron. "Do not think him a monster, for he was not without caring. Shelley took a loan—£3,000—and left much of the funds with Harriet and Godwin."

"I heard rumours about that," Byron said.

So he was not the only man of infamy!

"Yes," I said. "The rumour was that Godwin had sold me and Mary to Shelley." At the time, Mary and I had found this funny, yet as I said it, the words soured in my mouth.

Mary told me Harriet's letters to Shelley proved her to have the charm of a bowl of cold porridge. And that Shelley admitted he felt only friendship for Harriet. Since Shelley had left her, Harriet had run up a slew of bills at hat shops and hotels.

"My sister was determined," I said. "Once Mary sets her mind, there is neither soldier nor saint who might win against her. For sixteen, she was ever so clear-headed. So I agreed to go with her as she and Shelley ran away."

Byron clasped his hands together, fingers woven. I thought about the space inside, how warm and dark it would be if I could shrink and fit there. He saw me looking and unclasped his hands and cleared his throat. "And Shelley did not mind this—you coming with them?"

"Shelley said I ought think of myself in terms of the French Revolution—and be rid of slavery to thus enjoy freedom. My overbearing mother placed many demands upon me, which Shelley likened to slavery." Byron told me he was sorry to know this. This made my heart soar, for he looked so pained at my past expense. "Often the first coupling is mother and child, yet for me, it was me and Mary. So of course I agreed, and we left the next morning. At Calais in the hotel a man told Shelley a *grosse dame* had appeared to reclaim her daughter—me—how embarrassed I was!" I shook my head. Why had I thought only of my mother's big belly and not her desire to fetch me? "My mother had rapped on the door, pushed her way in to stay the night with me while Mary and Shelley were next door."

"Alone?"

"Yes. They had been . . . alone before." Another flick and the tea was cleared away. "My mother's threats grew louder; she would lock me away, she would involve the Municipality of Paris. Finally, Shelley knocked and asked to have a word with me."

Here I paused, remembering. Calais had been busy and damp, the sounds of horses clomping on cobblestones carried as ballast on boats and left behind. With the slim crook of moon out the window of the hotel's small, jumbled boot room, Shelley and I had a long talk—just us.

"Shelley convinced me it would be best to remain with them," I told Byron. "Back upstairs, Shelley met at length with my mother. She was convinced Shelley had inveigled me. She told me this yet did not ask me what was true." I felt a twinge as I looked at Byron but did not wish to break the moment so shoved the pain down to my knees. "She departed in the morning without a word." I crossed my hands in my lap. "That is the story."

"Part of a story, for one never has all the bits," Byron said. I nodded.

There was more to say but I did not offer it. He seemed satisfied enough not to ask.

Byron came to sit near me on the velvet chaise. I relished the feel of his thigh so near to mine. His forearm so close to my forearm that heat emanated into the fabric of my sleeve. I moved my hand just enough that my smallest finger touched his limb. He cleared his throat. "My house is large—yet you have seen only the entryway and this room." He licked his lips. "Perhaps you would like a tour of the upstairs?"

I took this first as a grand metaphor. He wanted to show me the rest of him, the other chambers of his heart. As he took my hands and pulled me towards the impressive staircase, I also knew he wished me to see his bedroom.

"Shall we, Claire?" Byron stood one step up from me with an outstretched hand. I looked at him but did not offer mine. He tilted his head and stepped down to the marble flooring where I was. I wished to go upstairs, for I knew it to be a place of adulthood, of bodily communing, of the natural progression of what was becoming a proper relationship with Lord Byron. Yet I also knew the blood rag I had pinned to my inexpressibles needed to be changed and, more than that, I did not wish to venture up those stairs quite yet. I opened my mouth to say as much but Byron spoke first. "Come to think of it, Claire, the hour is growing late."

I felt disappointment. I felt relief. I felt he had thought of me and understood.

"Perhaps another time." His eyes suggested *soon*, yet he said, "Only if you would like."

12

HAVING WHISKED THROUGH ALL my chores so as not to rouse discontentment in my sister, I sat in the corner trying to come up with a way to leave the house and again make my way to

Byron's. I wrote in my journal while secretly studying Shelley as he and Mary read in companionable quiet whilst William slept. Shelley's posture, his eyes flicking across the page—he read quickly when he was unable to control his anxiety. He worried about money—or the lack thereof—and I could see his financial woes on his face as he read. Still, if he had noticed I had not bought cheese and eggs and instead wrote, he had not scolded me.

"Madame de Staël is brilliant," he said to Mary, gesturing with his book. "To have such ability to write political theory, comedy, philosophy, tragedy. One barely fathoms."

"Champagne for her," Mary said, and touched her book to his as though clinking glassware, though her voice contained no celebration.

"And you, Mary, tell me your thoughts." He looked at her, and I knew he wished her to confess her true thoughts, not of the novel in her lap but the ache in her heart. I also knew my sister tried to protect Shelley from her misery, as though it were catching and they would sink in it together.

She gestured with her book. "Rousseau believes everyone is born free and equal—"

"Not true," Shelley said.

"Precisely. I find myself enraged by my own enjoyment. Passion and virtue, yes, but—" and here her voice rose in volume, her regular self suddenly visible as she went on. "My mother objected to his premise that we are born with particular traits, all fine and well yet women cannot only be born to nurture and denied an education!"

"He treated women like *a fanciful kind of half being*," I said. "That is what your mother said. There is an inherent enslavement to women, partly from their lack of legal standing and partly because of ignorance. She said allowing women only one way in the world, the fostering the libertinism of men, society makes monsters of them.

Mary and Shelley turned to me as though they had only just realised I was also in the room. This was not uncommon, for their intellectual discourses tended towards the exclusionary. "I read his novel last year," I said, and when Mary looked skeptical, I added, "I believe it is better in the original French."

Sensing an argument impending, Shelley said, "I shall read it next, Mary, and you read Madame de Staël."

They often read in conjunction with the other—when Mary had read Homer, Shelley had reread *The Odyssey* so they might discuss. I felt, with Mary and Shelley, an ever-enmeshing which left little space for either of their minds alone.

They returned to their reading and I to journal entries. Quiet rippled through the room until the postal knock interrupted. In one swift motion Shelley was out of his chair, to the door, then back to us with an open letter flapping in front of us.

"The trust money hasn't come through," he said, voice crumpled. He was a man of imbalances—strict diet and lax plans, wealthy and poor at the same time. His disappointment permeated the room. Mary rose to embrace him.

"Shelley," she said into his chest.

"Perhaps it will soon," I said. I felt I had to be the ballast for the room of woe.

Shelley tucked Mary's head under his chin. "How shall we be able to get away this summer?"

I felt a small relief rise in my chest. If we went away, I would no longer visit Byron. The longer it took for money to come through, the hungrier I would be but still in proximity to Mayfair. "Surely we would not need to leave right away," I said.

Mary was muffled against Shelley's chest. "I should benefit from a change of scene."

"Then we shall keep trying. I shall redouble my efforts," Shelley said. "For if we leave this spring, all the better." His confidence made me shudder. "Italy, I think, if it is preferable to you, Mary." He looked at me, and I feigned happiness. "I shall write to the bank again—and to my father." Mary looked pleased. It was my turn to feel crumpled.

If we departed London this spring, I would leave my heart behind. What else could I do?

13

I WAITED FOR BYRON AND gazed in what I hoped was a nonchalant manner upon his desk. Perhaps he had written somewhere his plans for the impending season. I saw a pithy invitation to Byron and his wife for a party—*carriages at midnight, ambulances volantes at 3am, casket carts at dawn*. Byron had struck through his wife's name but accepted the invitation and filled in the reply card, writing *casket requested*. Perhaps he would take me with him. I wished to go to parties that would go so late and contain such fervour one would require carrying out.

I looked to the door—still no Byron. With a quick nudge of the invite, I saw no evidence of travel plans, but I could read the first bit of the letter underneath.

> *At best one might say she is brisk-mouthed, which one supposes is uncommon for a girl of this age, so upon reflection I find this refreshing. Yet a curious divide in her mixes confidence with an undercurrent, a pusillanimous nature which only a certain kind of man would find enticing. Yet it appears I am that kind of man.*

I could not read more, for to move the page further would be too obvious. And I did not need to read more, for I had proof. He felt for me—and enough so to write about me. A brace of pheasants flapped in my chest.

When the door opened to reveal Byron in a lush quilted dressing gown and knee britches, I immediately imagined my own body inside that banyan and hastened to tamp down the fluster welling inside me. He walked to me slowly, each unhurried step a jolt in my belly. I could no longer hold back. Giving him no warning, I went to him and slipped my hands inside the loose folds of his dressing gown. My hands on his chest. My lips to his neck. With a groan he led me from the large room into the vestibule and to the base of the stairs and asked, "Claire?"

"I should like to see the rest of the house," I said.

His bedroom had the grandeur of a palace and his bed—oversized, plush with feather quilts and silk cases, which he told me kept his face from showing signs of age. White and gold, gold and icy blue. His usual calm demeanor had been thrown over for an excitable creature who brought me close. "Sometimes," he said, "I am subject to casual giddiness and swooning, which is so like a fine lady that I am rather ashamed of the disorder."

"I find you irresistible as lady or man," I said, to which, fully clothed, he kissed my mouth, my collarbone, and brought my hand into his britches, stroking him until he cried out. After this he pulled a hand from my knee to my thigh, inside my underthings, gripping me just firmly enough that I, too, cried out. Then, surprised at my own responses, I began to laugh. He laughed, too. He had held me in his arms on the bed but not in it.

"You are so different than one might expect," I said. I did not tell him I had read in the paper about lawsuits against him, about groups clamoring outside his house for a look at his fashion or those who approached John Murray's publishing place to gain early access to manuscripts.

"I might say the same of you," he said. "We do a disservice when we create a story about a person we do not know." He propped his head on his hand and looked at me. "This is always the way—my first collection had little to do with the one actually brought to the public. When I recollect on agreeing to remove those certain poems, I know I agreed to present a falsehood."

"What were the poems?" I reached out and touched the hair curling over his pale forehead. I had the freedom to touch his hair at will. I moved and kissed him and he kissed me back. Such permissions had I.

"Odes," he said, "thoughts. Many about a Cambridge friend, John Edleston, whom I loved." He gave me a look, which I took as a challenge, and I nodded without judgement. "We were together much of college, reading, writing—he sang, I sat with my bear." Another look. "Trinity would not allow dogs, ridiculous rule. Yet there was nothing written to disallow bears, so."

I reached out to touch him, mainly to prove to myself I could. He moved closer in response.

"I think it lovely to write about John," I said. I did not mind he'd loved another, for in some ways I owed that man a debt of gratitude for freeing Byron to wind up here with me.

Byron gave me a soft look. "We always write about our first loves," he said, "or the first to crush our souls." He drew a long breath. "In any case, my odes were passions fulfilled and, sadly, unrequited. And I cut and cut—and what was left was a tepid book. Still, one cannot regret completely, for I learnt from it not to pander."

"And you gave the world *Childe Harold's Pilgrimage*," I said. "Which I read with Shelley—we both adore it." It was the first time I had fawned over his work to his face and worried this cast me into a crowd. From the way he received the praise, I need not have worried.

"So you knew the work—"

I admitted. "How different you are with me to how you are mentioned in public."

"Well, yours might be the only favourable view," he said. "A publisher friend told me there is someone writing a novel about me—"

"I hope you don't think I am that person," I said, and sat up.

Byron took my hand. "Many people say they have a novel inside them. Few birth them."

"True. In our family it was believed that, contrary to what one might hear at a party, not everyone has a book in them. And, if one did have a novel or epic poem trying to claw its way out of one's belly," here I made my hands claws, "one ought to make damn sure the enterprise would bludgeon other works already on the shelf."

In truth Mary had reminded me of this when my novel, *The Idiot*, was forgotten on the Europe trip. That my story was lost did not seem a tragic loss to society—that was what I had told myself. Yet Mary allowed herself to grieve the loss of her own novel, confident the world was a worse place without her lost book entitled *Hate* in it. She had never let me read it, and because of that, I assumed it was about me.

"This novel about me," Byron took my hand and brought it to his mouth. "One assumes it is someone from my past who is—to put it indelicately—a champion cunt who never got over me and so turns her pen into poison." He turned to me. "Should you ever consider me a man-monster, you would not wound me by writing about me, would you, Claire?"

I shook my head. "I do not find you objectionable." I paused. "Yet." I took his hand and led it back to my breasts.

"I have no intention of becoming objectionable to you. I only wish you to touch my object." Here we both laughed. "My persona gives me the ability to behave however I wish. No one questions my poor behaviour now—though I do not experience it as poor at the time, you understand."

"Freeing?" I asked, with a slight gasp at his touch.

"Also a trap. They want me to be the vulgar-tongued ratbag they've heard about, and I find people are rather disappointed to discover I exist primarily in a realm of normalcy."

"So you are yourself and not yourself?" I paused, too caught in his touch to do anything other than moan. "I mean to say, do you perform to those expectations?"

He breathed in quickly as my pace continued. "Unavoidable," he said. "For we become what others believe us to be. I am a version of myself. The London version, I might add. Which is why—soon—I must take myself elsewhere."

This caught me off guard. I tried to hide my displeasure by chewing my lip. "Is there nothing that might keep you here?"

14

AFTER I HAD TOLD him over tea how much I enjoyed the tea trays with their currant jelly cubes, candied ginger slices, and nuts, Byron had given me a tin filled with almonds his servant had blanched and sugared for me. First I thought I would keep them near my bed and allow myself one per night, but as I reached for one, I felt bad for Mary and instead thought of what to do with them.

William had woken earlier in the night, and I had gone to him only to find Mary already with him as he coughed. We tried unsuccessfully to calm him, but when the coughing persisted, she bade me fetch Godfrey's Cordial. The bottle was shaped like my old schoolmarm, tall and indelicate, with stooped shoulders as though life had defeated it and the tincture within was the consolation.

She hesitated to put any on the baby's tongue. "What if the medicine is worse than the condition?" she asked. Never had I seen her so frantic. Still she did not wake Shelley. They handled their grief and concern differently. When her first baby had died the year before, she had written to Shelley's best friend, Thomas Hogg, who always made himself available to her. I had read her letter begging Hogg to come because Shelley was too afraid of catching fever from Mary's milk and so would not hold her. *Hogg*, she had written, *If one has a baby and then no longer does, am I still a mother? I cannot bear to think of this.*

"It is called Mother's Friend—would they give it such a name if it caused harm?" I asked.

She gave me a look which told me I was an idiot. "Claire, Mother's Friend and Godfrey's Cordial are laudanum. Sweetened with treacle."

"Oh," I said. I could not think of any clever suggestions, but I did recall having croup and my mother bringing me outside in the middle of winter to shock my lungs. In the end, that is what we had done, just the two of us holding Mary's baby between us on the front steps in our dressing gowns, with the street dark and quiet. I was sorry William had been unwell. I was grateful to stand there with my sister.

She and William were still asleep, despite the day being half gone. I did not feel I could keep the almonds for myself—partly I did not wish to be selfish, and also I feared their discovery leading to questions as to their procurement. So in midafternoon, I ground the almonds by hand and made a gingered bread inspired by the one in *Emma*, which I had reread in the night when I could not sleep—not from terror but from joy, for my days with Byron grew longer, fuller—and left it on a plate in the kitchen with a note for Mary, who still slept, and Shelley, who had gone to the bank.

This worried me, for at some stage some money would likely come through and he would announce our departure. I would be far away from Byron, and he would forget me. I took a slice of the gingerbread and wrapped it in a piece of cotton to bring to him. For if I might ply him with sweets and feel his body against mine as we grew ever-closer with shared stories, I might also learn whereabouts he planned to go when he, too, left London for the warmer months.

OFTEN I felt I wore my sister's doom misery like a cloak. I needed to rid myself of it before reaching Byron's.

As a child I had a proclivity for digging. I ruined roots of carrots, leek stalks, a small lemon tree my stepfather had procured from someone who had it on good authority that Erasmus Darwin had been the one to grow it. The tree, which seemed somehow elegant in its stout pot, sat for only a few days in the windows at the front of the house. My mother did not care about Darwin but cared very much about choosing the best pot. Everyone had spoken of what was to come—someone would admire the pottery (my mother), the fruit would one day prove the tree to be perfectly situated (Godwin), we might make a glazed butter cake with the lemons, tang and sugar ripe on the mouth (Mary, Charles, Fanny, our little brother, William, who had yet to taste a lemon). Yet as I stood with my hands pocketed, I had wondered only what lay beneath the soil.

Unable to help myself then, I had, in the earliest of morning, unpotted the roots and ruined the lemon tree.

I knew I would have to work hard not to dig too deep with Byron, though I needed—and I felt this to my core—to find out his plans for the coming months.

This was always the way with me. Yet time and again, when I came upon Mary and Shelley's journal, I regretted digging through it. For when I did so, I found dark thoughts wedged deep under my fingernails, and I knew I would be unable to scrub them clean. With sheer effort, I flicked her words—grief and more grief, and Shelley's fingernail moons and mush—off as I took the very familiar three steps up to the main gate of 139 Piccadilly.

My desperation to know Byron's plans did not entice him. Rather, when I asked again whether he had given more thought to his summer plans, he had looked at me the way one might a child who has asked for a pull of taffy without having the teeth to chew it.

His room smelt always of Bloom of Ninon de L'Enclos, which he slathered on his face. The scent was lavender and almond. The white lead in it gave his already pale cheeks an even lighter gleam, the properties quickly making it impossible for his muscles to move. He turned to me, unlined brow, pert mouth, overly awake eyes.

"Perhaps it matters not where travel takes me. I may as well throw a spear at a map and choose that way," he said.

"What about Italy?" I said, because Shelley had mentioned that climate befitting Mary and the baby. Perhaps I could lure Byron there.

He did not respond to my suggestion. "If I cannot assure against self-destruction, at the very least I could find a place that might benefit my work," he said. He shifted the papers on his desk, coming upon a stack of letters unopened. Perhaps mine was in there.

"Madame de Staël," he said, waving the letter. His tone suggested he thought he would catch me out—I surely would not know of her. I gave a self-satisfied, toothless grin.

"I know of her. Quite well, in fact." This refocused his gaze on me.

"You are more well-read than I might have guessed."

This pained me slightly, for I hoped I did not present as too light of mind, but I did not wish to object. "Have you received a letter from her? She must be . . . wise by now," I said. I used the word *wise* because it seemed the one people assigned to those who had managed to age without complete ruin.

Byron gave a half laugh. "Yes, she is very wise now. Still . . ." he thought it over. "There is something to be said for where she keeps herself, even with her advanced age she still holds her salons. And there are glaciers. Lakes. The rather ridiculous idea that one might be saved by a new environment."

I sat up straight. "Would her environment be a salve for you?" I asked. I needed him to say yes. To commit to a place for the summer that would allow me to join him. Or at the very least visit.

He pressed his fingers to his forehead. "Voltaire, Rousseau, they found influence in that environment. Gibbon, also writing in that same locale—and he was only twenty-one at the time! No matter my success, I cannot again achieve that age."

"That is older than I," I said. He held my waist.

"There is no cure for youth," he said. I knew not what to reply. I felt my brow furrow, mouth wrinkled in confusion.

"I was not aware of my illness." I tried to guide him to the answer I wanted. "Still, I believe you might write anywhere you bring your ink. Is that not the case?"

He had every opportunity to tell me of his travel plans then. Yet he did not. Instead, with his pale gorgeous expression frozen on the glacier of his unmoving face, he took my hand towards his bed, where I knew he would, in his own way, prove to me I would not stay young forever.

LATER, BYRON leaned against his headboard, rubbing his bad foot. I had noticed his limp—slight but plain to see. I asked if it ached him horribly.

"I am used to my deformity by now," he said.

"Would it help if I rubbed some lotion on it? For if your ailment freezes the muscles there," I pointed to his forehead, "would it not ease the foot ache?"

He seemed pleased. "I had not ever thought to try."

In what felt like the most intimate act, I took his twisted foot into my lap and, with two finger dips of paste, began to massage. He watched me do so and then, suddenly, reached for my hand. "Do you find your foot a hindrance?" I asked.

"This is my body, and I know no other way, so that is impossible to answer." He tugged at the front of his hair. "The hindrance was the others. I could have done without the wheyfaced devil children at school."

I frowned and held his foot to my chest a moment before continuing to rub. "I wish I knew you then," I said.

Byron gave me a long look. "Ah, yes, but that is not how time works." He pressed my hand.

"Do you wish me to stop?" I asked.

"No. I wish . . ." He chewed his lip. "We have not yet . . . consummated our—"

Relationship? Romance? Union? Please do not say dalliance. "Have we not?" I asked.

"There is the matter of duty, Claire. I wish to say you have none in this regard with this particular realm. For I believe people are comfortable with the duties of women yet have much discomfort in the pleasure of women."

I stopped rubbing. "And you wish only pleasure for me?"

He went to his knees, laying me down on my back. He parted my legs and his mouth as he licked my thigh. "I wish you pleasure, yes."

"I have been clothed with you all these times," I said.

Byron stopped mid-lick and looked me in the eye. "And? What does this mean?"

I blushed. "I thought it did not count if both parties remained at least partly clothed."

He scoffed. "It all counts, Claire." He held my knees in his palms. "Where did you hear that?"

He accepted my blushing as an answer and did not ask more. And when I made my attraction clear, arching my body towards his mouth, he kept going.

15

MY BODY WAS WONDEROUS and raw with desire. When I returned to our house, the others were asleep. Shelley's snores wafting down the stairwell. Mary had left a note on my bed.

> *The gingerbread was so lovely. I ate two whole slices! I could not ask for a more thoughtful sister. Please if you are going out yet again today can you find a cucumber, for I wish to slice it and put it on my eyes to reduce their puff. And Pomade de Graffa for Shelley.*

I wanted to be annoyed at her mixing a thank-you note with a shopping list, but below she had written one of our little symbols, a remnant from our long-ago disappeared language. A sort of half star, half flower that when I squinted in the half-light looked like a word I could not decipher. Perhaps we had embedded even our own codes with ones we did not understand. I slipped her note into my journal and, after more diligent documentation of earlier in the day, I wrote a letter to Byron.

I put my thumbnail to my lip as I thought of what to say, thinking of his lips on my inner thighs.

> *I do not expect your lordship to love me. Yours is a gentle disposition, perhaps more so than mine. You believe me to be*

carefree, and this is partly my fault, for you desire it and thus I become it. Yet I am not the messenger of all things young and sweet. I am Cerberus; I turn each of my three heads towards you when you call my name. Am I proud of this? No matter, for I seem unable to do otherwise. I wish to please.

Shelley said recently I am of a sweet nature. Do you agree?

Shelley's exact words: *There are two Claire Clairmonts. One who can be irritable, for she is prone to nervousness, and though you have not had an episode recently, one assumes the terror still lurks. This Claire can be quiet and withdrawn and with good reason, for the world seems to defeat you when really the world offers its embrace to you. The Good Claire is gentle and kind and cheerful, the most engaging of creatures.*

He says I am easily managed by the pers'n I love as the reed is by the wind—does this make me weak?

I knew Shelley was too fond of me not to be indulgent, yet I wished—what did I wish? For Lord Byron to know that he was not the only man who had ever thought me smart or capable or kind.

If I am weak and wish only to sit at your feet, kindly remember that you seem to enjoy sitting also at my feet.

Yours—

Of import: Shelley and my sister are leaving early with William for a day's outing in the hopes it will clear the last of the baby's ills. This provides us with such a long uninterrupted visit—I can scarce wait, C.C.

IT HAD taken the hours of first light for Mary, Shelley, and the baby to make the short journey from sitting room to steps. Mary jostled the baby on her hip as Shelley bid me farewell at the door.

"Worry not if we are late in returning, for if William—and your sister—benefit greatly, perhaps we shall stay the night and come back tomorrow."

I nodded, pressing him to leave so I might rush to Byron's. "Do not rush back—for I am quite content on my own." I thought of Byron dripping honey on my thighs. "No rush in the slightest."

Shelley went down two steps and then came back.

"She could not manage without you. And know this for certain, neither could I. We are so grateful to you, Claire." He went down a step and then again came back. Would he never leave? "I know that finances and Mary pull me away, and we have not had time for our private talks as of late." He put his hand on my forearm as though steadying himself in a rocky boat. I flinched. "Please know I haven't forgotten you. Ours is a shared mind—of books, of writing, of so much." Another two steps and back again. I fought the urge to push him off. Knowing his propensity towards injury he would break a wrist and then they would never go. "If you go out, do not be too long."

"Do you not think me capable?" I asked. "You needn't worry."

"But I do worry, Claire. I am sure of you, but I remain unsure of the world's intentions with you." I wished to silence him, and so I nodded. "Never underestimate your power, Claire. For you have such force—"

"We shall lose his nap if we do not leave now, Shelley," Mary called.

I gave silent thanks and watched until their carriage had pulled out of sight before heading to Byron's, where I could not wait to find him in a state of longing for me, near-panting at the door.

Instead, I found him spread like a sea creature on the floor of the big room. Fletcher led me to him and said only one word. "Laudanum."

From the looks of it, this was not the dosage Mary had given to William. For rather than loll in placid slumber, Byron moaned and spoke in muddied phrases, an odd sweetness to his breath when I knelt down to kiss him. First he did not kiss me back, and this pained me. Then with no warning he looped his arms over my neck and brought me down to kiss him again, this time hard enough our teeth clashed and I pulled back. He went back into a stupor.

This was not the morning I had wanted.

Fletcher left a tea tray, and once I had eaten, time enough had passed that Byron seemed more content, curled in a comma on the floor. With a sigh I thought that laudanum and grief made for poor companions to the sober and nonbereaved. I read a book, dozed for a few minutes, and then nosed around his desk.

Thinking I would find nothing of import, I saw he had written a poem. I was seeing a new poem before anyone else.

STANZAS FOR MUSIC

There be none of Beauty's daughters
With a magic like Thee;
And like music on the waters
Is thy sweet voice to me:
When, as if its sound were causing
The charmed ocean's pausing,
The waves lie still and gleaming,
And the lull'd winds seem dreaming:

And the midnight moon is weaving
Her bright chain o'er the deep,
Whose breast is gently heaving
As an infant's asleep:
So the spirit bows before thee
To listen and adore thee;
With a full but soft emotion,
Like the swell of Summer's ocean.

When I finished, I saw in tiny script at the bottom of the page *For CC.* I nearly screamed. This was not only a new poem. This was a poem about me. I could scarce believe it and instantly wished I could show it to Mary, to my mother, to Shelley, to say I had not imagined a great poet's feeling for me—it was there, on paper, proof.

I read it again and then once more before I saw underneath it the beginning of a note: *I shall arrive at Lake Geneva in mid-April.*

I was the one who then wished for laudanum. For that date was so close I could taste the departure on my tongue. Still, I knew the location of his summer, and as he slept off the drug, I clung to the poem like a piece of bow in a shipwreck. When my sister and Shelley returned, I would suggest Switzerland as the place we ought to reside for the summer.

WHEN BYRON roused, the morning had crept to noon. I wanted to ask about the poem, about Switzerland. Vowing not to dig too deeply, I kept quiet. Byron took my silence as offense and offered his apologies.

"Unseemly behaviour on my part," he said. "And I have only grief as my excuse." With that, he turned away. I could see from his shoulders heaving that he was crying. I went to him. "I have a dog," he said. "Had a dog."

"I did not know," I said. Had I been so entranced by Lord Byron that I had missed an entire animal roaming around his house? Had the dog stayed the past months with Lady Byron and baby Ada?

"No, no. Boatswain is long gone. Only on some days I find myself overcome with grief for his absence." I felt relief that I had not been so distracted as to miss a dog, but sorry for my new love. "There will be another dog in my life, and while I know this, my heart buckles under the grief, for he was like no other. Boatswain had a triangle on his snout." Here he traced this shape on my nose. "He seemed to know what I needed, what I wanted beyond need, without human words, without commands."

At this, I leaned my full body against Byron's, for Boatswain's was a gift I, too, had been praised for my entire life, and today would be no different. I would know what he wanted and needed before he had realised it himself. This was not entirely unselfish on my part. I desired Byron in a way I had never thought possible about a person. Only food or sleep. I longed for him even when he was there in front of me. I longed for him as he gripped me tightly and pulled back to kiss me. I longed for him as he asked if I wished to go upstairs, and I desired him as I told him yes with my eyes, my words, and, only a few minutes later, my unclothed body.

"Claire." We both lay on our side, faces so close together he became a handsome Cyclops in my vision.

"Yes," I said. "I am saying yes."

He put one hand on my cheek and brought the palm down my side, my waist, and rested it on my thigh. "You seem under the impression I am going to take something from you."

"Are you not?"

"I wish to give you pleasure—not take anything." He paused. "I am glad to have you in my bed." He began the slow journey of thigh to my inner leg, bringing his body closer to mine in the process. He put his lips to my ear. "I have no intentions of leaving you without your virtue intact."

Ever the gentleman, he kept his word. And at each movement, I felt new. I felt the same. I felt the best version of myself.

He moved slowly, yet as I noticed this I also knew the word was imperfect. Mary was always pecking at me about precision in my word choice, and I tried to eschew laziness in that regard. Byron was not merely slow. His limbs, his gaze, even his protracted sighs all made me think of taffy being pulled—that stretch and limber quality. Everything he did seemed to support the idea of grace. When I commented, he gave another sigh, this one paired with a leisurely drizzle of honey in my tea and then on my thigh. "Efficiency is a tool used only by the lower classes."

I did not dig out of him that he had been born to one such class before being given a title at ten years and an inheritance and the Newstead Abbey estate. I had heard it remained in a state of disrepair.

After another round in his bed, Byron watched me dress and donned his robe as he walked me out.

"Will you come tomorrow?"

I CAME back to Arabella Row to find the house dark and cold. A chill went through me. I considered returning to Byron's, for Mary and Shelley were not yet home and I had never been there alone. Tired and sore, I bolted the door and went to sleep, scarce moving until first light.

I woke with blood on my bed. Though I had thought ahead to this possibility a few days prior and placed a bolt of flannel on the mattress, seeing the slash of bright red surprised me. As a matter of propriety I ought to have disposed of the rag so soiled was it, perhaps burned it in a barrel in the side yard, or at the very least wrung it with lye and set it to dry by the fire. Yet I did not. I pressed a new guard against my opening and secured it with a string around my waist, folding the ends like a cravat. How jaunty my blood rags were. The height of fashion. I laughed at myself. I put on a thicker petticoat and hoped no seepage would occur.

I did not hear the door to my room open but woke with a start to find sunlight streaming in, and the hulking shape of Shelley's frame near my face. Still lying down, I immediately covered my face with my arm, which looked like a sleeping position, but truly I did so because I feared if he could see my face he might read upon it a change in me from my interactions with Byron.

Shelley buckled to his knees, conspiratorial. "Willmouse is well, Claire! Mary is recovered from her worry. They sleep upstairs. And you have also had a much-deserved lie-in, I see." He smiled at me as I removed my arm and showed my face. The world came into focus, and I saw Shelley peer closer, staring.

"Claire, you can always talk to me if you are unhappy. For your time outside the house does not go unnoticed."

"Rest assured, I am not unhappy. I only wish to keep the peace—especially as the house is small." He frowned, thinking I was critical of the rental.

"Next time we shall have better accommodations," he said.

I would tell him about Switzerland. How the glaciers would be inspirational. The lake transformative. The landscape and climate befitting to

Mary's mood and William's lungs. I opened my mouth to say so.

Shelley stood. "I shall leave you be—I only came to share such good news of our day away. And now," he brought a letter from behind his back, "even more fantastic news! For I have secured a loan, and we shall all go away this summer."

He had accrued so much debt I wondered if he should ever be able to pay it off. I wished to capitalize on his good mood. "In terms of travels, I have an idea for that," I said.

"You always have good ideas," he said. "Yet worry not—for I have booked already our passage to Italy."

My lungs became crow wings and flapped, taking my heart with them.

BYRON THREW off the coverlet, awake and alert, though we had been in his bed for hours, me presenting my virtue, he exploring all the ways one might keep one's virtue and still enjoy a buffet of skin on skin.

"I have some news," he said. "Late last night while you slept, I finished a poem. 'A Sketch from Private Life.'" He looked at me. "It is about the end of my marriage. Also, as of this morning, I have employed a personal physician. John Polidori."

I sat up, pulling the heavy coverlet to my chest. "This is someone to care for you now? Are you ill?"

"I will be ill at some stage. That is the human guarantee, is it not?"

He motioned for me to follow him into an antechamber with a large plunge pool at its centre. Steam rose from the water's surface. Petals from flowers I could not name parted when Byron sank into them. I worried perhaps he could not swim and I would have to rescue him. Then I would scream for Fletcher the valet, who would ring the emergency bell, alert the new physician, and then the gossip pages would catch wind and—

"Claire, will you join me?" he asked.

"Yes, if you do not mind a possibility of blood."

"A good name for a novel," he said.

I stuck a toe into the water, and he dragged his warm wet hand up my leg. "You are able to swim?" I asked.

He rolled his eyes. "Is this because of my foot? I am a champion swimmer," he said. "I do not wish to be a braggart, but truly, it is a forte. I crossed the Hellespont six years ago."

I slid in alongside him and began to soap his back. "I'm not familiar."

"Greek myths? Leander swam each night from the Black Sea to the Aegean."

"How tiring," I said. I could not have been happier. In warm water, in love with a poet who wrote about me. The only plague was our impending separation.

"He was visiting his lover Hero." He said this as though I were Hero.

I took this as my cue. "So now you have a personal physician. This Polidori."

"Hired and signed. Young, dark, sound of mind, unlikely to complain this summer as I travel." Byron leaned back into my bare breasts.

I bit my lip and took the risk. "Would you not also like a companion for those months?"

He stopped leaning and tilted his back, looking at me upside down. "When I leave England, it will likely be forever, Claire. And I think it best not to take England with me."

Byron would leave, taking his golden smile and wit with him. I would be forced back to my mundane existence of breast cabbage and hair pomade, stuck with my glowering sister and her smug betrothed, nothing to show except heartache. I kept washing his back, grateful we were not face-to-face so he could not see the water mixing with my tears.

16

I WOKE UP ON THE first of April, leaves unfurling, splaying themselves against the odd transom window in my room. I stood on my bed and cupped my hands against the pane, looking out on the musty green. Cold prickled the edges still; the stoop flowers had iced over, showing their stiff skeleton selves when I had gone to collect the first post. I hoped the days would grow warmer, for Byron had asked the unthinkable—to be seen with me in public, in a park, during prime walking hours tomorrow.

Yet I was caught in a web of my own thoughts—if the walk went well perhaps Byron might change his mind and invite me on his summer journey, wherever that might be. And layered upon that thought was Mary, whom I felt was improving in mind and spirit—a huge relief. And Shelley, who seemed pleased with Mary and with money and thus had not cornered me to ask where I spent my days. And layered atop all of this were thoughts of my mother.

Her broad hips and tight mouth, the way she wound her hair and clipped it at the nape of her neck, even though fashion demanded she wear it higher. The sloppy way she flung criticisms, even first thing in the morning; if she appeared at my door after two years she would spit out—*Enough of your betwaddled eyes, Claire, for you look like a cow in a courtroom—have you not been drinking milk? You grow paler by the hour—have you slept enough, for you are most unpleasant without enough drowsy hours. Scrub your cheeks, for no man likes a girl with yesterday's spots.*

She did not mean these as set-downs. This was all part of her perpetual fluster, as she always appeared crazed—or *dicked in the nob*, as my brother Charles said behind her back. My mother's was a loud sort of loneliness, meant to hide under an exterior of taut dresses, controlled exuberance for William Godwin's social respect, and facial pleasantries presented to the world. Each day, a facade of such a convincing manner that shopkeepers and strangers alike felt that they were in the presence of grace, where I saw only the emptiness underneath; this was amplified by her physical propriety, the superficial declaration of *all is well* which she carried like a war flag. She was, as Mary's father said, a church bell, constantly in a state of ringing.

She tried to impart wisdom to me: *Sometimes the easiest thing in life for a woman to do is to turn a blind eye.* This was because I looked so hard at things.

I'd watched my mother take old flowers, petals still clinging with colour, scents lingering, and slip them into muslin bags I'd sewn for practice. These sachets I had sold, and my mother pocketed the money, a new ribbon here, gloves Godwin had admired which she then purchased. Had she taught me the names of the flowers? To know just where to look for pungent herbs? She had not. She had meant to pass along resourcefulness in penny-pinching, but what she succeeded in handing down was shame.

Shame and emotional thrift. She had no excess to spend, cautiously guarding each love coin in a velvet pouch I imagined no one could touch, not even Mary's father. My mother wanted the clout that came with a class she would never have, to be the sort of person who—when they entered a room—would be listened to. She did not seem to understand, as I did even as a girl, that the poorest man would be more of an expert than the richest woman.

My mother was not without love for me, even when I was not with her. And yet. Her absences. Her harshness and blame. Her surety that I would—and ought to—see the world exactly as she did and find crucial exactly her areas of concern: money, a proper household, a proper husband, as though I might make up for her missteps. In some ways I pitied my mother. For so many years she did not register the ways in which she failed me and indeed carried not an ounce of shame or regret in that regard, though I knew she carried such shame and regret in other parts of her life (her illegitimate children, being born amongst the wrong class, her ageing body). After she'd left me with Shelley and Mary, I believe she wished she had been a better parent. And by then it was too late.

I thought of her perhaps because April was my birthday month, and she did like to fuss over that. A trinket rummaged from her bureau wrapped with a bow at the foot of my bed. A new bolt of fabric. I went to my desk to write my thoughts, only to find a parcel wrapped in brightest pink ribbon.

"I hope you like it," Mary said. She stood in her nightclothes and waited for me to untie it. When I did so, I saw a gleaming hairpin. The twin to the one I had taken from her years before.

"That is so kind and unexpected," I said.

"I knew you admired it and thought, well. It is the first of your birthday month, so." If she knew I had the matching one, she gave no evidence.

I felt a tear come to my eye, and I willed it away. "You know me far too well, for I had only just been thinking of her."

Mary looked at me with a mix of kindness and consternation. I thought of Mary's own mother, whose acclaim and literary merits loomed large, whose person Mary never truly knew.

We all one day will miss our mothers, the one we had or the one we wished we had. I wanted to thank her and also to acknowledge I could do no such gift for her, as there was no precedent to follow.

"I know you grew up without a mother," I said.

Mary crossed her arms over her chest. "No, Claire, I grew up with a dead mother. That is altogether different."

"You are aware that you did not kill your mother." I said this, though I had said it before, when we were in Europe and she had seen one of her mother's books in the rubble of a ruined book cart.

"My birth is responsible for her death." She sighed. "I did not hold the knife to my mother's throat—"

"How ghastly, Mary."

"But I was the one escaping her womb. And my exit proved her demise. Without me the infection would not have gripped her . . ." She trailed off. I wondered if she might be layering her own birth with her baby Clara's. "My father likely carries some resentment deep within him."

"Do you believe Shelley does?"

She looked away. "My mother's shadow is very long. And—I believe we all miss our mothers. Possibly forever. My father's grief gave him reason to build a new life for himself. Perhaps that is the solution to the problem of grief."

So she was speaking of Clara still, though she would not say the baby's name.

"What is your new life?" I asked.

"Leaving London. It might seem frivolity to go to Italy for the summer, but we must, Claire." She paused. "And I have William, of course." She looked over her shoulder, for when she said his name he cried on cue.

She considered Shelley and William hers. What could I say was mine?

17

IN MY NOOK I wrote in my journal, how I'd walked to Hyde Park with newfound confidence even in my sad sea dress. Wonderous clusters of ladies bonneted in jonquil yellow, azure silk dresses so that they appeared to be flowers and sky together. Men in hats so tall they verged on ridiculous. A couple on a horse, he facing forward in the saddle and she to the side in a pillion. Everyone out in the fashionable hour. I'd walked the Ladies' Mile to look for Byron on the footpath, aware suddenly of the women casting their pointed glares over me, men who purported to be gentlemanly, yet a flick of their eyes on my dress told me otherwise. So much in life was one thing disguised as another—how was I to tell which was which?

I'd come upon Byron at the centre of a group of fashionables, regarded his visage, smooth and lovely in the sunlight as though someone had taken care and carved him in alabaster and he would remain there forever. I had never before seen him out of doors. He called me bright and lovely right then and there and linked my arm through his.

It was not the thrill of his stunning face, not the memory of how his skin glistened round the clock, somehow defying sun or moon, and it was not even how he had given me the map of my body I had not even known I was missing. It was more the power I felt near him—I became the smartest and most vivacious version of myself.

But then Byron had guided me suddenly on a different path, his foot tripping up the pace. He cursed the dirtscum journalists who'd spotted us, chased us. I asked him if it might be possible to find a place between obscurity and fame. He told me if I found that country, I ought to live there.

We'd talked about the fine day, of pastries in a way that I knew meant we spoke of sex. He asked me to call the next day, which set my near-mind at ease, but there was still the looming future—this was what I wanted to secure.

As we'd walked in quiet, the newsmen tired of us. I asked about his writing, which Byron said he could do anywhere, *Childe Harold* having been written in Greece, Albania, Portugal, and Spain. I offered that perhaps there were more journeys for Harold—which I ought not to have said, for I knew from Shelley how frustrating it was for people to suggest what writers ought to take on next. But desperate as I was to fix the problem of our diverging summers, I tried again with drivel I made up on the spot—inspiring places, good company, &c. Exasperation. He told me plainly he was slow of foot but mentally sure-minded, so not unaware of my hinting.

I paused to dip my quill in ink, recalling Byron's taut expression that afternoon as he'd urged me to stop skirting at the edges of conversations and to just *say the thing.*

So I'd told him I wished to know his location for summer and to accompany him. He did not say yes, which sunk my heart, but it bobbed up again for he did not say no. I was learning to ask for what I wanted. I ended the day with a kiss and reminded him I only knew a little bit about love. "Ah," he said, "that is far more dangerous than knowing much or none."

I still had my head over my journal when I turned to find Mary watching me. I hadn't heard her. Only felt her. She was catfooted, so I never knew just where she was in the house or hallway. "You've given me a fright," I said. I closed the book. It was not for sharing.

"I came to ask if I might help with chores?" She waited, knowing this was not an offer she had made since I had moved in.

I gave her a grin, but that was all. For if I showed too much enthusiasm, I feared she would scuttle away. "Let me clean my foul mouth—" she laughed at me, for this was impossible, "and teeth and then yes."

We stood shoulder to shoulder over an unglazed brown bowl that had once stored salted meat and which caught the dribbles from our mouths. I stuck a finger into the jar of paste I made from crushed chalk and ash. Mary loathed the texture, so I loosed some with peppermint oil for her. I adored these times of simple domesticity. In the ritual, our vulnerability overlapped.

With her mouth full of paste she spoke freely. "I see you out and about these days—" Here I thought she would say she knew my whereabouts and lambast me for them. "And I feel, for the first time in so many months, that I might like to join you in the outside world."

Relieved, I spat, rinsed my mouth, and touched her shoulder. She did not flinch. This made me feel I had won at something. "I can see, Mary, that you are growing happier." She nodded.

We dealt first with the dishes and then the laundry.

"See what we have accomplished here," she said, and looked at the full basket of clean and tidy things. "When I sit to write—even if I succeed—I am left to wonder if there is merit, if anything will become of it. You get the benefit of a task completed, a job well done." She did not wait for me to comment. It was true that chores could give satisfaction, but her tone made them sound easy. As though linens or dishes were the entirety of my capabilities.

"I find writing a different sort of task," I said, "but when I write I am provided a true sense of accomplishment. A blank page covered in scrawl—good or bad—is still changed."

Mary barely seemed to have heard me. She looked out the window. She so often gazed out of the window that I wondered what she looked for. "Soon we will be free of London." Mary shook the next towel with vigour, snapping it and creasing the folds into squares. "We shall be packing soon—you know how much I favour a list."

"You are so much recovered," I said. Her whole body moved as though controlled by someone else. Younger, she had gone through an obsession with Luigi Galvani and his studies of animal electricity. Poring over pamphlets she read to me of electrical fluid coursing through dead frogs, muscled little legs twitching. My body felt now in some ways jolted by desire, the way Mary seemed controlled by an unseen force of doom as she helped fold William's clothes.

Byron was necessary and electric for me. Yet he would leave in a matter of weeks and did not wish to take me with him.

Mary and I ate during the small miracle of William sleeping, Mary seeming more herself with each slather of preserves from the small pot, forgetting herself enough that she licked the jam spoon as she had done as a child when my mother had her back turned.

"I've missed you," I said. What I meant was I missed the girl she'd been, long dead and suddenly back for a visit. What I meant was I missed the girl I had been, too, with her.

I felt convinced I could resurrect us both. I wished I could tell her about Byron, perhaps have them meet.

"Here I am," Mary said, "and Shelley misses you, too." My chest hurt when she said it. "He will be so glad when you are home more with us." Before she could say more, William screamed. Her smile fell. "Motherhood is a gut-tug at all hours, all days—for one never knows the threats of the world and how to keep a child safe." Mary rose as William screamed again. "Perhaps do not have a child, Claire," Mary said, and instantly looked as though she wished to retract the words. She had meant it to be wisdom, but I heard it as a warning.

THAT NIGHT I screamed. I sat up in my bed, lit a candle, my mind retracing a dream I'd had before. In October of 1814, I'd had a nightmare, Shelley's face too close to mine, hands on my pillow. I'd shouted, "You look horrible, take your eyes off!" Mary had come in, accusing me of nonsense. Shelley knew what I had shouted had come from a play, *Orra, A Tragedy*, which he and I had read during one of our late-night chats. We'd discussed it at length, how it was written by Joanna Baillie, a Scot who was considered to be second only to Shakespeare. In the nightmare Shelley was an evil presence, yet when I explained it to Mary, Shelley said I was the troubled one. And then—as though this were not enough—that same night Shelley purported to have a nightmare about me! He let out a scream, saying I was more frightening than he.

Mary had written an entry in their shared journal the next day calling me sullen, stating I would not speak the whole day. They had twisted it all round. And when I wrote to break my silence, I woke to find my pages torn from the journal—I could not recall if I had been the one to destroy them in a fit of anger or if they had been ripped whilst I slept.

Afterwards, Shelley made it into a joke about the skin of my face and my forehead being huge and wrinkled with a terror that could not be contained. He'd written in the journal that my eyes were wide and unblinking, ghastly sockets in my lifeless head. He had been so engaging we'd laughed.

Thinking back as I sat in bed, heart racing, I recalled his scolding journal entry. He felt I was insensible and had not the slightest capacity for the sort of friendship he offered. In the dark, I shivered. I wrote it all out but did not find myself laughing; in fact it all seemed terrifying.

18

I THOUGHT ABOUT BYRON'S BODY all the time. His hands. His fingers. His tongue. His manroot. I knew there was more to do together and wanted that. I also knew he was leaving. I was leaving. And I wished we were leaving together.

On each visit I fought with myself—if I pressed perhaps he would capitulate and take me with him. Or he might banish me altogether. And after each visit I again battled in my mind—if I told Mary and she then confided in Shelley, what would they make of it? Desiring a love of my own necessitated a break with my sister, which scared me.

I sat at the breakfast table with my journal. Shelley wrote near me in companionable quiet. "Is it possible to forget the self?" he asked.

Shelley and I had for years had such conversations, debates about writing, about nature, about love. About duty. "How could that be, when we are always ourselves?" I asked.

"We must free ourselves from societal trappings. In this way, I know my writing should benefit from my body being out of London. If we accept nature as being not only around us but above us, more powerful in its tangibleness and more representative in its beauty, then perhaps the self disappears."

I thought of my body with Byron. Of the sudden snow followed by spring heat. Of the ocean I had watched night and day back in Lynmouth, staring at it as I sat alone after Shelley had visited.

"Nature will always have power over us." I looked at him. He was beetle-browed this morning, all full of consternation. "Perhaps. Yet by the time you put lines of poetry on the page, they belong not to you any longer—so that is another way of forgetting oneself."

Shelley nodded. "Yes, Claire. Very good. For the poem is not for me, after all. I write it for the reader." Here he set his quill pen down and focused on me. I wondered if he could read my writing from his vantage point. He peered again at my pages, so I closed the journal. To distract him I asked if he had slept well and listened to him complain.

"I find I cannot sleep with too heavy a cover, and yet without it, my feet wake me with their cold in the night." He droned on. I had known right away that Mary cared for Shelley because of his intensity. His political tirades were nothing short of miraculous, how he'd gone to Ireland to aid the Irish Cause and push revolution, how his atheism had gotten him sent down from Oxford. Everyone loved Shelley for his passions.

But I had known Mary had fallen in love with him when she grew rapt with his monologues about the minutiae of his daily travails. On and on he went as I pretended to listen and thought of Byron.

Mary entered the room, glanced out the window as she always did and sat down. One would have thought Shelley was reciting *The Odyssey* from memory so rapt Mary became when he recounted his ailments and daily annoyances.

I kept waiting for the same to happen to me. But once when Byron had gone on about a blistered finger and how John Polidori, the new physician I had yet to meet, had dressed it in gauze and it was possibly better, but perhaps not entirely healed—I did not find it fascinating. I found I wished for a sandwich or thought about how I needed to urinate. There were parts of love I did not understand.

"I wish to know what tugs at your mind, Claire," Shelley said. I had made the mistake of not commenting enough on his sorrows. "I am here should you wish to spill." I imagined myself as a pitcher tipped on its side. The mess I would make. "It is not my mind being tugged upon, it is my heart," I said.

I should not have said this, for Shelley leaned closer, lapping up the truth.

I faltered. "I feel . . . torn about leaving England. For last we did so was the end of my time with my mother, with our family, and now I wonder if . . ." I made this up as I went along, for I could not say anything about Byron. He was too famous. Too successful and possibly commercial for Shelley in the writing realm. And Shelley far too protective of me for me to admit anything of our romance. "What if I cannot survive without . . . London? For this is the city I love."

He went on with his boring blanket of reassurance. "If the world is ever cruel or inhospitable to you, should your heart require mending, I will have needle."

"You cannot sew to save your life," I said. Mary coughed as she cleared our plates.

"Then I will be balustrade—for surely my height allows me that."

I had not told him the core truth, I had not said the thing. Still, Shelley's kindness was a kind of death to me. A puncturing I could not name.

"IT IS the poet's duty to describe the ineffable, to memorialize ideas," Byron said to me. We were unclothed, the perfect amount warm and relaxed, though still—as he had assured me, despite our entwined legs and roaming tongues—my virtue remained intact. More and more I felt this a silly judge of what mattered, for my soul had burst open with him, shone and grew, and my body felt invigourated with lust.

"This means nothing if the poet does not move the reader," I said. I thought of Shelley's words. "For the poem is not for the writer, it is for the reader."

"You do have keen insights to the writing mind," Byron said.

"May I admit something? I know I mentioned in passing, but when we went across Europe I wrote an entire novel. *The Idiot.* Mary wrote one also—hers was called *Hate*, and I don't know what became of it nor if she even finished. But mine I completed."

"And who was this *idiot*?" Byron asked.

My mouth was a question mark. "Likely I was," I said, but could not say more, for the writing of the novel had occurred mainly at night, with Shelley hovering and eventually putting me to bed.

"And might I read this novel?" Byron touched my chin with his nose. "I have connections."

My heart soared and then smashed its little face in the wreckage we'd walked through abroad. "I fear it is lost."

"How unfortunate—and fortunate, too." He saw my confusion. "Unfortunate, for you likely toiled long over the work. Yet in all likelihood having lost it is pure good fortune, for you will never have to deal with the rejection from publishers and public."

I sighed. "That is a sad state to be in."

"That is how art as commodity works, Claire."

"Well," I said, feeling desperate to prove him wrong, "I am glad to have written it, for I learnt much about how to write from doing so." Surprise tears threatened to fall. "What if my novel was good and true and had survived?" I willed the tears away.

"Oh, Claire, such accidents happen. One has only two choices—trod on or rewrite from memory." He paused. "Sometimes I wish you were only frivolous. Easier that way."

"Surely you know by now I care too much to be concerned only with light matters," I said. I did not want to be thought of as easy, as simple. I mustered up the courage to push forward. "I should think you would want me with you this summer."

He sat up. "You have no idea the pressures I feel, Claire. You think of this—" he gestured to the room, the bed, my body near his, "as the bulk of my day. Yet there are hours I live that do not concern you. Legal matters. Financial issues far from your purview. This is all alongside my growing disdain for the ruling class in this country."

"Are you not a part of it?"

"I wish not to be. I feel more akin to the masses than the idiots in Hyde Park," he said. "I feel the pain of the oppressed, though I realise I have borne nothing in comparison with those who have truly suffered." He took my palm and flattened it on his bare chest. How familiar that space, the small dip in his form. His look was far away, but his mouth looked hungry for me. "Likely you have not read my *Hebrew Melodies*." I had not, but he did not wait for my response. "I gave the poems to Isaac Nathan because he wished to adapt tunes from the synagogue."

I had never said the word *synagogue*. It was foreign and bulky in my mouth. "Yet you are not a Jew."

"No." Byron looked at me with something close to sorrow in his eyes. "Yet I fear sometimes I might have been born in the wrong religion. Lord knows I was born to the wrong mother—alcohol was her adopted religion. Anyway, I gave Nathan thirty poems, and he set them to traditional music—which turned out to be more of a commercial venture for him. And he scored with John Braham—he of the wonderful tenor voice, and himself a Jew! For an oppressed people, one finds them everywhere." Byron's hand gripped mine. "Such determined people."

I felt my cheeks redden, for in an earlier journal, one I shared with Shelley and Mary on our trip, I had written disparaging remarks—something about a Lord Jew from whom Shelley had borrowed money and, when the man and his associates wanted to be paid, Shelley had urged us to leave that town. Despite the facts, I had sided with Shelley.

Byron touched my cheek, noticing the blush. I did not mention my embarrassment—had I truly written about the way one could spot a Jew by their features? Had I participated in group hearsay and cruelty? I had written the word *dirty*. I fought my shame with a statement. "I should do better by people different from myself."

I imagined crossing out the harmful words I had written years before but then realised that would do no good—for I knew the words still existed in my head. I would always know I had once been cruel and dumb. I could—I would—be better. "I should like to hear Isaac Nathan's music."

"Perhaps you will. Still, do not be fooled. This was a financial venture for us. If Britain is going to put clout and cash on a minority culture, if those of the old guard and title make fetishes of difference, then why should Nathan—or myself—not fill a pocket?" He paused. "And it was an enjoyable experience. Nathan is not particularly God-fearing, yet he remains a Jew."

I felt I was maturing during the conversation. "So there is a culture apart from the faith," I said.

"Exactly," Byron said, lighting up with my understanding. "And now I can add that to the list of closed and done." Byron brushed his hands as though he'd laid a fire and wished to be free of the peat particles. Only, I was the peat.

"Surely London is not all bad," I said, feeling silly for defending a city that had not once made me feel anything other than a girl in a ragged dress off to shop for a scant piece of meat.

"Not all," he said. "Yet one feels plagued daily by the grime and emotional fury. The invasiveness of too many eyes and mouths."

"Am I not a relief from those plagues?" I asked. I could hear the distance growing in his voice. This sent a panic into my stomach. How could he write a poem about me and then not want to keep me near?

"It is decided. I leave for Switzerland on the twenty-third. Lake Geneva, nearby to old Madame de Staël. Davies and Hobhouse have sorted it. They will see me off."

He had spoken about his closest friends, Scrope Berdmore Davies, whose name, Byron said, sounded like a diseased testicle, though he was good-natured, and John Hobhouse, whom Byron had known since Cambridge. When he spoke of them I felt jealous, for they had years of shared history and could travel and talk together in public without fear of gossip.

I did not press further. I had only a fortnight to come up with a plan.

19

C—your anonymity cannot keep—the needlepens have seen you coming & going, so if you visit, come in the back way near the delivery door or under cover of night or both. I am not suggesting you hold off seeing me. You are my little fiend in certain matters, so do come today, only not the front. Yours ever, &c. LB

I had read his words and started a response.

LB—
No one knows who I am so I find difficulty in believing the gossip would begin. I fear myself unknown and forgettable but of course I can enter through the back. And while I admit to rather liking the possessive "your fiend" & I feel myself yours &c., I resent the "fiend" for if a man thinks of the bedroom as much of the time as I do, he is only a man yet if I do so I am a fiend. Honestly, I had ten times rather be your male companion than your mistress. Then I might be with you in public at all hours, enter any door without remark & still share your bed. Remember I have withheld nothing—can I help therefore feeling utmost anxiety with regard to your sentiments & opinions of me? Think of me not as your fiend but as one who cares about & for you. —Clara

I HAD WRITTEN *CLARA* BEFORE my mind caught up with my hand, as though my quill remembered only who I had been before Shelley had changed my name. I splotched it with ink and it looked dramatic and messy, which was preferable to one who cannot keep one's selves straight.

I went to post it, passing Mary in the front room. She sat looking out the window again.

"What are you looking for?" I asked. She did not answer.

"To whom are you writing?" she asked. I gave her the same response.

I KNEW two things: the first that Mary—and therefore Shelley, for they were of one mind—believed me to be keeping secrets, and I could only hold them off for so long. The second that I was more than ready to hold my virtue once more in my hand, thank it for keeping me company lo these years, and then hurl it out the front window of Byron's outrageously large bedroom.

My mother had not used the term *virtue*. She had instead focused on the body part. My Area of Distinction, my mother had called it. *Your cat-hole*, Byron had said. "The folds of a woman," Mary said as she wiped William, whose gummy smile went unnoticed by her, "are so much more complicated than what a man offers."

The Folds of a Woman—as though I were a letter to be written, folded, unfolded, and opened again, which perhaps was the most accurate of all of the terms.

"Will you take William for me?" Mary asked.

I wanted to please her yet wanted to be free enough to go to Byron's later. When she asked me to be with William, her work time grew longer and longer, though I knew not if she wrote or only thought about writing. "Could we not take a walk together with Willmouse?"

She gave me a look which suggested that was a poor use of both of our energies yet agreed to go as long as we bundled the baby, for while the sun tried to shine, the air grew colder still.

Tufts of last year's grass poked through the carriage path edges under a wary plump of clouds as we went past the fishmonger's buckets of eels writhing in the chill. Though they had not been used as currency for so long, the Thames still roiled with them, so they hauled them early. I watched the fishmonger chop off an eel head. Mary turned away.

A sharp cold gust churned up old leaves at our feet. "Spring appears to have forgotten her duty," Mary said as we strolled William.

I scolded the air. "How dare you, April? One more cold snap and you shall be demoted to winter."

Mary laughed and then, still laughing, turned to me quite serious. "Are you keeping something from me, Claire?" My breath caught in my throat as another mother pushed her grinning young boy on a wheeled wooden horse. Mary looked on, enviously I thought. There was always another, better mother somewhere nearby.

I tried not to falter in step or expression. "Some things are best left unsaid," I told her. I felt power creep up my leg and curl in my lap like the best, warmest cat.

Mary arched her eyebrows. "Are things truly being left unsaid if they are written about? For one assumes you are writing about them in your blue journal."

This annoyed me, for it extinguished the cat warmth. "I write only for myself."

"That is not real writing then. For writing is meant to be shared."

And I did wish to share my heart with her. I longed for her to know my hours with Byron, how I was growing more and more myself. Yet Mary was also put off by my wish to be close to her.

This fact annoyed me, for I felt childish, yet I wanted to be the sort of adult sisters who relied on one another, whose children played side by side, so I persisted. Before Scotland, Mary had had a friend whom she enjoyed most because the friend did not need her. If they played, that was fine. If they did not speak for weeks, that was also acceptable. And when they did spend time, there was an arm's length—or leg's length, really—distance in their conversation.

Mary somehow wanted to have closeness without intimacy. To be afforded great love like she had with Shelley without great vulnerability. She saw this as a strength. The more vulnerable and open I became with Byron, and the more I understood I also had allowed myself to be vulnerable with my sister and with Shelley, the more I saw my sister's inability to be open as a personality deficit. How might one truly be close to another person without laying oneself bare, scars or ugly thoughts shown while still hoping to be loved?

"You asked to know what I am doing and keeping secret, so I should like to tell you," I said. I felt grimy knowing I had to lure her with my verbal offering.

This piqued Mary's interest. "So what is this great mystery, Claire?"

"I have . . ." I stopped. If I said love she would demand proof, and what did I have? I did not have the poem with me. Did not have in my hands the hours of talking, of touching, of storytelling Byron and I had shared. I thought better of it and said, "I have an idea of the summer."

Mary frowned. "Shelley has worked feverishly on our plans—you know full well we are due in Italy in May."

"My idea would require a change of plans because . . ." Here I paused for dramatic effect. This worked and piqued her interest. "I have been in close acquaintance with Lord Byron."

I could have said I was a duck in human form and she would have looked less shocked.

Admittedly, it would be a surprise to learn one's sister knew intimately a celebrity—yet her disbelief was also due to Mary's constant underestimation of my appeal and intellectual capacity.

I gave her the bones of the interactions—I had written a fairly common letter of admiration but one which held a resonance, he had asked to meet, we had begun a friendship.

Here Mary looked skeptical. "And what does this *friendship* entail?"

"You mean to suggest he could not possibly find me interesting enough to warrant the time spent?"

"Stop it, Claire, I said no such thing. I mean to ask what the purpose of the contact. If his reach is too long."

"Say the thing, Mary," I spat out. She did not, so I filled in for her. "My virtue is intact, if that is what you mean to say." Virtue! Cat-hole! Area of Distinction, whose architecture was both mine and Byron's. I fought to stay focused.

She seemed satisfied. "His writing is not outshone by his notoriety. Is h— Is the truth of him the way he is portrayed?" Her voice was a bit too eager. Ha ha—so my erudite sister had known of the gossip pages, of the rumours pecking at him. "Is he ever-so-brilliant? Does he have a cadre of lovers? Is he diseased from running rampant?"

I pursed my lips. "He is not." I did not think he had the clap, though it had not occurred to me to ask. "Though he is very pale." Mary drank in the information I provided. "And every bit as handsome and well-to-do," I said, and then, in case this made me sound too fawning, I added, "There is a depth to him that is never reported upon and a sensitivity—this is a man who still cries about the loss of his dog. And has such generosity . . ." I thought of his tongue. Of the pastries we had shared. Of his curiosity about my past, my desires. "Of spirit worth remarking on."

Mary nodded. "I should like to meet him," she said. And then, offering me a bone, added, "Might you be able to organise a brief introduction?"

She had never asked for anything of the sort. "I shall see to it at once," I said, pride unmistakable in my voice. Part one of my plan was settling into place.

20

GRASS AND NEW LEAVES were bright, defiant green in the grey rain. Mary and Shelley focused all their energies on procuring items for our summer trip: lightweight clothing for William, a day dress for Mary, softer boots for Shelley, a mess of new quills, as though no other country had pens. So busy were they that they hardly noticed I came and went.

In each step I took notice of my surroundings. Past the fishmonger and ice merchant, poulterer with open door so feathers gusted out, fruiterer at #6 offering greengages and gooseberries, boot maker, saddlery, milliner with new looks for spring, dentist, stationer where first I had bought paper to write to Byron what felt like ages ago, and confectioner. In short, everything was available to me with barely five minutes' walk. And nothing I wanted. For I wanted only Byron.

April brought with it all the expectations of spring, woozy with cow parsley umbels and heady scents as I visited him, entering not near the flowering vine that wound round the front gate but at the back with a view of only the rainwater barrel. Any feeling of oddness I had about coming in the servant entrance was quickly overshadowed by my simple desire to be in the house with him and the knowledge he was keeping me safe from prying eyes.

He refused to open his arms to me when I entered the room.

I waited. I asked what troubled him. I touched his shoulder lightly. He pulled back. "*The Champion* has published my poem 'A Sketch from Private Life.'" He motioned to a stack of post on his desk, some opened, some torn, others untouched. "Already the rants begin. For as it happens, writing the truth does not suit polite society. They—" he motioned to the world outside the window, "feel the dissolution of a marriage is not a fit topic for a gentleman." He shook his head. "Do not become a writer, Claire. Or rather, know this—writing is one profession, publishing another." His shoulders flumped, defeated.

I fought his coldness and embraced him, my mouth upon his neck. I knew he liked this. He put my face in his hands and brought my mouth to his. As we kissed I became aware of a hulking trunk on the far wall. New since yesterday, it filled me instinctively with dread.

As our tongues moved together and his body responded to mine, I was caught in thought. I retraced my walk from Arabella Row to his house. The shops. Smells. Items on offer. My desire. My need. Then I understood. All the time I had been on my way thinking only of him, he had been going about his day—toast, marmalade, tea too hot and abandoned on the tray, the trunk. With a stabbing pain I realised what was happening in my head and what was happening in his were not the same. What a distinct ache to know this.

With this revelation, I pulled back.

"That is a huge trunk," I said, trying for levity. His lips were wet. His trousers bulged. He turned to see what I pointed at. "Oh, yes. Switzerland, as I've said."

I touched his mouth with my fingers. "You ought to come to Italy with us."

He kissed me and then broke off. "I know not what to do with you, Claire."

He would not acquiesce and change his route. "Do you know what Shelley wrote in his notes for *Queen Mab*?" I said. It had been a successful publication, well-received, though we did not much mention it in the house, for it had been dedicated to his wife Harriet Westbrook, and Mary found it distasteful to bring her up. "Shelley wrote *to promise forever to love the same woman is absurd*." This caught Byron's attention. "Milord, you think I wish to be yours and yours alone." I did, but I went on. "Yet I have been told from the time I was not yet table-high that one cannot exclude others from the heart." I swallowed. "Nor the body."

"And this is what Shelley believes? As devoted as you say he is to your sister, does he subscribe to the idea of monogamy?"

"No. Devotion and monogamy can exist together and apart," I said with conviction, for I had been fed the meal of it for as long as I ate.

"And what reason does he give for this?" Byron had his author voice on, one which came out when he spoke of ideas, of literature, when he needed to convince or to be convinced.

"Shelley . . ." I thought about meeting him first when Mary was away. About our walks. I thought about the long night in Calais and how he had definitively told my mother I was to stay with him and Mary. The comfort he pressed on me with my terrors. How he had visited me in Lynmouth—still wholeheartedly devoted to Mary yet convinced he would provide solace in my exile. "This is what you must understand. Shelley—and also Godwin and Wollstonecraft—does not believe the boundaries of a relationship are fixed. You are also against tight reins. I mean to say I understand the idea of marriage, of singular union, is but a societal expectation."

I was instantly proud of myself for my explanation. Also horrified. For I had spewed the rhetoric of my childhood without much pause to consider my own views. Was it possible to live what one did not believe? I wanted Byron, and if he, like Shelley, would not believe in attachment to one person only, then I would have to try.

"That is reassuring, Claire," Byron said. "And refreshing—you are always refreshing. Still, I cannot ask that you include me in your Italian plans. I have so enjoyed this spring-muck season with you, yet my departure is so soon—" He took me in his arms and held me so I could not see his expression.

A panic match struck in my foot and lighted the edges of my underthings. I was running out of time. "My sister, the brilliant Mary Wollstonecraft Shelley, wishes to meet you. She needs proof you are real." I said the words into his chest as though they might plough into him. "Might you agree?"

"If that is what you wish, then yes. You may visit me tomorrow and then perhaps Mary a day or two after that."

I felt relief until Byron pulled back to look at me. "Claire, I ask you not to speak of our—" Union? Future? I had high hopes for the word he would choose. "Interactions these months. Even with your sister."

Interactions! "Your phrasing sounds as though we are already in the past tense," I said.

If there existed a look caught between dismissiveness and pity, that is what crossed Byron's face. Rejection scythed me open, and I wished for a sewing kit to suture myself closed.

Half of my body stayed with him in that familiar room with its gilt-edged tables and ornate carved mantel, the familiar pieces of furniture I had sat, lounged, and sexed upon all phantom-clad and ancient.

Then the other half of me felt the terror of night, though it was daytime, and I wished the ground would swallow me whole, tug me out to the ocean. That was the insecure Claire, the one Shelley had spoken of. I held her underwater until she quieted.

21

WITH MARY SET TO meet Byron in two days' time, I went to Byron's back entrance with the relaxed feeling of knowing I had all afternoon with him. The morning sun had sucked itself back into clouds, and I drew my shawl closer as I waited in the cold for Fletcher to bring me inside.

Tea. Fire. Sweets. Everything I had grown accustomed to save for Byron in a full-on rage, which I had not yet seen. He paced by the fire, too irate to hold his tea, so he set his cup on the mantel with a great clatter. Before I could ask what the matter was, a fluster at the door. Dressed in what looked to be the outfit winner of the Person Dressed Most Like a Well-Fed Pheasant contest was a man who entered the room and, without pause, greeted me by my first and last name. Byron's people knew my name! This was a point in my favour surely, for though he had asked me to keep quiet, he had been unable to do the same.

"Scrope Berdmore Davies," the man said. He had ruddy cheeks and a chin that spoke first. "Forgive our Lord, for he is seething from this." Scrope held out a manuscript bound in pale blue silk ribbon, which announced it had come from a woman. I pressed my toes to the floor so my mind would not run away to bash this other woman over the head with the pages.

"Scrope is too close to Beau Brummell to dress like a normal human," Byron said. Beau Brummell might have been the arbiter of men's high fashion, but upon seeing the exaggerated military boots, the elongated lace trailing from Scrope's neck, one wondered. "Fashion has reached the point of insanity," Byron said. He charged over to his desk, grabbed a handful of quill feathers, and chucked them at Scrope. "You seem in need of feathers."

I picked one from the floor and stuck it behind Scrope's ear. "Fly free, little birdy," I said. If I was to meet Byron's friends, I would endear myself to them.

Scrope laughed. "She is a proper slice of cake," he said to Byron, though I stood in front of him. Byron's ire continued. "Besides, LB, do not take your outrage out on Brummell, for he has fled to Paris in a sea of debt." Scrope gave a pointed look at Byron.

"Caroline Lamb is a fool," Byron said. I did not recognise the name. "This is why I must leave England. This is why I need a dog—for if Boatswain were here I could slather the pages with jam and command him to eat them."

Scrope patted Byron on the back. "Never mind Lamb. For her novel will publish after you leave." He turned to me. "You no doubt know I would defend Byron on all things—for what is a friend if not one who might clean up another's mess?"

I wondered if I was also someone's mess to take care of. I could fight my curiosity no longer, and I asked, "What is her novel?"

Both men turned to me. Byron came improperly close to my face, and I realised Scrope not only knew my name but details of our *interactions*.

"Caroline Lamb is a parvenue—she knows she is nothing without using me as her claim to celebrity." Byron showed me the bound pages but did not untie the ribbon.

"She sent you her pubic hair when you rejected her, Byron—" Scrope coughed. "Apologies, Miss Clairmont, but this is fact. She is a louse."

I was glad I had not found that amongst the papers I had looked through on his desk. Just when one imagined oneself as the most forward, the most outrageous—kissing Byron, putting feathers in his friend's hair—one came to understand there would always be another more forward, more fetching at the ready.

Scrope explained. "Her novel is set in the Irish rebellion. Yet the focus truly is upon the disreputable Lord Glenarvon, who bears a rather uncanny resemblance to my friend here."

I recalled Mary's father Godwin once quoting playwright William Congreve's *Love for Love*: *O fie, Miss, you must not kiss and tell.* Godwin would be content to know I could quote him, too.

"So the novel is a kiss and tell?" I asked.

"More like fuck and publish," Byron said. Scrope snortled, a word I gave to the sound men made when their nose and mouths sounded off together and produced a spitty cacophony.

"You need not worry, for I am sure the book sales will be naught," Scrope said. Given Byron's fame and Lamb's subject, this seemed rather optimistic, but perhaps that was part of friendship, soothing the other even when ruin or embarrassment seemed likely.

Scrope adjusted his silly hat as though only just realising he ought to have given it to Fletcher and perched tall in his false military boots, which went over his knees in a style I wished to describe to Mary as bovine.

"Ah well, Miss Clairmont could run circles around Caroline Lamb," Byron said, and I thought I would break my face with my giant smile. I shoved it away so as not to look too prideful. "This is a girl with vivacious intellect who can speak equally of Coleridge, of how best to bake with almonds—"

"Playing to your sweet tooth," Scrope said, as though *sweet tooth* meant pole-sucking.

"And lecture about Joanna Baillie."

"Forgive me," Scrope said, "For I had neither the marks nor the brain of my friend, so I am at a loss."

"She is second only to Shakespeare," Byron said, and to Scrope added, "Heathen. Shakespeare who was also called Shagspeare, I should have you know."

I sighed, shook my head, and soldiered on. "Joanna Baillie's work suggests that inherent to the masculine is a violence." That last word caught on my tongue, yet the point seemed relevant considering Byron's reaction to Lamb's manuscript.

I thought of Byron being mocked as a child and of Shelley's visit to Lynmouth and remembered him saying, *Did I ever tell you I was bullied at school?* He had, but I had let him continue. And he had told me again about being chased at Eton, hit when he refused to perform on the older boys—no fagging for him, he had said. Oh how I felt for Shelley back then. He'd earned the nickname Mad Shelley, for he was prone to violent rages—*it's to be expected* he'd said to me. I had nodded, drinking in this knowledge from one far more experienced than I.

How I felt, too, for Byron. Both men inspired in me a loving pity. Did being mistreated as boys cause anger in men, make them entitled to going through the world hands first? Was that what Baillie had meant?

Seeing I had their attention, I went on. "Baillie wrote, *I am strong and terrible now: Mine eyes have looked upon dreadful things.*" I thought of my nightmare when I had woken screaming those lines and of my bad dream only recently.

"Impressive," Scrope said.

"Baillie?" I asked.

"You," Byron said with an approving look. "For I defer to Baillie in every way. When first I read the work—published anonymously of course—I thought the writer a great man. To later learn that the pen was held by a woman's hand . . . well, surprise does not cover it."

"Why ever not?" I asked.

"Writing tragedy demands testicles," Scrope suggested.

"Lord knows how Joanna Baillie succeeds," Byron said. "Perhaps she borrows them."

Byron gave to me then a look that said that I—testicles or not—could approach him, which I did. The men exchanged a glance that contained words in a language I did not understand, and Scrope took his leave, taking the manuscript with him.

WE WENT upstairs to his room yet not to his bed. Instead, we lay on the floor, dust motes swarming in the shafts of late afternoon light. I enjoyed his touch. The gentle but sure way his fingers dipped in and out of me that brought me in and out of myself until I cried out his name and he grinned with amusement or power. He drifted into slumber right there on the carpet.

I looked at the room from the vantage point of the floorbound; lion's footed chair legs, a pewter button under the bed, blue and white drape hem in need of a small mend, and nailed to the bottom of an enormous looking glass a small brass placard that read *A. Jessup—Gilder, Carver, Looking Glass Maker—Fargate Sheffield*. Someone had made a thing and someone else had bought the thing and still another had moved the thing into Lord Byron's room. I tilted my head back and could see myself upside down, Byron's steady warm breath nearby.

In two days my sister would meet Byron. This was necessary because somehow as sisters it was as though nothing really happened to one of us until the other knew of it.

And in two weeks' time I would turn eighteen. What would the future bring to me with this newfound age?

THE ROOM had darkened. I sat up and poked Byron, for we had both fallen asleep on the floor. I stood in the eerie quiet. Could it be dusk already? I needed to leave and rush home in order to make dinner. I went to the window, hiding my frame behind the thick drapes in case someone peeked in from the road. Only the road was not visible. Roofs and wrought iron alike coated in thick snow.

"What in the devil?" Byron came up behind me. He tugged the embroidered bellpull near the bed, summoning Fletcher, who explained the sudden storm had all but shut the city, stranding horse carts. Byron asked that dinner be brought to his room.

"I believe this means you're stuck with me," I told Byron. Ought I send word to Mary? I could not, for the post could not get through. Perhaps she would know where I was.

"Lucky me," Byron said. He closed the drapes and regarded me fully. "A full night with the irrepressible Claire Clairmont."

I imagined telling this to Mary. I knew I was not alone in bedding down with Byron—his ex-wife, highly painted men at masked balls, barely rouged women in polite society, rumours of his distant half-sister Augusta. I did not read too deeply into Byron's antics nor focus on the tawdry laundry he'd hung in society, for I began to realise that my mother had been correct: Love involved a certain degree of looking away.

Byron, I felt, was wholly and truly mine. And in my core I felt I was known to him.

He said my name and began to recite the poem he had written for me, not knowing I had already snuck a read of it. His face was so close to mine that when he spoke his words went directly into my mouth. Had I not been bound by my physical form, I felt sure I would have floated upwards, angelic and sweet, and then, when he held my hips, his gaze grew in intensity. "You have me, Claire."

And if there is anything more alluring to a woman than being told she had the power to turn a distracted man's attention into true devotion, that she has tamed a wild celebrity, I do not know what that would be. Somehow I would be with him this summer—that I promised myself.

And so began another step for me. This was the end of something yet also the beginning, I knew.

I had seen on his shelf a book so well worn I had grown curious and read it—Giovanni Giacomo Casanova, who wrote of his life, which seemed based on sex. He had described placing lemon halves—half emptied of juice and pulp—over the inside parts of a woman. Until then I had not even known I had those parts within me. I thought back to school and rumours of beeswax, sponge, rock salt, all used to prevent someone falling pregnant; in Europe Mary had met a woman who used a ball of opium to ward it off—imagine! But Mary had said pregnancy did not happen most of the time. My own mother had told me of her struggle to bear a child. It seemed largely based on timing of courses, and that day—when Byron asked if I was ready—I nodded. For I well and truly was.

22

I WOKE A FEW HOURS later and found myself alone.

I gave myself the small gift of stretching my legs and arms out like a star ornament and breathed in the experience of waking in someone else's bed, having been there all night. Byron's scent lingered: cloves and citrus from the tea we had shared in the early hours, and always lavender almond from the spray kept on the mantel, which I had noticed and wondered if another woman had left behind. Under those smells was something different, more intimate, and I recalled with a flush the way Byron had first pushed into me and then rolled me so I sat atop with my hands on his pale gorgeous chest as he moved my hips.

I felt like a house one walks by during the day and thinks, well, that is no place special, and then at night happens by the same and with the windows aglow with light thinks, how charming, how magical, those walls, that structure. I was lighted from within.

I brought the sheets to my face, trying to identify the smell—a baked good? Flour or dough and that magic when one mixed ingredients and a small squish of dough set to rise became an elastic puff of possibility.

I felt the same magic. I could not go back.

IT WAS difficult to pin down exactly when I left my childhood behind. Perhaps when my father died, though I have no memory of this, for my mother fled and scurried, scrounging food and housing for us, yet I was too young for memory, so likely not then. Or when she married Godwin and I found myself raised with Mary yet often alone. Or later, when Shelley came to live with us and I witnessed his pull over us all, Mary's growing devotion, his admiration for the darkness in her that repelled many others, and I realised I might not ever find that loyalty for myself.

Or I might have left childhood behind when Mary and Shelley deserted Skinner Street and brought me with them, a literal door closing behind us, Shelley as our lifeboat. Yet still my childhood lingered on me.

I neither wished to hang onto childhood—one of those odd girls who played with dolls or drew horses far too long—nor was I precocious in my attempts to shed girlhood. I simply was without thinking in this regard.

This lack of thought about my own girlhood was the saddest part of my childhood. For even if one understood one's own gentle interior and the body paired with it, even if one felt entirely sure of being ready for any-and-everything the adult world offered on its manly palms, one could never take enough care.

Perhaps childhood's end came with a certain amount of breakage.

All of this had led me to the quite happy day and night I had spent with Byron. Again we had joined in his bed before the sun rose, bragging newly strong rays which melted the snow.

Still, that was not the moment.

When I arrived back home to find Mary in the sitting room with neither book nor needlework in hand as though waiting for me—she did not ask where I had been. She did not ask after my well-being.

I stood in the sad quiet near my sister without shared confidences in early afternoon light, and I realised that moment was the true end to my childhood.

23

HAVING BEEN DELAYED BY the snow that then caused raging high tides, Byron agreed to meet my sister.

I took Mary in the front entrance and pretended I had not been in the house so often. I pretended I had not—hours before—been in the bedroom lounging together, reading bits of Shadwell's *The Libertine*.

Byron voicing the letch Don John, whom he thought fearless and as such free. When I said that he and Don John had similarities, he looked wounded, so I had amended my observation and added that Byron was far more sensitive and sweeter. It was exhausting reassuring men that they were good and well-intentioned and ever-admired.

And before I had dressed to collect Mary and return with her, both Byron and I had remarked on Don John's shifting from man to devil. How blessed I had felt to read with a man other than Shelley, to offer my opinions and have them met with agreement, all while relishing a man who kissed me as though he were shipwrecked and drowning and I a plank of bow.

In Byron's large room, Mary waited for Byron to approach her, and though it was their first time meeting and she might have given a small bow or deferred in some way, she instead shook the hand that had recently held my face so gently in sunlight.

"Lord Byron, a pleasure," she said, and was so self-assured in voice and shoulder I prayed he would not fall in love with her. There was so much to love—Mary's handsomeness, the way she spoke rapidly about his work, about her own ideas, about the very nature of crafting the written word with such ease that she made me feel like a pigeon.

"Mrs. Shelley," he said, though he knew full well she was unmarried.

I clucked around the room, feeling ashamed by my insecurity, as they were clearly enamored with each other. For a moment I worried, for when I had anything worth taking, Mary did so. The doll I had sewn with Godwin—rag-stitched with a button-nob nose—she'd claimed as hers because, after all, Godwin was her true father. A neighbour girl I liked to play with became Mary's friend after I fell ill for one day. I did not see this as malice on Mary's part, more that her combination of wit and aloofness made people try harder and want her more.

I watched Byron. He listened, interested, but caught my eye. "Claire, your sister is every bit as clever as you offered."

A barely perceptible smirk tucked into the side of Mary's mouth. She wanted not to care what I, what the world beyond Shelley, thought of her, yet she did.

"And Claire had only accuracy when she told of your generous nature, your commanding shine, which one finds is rather quite ordinary."

This pleased Byron greatly, for it was a cake-and-eating-it compliment. He was famous and an everyman—perfect, in other words.

That the two of them were taken with the other only strengthened my resolve. For as I sat with them I understood: Byron would not come to Italy. Shelley and Mary were hellbent on a holiday there. I would do anything to make our holidays one.

Mary did not accept the *langues de chat* from the tea tray, nor did she truly sip the blue tea he offered. She brought the cup to her teeth yet never swallowed. After a time Byron had likely decided upon beforehand, Fletcher appeared to show us out.

"Perhaps we shall see you again," Mary said, and with her head told me I was to leave with her.

"I should like that very much," Byron said, but instead of looking too long at my face, as he often did when we parted, he grew distracted by the hulking trunk that stood then in the entryway. I felt my heart about to slither out of my chest and knew I needed to redouble my efforts. I reminded myself I was not without power: I had just this winter been a poor girl banished to the ocean who then came to the big city and wrote such a convincing letter to a celebrity that he invited me to find his ordinary heart and I had made it mine.

"HOW MILD he is—how gentle. So entirely not what one might expect," Mary said over and over again in the carriage on the way home.

"Mary," I took her hand, and she did not pull away. "I need your help. You have far more sway than I do. Imagine if we did not go to Italy and instead took the calm air of Lake Geneva. Consider the majesty of the Alps, how easy William's breathing should be away from cities. Greenery, such placid space." I was being conniving.

My skills were improved from my *Idiot* days, and as we arrived back home, Mary had agreed to push Shelley in the direction of at least a visit to Switzerland.

OUR OWN front room also had the stuff of journeys: trunks, cases, book stacks, and two apothecary cases.

"Lord Byron is entirely a gentleman," Mary announced to Shelley.

"He is an important friend," I said.

"Quite a literary accomplishment," Shelley said. "Meeting one whose work has been so widely circulated." He did not praise its merits more deeply than that, yet I knew he truly admired Byron, for he was so far ahead of where Shelley was and where he hoped to be. Shelley wrapped bottles of ink in tissue and when he ran out, reached for the daily paper.

I saw a headline on the top of the page. "See that," I said. "The paper says, *The number of English men who are now living at or passing through Geneva is immense. Crowds of travellers visit the lake, enjoy the temperate climate, and visit the stark beauty of the Glaciers of Chamonix.*" I made eyes at Mary—*ask him*.

Shelley paid me no attention. He arranged the books in one of the trunks. "Shelley," Mary said, "Claire's many visits with Lord Byron suggest he would like to meet you."

Shelley's face remained fixed, but I saw his hands twitch. "So now we know what has been distracting you." He gave an audible nasal sigh for my benefit. Disapproval.

Mary tried again. "Would you like to meet him? He was most agreeable."

Shelley set the books down. "Perhaps in autumn when we return I might meet him on my own."

So Shelley would claim him. I twisted my mouth, and I had to interject. "He is unlikely to return to England at all," I said, thinking quickly to entice him. "He has new works, however."

Shelley considered. "Imagine reading the work before anyone else—that would be something."

It *was* something, I wanted to say, but did not.

"He will be at Lake Geneva this summer," Mary said, in the high register she only used when she meant to sell an idea. We were a pair, working together.

I brought the paper to show him. "This is not a remote spot, Shelley. And you should know Byron has his own physician who travels with him. John Polidori."

The hypochondriac in Shelley grew enamored with this idea. I felt I had won. Mary crossed her arms over her chest as Shelley began to pace.

"We have our plans, though, do we not? And Italy is always such a salve for the soul, is it not?" He did not ask this of me but of himself. "It is a nice idea, Mary, but my answer is no."

The timbre of his voice changed, and it sent a chill through the room. For if it is terrifying when any person grows angry and loud, it is perhaps scarier still when a man—a mild-mannered man who prided himself on being so—turned stern. Shelley did not have to explain himself. Mary nodded and went to fetch William. Shelley came towards me.

"I fear you are in a muddle, being tugged this way and that." He looked to see if Mary approached from upstairs with William. "There are friendships which simply run their course. One mustn't spend effort trying to exert force over what cannot be controlled."

He had laid down the law in our lawless home. I wanted to scream. I opened my mouth and no sound came out—what power did I have? Not as much as I liked to think.

24

"THE WORD *MEDDLING* COMES to mind," Byron said days later. "You ask for favours when I have none to give."

"Forgive me—I did not think I was overstepping." I reached for the pages I had brought to share. "*Daemon of the World* is part of *Queen Mab*. Shelley has revised it since the original from three years ago and I thought . . . I thought it might interest you." From Byron's face I could see this was not so. "He is twenty-three years and ever so gifted."

"As he is sure to have told you." Byron paused. "In truth I quite enjoyed *Queen Mab* when I read it."

I chose not to tell Byron that when Shelley had sent *Queen Mab* to him years before, the book had been accompanied by a letter detailing all of Byron's societal errors and lapses in morality—so detailed it seemed almost admiring. Shelley had gone on to write that should those accusations prove untrue, he would love to meet Byron. The letter had come back to our house on Skinner Street undelivered, and I had found it in the bin and read it. Byron had read the book on his own.

"You and Shelley have much in common," I said. Byron did not respond. He had been in foul temper all day, tired from farewells and legal issues, and it seemed to me he had packed his heart in advance of packing the trunk. "And these pages are sure to provoke thought."

"I shall take your word for it," Byron said.

"Will you?" I asked, pleased I had more pull than I thought.

"No, Claire, I will not. If I read the work for myself and am so moved to comment, then I shall. I do not require your errand services. Your wheedling is not appreciated."

I had brought the work thinking Byron would take a shine to it and invite Shelley to join him. I'd used up one of my last hours with Byron trying to sway him. "I am sorry for your woes."

"My woes. You make it sound as though I've got gout. It's been an entirely disastrous year." In the breath he drew I felt myself bundled into his bad year. "Marital torment, a flock of legal cases, humiliating public scorn, all while that same public only waits in front of buildings to get a better look at the ruin of a man they wish me to be." He at last looked at me. "It is only my privilege and rank that save me from prison—how might this marry with my wish to be admired as a commoner?" His beautiful face was a portrait of despair. "I have nothing."

You have me, I wished to say. "You have writing," I said. It was a peace offering, a reminder he was not a cad in my eyes. Shelley often said writing saved him from himself.

"Writing is a poison I must purge myself of—I enjoy neither the ingesting nor the vomiting of it."

I had tried to be pleasant and descriptive and cheerful. All unsuccessful. I kissed him. His mouth met mine with familiar motions yet without fervour. I tilted my head back to catch his gaze.

Byron looked at me with a kind of flatness that made me feel I was paper. A story he had no desire to read. I, too, had told myself a story of Byron, and I had believed it.

I felt part of me cave in: a peculiar sharp pain from the quiet ambivalence in the way he gripped the chair to stand up, his sigh as he looked past me out the window. Was this part of the adult world, the hasty retreat of passion and possible future?

He would not hold my face and put his mouth to mine. Not only would he not invite me to Switzerland, I understood right there that he wanted nothing further to do with me.

25

For reasons which are plenty I cannot see you again. I shall be away for some time which would preclude our meeting. Rest assured I will send thoughts upon arrival in lake Geneva. —LB

Dearest Claire—I am loathe to say the events of our last embrace will haunt me in the purest way as I depart for Lake Geneva. Whilst I shall think fondly on our meetings please know I will be away for an indeterminate number of months or even years so let this note be our goodbye. —b

Come away with me. Love, you are water or air &
on any given minute I am torn as to which I need
more. I should give this body up to beasts if it should
mean the trade brings you to me one more time—

NO, THAT WAS too much, even from my own imagination.

I received none of these letters. No post. No footman nor ragged message boy brought word. No trained crow with bobble on its claw and love note in its beak. I was the recipient of a bundle of emptiness—the kind that plagues like illness as one wonders and mulls and tries to unwind and pull the thread back to its start to find what happened to cause the ensuing silence. The more I endured days of waiting, the greater my palpitations.

My pacing—which greatly annoyed Mary which in turn annoyed Shelley—turned to floppage. I slumped by the front window as though at any moment a letter would arrive explaining the sudden cut off from someone who had so recently had parts of his body in mine.

Yet I once overheard him in the entryway speaking to his friend Hobhouse. I knew Hobhouse had come by, knew he and Scrope Davies would send Byron off on his travels, but I had glazed over what I'd heard as I stood in the hallways upstairs, eavesdropping. *It is but a brief diversion with an unattached girl of indeterminate class and unconventional views who offered herself to me—how might I be at fault for accepting?*

I could overlook his snideness, for I knew the heart underneath belonged to a man who wrote poetry about me, who held my face and let himself be at his most open. Now he was sailing from Dover to Ostend, hoping to avoid the public eye as he went through Belgium to Switzerland. And where was I? Exactly in the same sad writing nook I'd started in before I lost my heart.

26

THE LAST DAYS OF April slipped by. On the twenty-seventh I put a thin layer of raspberry preserve over the top of a vanilla cake base and then thunked the next layer on, not caring that the cake looked a mess and that my eighteenth birthday had arrived not with fanfare but with vomit. For the baby had started the ills and Mary had succumbed and they slept upstairs while Shelley had all but barricaded himself in the downstairs front room, wary of even approaching the stairs. An inauspicious start to my year.

And yet I had the tiniest crocus bloom of an idea in my mind. I found solace in writing and kept doing so, even when I could not sleep. What if I wrote more and one day produced something worthy of publication?

As night crept in, I ate another slice of cake (secret ingredient: doubled sugar, cost be damned) and thought of the encouragement Byron had given me. I scratched at my arms. I needed to bathe, yet I did not want to, for then Byron would not have touched my current skin.

This annoyed me more than it made me sad—for I wished to be the powerful being I had been discussing Shadwell, impressing Scrope. I did not want to be a mushy soft thing in a small, dark room. A raft of desire and ache too large to fit anywhere in the house threatened to break out of my chest. Who would clean up the mess of me? Mary I supposed.

Shelley appeared in the doorway, surprising me. "I braved the upstairs and gave her Godfrey's Cordial," he said. "She should sleep soundly through until tomorrow."

I closed my journal and leaned my itchy forearms on it. "Then I shall not worry about her," I said, though I would.

He presented to me a pair of new calfskin ankle boots the colour of a bruise. I saw in his eyes that he had taken too much care with choosing them. That he needed me to adore them. This frightened me.

"Perhaps I ought to check on Mary," I said. I picked at the skin on my thumb to give myself a pain on which to focus.

"Such a shame she is ill," Shelley said, and frowned but only for a moment. "Still, I am glad to find you. I do so miss our long chats." A particular smile crawled across Shelley's face.

I nodded but did not look at him. For I did not wish to have one of our chats. In truth I sought to forget them. And I did not wish to clean up more vomit from my sister. I did not wish to be apart from Byron. But perhaps I spoke too often in the negative and needed to express in the positive what I wanted, plain and simple. I needed to *say the thing.*

"Shelley, I wish to go to Switzerland. You and Lord Byron would, I am quite sure, form a fast friendship." I had treated the men as separate, but I realised I ought to treat them as one. "Surely writers benefit from the company of other writers, especially of similar political minds." I turned to face Shelley. As I sat at the desk and he stood filling the doorway, he appeared even taller. If only I could see Byron outside of London, I knew we would not be finished.

"I do not know what else to say," I told him. "We have outgrown this rental. Italy is not where we ought to base ourselves. Lake Geneva is the place, Shelley." I could hear my own breath as Shelley did not reply at first. He did not move for what felt like such a long time my fingers grew cold and I laced them together.

Finally, Shelley took a step closer. "Oh, Claire," he said, with the voice he had used to comfort me in Calais, at night in Europe, last autumn in Lynmouth, "you know I only want good things for you."

Shelley gave me a familiar look—one of gentle ownership. It was a look I had come to dread.

"Then why not follow Byron to Lake Geneva?" I asked for something large, yet the words felt so small for they came from my mouth, which belonged to my body and yet did not always feel as though it belonged to me. It was quite a narrow space a girl lived in, wedged between amiability and susceptibility. Shelley faced me, tall and gaunt, closer still. "Claire, you were always able to convince me of anything."

PART TWO

MAY 1816

LAKE GENEVA

1

THE OCEAN ALWAYS SEEMED a country of its own: not the place one had left and not yet the place one was going. One week into May, my world was a confusing chop of waves. I slept poorly again, with night terrors, unsure which way I lay in the small berth.

I stood at the railing feeling not quite myself as we sailed to France.

I had written to Byron: *Convincing Shelley to meet you in Geneva did not take long.* I paused too long there and bent the quill tip. Then went on, messily. *I know not if I should call you friend or which word is most appropriate. Though I love you, I fear you have lost interest in me. Were I to float by your window drowned all you would say is, oh, hello there.* I paused again. Not my best work. I had tried to come off nonchalant. *See you shortly. Safe travels.*

I wore a heavy shawl over the same sea bathing dress I had worn with Byron, only since the marriage of Charlotte, Princess of Wales, to Prince Leopold of Saxe-Coburg-Saalfeld the week before had made the colour Coburg green so fashionable, I received compliments and smiles. Byron had described such plaudits as invasive, yet I rather enjoyed the adulation.

As I looked at the expanse of water, I pictured the sand underneath rising and settling. I had made myself into that sand, pushed and pulled by others. From Paris we would go to Champagnole and then the Jura. What would happen in this new place?

The ocean did not give me the answer but bubbled up froth and slap-waves onto the hull.

Once I had overheard someone describe me as a bubble. Oh, how we believe the versions of ourselves told to us by others! Mary and I were young. Her father applied for tickets to the British Museum. He wanted us to see firsthand the department of antiquities, offering that what society chooses to display shows not only the merit of the art or object, the use of such things, but indeed what that society itself values—what that was, I did not know. Mary and I took to waiting for the post by the Skinner Street front door.

We'd stood like footmen awaiting royalty until my mother's many sighs burst from her. *Enough,* she'd said, *come inside—there is no news so important one must stand and be assumed to be blobbing for coin. We aren't begging,* said Mary. And to this my mother replied, *What you* are *doing is never as important as what you* appear *to be doing.*

We obliged, waiting inside for entry tickets. Of course the new museum was free and open to the public, Mary's father explained, yet one still had to apply or know someone who had the clout or connections. Finally, we journeyed to the formidable building to see some of Sir Hans Sloane's collection: agricultural tools and implements, bill-hook and sheaths, a special needle with carrier. This last, Mary could not pry her eyes from, her ferocious gaze upon the object as though willing it to speak. *Mary, Mary.* Her father had poked her shoulder gently at first, and then his voice switched from questioning to near pleading with her to move. She'd held fast, oddly focused, until she placed her hands so near the object I pulled her away lest she be escorted out. *We ought to be able to repair things better,* little Mary had said, and stepped away.

I hadn't known if she meant stitching cloth with that needle or sewing together the wounds that might have caused her mother's infectious situation—perhaps Mary felt that overlarge needle might not be dangerous but instead prevent death. *Now you know what society values,* her father said on the way out, but I did not quite.

Yet I did not say as much. Close by to the museum was a spacious set of windows displaying paintings. We stood as Godwin tried to engage Mary. Then a man known to Mary's father appeared. I knew not his name, and, as I was a child and he an adult and therefore by default boring, I turned my attentions to the art. The men stood behind me talking, perhaps also looking at the paintings on display. Work by Jean Siméon Chardin. *The Water Cistern. The Young Schoolmistress. Soap Bubbles.*

I heard then Godwin describe Mary's intensity, her adult language, her dark moods. They were not such favourable words, and yet he said them with love—this was who his daughter was, and we all ought love her as such. *And the other girl?*, the friend had asked. I waited as one does—with equal parts hope and dread—to find out how I was seen. A cart and horse went by at that moment, so all I heard was *she is like that . . .* and he pointed to the window where the art was.

A bubble, the man said with a laugh. Mary's father, perhaps grateful for the break in mood, laughed, too. And Mary suddenly giggled, which only set her father off more. They waited and I understood I ought also to be laughing. So I did.

I had looked at the paintings, which depicted domestic scenes far more applicable to my life than any elevated renderings: the man in the oil painting, brown coat, hair curled, as was the fashion back in that day. Out of fashion, as everything would one day be. He was blowing a bubble, and the painter had captured that moment right before a bubble bursts.

I felt a child's version of sorrow then—for what the painter meant was not the happiness of bubbles on a warm day but rather the sure end of both. I did not speak up. Instead I kept up the laughter that had been asked of me. Mary had turned to her father and his friend. *It is the ephemera of life, is it not?* young Mary said, and her father had beamed.

I had spent my days being the bubble to Mary's brain. A family axiom brought forth from childhood to now, when we wore the flags of our given personages without much thought to donning them each morning.

I looked at the country of ocean and vowed to reach the shore and find the courage to puncture, somehow setting myself free.

HAVING BEEN ill alongside Shelley during our crossing, Mary steadied herself, gazing over the ship railing the way she had looked out the windows in London, waiting for something.

"What are you doing?" I asked, weary of travel, of being awake and alert at night.

At first she did not answer but then put her hand over mine on the railing. I lived for that, the two of us facing the dominating ocean together.

"I admit I am looking for my mother," Mary said. When I thought I had misheard her I put my face closer to hear better. "I have come to think of her as a bird." She did not say more.

Here was the sister I thought only logical, yet even she had some mysticism, the ache of loss that required finding signs or meaning where there might only be scrub grass, waves, or wings. "And what does she say to you in these winging moments?" I asked.

Mary returned to me befuddled, "I have never thought to ask. Perhaps it is just enough to know she is nearby watching me."

This would not have satisfied me. I would wonder if the bird could talk, what it would say. "I've been reading my mother's posthumous novel, *Maria, or the Wrongs of Woman*." She shook her head. "Do you know my mother referred to me as an animal when I grew inside her? I found a note from her to my father—she wrote it waiting for the midwife." She looked at me. "Was I feral to her?" Her grip loosened. I recalled reading lines Shelley had written and left in my room in Lynmouth after the baby died: *Every articulation from Mary's body aches with grief. I wish to be sympathetic, yet in my chest I feel a repugnance which forms into bricks with which I build a wall. Such crenellations through which I might see out yet let nothing in.*

I took my hand away before she could, just to save myself that slight. "Perhaps, Mary, if you wrote of grief—as you did once in the journal—you might find relief in the day-to-day."

Instead of swatting my arm or telling me I did not know about writers, because of course she knew I had spent much time with Lord Byron so must know something, or because her bird-mother hovered in the air, Mary nodded. "Perhaps yours is a good idea." She rebuilt herself in front of me. "Everything is well, is it not?"

I gave her the assurance she needed with a smile she accepted, though it was false. If all was truly well, why had my night terrors returned? I begged the Gods of Sleep for a chance at a full night when we reached Geneva.

Land came into view. I felt myself split in two: Half of my heart filled with anticipation of the love or adventure waiting for me, with the other half packed full of dread for a reason I could not name. Perhaps the unknown. I wished I had a word that encompassed both.

2

WIND AND RAIN VIOLENT and hard made the mountain journey in the berline longer and more arduous. I held William so Mary could sleep on Shelley's shoulder as the carriage jolted.

"I hope this is not a mistake," Shelley said.

"I could not have predicted this weather," I said. Our passports, written in the universal language of French before our departure from England, had been for Gex in France. Shelley had bribed officials and changed our destination to Nyon in Swiss territory.

"I do not blame you, Claire," he said, as a crack of lightning broke the sky in half, though his tone was not convincing. "I only wish for quiet."

Outside was loud. Inside my head, too. For I could scarce wait to reach Geneva and see Byron. In my note to him I'd reminded him of his praise for *Queen Mab*, assured him this would be an introduction of literary minds, lest he get any wrong ideas of my motivation, although wrong ideas were precisely my motivation.

"This is a fine sonnet," Shelley said, rustling the paper in his hand. Nausea had overtaken him on the ocean crossing, yet he could manage to read in the carriage and had balanced well enough to use the carriage pot, creating a stench. I did not understand how he managed his body.

"What is it?" I asked. I willed my nerves to settle, but the fierce wind precluded any such possibility. William shifted in my arms. He needed changing.

"A new poet. John Keats, a medical student. First publication, and Leigh Hunt agrees to put him in print in *The Examiner*!" Shelley sounded both impressed and annoyed.

I read the title upside down. "*O Solitude*," I said, and wished I had it.

We pushed on along the mountain route into darkness as snow began to cloud the way. *Bad inn, dirty beds*, my sister had put in their journal, while Shelley had added lines about spending money we did not have: fresh horses and ten men to keep the carriage moving in the snow.

I looked out the window: Only wooden poles lined the steep road edge—hardly enough to keep us from careening off. My hand gripped tightly to the carriage handles. "Keep doing that and you'll break it," Shelley said, and swatted my hand off the handle.

Mary held William like a shield against her. "Claire doesn't know her own strength."

3

At last we arrived at Lac Léman, hot air flowing into the carriage as we lowered the windows. We would have the cheapest rooms at the best inn, Dejean's Hôtel D'Angleterre in Sécheron, just outside Geneva's city walls, where the gates were locked from ten at night until six the next morning.

We approached over cobblestones through the most fashionable garden suburb of the city: women in high-waisted summer frocks with sheer sleeves and bosoms higher than back home, furniture boasting jaunty green and white silk stripes, outdoor chairs set at just the angle to catch the procession of people on holiday who had to fill the time between meals and so changed clothes and walked until they might justify another sit-down.

We could neither afford such changes in wardrobe to keep up with fashion nor did any of us wish to be the sort of people who kept up with fashion. This did not keep Shelley from noticing a man's fine summer-weight jacket or offering to buy us both a pair of gloves should we require them. My own dress was lightweight, the colour of off-season beachside sky, faded from too much washing, which only gave it a more tired presentation. Our carriage pulled into the circular drive at the Hôtel D'Angleterre. We stepped out, and I noticed interested glances from passersby.

Perhaps our bonnets or boots gave us away as not being local, nor French, or we possessed the queer speech and the pigeon-darting gaze of the recently arrived. As we were obviously foreigners, I hoped my lack of fashion would be overlooked, perhaps misunderstood as relevant elsewhere. I hoped this until I looked down and noticed my hem, ragged and growing still dirtier as I stood in the remnants of a puddle. Foreign fashion was one thing; dirt was universally understood.

The hotel was finely appointed, with velvet chairs and towering flower arrangements, staff at the ready. While I did not expect a theatrical performance—harpsichord music! butlers with champagne!—I was disappointed to arrive hot and perspiring with no sign of Byron.

Shelley said he was anxious for us to explore. He gave a side smile while Mary held William tight against her, using her hand as a shade for his small sleeping face. I could feel sweat pooling under my breasts, and trickling down my back.

"I should rather rest," Mary said. "Willmouse, too."

She was a terrible traveller, unable to face boat or carriage without stomach ails, unable to sleep at the proper time. All I wanted to do was to clean up, find a dress that did not give me the appearance of a penny-pinching old maid, and look for Byron. I imagined him in the perfect pair of tight britches that I had already seen worn by a few men outside. He would have a linen shirt that would complement his physique and be easy-fitted enough to shuck off quickly. I shook my head—I had to stop thinking of the story of him and simply find the real him. But not until I had freshened myself.

"If you are too tired, Mary, perhaps Claire will walk the grounds with me," Shelley said. He pointed to the pass-through. "Just through there are gardens, and the lake!"

Shelley stepped away to the front desk, leaving us in the city of our trunks and cases. On the curved wooden counter was a solid slab of marble, and on top of the marble was splayed a ledger. I saw Shelley trace a finger down a page and then another. He came back to us. William fussed and Mary shifted, uncomfortable in the heat.

Shelley returned. "Lord Byron isn't here," he said.

"I am not bothered," I said. This was a lie. The question was whether he would show at all.

My body wilted, and I felt on the verge of asking to return to London. At least it would be familiar. Then I thought of the carriage, the mountain pass, the storms, the churning ocean crossing—it was so far back. Shelley dashed to the desk and then back again. "Someone mentioned Byron's carriage has broken down and needs repairs."

WHILE WE waited to see if Byron would appear, my sister and Shelley acted as a couple on holiday. They slept late, lingered over currant-studded rolls, admiring the jams as though no one had ever seen preserves before. That was the glamour of being away from home—the ordinary felt special.

Still, I felt at loose ends. Shelley removed himself to see to more permanent lodgings—we would only be in the hotel a few days. I documented the days in my journal, strolled the grounds until the heat proved intimidating. Once I realised I was walking only to look in the faces of passersby to check if they were the face of my love, I felt silly and returned to the room.

I opened the apothecary cases, while Mary sat in her chemise and nursed William. Mary's case, a wedding gift from Shelley, had her initials MS on the silver lid. Inside stood an army row of blue glass bottles with matching silver tops and a tiny amethyst from Mary's cousin Edward Wollstonecraft. I picked up the jewel.

"Where is he now?" I asked. Her cousin had been ashamed of Mary's mother's fame, so he had hidden in Portugal, away from any maternal connection.

"He and his friend, Mr. Alexander Berry, have lived together some time." She paused, and in that pause I understood she was waiting to see if I understood her.

"If you wonder, Mary, if men love men sometimes, I can assure you, they do. Even in London." I thought about Byron's first love, John, and bit my lip to keep from using my information to prick her.

Mary switched William to her other breast. She was disheveled, hair slipping from its ribbon, chemise pulled to her waist. "Now Berry is infatuated with my cousin's sister and all three live together." She sighed. "He is hoping to leave for the colony of New South Wales and then I shall never see him again." As she said this, a tear slipped from her eye. They were not close, but any mention of leaving seemed to wound her.

"I can see you are tired," I said. I poured her a glass of water from the pitcher and dampened a cloth in the basin and put that on her neck to cool her. She thanked me and looked out the window as I unpacked.

"We brought too much," I said.

"We had to clear the rental," Mary said. "Also, one never knows quite what will be available abroad."

"We are in Europe, Mary, not the Russian Empire," I said, and kept unpacking. Here was cream in a small amber pot. A new perfume, which smelt of freesia and bergamot. A manicure set Mary and I had used for years, trading turns. Mary did not wish us to have the chapped lips of the poor, so we had many lip salves between us. Castor oil for our lids and lashes, rice powder if we freckled in the sun, piles of undyed cotton flannels—more than Mary and I would likely need because of course we would wash and reuse them. A small silver vial filled with pins to hold the rags for our courses in place.

"No matter how carefully I calculate dates, or study the moon," Mary said, "It is always a bit of guesswork, is it not?"

"Indeed. I have a complicated system of markings in my journal. Monthly blood maths."

"It is an unfortunate disease," Mary said, and looked ashamed. My own mother had been told she had a wandering uterus. This would have been amusing had she not believed it and told me the same. I did not confess I pictured my innards with their carrying case boarding a train.

"See what I have there?" Mary said. She pointed to a bottle. She favoured Mrs. Mallory's Sanitative Wash because she thought all women had an odour, so she had two bottles. She brought lime-scented soap, which hid the smell of the tallow. So much of what she brought seemed to cover up something else.

I had tooth powder from crushed oyster shell and bones and a glove stretcher from my mother, which as far as I knew neither she nor I had ever used. Part of being a woman seemed to be accumulating tools and potions for betterment, only to have them lie useless in a case of fruitless hope. I touched the nailbrush with its inlaid onyx, a hairbrush, and a tendril trimmer set and thought of Byron fingering each front lock of my hair, smoothing it only to have it refuse to stay put. I wished I had clipped and stolen a piece of his hair when I had the chance.

My mood fouled, and a cloud came outside the window in agreement. I took the clippers and set about trimming my fringe. One piece. Then another.

"Claire, stop before you become a head of regret."

I stopped mid-snip. "Fine." My sister was correct—I should not take my stepped-on feelings out on my hair. Mary, however, might benefit from a redo. "Shall I tidy yours?"

At this, the tears that had only leaked out before fell in big blobs onto William's head.

"I do apologise," I said, though I knew not what I had done.

"I cannot cut it." She let go William, who flailed on her lap as Mary held her hair. "If you cut it and cut it, eventually there will not be a hair on my head that the baby touched."

And then I knew. Mary held one baby in her arms but thought about the one she had lost. I put her to bed with William and cleaned myself up. Mary was not as brightened as she had appeared in London. This was perhaps a new stage of her grief.

I would sit outside and read or at least pretend to read whilst I watched people. I had packed the volumes of *Pride and Prejudice* and *Emma*, which, though I held it in my hands, felt far away. The girl who had pored over those pages was only a shadow of the me standing in the hotel waiting for her would-be lover to arrive. I placed the book back in the trunk and went to check the guest log again for Byron.

4

Days passed and still no sign of Byron. Worry had its own mouth, talking to me late at night when others seemed peaceful in slumber. I put my worries in my journal: What if I had been wrong to come here? What if he would never look my way again? What if I had given myself to someone who would never give back what I wanted?

According to the dailies, we had left London just in time, as the food prices were again on the rise, crowds hungry and demanding food yet without the ability to pay the hefty fees. Shelley had said we would be better off in Europe, but this had not proved true, for the harvests were said to be poor here, though we had been saved the protests and riots. No spears on the shores of Lake Geneva, only small hard rolls and butter in dainty pats that looked fancy and also kept diners from taking too much. I wrote to our sister Fanny about the hotel, the salted sliced marrow at breakfast, the poached fish, about the undercurrent of Mary's mood, about Shelley having been unsuccessful in finding lodging for us. *I long to leave the hotel*, I wrote to my brother Charles. I longed to see Byron, longed for Mary to brighten and hold my arm as we walked and told our dreams of summer.

Day in day out I waited, checked the guest book, found no evidence of Byron. And then, when I had given up and sat naked in a tepid bath in a useless attempt to stop perspiring, arrival horns and a burst of noise outside. By the time I had dried and dressed, the noise had settled. I checked the guest log. There. His name. Next to his name he had entered his address as *unknown, you tell me* and his age in the hotel register as *one hundred years*.

I laughed and felt love for him, though I was sorry I had missed his arrival, for the guests swarmed like starlings chattering—*his coach is far too large, it is modeled after Napoleon's, he is fairer in person than in papers.*

I wrote a note to be sent to his room: *I am sorry you are grown so old, indeed, I suspected you were 200 for the slowness of your journey. Well, I suppose your vulnerable age could not bear quicker travelling. May heaven send you sweet sleep—I am so happy you are here. Shall I introduce you to the Shelleys today? Let us meet on the dock at two o'clock.*

FINALLY, I would see Byron. Shelley and Byron would meet. I had succeeded in getting my sister to Lake Geneva, and she, amidst all of the literary shine, would be well. Shelley waited for the moment of my introduction, while Mary stood before the looking glass.

"Do you care much about your appearance?" she asked me.

"Not as such," I said.

"Nor do I," Mary said, as she switched bonnets last minute. Shelley witnessed our mendacious exchange without comment.

"Could we not go faster?" I heard the urgency in my voice, but it seemed to have little effect on Shelley, whose long, unhurried stride across the hotel lawn filled me with fury. I had worked so diligently, put forth so much effort for this meeting. We could not be late. At last, we arrived at the hotel dock, where a small crowd of onlookers had already spotted Byron and oozed closer for a better look.

He was every bit as resplendent in the present as he appeared in my mind. He wore an inconveniently sized hat which spoke more to providing some privacy than grandeur. Curved half smile, confident gaze, jaw set the way it had been in his bedroom. He paid me no notice.

How could a man who had bared his soul to me, given me his body—bad foot, too—and entered mine, a man who had expressed his feelings for me in a poem, his own famous art form, look away from me? I shoved my rejection deep into my belly.

Alongside Byron was a man who seemed not only to notice the people noticing them but to court it.

In the heat and sun at the hotel dock, the lake rippled gold, casting us all in warm light as though we were too wonderful, too young to require hope as I presented Lord Byron to Shelley and again to Mary, and Byron in turn presented the young Dr. John Polidori, twenty years of age and hired as Byron's personal physician. All were known by what they did—writer, poet, doctor, mother. What would I be known for?

After we all made a strange spider of our arms and hands shaking with introductions, Polidori turned to me. He wore no hat; his hair curled tentatively over his brow as though skeptical it was up for the companionship. "*Miss Marisol*," Polidori said, overly enunciating each *s* as though that would change the fact that he did not know my name. I gave a confused look. He answered with a definitive chin tilt.

"Miss Clairmont," I said, when no one else corrected him.

Polidori nodded without seeming to absorb what I had said, for Byron had launched into a tale. He had on his performance voice, which was at once enticing and yet also filled me with such sadness for I wished to run into his arms, the story meant for me, but could not.

Byron brought everyone around him. Polidori edged through Mary and Shelley, vying for a better position. "While travelling I came upon a man," Byron said. "A man who admired my coach, for he, too, was enamored and influenced by the heroics of Napoleon. This man—"

"He's very famous," Polidori interjected. "Considered most important—"

Byron pursed his lips—the famous needed not to recognise their own. "Yes, a musician of renown, you know he had set one of my poems to music."

"Which poem?" Mary asked.

"'Dark Lochnagar,'" Byron said. "'Lachin Y Gair.'" It stung me to know there were words he'd penned that I did not know. "About my childhood, really. I am half Scot." He turned away from the shore, where the group of onlookers pointed at him—one of them shrieked. "Is travel not extraordinary—for one believes one will be far from any known person or thing and then the world proves so small," Byron said. "In the middle of Belgium, a country that was not mine nor his, we found each other quite by surprise. And drank together all the night long." He paused. "Though his taste in wine is cheap and he added lead sugar to make it palatable."

Polidori made a face and quickly erased it, adding, "This famous musician is also deaf."

Byron nodded. "Deaf! Imagine being locked out of one's own art—he is writing a story he can never read."

"That is heroic indeed," I said. Byron flashed me a smile but only tolerant, not warm.

Byron was more than happy to make Shelley's acquaintance but clearly not so pleased to be in my company. I would have to remind him of his good feelings about me. Byron continued, "The composer carried with him a new invention, and I find myself thinking about it far too often since. What was it, Poli?"

"A metronome," Polidori said. "Newly patented by a German. Johann Maelzel." Polidori had revealed himself to be the kind of man who used knowledge as protective weaponry.

Byron held his pointer finger in the air. "Back and forth it went, counting time the man could see, though he could not hear the rhythmic tock. Hypnotic. I shall wish to hear the piece he wrote—there is a particular thrill to having one's writing translated into the language of music."

"This composer who loved Napoleon and made music and could not hear it, what was his name?" Shelley asked.

Byron thought a moment. "Beethoven."

Beethoven had been so moved by Byron he had composed music. Byron had been so moved by me he had written a poem. Did being his inspiration mean nothing? Did ordinary humans exist in proximity to artists only to be momentarily useful for their art? What would happen to me now that I was no longer useful?

We removed ourselves from public viewing and into the shade of a pergola on the backside of the hotel. Byron had plenty to say—his travels, his procuring of a new dog, the details of his rental lodgings. He only did not have much to say about or to me. I had brought about a miracle of literary introductions yet would not be in it, it seemed.

This crushed me, and yet I did not, like Mary, retreat inside out of the heat. Discomfort or complaint of pain had not served me in the slightest as a child, for there was too much chaos already and, with Mary's ailments and Shelley's perpetual issues, I only furthered my skill. I could bear more discomfort than anyone.

"I almost rented Villa de Saussure, Madame Necker's place," Byron said. Shelley was impressed. The look on Polidori's face suggested he was bitter at not knowing whom Byron spoke of.

"Madame de Staël's mother," I said, to clarify and annoy him.

Polidori was a tall man with a solid form and a plinth-like body, as though his head were a memorial to himself. A memorial to an unremarkable man. I knew this was an unkind thought, yet his lack of exception came forth in his eyes, in his step, every action an apology for not being better. This kind of insecurity caused people either to buckle or to become bitter. As he pushed past me to keep pace with Byron and talked over my words, Polidori was on his way to doing both. Still, he had quite a handsome face—at twenty years old he had the slightest bit of childhood left in his cheeks.

"Regardless, hers was already rented for three years to a British family." Byron turned to Shelley. "That's the trouble, the English are everywhere."

"Are you not also English, my lord?" Polidori asked.

"Yes, in fact—so I, too, am everywhere, Polidori. And withering, perhaps as my doctor you might anticipate my parched state and hydrate me."

Polidori dashed off to meet his employer's demands. I stood so close to Byron my gloved sweaty hand nearly touched the edge of his linen banyan. Shelley towered over us both. Byron mentioned dinner. I smiled and pondered immediately what I might wear. Polidori returned with a silver pitcher of water and a glass goblet. While Byron gulped, Shelley looked at me.

"Dinner sounds promising," I said quietly.

Shelley rested his hand briefly on my forearm. "It is an invitation for me, Claire. Only for me." Byron wiped his mouth in a way that made me think of him between my legs. I fought mightily to rid my brain of such thoughts but failed. "Perhaps you ought to check on your sister," Shelley said. "Dine with her in the room this evening while I am out."

SHELLEY CAME back drunk, with his collar soiled from wine. Body like a weak bough, he swayed and looked at me too long—as though he knew I had shed tears over Byron's dismissiveness. I wriggled my bottom to try and correct the pin that had come loose from the slip of fabric I'd positioned between my legs to catch the blood spots I'd noticed after the dock meeting.

"We are sorted," Shelley slurred. Mary roused enough to hear him but did not sit up fully. William lay alongside her with his arms above his head. "I've rented us a cottage. Maison Chapuis. In Montalègre." He steadied himself on a chair. "On Lake Geneva. Just the other side from here."

"Is it too remote?" Mary asked. "For the baby's sake."

Shelley shook his head. "Near the village of Cologny."

"And Lord Byron will visit?" I asked. Shelley shook his head again, and my hopes sank to the far reaches of the earth.

"Byron does not do things by halves. He's rented a mansion. A villa."

I pressed my eyes, for tears had welled again. I was not prepared for an ending so soon.

"Poor Claire," Shelley said, the words sloppy on his drunken lips. "You look so disappointed. You think him avoidant of us. Never fear," he patted my head in his inebriated fashion. "Byron's villa and Maison Chapuis are neighbours. So meeting up shall be unavoidable."

Mary drifted off. "We leave tomorrow," Shelley said to me. "Byron insisted. For they have already printed *mill-icince*, no, *millishinace*. *Malicious*—that's the word—items about us." I was taken aback. How soon word had spread. How quickly gossip formed. "Some Lord Glenbervie, whom Byron called Lord Pervy, told his lot that Byron and you were—well, one could not imagine such nonsense." He clutched his stomach, and I knew he would soon purge himself of drink and be difficult to rouse in the morning. "The gossip was printed that you—misprinted as Mrs. Shelley!—and Lord Byron are involved and now all of us are in a whirlwind of confusion—and I am going to be sick." And with that, he heaved onto the floor and lay down in a puddle of his own making.

I was disgusted. I was surprised he and Byron had been out for so many hours together. I was concerned about the news. And yet, I glowed. For if I knew anything about public opinion, it was that if people believed something to be true, it was possible.

5

OUR CARRIAGE BUMPED AND jostled us along, out of the city area and towards Montalègre and our cottage, Maison Chapuis. "One hears rumours of fame poisoning the person, and I admit readily to judging Byron as profligate before meeting him," Shelley said.

"Hours and hours you were out," Mary said, with scorn so slight it wafted over Shelley's head and out the window.

"Such a fine conversation partner," he said, "I barely feel the effects of drink this morning." I had cleaned up the effects of his drink before he'd awoken. "So caught up with him was I that time slipped by. What chance. What pleasure—for the man can speak of Locke, of Hume or Drummond, the agency of the individual, or recite Wordsworth, all while eating a tray of chocolates procured from a local confectioner."

Mary looked away, and I knew her to be annoyed to be left out of their writerly discussions. I waited for him to thank me for the introduction. I kicked one boot against the other as we made our way to the small town of Cologny.

Finally I said, "Well, I am pleased I could connect you with Lord Byron—all those many weeks I had spent in his company did make me think you and he would have much in common."

Shelley's mouth soured. "I had quite forgotten you knew him," he said.

The carriage bumped along slowly. Shelley and Mary dozed, with the baby sprawled on their laps. I watched the haze of buildings give way to greenery, mind wandering. In my body I felt a heat or smelt a smell that transported me to our sojourn two years before.

We had traversed war-torn Europe with no intention of visiting the Sacred Wood of Bomarzo. We had never even heard mention of its existence. Yet in front of us, the monster park lured us with magic and moss. We entered through a stone archway, and walked through fields dotted with the labyrinth of symbols. Shelley said the layout came only from a muddled mind with money. Mary appeared shrunken near the sculpture of Hannibal's elephant; the height of a house, it rose high up in the air, complete with stone carriage on top, defying the heaviness of stone itself.

"Vicino Orsini commissioned the park—a gift for his wife, Giulia Farnese," Mary had said, with a sly grin that I understood. I took my leave, allowing her time alone with Shelley—it was their elopement after all. I was not without insight into their connection and saw the spark that lingered, even when Shelley asked me to keep him company by the fire if Mary slept. He always came back to her.

I had left them and walked through the park without direction. This was a delicious roaming, as we had been walking with great purpose, town to town each day on the European trip. At Bomarzo, I saw the temple with its solid pillars, the Leaning House, narrow and white and oddly angled, which seemed to grow from the earth in such a way to knock the viewer off kilter. I could only visit there a few moments before feeling ill, a whirl of worry—we needed food and shelter, we seemed at the mercy of nature, and I had followed Mary and Shelley, who had each other as mutual anchors. Who or what was mine?

I had walked on. The Fury with her scaly tail covered in moss, unabashedly displaying her breasts for all to ogle. Yet it was not her breasts that captured my attention but rather her wings—elegant, regal, enormous—giving her perfect posture and a steady gaze. I wanted that balance of grace and strength, an impenetrable exterior despite baring nearly everything. Yet she was, I realised with sadness, stuck there forever, unmoving as statues are.

As my boot had sunk into damp ground, I thought of Orsini, the creator of the place. Had he been mad? A creative spirit stuck in the wrong time? Did he mean to say the only way to achieve that balance of fury and poise was to be imaginary—that I might need to reinvent myself as a mythical creature? I passed oversize tortoises, obelisks pointing hopefully towards the bluest sky, and I craned my neck up to see until the brightness was too much for my eyes and they began to water. On the obelisk was written *sol per sfogare il Core* ("just to set the heart free"). Stone nymphs and giants struggled or frolicked, though they did not move. Somewhere my stepsister likely lay on her back on the cold stone, perhaps in the temple. She and Shelley had first consummated their love at Mary's mother's grave, so they found odd places to replicate this. I did not question her desires, for I was grateful she confided them to me.

I went past Proteus and wished he might tell my future, saw stone dolphins, the sleeping woman, and, at Cerberus, I recoiled as he both scared and beckoned me. I thought of an old song my mother sang, *all wilds wish to be tamed*, which I wanted to believe. I had stopped at the Etruscan bench and thought I would rest there until Mary and Shelley emerged, yet I wandered further to a tree sculpture and found myself in a folly. There in front of me, a mouth the size of a castle door. Orcus—I said the name aloud, then put my hand to my mouth as though I had been too crass.

"God of the underworld," Mary had said, appearing next to me quiet as an apparition. Vacant eyed, snaggletoothed, with steps that led into the mouth.

"Shall we?" Shelley had asked, as though we were setting off for tea and not into a hellscape. But I had smiled as the three of us had held hands and stepped into the dark.

In the carriage to Chapuis I looked at my sister and Shelley and William and realised the Bomarzo trip was not simply the pleasant outing I had fashioned it into in my mind. We had been lost but pretending ever so well to be explorers. Why, in memory, did the mind try to smooth out the rough edges of feeling? Perhaps this is what the brain did, allowed us to pretend through our fear, through our sorrow, until we reached the other side of it.

Yet as our carriage wheels veered right, nearly going off the path and then correcting with force, I recalled the tilted house and understood—there was no other side of anything.

And there was a danger in pretending to be explorers, pretending to be anything—as it was all too easy to believe so wholeheartedly in the mirage that one lost sight of the truth.

6

THE CARRIAGE SLOWED, PAUSED between two columns. Letters carved into one read DIODATI, all big letters as though the pillar had a deep voice of warning. The others awoke.

"Ah, we've arrived," Shelley said, bright and ready. We pulled into the half-moon of a sandy drive and stopped near a stone portico. I wished to take a good look at the place, but we had arrived before Byron, a faux pas, and so stood feeling awkward for a moment until an enormous, lumbering coach appeared.

Two imposing back wheels propped the body up high, with two wheels with slightly shorter circumference at the front. A full set of stairs was required to allow Byron to step down. Polidori followed, pausing on the steps as though expecting to greet an adoring public.

"I'll be damned," Shelley said. "It truly is a replica of Napoleon's carriage. I thought that would be an exaggeration."

Shelley did not wait for an invitation and went to greet Byron, who propped his hands on his hips and waited as a bevy of staff arranged themselves near the pillars. Mary and I followed with William.

"As for them." Byron pointed to the line of staff in an expectant row. "Berger, a Swiss steward, William Fletcher, my valet—" Byron paused to see if either I or Fletcher would acknowledge each other. The man had seen me at all hours in London. Neither of us gave any signal. Satisfied, Byron went on. "Robert Rushton, a butler. John William Polidori, MD, whom you met, is here yet—" Polidori suddenly scooted away, "it appears he ran off inside. Pity we won't witness him as an Ode to an Englishman in the Heat. Here are the yeoman and page, my English servants, who are the very same who travelled with me back in '09—for one cannot reward enough the bonds of loyalty."

"Quite right," Shelley said. "Loyalty is to be commended." He looked at me as he said this. I did not meet his gaze. Byron's crew scurried—trunk after trunk from the carriage, towers of parcels wrapped in brown paper, a raft of books and papers.

"And to think we worried *we* had overpacked," I said, and Mary laughed her glittering laugh that shone on me.

And then, just when I thought we would make our way to the grounds to see Villa Diodati and our Maison Chapuis, a great cacophony.

"At last," Byron said, as another carriage arrived. Out came ornate cages: peacocks and guinea fowl immediately released and pecking for bugs near our feet, a monkey with a question mark tale who went right to Byron, and a dog the size of a steed. I had known him so well in London, but only in those two rooms of his home. Perhaps I did not know him at all elsewhere. "May I introduce the animals!" Byron looked so gleeful I was jealous.

"So you have a new dog," I said, when I could hold off speaking to him no longer.

"This is FF," he said, giving me a slight acknowledgement. "Finest Friend." He turned to the dog's massive head and addressed him directly. "Good dog."

I knelt down to look in the dog's amber-brown eyes and wondered if Byron knew my wish to run my fingers through his hair rather than the dog's soft fur.

We followed Byron through a ring of wet, ragged weeping willow trees to the front of the house. Why were they wet? Had it rained here and nowhere else? The trees gave way to reveal Villa Diodati: huge, orderly, elegant. Tall pillars evenly spaced all the way round the bottom of the house. Two-over-two windows, each framed by a set of dark green shutters, gave the villa a well-ordered appearance. The roof was red, and on each side three small dormer windows popped up like ill-fitting bonnets. A wide balcony, lawn rife with blushing pinks and lightest green.

And spread out in front of us, pulling us in, was Lake Geneva. The water this side of the lake appeared darker than at the hotel. The enormous jagged mountain peaks had the odd effect of looming over the lake, teasing, for we might never reach them no matter our trekking skills.

Shelley stood agog. "I am awestruck." He turned to us. "Truly." In that moment I saw him as he had first appeared at our house on Skinner Street—humbled, passionate, a man laid out open to the world. He turned to me. "You wrote of the Alps in your old journal, did you not?"

I nodded. "Sublime." I knew what I had written and felt embarrassed he remembered it from two years before. Mary had gone through the pages and struck through certain lines.

"*Oh, the terrific Alps*, you wrote," Mary said, her voice playful in tone but stinging to me. This caused Byron to roll his eyes. "Hardly poetry, is it?"

"Claire is a fine writer," Shelley said, but could not turn away from the landscape. Shelley's words in my defense seemed to startle Byron.

"She is a person of many talents then," Byron said, with a wink in my direction which caused my hopes to rise. Contrary to what Mary said, I had written well about the Alps, calling them *peaked and broken, the light, airy clouds arrested a few moments on their aspiring France, and then fled away, but we might better behold the sublimity of the scene.* That is what I had written, yet I could not force the words out.

"John Milton once lived here," Byron said, finished with any attention towards me. Polidori emerged from the villa holding a ball and presented it to Byron, who threw it for FF. The dog lumbered towards the lake and came back sopping. "Good dog," Byron said, this time to Polidori. I took a side glance at Byron's face, his mouth, his plummy lips. "We shall reconvene later," Byron said, without looking my way.

"I shall make you a medicinal tea, my lord," Polidori said.

"I shall hate you for it, Polly," Byron said. "Shelley—boat?"

It was not a full sentence, yet the men had agreed on something. Already Shelley and Byron rejoiced in each other. Each man's suit of insecurity could be set aside in the presence of the other.

"Then I shall report back to London," Polidori said, clearly annoyed he was not asked on the one-word adventure.

"Only tell good things," Byron said.

"Only say what must be said," Shelley said.

"Only leave me out of it," Mary said.

"Only—tell me why you write?" I asked.

Polidori turned to me. "Well, Miss Godwin—"

"Not my name," I said, and Shelley shot me a look, for it was rude to point out this misstep. "I am not Godwin. I am Clairmont."

Polidori kept going. "Mr. Murray, that's Byron's publisher—"

"I know who John Murray is," I said. "I have met him in his offices."

Polidori regarded me with doubt. "He offered me no less a sum than £500 for an account of Byron's life this summer."

"Polly here is a doctor of medicine with an advanced degree in gossip," Byron said. He did not seem displeased, rather amused and resigned, yet this news made me check myself.

For my feelings were so close to the surface of my skin, I worried I appeared like a bird whose new heart was visible from the outside. My own selfishness that I wanted a showy spring into summer. I wanted daring magenta and that almost-vulgar pink so ripe I imagined gentlefolk turning away, embarrassed by the crassness. I wanted warm breeze that foretold of summer's burgeoning heat, which in turn brought thoughts of nakedness. I wanted green lush grass and clover thick on the foot soles as Byron took me on the lawn at dusk. But I did not for an instant wish this to be reported back to London by Byron's charmless physician. Although I did take solace that he had yet to learn my name.

"Go off then, and write, Polly—" He put on a voice. "Byron stood with his monkey, staring out at the lake as a storm threatened to come in."

"There is no storm," Shelley said. "The day is blissfully warm."

"It won't last," Byron said. I could have sworn he looked at me.

7

My room was simple and clean. A bed slightly larger than I'd had in London. A desk missing a chair, as though Shelley and Mary thought I would not require one for writing. A chiffonier with high drawers and a small looking glass on top. I willed myself not to look out the window to see if Byron just happened to be walking through the orchard to find me.

"Just seeing how you're getting on," Shelley said in the doorway.

"Fine," I said. I draped a pair of stockings over my arm like someone's shadow as Shelley watched. "A chiffonier—it means ragpicker and a place to store odds and ends."

"I always appreciate your knowledge." He looked around and, as there was nowhere else to rest, sat on the bed. I turned away from him as he stretched out on the mattress. "This is quite comfortable."

Mary appeared at the doorway, eyes trained on Shelley. "What are you doing in here?" He sat up and stood up in one motion. I blushed, though I had not done anything wrong.

"Bad dog," she told Shelley, but her face softened. "One of you come help with Willmouse."

I went to my satchel, found ink and quill and journal. "I need a chair for the desk, Shelley. I intend to write all summer."

Mary crossed her arms over her chest. Shelley gave me a nod. "Very well, good idea. I shall see to it at once."

They left me to finish unpacking. I hung up the sea dress, set the calfskin birthday boots near the narrow wardrobe, put my silver tin on a shelf set into the wall. I looked inside it at the wooden horse and the hairpins. Everything I called my own had once been someone else's.

I KNEW not what to do with myself. Mary had William to contend with. Shelley found a chair for me and set about checking furniture—which chair wobbled, which table might need wedging—unintentionally comedic, as he was not skilled in labour nor particularly handy yet took the task seriously, brow furrowed, mouth tense. I stifled a laugh and took my leave.

The tidy grounds at Diodati displayed refinement—stone urns with interesting though not ornate spring blossoms, lawn that rolled to the lake, clipped hedges between the side and back. A wide stone slab terrace faced the water. Not a twig nor errant leaf besmirched the lawn. This was a beauty that was easy to admire yet hid the labour necessary to keep such a place in order: groundskeepers, gardeners, scullery maids awake before anyone.

I thought more about Shelley attempting to be handy and began laughing again. Not wishing to be overheard, I stifled myself and so began coughing.

Dr. Polidori emerged from behind a sculpted topiary. "Are you quite well, Miss Clerment?"

"Clairmont," I said. "Miss Clairemont." I saw he had a thick diary. All those empty pages—what would they be filled with come August? "They really wish you to report back on his dailies?"

He arranged his shoulders and held his head high. "Five hundred pounds." He paused. "Twenty ponies."

"A monkey." He looked surprised. "I do know how currency works, Doctor. Twenty ponies is a monkey, which is £500. A £500 book deal. And yet—your employer truly *has* a monkey. Which is just brilliant."

My joy at this silliness deflated his chest. "Well, Miss Clermont, I bid you good day."

"*Claire*mont."

He did not respond. He closed his diary with a thud and held it to his chest in a manner unbecoming to a physician. That is, he looked unsure. And one does not expect nor wish to have a man of medicine who is unsure.

"Good day," I said, and went off to look around the grounds.

I SAW no one as I explored; Mary and Shelley—keen to think on the impossible beauty of our surroundings—had taken William for a nap. Maison Chapuis was set to one side of Villa Diodati and closer to the lake, although it had no direct access. The cottage was a churchgoer's summer bonnet, replete with climbing roses inching up the sides, wisteria heavy on the ratty trellis at the back, and a simple stone terrace. From the terrace and side windows, one could see the small thick orchard that separated our place from Byron's.

I looked over the grass, the clipped hedge, the orchard branches with their buds and bright green leaves, everything elegant and subdued enough to scream money. From the vantage point of Maison Chapuis the orchard rows appeared ordered; yet when I moved closer, the corridors of trees and bush vines were overwhelmingly tall, a near-maze. A set of wide stone stairs set into the hill provided the way from the orchard up to Diodati. A set of small trees flanked the stairs, both with floppy flowers that resembled nothing so much as fried eggs, yet the flowers were pink. This was a place with egg trees. I expected fish to sprout from the green stalks that struggled to push up through the earth. I had stumbled into another version of Bomarzo, this one not entirely realised.

A motion from my side view startled me, and I turned. There, in the centre window, was Byron. He moved the drapes deliberately, letting me see he was there. I knew he had seen me and knew he stood there still, yet I tried to give the appearance of caring not a whiff. In fact, I tried so hard not to care that I likely exaggerated my traipsing, possibly looking confused or drunk as I swayed this way and that: oh look, the lake, how lovely! and what a fine day and oh, see here a small rodent eating the not-too-ornate plants—someone will kill it for that.

As I meandered, first as a ruse to appear busy, I soon found myself truly entranced. Between moss-cloaked stones by the drive, I noted the tiniest of blue flowers. And near the orchard edge, an old wall missing a few stones and in those spots there grew a thick scrub of blue-green grass. And around the bases of some of the orchard trees twined a kind of ivy I had never before seen. On the boughs of many of the trees, a thick shag of light-green lichen. From a stone wall protruded a copper spigot that once had shone and had turned a mossy shade of blue I wished I could wear but had never seen replicated. For a moment the sun broke through the heavy layer of clouds, illuminating the entire villa. As the exterior was the colour of fresh cream, it glowed.

Gravel beset with lavender bushes already in bloom, heady-scented but delicate. Huge clumps of rosemary that begged me to touch their strong stems. I pinched the slim leaves as I pulled my fingers up the length of one and breathed in the delightful scent.

A clutch of chicks nestled in the small space between firewood logs and a large stone at the edge of the mossy slope. I stood as though at that very moment the stone would roll down, but of course it didn't. I realised I liked the tension in hoping and then un-hoping it would go. Everywhere there was evidence that this place had once been wild. I tucked this knowledge away, pleased as though the outside world and I shared some secrets.

8

IN BED THAT NIGHT, my upper body straight, my legs spread, I pictured myself a human letter, a Y. Though I was tired from the journey, I could not sleep—such quiet that each small noise seemed grand, wind on the ash trees with their new leaves, a stray branch scratching the windowpane as though the tree wanted to come inside, scuttling animals on the thatched roof, the odd night lullaby of arriving somewhere new.

I gave in to the game of overthinking. One could play this game for hours, especially when sleep evaded, and I sifted through old embarrassments, conversations gone awry, the look Mary's father and my mother had given me when I'd told them years before I was leaving. Did Mary's father lie awake with regret at having brought Shelley home?

Once engaged, my mind mechanics had controls out of my reach so all I could do was watch as my brain spewed sludge: an argument with Mary this March when she'd accused me of being like a vanity jar, the one on my dresser with guilloche lid—*gorgeous on top but empty inside* were the words she'd used, and I could recall them at any time, tiny tacks that would never leave me. I would be an eighty-year-old hunched lady and still dredge up that description. She thought me vain as I changed to go out—she did not know I was going to see Byron—while she stood in her nightdress, breasts swollen and leaking. I could have lashed out, but love and pity kept me quiet. And then Polidori unable to fix my name to his memory. Was I forgettable? Would Byron, too, let my name slip away from his lips?

My feelings towards Byron had started like any raging fire—the tiniest of sparks. Almost manufactured. I roamed the great hellscape of hearts tromped with Byron's infamy, and while the crumpled hearts of strangers ought to have served as warning bells those months before, I found myself oddly detached in my continued pursuit. Because I knew I would pursue him again.

Rather like the child who is convinced the stove will provide only heat not burn, I did not quite believe Byron's past indicated his future. In the dark, I thought of myself. I thought of Mary and Shelley—he a most handsome man with political fire—finding each other, their passion great enough to elope.

Wasn't my greatest strength understanding how people worked and using that knowledge to befriend them? I learnt their ways—who might be shy and need coaxing, who preferred light humour as the coating for depth of feeling.

My body was straight, a capital I. Alternating I and Y over and over until the sheets warmed, I pictured Byron's face when once he'd come to his sitting room and found me—not standing as I ought to have done but on the settee as though the room were mine. He had stared at me from the doorway. *I don't know how you've got here*, he'd said, for truly he was trying to be out of the public eye, too great was his fame. *By carriage*, I had said, as though I were only witty and cared not if I stayed with him.

I thought of my heart protesting, irregular and agitated. I had wanted to prove I could get him and succeeded. Only in a new country, I felt I'd quite underestimated his power. I called to mind his hands in his pockets, his stance, his eyes never breaking gaze, his mouth slightly parted, his consideration for my physical presence. How he'd said, *So you've come for me then?* How I had opened my mouth only partway as though I possessed a bird beak, only I was songless.

At Chapuis, the ash tree scratched the window again, the wind whipped stronger, and I heard Byron's words again and again as I rolled over, my hands between my legs *so you've come for me again*.

9

IN THE MORNING THE sky was blank as scalded milk, the air odd and thick enough to make walking feel effortful. I went out the side door of the cottage and stood on the small stone slab terrace, which was bare of anywhere to sit or take a meal—we would have to improvise and bring chairs from the table. The lake watched me as I stood breathing in the damp. Already my hair curled more, my skin warmed, my feet longed to be bare on the wet lawn. The trouble was the feeling reminded me of being unclothed with Byron, bodies slicked together, his mouth on mine, my hands on his sure back, one thumb flicking my nipple as his fingers went inside me while his eyes told a story of us being together. The lake's watchful eye stayed flat and judged me for my thoughts, which made me ache with a longing of unmet feelings.

ONE OF Byron's cooks had left a basket of items for us: dark bread, mixed berry preserves, a crock of butter. Mary and I ate together, while Shelley only gave a wave on his way to Diodati. I did not know if he had received an invitation or felt entitled to show up when he so pleased. Jealousy made me rip my bread into pieces.

"Claire," Mary said. "Should we dine with the others, please do not show your feelings on the plate."

"Only you would notice," I said. "For I am an apparition to others—barely here." I pushed my plate away and went to open the window, for the air was stifling in the cottage. Already I felt trapped as I had done in London. I felt the air, its undercurrent of cool a welcome wash on my face as I looked out on the lake and orchard.

Mary rose and stood behind me. "I feel a similar frustration." She shook her head. A familiar sigh overtook her body. "So much discussion already about writing. Yet who amongst the men has asked me about my work?"

DISAPPOINTMENT IS entirely relative to expectations. For what I had pictured was in the realm of jasmine perfuming a hot day so much that Byron's soul might need to be bared only to me and, once exposed, he would also need shed his shirt, perhaps pulling me into the lake with him.

Instead, we were simply cold. The mild early morning had given way to midmorning chill. The sort of cold that inched up the leg, embracing the knees to suggest instant ageing. The cold that went from my unkissed neck down my arms, circling my wrists and stiffening my hands. I might've withstood the chill so much better had I not been picturing the warmth in the first place. It seemed that when I expected something, when I allowed myself to imagine that particular future, I grew all the more devastated to find that reality did not match.

If I had imagined layers of muslin and wool, if I had imagined us, each cold-cloistered in our own attempt to keep warm, I might have imagined who would lay the fire, who might restock the wood, who might huddle alone under a blanket, and I might have had a picture that, while not exciting, was tolerable. But that was not what I pictured, and for this morning, it seemed I was not alone in misguided visions. I tried on my birthday boots, but the leather was so thin it felt like a betrayal, and I not only put them aside but put them out of sight in the wardrobe.

The belly of sky grew purple, the sort of odd air that set Byron's peacocks screaming. They ran down the slope from Diodati to the cottage with the clomping Faithful Friend running behind, yet the dog was so large he could not truly run and so appeared to be acting out a charade of the word *gallop*.

When Polidori came to see if the screams were human and perhaps thus requiring his professional skills, he found us at the cottage quite well, if cold, and invited us to sit by the fire at Diodati, where I arranged myself and sulked in the miseries of my ruined expectations.

Shelley wrote in one corner, Byron at a double-sized desk that bumped against the oversize middle window, facing the lake and darkening sky; Polidori wrote on his lap with the ink on a drinks table.

Mary wrapped William and told us she set him in the bottom drawer of a large sideboard in the dining room that was next door to us. She pulled a book from the shelf and wrote on her lap, borrowing Polidori's ink. At first he made a face and then, when Mary's sweet eyes and hair cascaded so near to him, he was a moth and fell for her light. They alternated dip, write, write, dip, and every so often Mary set down her quill to check on the baby.

"Are you not going to write in your journal?" Mary whispered to me.

"I worry it would ruin in the rain." In truth I was too distracted.

Mary looked over Byron's head. "I see no rain."

At her words, the sky broke. A shock of thunder set the peacocks screaming again. Fletcher appeared, and Byron nodded at him. Within moments, the birds came inside, fanned their ornate tails and walked among us as though proctoring a written exam. The rain continued—patters turned to slamming.

"Hail!" Polidori stood up.

"I am not Caesar," Byron said, though he rose, too. Shelley lanked his way to the tall window at the front and put his face to the glass. "How perturbing."

The peacocks settled on either side of me as the others returned to their writing stations, but without the same focus, for the hail's clatter increased with a ferocious wind, drum beating the frozen pellets against the windows until one such shot—hail the size of a new tomato—broke the pane.

Mary gave a scream, which in turn made me echo her, and our noises ignited passion in the fowl, who spread their feathers and were either dancing or close to mating. FF startled himself with snores and began to pace with Aurelia and George, the peacocks, while William fussed and a servant swept up the broken window glass.

"How is one meant to work with all of this commotion?" Byron asked, as though the animals were not his.

And then, just as quickly as it had started, the hail stopped. The sky's dark cape fell, and the flat light from morning returned. Not sun—for that would have been too lovely, too much a reminder of my lusty thoughts and hopes for reconciliation with Byron—just a blankness.

"So great is my employer's reach that he controls the weather," Polidori said.

"Would that were so," Byron said. "But please refrain from stating again and again the reason for your presence."

Shelley's taut mouth told me he agreed—it was uncouth to mention the roles.

"I've finished," Shelley said. Byron offered him wax and seal. Shelley again sat down. "The change in weather offers a few lines in my mind." He reached for the pen again. "I cannot express enough gratitude for this unfettered time." He looked at Byron. "Perhaps I shall have another volume by summer's end."

"An addiction to poetry is very generally the result of an uneasy mind in an uneasy body," Byron said. "Still, I should like to think we shall encourage the other to be productive."

Though there were five of us in the room, Byron only looked at Shelley, who glowed in the halo of his words. I knew that haloed light.

Mary folded her letter—she'd written crosshatched to save paper and postage—and placed it with Shelley's. Polidori put a dramatic full stop of ink at the bottom of his page as though he expected a round of applause. It was tedious being near someone who quietly demanded attention and praise for simply being a person and doing person things.

When no one commented on Polidori's flairful folding of his letter, he offered, "I have finished my report for Mr. Murray. The first travelogue episodes."

"I hope I am not included," I said. Polidori did not answer. Byron sealed his own letter with wax. Mary went to the bookshelf and considered a few volumes before settling on Milton's *Paradise Lost*. She showed it to Byron, whose nod suggested she had made the correct choice, a test I had not known was being given.

Polidori leaned towards me. In his palm he held a few mailing wafers, flour and gelatin in discs. "Miss Godwin," he said, and I shook my head. He cleared his throat, corrected. "Miss Chermont," he said sotto voce, "have you anything pressing at present?"

"Clairmont. My name is Claire Clairmont. We have been here long enough to have that name sink into the lake of your brain." I raised my eyebrows to show I needed an acknowledgement. Polidori stared at me. I did not see his lips move to sound out my name, but I believed him to be reciting it internally.

"Now that the storm has broken I believe I will go to the cottage," I said, and then, because I knew from the pull of his shoulders that Byron was listening, I added, "I crave sweets—I should like to bake something rich and scrumptious." I drew *scrumptious* as though I meant to say *fuck me* and saw Byron flinch, though he refused to look at me. I sighed.

"If you are determined to sulk and are heading out anyway, be useful and send these off," Shelley said, and handed me a couple of letters.

Polidori quickly licked a wafer and used it to press his letter to John

Murray closed. He handed me the rest as an apology. "In case you need more, I have plenty."

Byron handed a letter to me. "The postal carriage is at the crossroad of Chemin de Ruth and the small path that has no name—you will find it past the cow field on the right-hand side."

"Perhaps you might show me out," I said. Mary looked up over her book, and Shelley watched as Byron soldier-marched with his bad foot. He walked me not to the front entrance but to the back door.

I wanted to give him a carefully crafted speech, but all that came out was, "You are being very rude to me."

He smelt the same, vanilla and almond laced with condescension. "One cannot be angry at a dog for behaving exactly as one expects a dog to behave."

"Your dog has far more manners," I said, and looked him up and down. "And better hair."

10

I HELD THE LETTERS IN both hands. Out the back entrance, a solid door flanked by two glass lanterns, I turned to look at the house from this perspective. Five windows—three above and two down. Just as there were five of us. Intricate metal fencing cornered by interwoven vines that appeared sharp. Perhaps for decoration or to discourage birds from roosting. Everywhere the lake beckoned, an artist's palette that shone in the burgeoning sun. From Diodati's roof, two pointed knobs rose out like snails. I touched my palm to a rose bush struggling in the cold but did not pick any, for each thing here seemed to ask, most respectfully, not to be disturbed.

Out the drive, spring's sad attempts at flowers nodded at my ankles: slim stalks, bushes with almond-shaped leaves and tiny white buds. I knew not the name of these plantings nor if they grew wild or at the will of man. There was too much I did not know—at what age would I be able to recite the Latin, the common names, harvest anything useful?

I vowed I would go to the library at Diodati and find a guide.

I followed Chemin de Ruth past houses, fields with horses but no cows, walking with heavy steps, conveying my anger to no one save for the dust-grime wheel ruts and scattering of new horse excrement and old snowdrops with their embarrassed dipping blooms. How could I possibly stay all summer when I knew nothing of Byron's heart?

All four of the others thought they were too busy to walk their own post in. I was more than an errand boy, that I knew. The sheep, fleecy white on the ice-crusted field, seemed to think otherwise and barely noticed me as I walked by. The colours were off—where there ought to have been bright green and fruit-jam flowers the grass was a concerning pale yellow. I was in a season no one had yet named.

The unknown stoked in me a fear, that same oddness Mary had felt with screams and wild wind and hail. I hurried past the cow field and came finally to the crossroads. A ways up the road I could make out a carriage and presumed it to be the postal carrier, so I waited with my stack of letters. Oh, how I wanted life to be exciting—yet so much of it was errands or waiting.

Afraid I might drop the letters, I pressed them to my chest as the sky began to darken again. It was a threat I did not take lightly. The plane trees whispered around me as the mail truck drew closer. Even the slim trees leaned into each other, conspirators noticing my foolishness going out in such weather. The others ought to have protected me.

I waved for the carriage to slow, at which point a light rain began to fall. I gripped the letters tightly. Too tightly, for Polidori's came unstuck, and when I frantically began to try and smush it closed, Mary's opened beneath it.

"It's come unsealed," I said to the post driver. The rain came down faster.

He was unfazed. In French he said, "I have a trick for resealing. If you want to sit for a few minutes and get out of the rain, come in." I climbed up into the carriage and wedged myself on a bench seat alongside a burlap sack of parcels and an open crate of letters. So many words people sent back and forth, so little I had heard from Byron's mouth. I pawed at the letters in my lap. The driver handed me a small pot of glue. "Colle de poisson," he said. "Ça sent mauvais, mais ça marche." Fish glue. It would smell, but it would work.

As the rain spattered the carriage roof, I studied the pot of glue and damaged letters, holding each note in my hand. How shut out of Byron's mind I felt. How annoyed at Polidori's very presence and gossip contract. How little Mary had told me of her own writing these days. How much and how little I knew of Shelley's thoughts. Yet there, in my hands, were those very insights.

I checked around me as though the lowing cattle would judge me. I began with Polidori's and took a quick peek.

> *Dear Mr. Murray,*
> *Arrived at Diodati. Who said money cannot buy happiness surely had none for the place is fit for a king. Or a Lord! Byron is well though sleeps not enough in my opinion and wakes far too early for a good constitution. This I will work on with him. Shelley, heir to a baronetcy which alone would alienate a lesser man than I, is also far too tall. He has one wife in England and keeps two daughters of Godwin—a Miss Godwin or Shelley?—and a Miss Chermont, both who practise his theories; one is LB's.*

I could scarce believe my eyes—here were Polidori's unfiltered thoughts, here were his incorrect assumptions about Shelley, and, again, he could not get my name properly. And yet what really struck me as the letter shook in my hand were the last three words. One is LB's. I was Lord Byron's! Hope ran fresh through me and, so inspired, I read the other letters.

Mary wrote to Thomas Jefferson Hogg:

I hand off the writhing breadloaf of my baby son who eats and eats at me and I love him and he wants only more yet I can scarce bear to put him down. Without a mother myself and now being one haunted by the death of her own daughter, I want only to write of this. Only who wishes to read the plight of mothers? Over and over I see my mother in birds, hear my gone baby's breath in the sighs of wind. I have been advised to write of grief—this feels at once daunting with extreme pain and also tantalizing for its possible release.

Mary's letter went on but I caught the gist. She had not admitted my suggestion had worked, but knowing that my sister tried my grief-writing idea meant so much. I was helping her.

Shelley had given me two letters, both to Hogg. I read the first.

Hogg—Lord Byron is far better a man than one imagines, managing to suck the day dry of hours, rising earlier than the rest of us. He swims, rides, plays croquet, writes when the rest of us merely breathe and then returns to the house to dine at length, gossiping until day beckons again. This schedule will probably not kill me as we are here only the summer, yet I should not try it longer. Lord B's establishment consists of servants well-paid for he rails against slavery, has horses too many to count, a dog so enormous he might in fact be two dogs, one monkey, a feral cat he has begun to tame, a crow he only just yesterday lured with a silver button that will no doubt become his, and two peacocks—George and Aurelia. All of these (save the horses) walk about Diodati, which every now and then resounds with the menagerie's unarbitrated quarrels . . .

PBS

P.S. I find that my enumeration of the animals in this Circean Palace was defective. . . I have just met on the grand staircase two guinea hens and an Egyptian crane called Ned.

I sat laughing in admiration of Shelley's description. True, it made no mention of the humans at the house, but the letter would have been far more useful to John Murray than what Polidori had written.

I read Shelley's other letter and the smile went from my face.

> *I am of the belief that man is born selfless. And so I shall remain. Moreover, I am of the belief that one must create an environment in which there is no room for grief to grow. No tendrils, neither root nor shoot, no tentacles disguised as slow leaf. My beloved seems to cultivate her grief, and I find I begrudge this, for we have a living child and each other and this new place—is that not enough and if it is not, then what would be? Save the return of___ which would mean no William so what then? Starve grief, I say. And swim on without comparison, for whom does that serve? We have here the possibility of a summer group and what good would it do to say which of us: Which of us is the better swimmer—*

I paused here, for I knew the answer: Byron had swum across Hellespont—a great length and a tumultuous churn—but Shelley had not the information I did. I read on.

> *Which of us the better lover? The better writer? Are we to be judged by our work, our words on the page or strength in the field? Are we the sum of those crowds who view us cheering or jeering or—am I to be looked upon as hero one day by the masses or a scoundrel by one woman? Who is the better man, I wonder. Are we opposite sides of the same coin?*

I had not time to reflect on the one woman judging him because the carriage driver pointed to his pocket watch—he had waited the required length of time for the mail stop and the rain had ended.

Quickly, I read Byron's to Scrope Davies:

Diodati is finely appointed and the animals are well. I needn't have brought my books; library is stuffed and I a glutton for its offerings. Grounds well-kept, too well in fact, for one waits for the hedges to push free of boxy form and anticipates a great and terrible fish-man to rise from the eerily still lake. I have let FF free to run. He will muddy the lawn soon enough.

Already received word from Madame de Staël, who has now read Caroline Lamb's <u>Glenarvon</u> and informs me Lamb writes I am '<u>mad, bad, and dangerous to know</u>.' I begrudge her only the rhyme. Mme says the book is marvelous in its atrocity, grievous in its truth. Perhaps I shall learn to act in ways more befitting of a gentleman away from London? As for my mood—upon arrival I got a pestering ex-lover and a knee ache on the same day—one is more easily shaken than the other.

I recall hearing that Godwin made £1,500 selling Mary and Claire to Shelley. This cannot be true yet when I see them together I have the feeling that whilst no money changed hands, he was still the benefactor. I am louder and more skillful in most regards than Shelley (save for height which, while not a skill, is one thing a man can offer which is never turned down) yet I have not half the control over the room that he does. He controls with his silences.

I am ashamed of my egotism in this writing—blame it on the view of the magnificent Alps across the lake which makes one believe all is possible while also suggesting one has done <u>nothing</u> of worth.

I fear there are storms brewing here—weather and other. All of which is to say I hover on the verge of feeling (oh God, too much feeling and I shall vomit a poem)—all purple and gold this morning with gilt-edged lake which urges one to feel one is capable of great depths when actions are contrary. Some writers start with the Great Nothing and mould an idea on the page. Perhaps I ought to try this—take a blank page and treat it as my own. Rather like one can do with an eighteen-year-old plump girl who travl'd 800 miles to unphilosophize. Nevermind. I shall tell you the news shared from Fletcher: The hotel across the way has got wind of my whereabouts and, knowing I have others with me, is plotting to send gossip boats complete—binoculars for better viewing are extra. And you ask why I have not produced more poetry— Yours&c. LB

I bit the centre of my top lip, willingly bringing pain so I might avoid tears. Where had the Byron I had loved in London gone? Did he profess to bitterness on the page and tenderness only in the sheets? I resealed the letters and handed them back to the postal carrier.

I KICKED a rock on the way back, playing a game with myself on the dirt road that led up the brambled back way to the cottage. I understood that even the misfortune I would bear from knowing someone's cruelties seemed like a collection I could make—some gathered feathers or marbles. I could gather words and use them to my advantage: If he mentioned a particular element of my character which he did not like, I could mute that part. Conversely, if he admired in someone else an attribute, I could don that like a borrowed hat. Reading the letters was entirely self-serving, an immaturity prickling my neck and travelling down to my wrists—the same wrists Byron had kissed in rounds as an invisible bracelet I would wear forever.

I worried for myself—for I was so skilled at knowing how to be what others wished me to be, it was easy to lose my own voice. I had been taught to be good and agreeable, and I clung so to those ideals that I had not questioned them.

As I approached the villa, I licked my fingers clean of any disgusting remnant of fish glue and told myself I would not snoop again. I knew also this was a blatant dishonesty to myself.

The group lounged in the struggling sun on the lawn, and I felt the prick of shame. I wanted to know what people said about themselves, about me, *if* they said anything—for is it worse to find ill will written about oneself or is it worse to find nothing?

What one person said to the other in private only told a half story. What one broadcast to others, that was the truth. I thought of a line from Mary's letter: *We know best what we want when it is taken away.*

11

I WOKE EARLY THE NEXT day and found the cottage quiet. The hearth cold.

Nearly the end of May yet I layered a shawl and a blanket over my dress. I dashed up to Diodati and let myself in the servant entrance. I held my breath as I tiptoed to the library—for while Byron likely slept, it was possible he would find me and think my intrusion was for him. It was not.

In the library, I dragged my finger over the gilt-edged spines until I came to *Elements of Botany*, a two-volume set by R. J. Thornton. The mottled cover looked like rock itself and gave way to pages with sketches, everything named and labeled, uses medicinal and gastronomic. I bent my head down over Linnaeus's sexual system of plants. I could become a person of my own making: learn the plant kingdom, the groups of stamens and pistils, force myself to memorize the book to know better the world around me.

Between the cottage and the shore, a coppice of trees to the right blocked what should have been the best view from the sitting room, so I arranged myself at the breakfast table, writing in my journal until hunger roused me. I wrapped a slab of bread and wedge of cheese in a cloth and went outside, where I saw no trace of anyone—no Byron stretched on the metal summer chaise, no Polidori glowering nearby, no Mary nursing William, no Shelley catching me looking too long at Byron. Alone and fearing more weather, I pushed on, feeling the metronomic sway of my hair on my neck, and decided to have an explore.

Moss-splotched roof, wall creeped with tight patches of lichen. Great stone plinths with ivy running down the length of them, each topped by an enlarged stone circle, giving them the appearance of a creature with no arms, or one whose arms had been cut off. Turgid lake with its reflection of the intricate cloud layers above. It did not threaten me yet did not beckon either, and so I bypassed the narrow path that was barely discernable from the cottage back door and that led through scrub down to the shore.

On the ground and winding along the path were flowers—*Helleborus*, I looked up—often called oracle flowers. They were that green laced with pink, wind broken, strewn at my feet on the cottage grounds. Next door, Diodati's lawn rolled with gentle clipped grace, enormous urns beset with trailing licorice plants.

I was not religious, but it seemed to me when I was outside, I was always praying. This was what happened with noticing—if one saw the tight-fisted buds on the Ranunculaceae one felt a twinge of hope—please let them open, let me be there to see them tomorrow. Was this not a prayer? And if ever I saw recognition in Byron's face or my sister's wry smile, this too was prayer—he would love me, Mary would be okay.

I turned to look back at the cottage and Diodati inescapable in its hovering and realised I was quite out of sight. In front of me, the coppice of trees. I walked up to the edge of the forest. The cool damp from the trees touched my face first, a chill mist with birdsong and dripping that pulled me in.

I sat in the coppice and wrote neatly, as though writing a letter to Another Me.

> *B— has the properties of liquid, filling up any space unoccupied by anything else. This is both beautiful and suffocating. I want to be repulsed and yet am drawn to him the way one might've come to long for a scent. Or no, that's not what I wish to say. What comes to mind is a long-ago ingested meal in Bath with salmon we caught in the River Avon. Those*

dead eyes. Pink flesh peppered with salt grated by blade. Dill from the garden. Sugar from the tin. Two fish slabs skin-on-skin weighted by bricks for three days during which the mouth waters. Then the dark bread heavy with soft butter. The cured fish perfect on the tongue in the mouth. Nothing so perfect had ever been prepared. And the chew. And the need for more and then the seemingly unquenchable thirst. Water and water and water and water. I went to bed that night dreaming not a bit of the fish but only of the water required after its enjoyment. Rather how pleasure quickly becomes need. So B— is liquid—that particular liquid for me.

12

"I REGRET TO SAY," SHELLEY told us upon his arrival for dinner the following evening, "the hotel proprietor has set up a large telescope. Like a church spire and just as cruel, it is resident on the shore and will provide everyone a view of this—" He swung his long arms this way and that as though threshing.

"Why bother with truth at all when one might invent a better one?" Byron said. In the chandelier light his anger shone on his face.

Polidori frowned. "I worry my employer will do ill to himself should he not settle down."

"Your employer is about to burst into flames," Byron said. He pointed to the other side of the lake. "They make my life a hell. Above all, the Gossips enjoy inventing stories. And at what cost? Only my own. For truly the most entertaining villain is a lordly one."

I saw Polidori mouth those words as though saving them for later.

The wind's violence became the backdrop of our dinner. Mary fretted it would wake William, whom we had settled in the drawing room away from our boister. Shelley, despite saying he regarded Mary as his equal and thus shared all parts of her life and work with her, had not offered help in this regard, and Mary had pocketed her grudge like a miser with coins. As Byron's rejection of me persisted, I found my personality shifting. The alacrity with which I had spent my London days, the arrangement of the trip, the hopeful meeting at the hotel dock gave way like a sand dune, leaving me a bit flatter.

I had been bred to present with cheerful fervour at all times—balancing my family's pain or distress with anything I might feel myself. And I had accepted that as my job, day in day out, without remuneration. Only at Diodati, a creeping voice had suggested in my mind that just because I excelled at something did not require me to do it.

"I apologise for the cold," Byron said, as though he had made the weather. Given his ethereal beauty it was possible he had. "The fireplace was cleaned and readied for summer and needs redoing, so should you require a layer, Fletcher placed some items on the sideboard."

Where there might be a floral arrangement there was instead an array of cold weather items: boiled wool mittens, folded wraps in autumnal colours, a sealskin coat, a cap Polidori tried on but put back when he noticed the rest of us did not take anything. I dropped my napkin, and when I bent to pick it up I saw Byron rested his feet on a foot warmer under the table—his stockinged feet rested on a pottery shelf heated underneath by boiling water. I had held those feet in my lap, massaged them.

I ladled some Potage de Bonne Femme into my bowl, wondering which good woman had been the source for the name, and spooned some into my mouth as each person set about creating their plate.

All of the dinner dishes were set on the table at the same time: spring soup, rabbit cassoulet, Velouté de Chou-Fleur, small artichokes crisped with onion, a white fish with dark sauce, a dark meat with white sauce, duck with watercress, endives dressed with shallot vinegar, *les asperges en bâtonnets* with the spears done in simple melted butter, but rather than green, they were white.

"Etiolated," Polidori told me when I studied a spear before putting it on my plate. "Grown in the dark." I had not asked for this information, yet he seemed to wish to be thanked.

I piled food on my plate—rapturous as only the love-hungry can be—and fought a look of admonishment from Mary with my own wide eyes.

"Eat up, friends," Byron said, "for I hear the scarcity is ever-encroaching."

"Did we not leave Bread or Blood riots behind?" Polidori asked.

"Have you been practising medicine under a rock?" Byron said. "Take a look outside."

I looked at the frozen slop on the window. "How can crops survive with continued cold and wet?" I asked. "Without a proper harvest, only famine can follow."

Byron gave me the smallest acknowledgement with his eyebrows as he held a piece of duck near his mouth. I thought then that the others were surprised I paid attention enough to what was happening in the world to be able to comment. I did not know what to do with the flicker of rage this sparked in me.

Byron selected some fish, told us it was called *gravenche* and then spoke. "The devastation from the wars here leaves the land, the people, all vulnerable. Germans are eating bread made from sawdust."

"There's hardly a full day of sun," Mary said, as though her own small face belonged in the centre of a daisy and she, too, withered.

"Shall I pass you a plate of doom?" Shelley asked, and held out a conciliatory basket of bread, which Mary accepted, testing it to see it was not made of sawdust. He placed his hands on the table as though at a pulpit. "Violence and riots are not the answer. Social reform comes from art, from creative thinking." His passion was so great in these tiny, atheistic sermons that one could not help but fall prey to him. Shelley seemed to woo even himself.

Shelley barely touched the asparagus on his plate, while his wineglass was in heavy use. Byron set the pace of drink, offering vins de Graves, while Polidori struggled—a man always trying to keep up with other men. If they set out to walk, he took a knobby stick and tried to lead, only to realise the other men had held back, having a conversation of which he was not a part. If they drank, he swigged furiously, becoming, as Byron had said, an admiral of the narrow seas—heaving onto the person next to him, who of course judged his lack of skill for the drink.

Mary ate angrily, attacking her duck with an urgency that set Shelley on edge. He fussed with the food on her plate—more fish, for that was kinder than fowl, and did she wish seltzer water from the aerating apparatus on the sideboard?—all while keeping an eye trained on Byron.

Polidori watched each move. "Shelley, your uxoriousness is commendable," he said, but in the tone men have that meant he pitied him for it.

Byron did not miss a beat and threw his napkin at Polidori. "Use it to wipe up your envy."

Shelley's devotion to Mary had always been a thing of beauty to behold, but in my dwindling alacrity, I questioned his motives. With the tang of the endive's vinegar on my tongue, I watched Shelley cut the food on Mary's plate. He had gotten to Mary when she had been so young, perhaps she had not entirely developed a full self and had instead grown from him like a needy branch that relied on the trunk to bend in order to find sun.

His attraction to her was in direct relation to her admiration of him—the more besotted she became, the greater his love. I saw Polidori and even Byron falling prey to Shelley's demeanor, the way he doled out compliments or preached progressive politics or took interest in another man's ideas—whatever was required to make a sycophant of the person in front of him. I, too, had succumbed to this—all the way back when Mary was in Scotland and Shelley had convinced her father to let me join at the dinner table rather than sit with the children for their earlier meal.

I hated myself for being in the troupe who followed Shelley, yet my life required him, a need that only made me loathe myself rather than the person responsible.

Dinner progressed from gravenche to celery salad that crunched in my mouth as I thought of how long it took to grow each stalk, how quickly the salads were consumed. Shelley and Byron discussed the experiments of Darwin. Mary spoke of Galvani, while outside the sky appeared broken by lightning and then smoothed over by heavy rain as the debate circled about what made the principles of life and if it was at all possible anyone would discover it.

"And if they did," I said, "how might they communicate it?"

"Is not character built into Men? For men have passions so fierce they cannot control them," Shelley said. He looked at me, and I chose just then to knife my lamb.

A quick cloud came over my sister, and she looked as though she wanted to slap him but she did not speak.

"Medically I believe this to be true." Polidori's words blurred at the ends. "It is a simple matter of the bodies. Our blood is different."

"I cannot believe you have blood different than I," Mary said. "I am nearly nineteen yet have far more experience with blood than you—for you describe the dead who have no moving blood. Women have blood all the time."

The discomfort on Shelley's face distorted his mouth. Even Byron saw it and rose to the occasion. "Come on, man, surely you cannot be so squeamish about a monthly cycle? How is their mess different from ours?"

Polidori began to explain, but Byron swatted him on the arm.

Rain slapped the windows. The pervasive dark came from everywhere all at once—the sepulchral outside, the room with its sloppy candles, the fireplace smoke which puffed into the room with each gust of wind. I refused more wine, for my head was swimming already. Polidori, seeing that the men had begun another bottle, redoubled his efforts as they talked of the experiments of Dr. Erasmus Darwin, and if one might reanimate a corpse.

"There is no blood in the dead," Polidori said.

"A collection of poetry by Dr. John Polidori," Byron said. "Likely *not* a bestseller."

"I am the only one here with the experience of a dead body," Polidori said.

"Not true, for we are in proximity to you," Byron said. I looked at Mary, for she, too, had held a dead body—a tiny one. She said nothing.

Instead of being put off by Byron's continued remarks, Polidori took them as a sort of praise and closeness, as though he rewritten the intent to suit his wishes.

"We shared cadavers," Polidori said. He stood and came to Byron's side of the table, closer to the dead fireplace. "In medical school—"

"When you were four," Byron interrupted.

"When I was fifteen," Polidori said. He sounded only half-prideful. The other half mournful. I understood. We had both given away our childhoods too early. "In the dissection, the peeling of the skin and examinations of the muscular systems—sorry, not meaning to offend you, gentle ladies."

"You aren't," I said. "I have a strong stomach." The sweets were set before us, soufflé au citron and perfectly soft gâteau à la Manon—I could smell the yogurt and sugar from where I sat and my mouth watered. "I was the only one of us who did not heave on the boat nor in the carriage in the stormy mountain." No one congratulated me.

"I have not a strong constitution yet am too interested in what the doctor has to say to be bothered," Mary said, which stoked Polidori's fire. "Yet I fear, Shelley—you've got a weaker stomach." He could not object, for this was true, and his face looked as though he, too, had been grown in the dark.

We listened to Polidori describe cutting, dissection in honour of learning, the deconstruction of a human, working together with his fellow students for a better understanding. My stomach was indeed fine. As I looked at each of the people around the fire, it was my heart that ached. It ached so that pain spread to my jaw. Soon my teeth throbbed. I put my hand to my face. "It would be nice," I said. "Except for the dead part." Everyone turned to look at me, Mary embarrassed for me as I went on. "To be known so well."

"You can tell so much about the life someone lived by looking at their organs," Polidori said. Shelley promptly clutched his stomach and rose, only to become woozy.

"I am unwell," Shelley said, and clutched the chairback with one hand and his chest with the other. Mary went to his side; any anger she had felt was gone from the concern.

"Can you not help him?" she asked Polidori.

Polidori, swaying a bit himself, charged into action. "I have just the thing," he said. "Allow me to grab my case."

He returned a moment later with his leather satchel, from which he pulled a narrow case and unlatched it.

"Ah, Polidori is going to play the flute—that will surely cure us all," Byron said.

"It is altogether a different kind of instrument," Polidori said. He removed an article which had two tubes, the ends of which Polidori pushed into his ears, and a small disc, which he pressed to Shelley's chest. He moved it around and then without asking lifted Shelley's shirt. Pleased with his findings, he nodded. "Shelley, you have a problem of agitation. You ought to rest and settle your heart."

"What is that thing?" I asked, and held out my hand, for I had never seen an object similar.

"It is called a stethoscope. Invented only just this year." Polidori began his usual information spewage. "René-Théophile-Hyacinthe Laënnec, a French physician. My father thinks him brilliant. The instrument allows one to better hear the sounds made by the heart and lungs."

Shelley and Mary stood in the doorway.

"I should put Shelley to bed," Mary said. Polidori, seeing Mary's smallness next to Shelley's height, even while hunched, said he would help her.

I rose too, but instead of leaving I went with the stethoscope over to Byron and caught him off guard when I held it to his chest. "How odd," I said to Polidori. "It must be broken."

Polidori paused in the doorway, concerned. "I dare say I used it only just."

I leaned in again, and pressed it to the heat of Byron's skin. "No, you are correct, Doctor. The instrument is in working order—it is the subject who has no heart, and that is why I could not hear it." Byron looked sour. Mary snickered. I loved the sound of her wicked laugh, and she caught my eye, giving me invisible points in a game begun long ago.

13

THE NEXT NIGHT, THE fingernail of moon out my bedroom shone a scarce muffled blue light as though someone had put a hand over its moon mouth. I sat at the desk and wrote.

We never know how we appear to other people. We can look in the glass, study ourselves, I could notice my eyes, which were not only brown as I had been told my whole life, but rather green-flecked, too, enough to notice, enough to make me wonder if the colours did battle and eventually gave up, neither winning. I could notice that perhaps on some days I was quite pretty, not the sort that makes other women cruel, just a regular sort of palatable attractiveness. Yet every step I took at Diodati was inhabited by a certain degree of doubt, a kind of doubt that I supposed came from knowing I was not gifted as the others. In my earliest memories, Mary was already collecting words on scraps of paper, the inside of her fingertips already ink stained. Each of my uncertain steps held echoes of my mother's combination of overpraise and marked criticism, this mixed with the uncertainty people possess when they know not where they come from. I might never learn who my father was, as though my mother created me from a witch's brew, or conjured me in a spell, and in Lake Geneva I was given the title of Ordinary Girl. I felt myself as the admiring centre of this group: entranced not only with my sister and her obvious talent, but with anyone whose light beckoned, whose ideas drew me towards them in a sort of miracle and disaster of an epic storm.

I lay awake willing myself to be as still as possible in the clotted moonlight. Byron's rejection weighted me, and I thought if I could lie flat and calm I would somehow rise in spirit. This was an ill-fated experiment—my stillness, the villa, trying to infiltrate the group.

"Claire."

My stomach lurched, but I refused to flinch when Shelley appeared at the door. "I fear you are in poor spirits—remember, I have known you since you were a young girl." The fact of Shelley's knowing my thoughts made me bristle. Shelley sighed. "You must understand that men—even men who strive for a sort of equality—can grow tired of women."

"So I am tiresome."

"No—what I mean to say is that all people can become tiresome, but you yourself are not. So if you feel compelled to wither at the table or by the lake with us," he paused as though he had designed the group and I was a tourist, "do not." He took a step into the room and reached a long arm out to grip my hand. "Never forget you may rely on me. I have always made you a priority, fought to have you near—in Calais, in London just before this trip—"

I blushed in the dark, glad he could not see. "I am fine," I said. For part of growing into my adulthood seemed to be lying about pain. "I made a choice to come here, a choice to arrange it."

Shelley withdrew his hand. "We all make choices that we cannot defend." Down the hall, I heard Mary cough. Shelley left and closed the door behind him.

14

THE DRAWING ROOM AT Diodati reflected the idea that it was meant to be a room of femininity. Unlike the dark dining room with its heavy oak table, pawed armchairs, and maroon and mustard velvet wall coverings, which kept it securely masculine, the drawing room was all looking glass and light. Lightest pinks, barest hint of lavender—a tufted bolster here, a pillow fringed in lace there with a needlework flower, insipid with pastel petals. I knew this from the botany book to be *Passiflora pinnatistipula*. Passion flower, a climbing perennial that looked so harmless yet could grow so vigourously it might smother anything in its path. It could weaken the stone and eventually cause structural damage. I hated it both for its daintiness and metaphor of disaster. For I wished to think that passion did not mean ruin.

The drawing room only had its name from the withdrawing room. With the men and Mary again ensconced in letter writing, I situated myself in the corner at a table built just for that space and with a corner chair that allowed my back to rest but demanded I sit astride the seat. This did not help the lingering thoughts I had of the stethoscope on Byron's chest.

I wrote: *Is this how you see me? Compliant flower stalk swaying this way and that?*

Byron walked past and without warning reached for my journal, held it aloft, and read my words aloud: "Stalks. Hmmm. I suppose. Oh, here is more from the mind of Claire! *If men have desires that cannot be tamed that is to say they are wild and provoke an image of a handsome rogue. And if women have desires they are desperate sad puppies whining to be let out.*" He looked at me. I wanted to jump up and grab my book, yet I could not reach and knew this would only make me appear as desperate as I felt. "Are you a puppy, Claire?"

Byron held my book and gestured to the door. "Do you need to be let out?"

Shelley rose and gripped Byron's shoulder, but Byron broke free and went so far as to open the heavy door, letting in a gust of afternoon air, cold and damp, bits of grass and leaves skittering inside for warmth. We all looked at the windy outside world for a moment before I went to Byron and grabbed my journal. He did not show remorse for snatching it.

I spoke my words with care and calm. "That is mine."

"All words once written become public, Claire, that is the way of all writers," Byron said. This time Shelley did not reprimand him, for he believed it true. Mary and Polidori nodded.

My will was useless against the blushing that rose to my cheeks and spread down my neck. "My thoughts are my own," I said.

"True," Shelley said, "yet if you put them to paper this changes everything."

I wished he would go closer, tower over Byron, and smack him for me. I seethed, my voice louder than the wind which whooshed and howled. "So I might keep my thoughts imprisoned in my mind, then?"

Polidori stepped in. "Or you might let the little puppies out . . ."

He was rewarded with a smirk from Byron. I looked to Mary for help.

"One ought to be able to write freely without prying eyes," she said. She looked hard at me, and I heard her words as a question. Did she know I had read her letter? Had read the words of everyone here? Mary went on, "However, it seems very little is private—perhaps it is best to go through life with understanding that secrets will out."

I looked at the others, memorizing my thoughts so I could write them in the safety of my own room when I had my journal back: *the whirlwind of a man's wild passions provides ample cover for his confidentials. Unlike a woman, whose body bleeds or grows, whose heart breaks open on the page for all to read, men may have public scandals yet are granted secrets they may keep with them till the grave.*

15

With the ground too sogged to venture to my coppice of trees, I sat at the kitchen table. My back and arms ached as though along with my journal I, too, had been pried open the night before. To soothe myself, I angled my view so I could pretend to shelter between the boughs as I wrote about all the plants I had seen so far, committing to testing myself on their names, which read to me like poetry: *Corylus avellana* with its edible hazelnuts I hoped to pick by August, *Trifolium pratense*, clover, *Lotus corniculatus*, bird's-foot trefoil, also known as ground honeysuckle, as though it could not determine where it ought to be. Just like me. Perhaps, too, there was a way of classifying people—how would I do that with those of us gathered?

Shelley came in holding William and a letter addressed to me and

Mary. "I am letting Mary sleep," he said, "for she could not last night—"

"Too much wine?"

"Or too much thought," Shelley said. "For though she likes a deep conversation, the croquet mallets of men exhaust her."

I finished my sentence and nodded. "I agree."

I quickly read Fanny Imlay's letter, which dealt largely in commenting on Byron. Was he like the London scandal-mongers described, was his face as fine as the portraiture she had viewed? *I cannot help but think, from his writings, that he can be such a detestable being. Do answer me these questions, for where I love the poet I should like to respect the man.*

I reread those words with Shelley watching me. I chewed on them. I swallowed them and knew they would float in my belly forever.

"Is all well?" Shelley watched my face as I closed the letter. I nodded. I could not discuss the separation of man from art with him.

Shelley stood William on his lap, dancing his small socked feet, and I thought what a good father he was in some ways and how lacking in others—for what would become of the children he had left when he had abandoned Harriet?

"Are you entirely devoted to Mary?" I asked.

He turned William away from me and glanced outside as if both baby and man could not believe my question. "You are well aware of that answer, Claire." I raised my eyebrows as a response, a silent parenthetical. He softened. "Men tire of men—look at Byron with his physician. Men grow weary of pattern—they require excitement from time to time."

"I care not if I am exciting." This was a lie.

"You misunderstand, Claire. Byron's capriciousness is vexing, I am sure." He reached for my hand, and I let him take it. "For while he seems a fine gentleman and sure-hearted in his work, his is a record marred with poor decisions."

I withdrew my hand and clutched my journal. Did Shelley know about my visits in London? Was I only another of those poor decisions? "Well, he is unkind—to Polidori, to me."

Shelley perked up. "Is it possible you have made Byron into a villain when he is merely a man, flawed as any other?"

"You give me far too much power—I have not made anything."

"You are special, Claire. I have always felt this and always told you so. Of course I am devoted to Mary, but you have so much to offer the world. And unlike your sister, who plays her cards so close to her chest, you let the world in! That is a beautiful thing to behold."

I heard his words and realised I had outgrown his praise, so I kept my face unmoving. He was not used to this reaction and said, "Does it wound you that Mary did not wish you here this summer—" He saw the pain on my face. "Do not be wounded—for you have every right to be here with us."

I turned to find Mary at the door. She came and reached for William. "How long have you been there?" I asked.

"I see you are writing again," she said. "You've cut the nib so many times you look to be writing with a child's quill."

I looked at the trees outside as though each point in the coppice were a quill waiting to give me a story, a line, a thought. "Then I shall go into town and buy some new pens—if the ground dries enough."

"Well," Mary said, and looked at Shelley, "make sure you purchase ample for us all—for I am starting to write again, too."

BEFORE CONTINUING to town, I took everyone's mail—for they assumed I would provide this service—and walked their letters again to the postal carriage. I knew that though I had told myself I would not pry, that I would. After all, hadn't the real writers told me what is on the page is for public consumption?

With a fingernail, I gently undid the first wax seal. Mary's penmanship was tight and contained, and I gasped at her words to Fanny Imlay in the presence of the postal carrier, who did not appear to judge me for my indiscretions.

> *What is it like then to be merely average? To only hold simple expectations of the self? Why does she continue to expose herself to others' greatness when she herself is merely moon reflecting the hidden sun? She seeks knowledge and wisdom*

as I once did yet seems not to fathom the price attached to knowing—for one cannot unknow. And Claire—of course everyone finds her charming. She tries so hard at it.

Oh, Fanny, I want Claire to have everything. I wish her health and satisfaction in her endeavors and, should any true harm come near her, I should like to think I would wall her from it—keeping in mind my body is considerably smaller than hers and thus I might not provide perfect coverage. Of course I love my sister. I love my sister and I say this like a prayer. I want her to have everything. Or, if not everything, then just slightly, ever so slightly less than I want for myself.

What a clean wound those words produced—for this was not all a surprise, yet reading something is different from thinking it. I moved to Polidori's letter, thinking it would be clipped gossipy sentences—Byron drinks! Shelley coughs! Instead, his letter to his father surprised me.

I could be Byron, viewing each room as though laid out just for me, as though the world knew I was coming and had gone to extra trouble—guest trouble—royal trouble!—to show me its best. Or I would be a Shelley-sort with tender heart, eating only vegetables for wont of being careful with animals though ravaging breasts as beasts as though as a writer I would be forgiven for forgetting "r."

And I would be sure of my politics and not a little smug at being on the correct side of arguments and taxes, social reform, and so I would put my stocking-clad feet into shoes daily and walk with footsteps proud yet not too proud—for that would not suit me. I should wish to be seen as the epitome of realised maleness, borne of woman and loving women, committed to their bodies even as I gave my heart only to one, and should I ever waver—though I oughtn't properly, not in the way a woman worries with her whole mind & body verging on ruin—

I would comfort myself in this wavering to know I had

allowed my heart to be given and to that woman. To Mary, I admit, I would allow the same bodily freedoms afforded to me. Though I might pause to say I would not raise another man's child as my own so let Mary be smart in that regard—perhaps curtailing any s-explorations for the few days she would be neither fertile nor bleeding and in which I would not be there, connected as we are each time with me presenting her with a key to free her from such simple-minded relational constraints as monogamy with its yoke and burden.

Oh, to be these ravenous men. This is pure folly on my part for the woman has not looked my way except in the interest of medical information. I shall cling to that.

So Polidori had fallen under my sister's reproachful gaze and thus her spell. It was inevitable. I feared not about that—but what if Byron had written the same? I opened his next.

Polidori is adequate as physician. No more than that for he is a gentleman of three outs: without money, without wit, and without manners. A prediction: His overfondness to his employer causes intemperate remonstrances in regards to Shelley. For a man cannot bear another's bonding with the object of his desire.

And I know Polly Dolly studies us all with the job of writing about the group—a conflict of interest I feel. For he wishes to trounce fame and *to be part of it.*

Fame is foolish, true. Yet provides the fodder for outliving the body, surely. Castles may be razed. And if one leaves the written word, it might be published yet then lost. Yet infamy outlives all of that. Might I like to live beyond the norm? Wander in a field alone as everyone around me suffers or slips away wordless as grey overtakes the body and the mind's candle dampens with that simpering hiss? What fool would I be to say no.

I shared with Shelley what truly keeps me awake at night: We fail time and again to recognise the effects of our actions on the world in which we live. What destruction have I personally wrought on land and earth? Mass enslavement, war, chemicals, pikes and gunpowder, these are weapons now yet the way Polidori writes falsehoods and sends them to London to be printed as fact disseminated for all to read or hear of secondhand, the thrift of language, believed to be true. Who is to say what this aching planet will look like after I am gone? One moment I think I have written something profound that will strike a chord for decades to come. And yet I might read the exact same lines an hour later and find I have written sad dross. How might I go on when I cannot know how—or if—I be remembered? And if that be the case, which part false and another part true?

The postal carrier gave his watch tap—I almost didn't bother to read Shelley's but gave in to curiosity when I saw it was addressed to himself to be held at the publisher's until his return.

This letter is only for the me of the future, and thus I do not address myself by name. Of note about Claire: She regards me—not only me—all of us with the keen eye of a lapidarist. Part of her allure is such wondering as to what she sees. In her eyes I might be cabochon-shaped and polished or still in raw state. I fear she hopes to gain by surrounding herself with excellence here, as though she thinks it will rub off on her like the brass cleaner Polidori used yesterday on the lantern he found whilst rummaging in a blanket chest in my room—why he was there is another thing altogether—he is an excavator, a poker of fires and issues.

These people inhabit my soul in a way that forces will out of me and I fear I lose myself within the group. I shall redouble my efforts to be a man of goodness, one who tries wholeheartedly to capture nature's great expanse and sheer power on the page.

Also, I shall try to encourage Byron to quit meat for he is a carnivorous glutton.

I stuck my finger in the fish glue and resealed each letter before I set off for town.

16

COLOGNY WAS NOTHING SO much as a model of the word *town*. A centre with an unremarkable fountain whose water catcher could not keep up with the rain and so overflowed, drowning the flowers beneath so it looked a monument of decline. Shops neither many nor few. Town flats for the shopkeepers. A restaurant Polidori had said we must try, for it was known for being the best in town. He hadn't realised it was the only place in town.

I entered Swain's Stationers and found it well stocked. A wooden counter stretching from front to back, behind which were glass cases that contained rows of flower vases empty of blooms, instead displaying clutches of quills arranged by origin: swan feathers tallest and bright white and labeled *primes* and thus most expensive, ordinary goose quills, a drama of crow feathers that would provide the finest lines. I coveted those but could not justify the expenditure—for what I wrote was drivel. I suspected Byron used crow quills even for his drafts.

Each type called to me, yet I thought, too, of the birds. For each wing only gave a handful of suitable quills—where were the rejected ones? The tins had signs, *gauchère* for the right-handed folk whose preference was for left-wing quills and *droitière* for left-handed people whose writing improved with quills that came from the right wing of the goose. I scanned the offerings. The quills were further separated into country of origin: mostly from the Netherlands and Norway.

"We have highest grade quills from Germany," the stationer said. He produced an exquisite grey feather.

"Have you any seconds?" I asked. The stationer nodded and crouched down, standing up with a can of mishmash feathers of mixed colour and height, quality diminished by a bent top that would weight it awkwardly in the hand as one wrote or quills that needed a penknife slice right away to sharpen enough to use. He watched me, a ragpicker of writing implements.

"We have pinions, too," he said. I considered those—the smallest and least desirable—but could not face returning to Byron, even to Mary, with those. "Our pen cutter is excellent," he said. He took the quills I had chosen. "Even with the seconds. Leave them with me a spell and you shall find them all to your liking."

I added some paper to my purchases, including a leaf of rose-scented for Mary to use in writing to Fanny Imlay. Perhaps I did this out of guilt for reading her letters.

I went outside while I waited for the pens, following a path cobbled with a mix of brick and rock done haphazardly over time with whatever material became available. A wheelwright, a small inn. A wall of severe white stone stretching on and on with no blemish until a small section appeared, splattered with all manner of colours: puce swath here, a constellation of green splotches, thumb swipes of cobalt. I stared at it.

"Some of my best work," a voice said. A man in an immaculate suit wiped fresh paint—violet—on the wall. "I cannot touch the other sections of wall, but my studio rental allows for this part here, so I use it like a rag."

"It is most delightful," I said. "If only I could have a chunk of wall as a piece of art." I followed him inside his studio. A series of canvases—some palm-sized, others tall and narrow as doors, had intricate arrangements of what appeared to be shades of darkness.

"The rain," he explained. "For it infiltrates the mind, does it not?"

"And the page," I said, as though I were a real writer.

He took up a brush and made an adjustment. "Everything I paint is already a memory."

"And then you sell your memories?" I asked.

"I paint only paintings for myself. I do not make a living here but rather at my forge—this is for my own enjoyment." He added a splotch of grey which illuminated the patterns of water on the board. "I feel compelled to explain what I see. When I do this, I have a better understanding of rain. Of my wife, of hanging laundry, or the way the snow ruins the edges of *Carex* grass just so."

I looked on the wall at the back of the studio, where there was a small framed painting.

"That's Japanese," he said. The image depicted a woman in a robe red as new blood, yet looking more closely I saw she was not still, near her on the edge of her glorious garment was a cat, coiled and sleeping. "She is cutting the dress off of herself so she won't wake the cat."

I stood still to absorb the painting. I stood longer than was appropriate. He appraised my studying.

"In life," he said, "we are either the cat or the woman."

I gave one last look before leaving to collect the quills. "Or the dress."

17

WE HAD LIVED A year of season cycles in a matter of days; our only proof it had been just over a week was William, who appeared the same. The rest of us, however, had begun to change. Mary went to Diodati without invitation. Polidori sat with Shelley on the lawn and listened to his aches and moans. I wandered free as a ghost from room to room, cottage to villa and to my coppice of trees.

Byron rose earlier and earlier, awake in the night and greeting the dawn. Once when I could not sleep I went to the terrace and saw him down by the lake, stripping down to skin yet covered by night to avoid prying eyes. He waded into the cold water. I could not break away until I heard a door whine open and I worried I would be caught spying.

In the coppice with dank lichen and the familiar twinkle of rain remnant runoff, I wrote in my journal about the group. I had studied them, surveyed their actions, and as I was a part of it—albeit one still at the edges of the whole—it was altogether darker. For part of the genius was a collective mind.

With our laundry overlapping on the line, it was already growing more difficult to know which articles belonged to which person. I could no longer discern which man's shirt was pinned to the rope—this was of little consequence, mainly because the chill prevented much from drying fully. A maid would take the lot of it inside downstairs, where the clothing tumbled into a messy heap. If I entered Diodati by the back entrance and saw the basket, I could not ascertain which one was what article nor to whom it might belong, as though we were all one beast.

So, too, the writing. I had seen Shelley scratch out some of Mary's words and replace them with his own and seen Byron do the same with Polidori, who continued his mission. I had to sequester my own writing, shelter it from rain and from others after Byron's thievery.

I LAY back on the cold moss, the damp seeping into my shoulders. I would pay for it later—that unshakable chill creep. I'd have to bathe. But I looked up at the branches and leaves that struggled to stay attached, confused about the season.

The collective mind was powerful yet also dulled the sense of self. For all the charge of ideas and excitement of *yes*, or *consider this*, adding brick upon brick in service of building a towering novel or epic poem, there was the question of just whose hands were on each brick, what each person had truly contributed to the structure. Were we meant to be free of ownership in the name of creation—who had done what part—or did we create in order to claim the finished product as our own, seeking credit for years to come?

After a night of revelry, Shelley had cornered me in the cottage. "We must admit the individual is the core of everything." He'd been drunk or inebriated by his own thoughts, a scrawl of pages on the floor, the desk, as he'd brought his face too close to mine. "Surely it is a mistake for people to follow rules and adhere to societal convention instead of what each person believes to be his ideal. Liberty of the imagination, of the self. That is the crux, Claire."

I had freed myself, not from Shelley's imagination, which had clearly gone wild, but from the cottage and gone to find solace on the terrace at Diodati. There I'd sat, trying to clear my head whilst looking at the lake, only to encounter Byron bursting from the glass doors. He went on a tirade about slavery and the ills of man, ranting at me, though I might have been anyone. Polidori had arrived, Shelley and Mary quickly at his side, the baby between them as Byron went on.

I felt compelled in Byron's rejection of me to remind everyone that while Byron had last year published *Hebrew Melodies*, it was Anne Isabella Noel Milbanke, the Lady Byron—now ex-Lady Byron—who was a major proponent of antislavery legislation. This silenced the men, and I relished a twinge of pride.

Mary had engaged with my idea, wondered aloud if Byron's views were influenced by but not accredited to his ex-wife, whom he had disgraced with his behaviour. Byron said, "We are measured by what we leave in the world. How one treats another person one day to the next is only temporary."

Polidori had stepped in and said, "What a man believes far outweighs how he acts." And then he'd given a schoolteacher's look to me—would I be able to follow his complex suggestion? I'd wanted to knock him on the head with the fire poker but feared he would not understand the action.

At that point, Mary had not broken her gaze towards the baby. William—a new boy in the world, but yet, a boy—was still perfect. An achievement attained simply by being alive without yet being horrible.

Mary had spoken: "You confuse global good nature with personal profundity and halo-grabbing. You all have the great blessing of being able to believe one thing in the mind and quite another thing in the body." At this Shelley made eyes at the red and gold carpet of sunlight on the ground, sure he was excluded from the grouping. Yet Mary studied each man's face in turn, continuing, "Women have no such luck, for we have no control over our bodies, which in turn imprisons the mind."

Byron sucked his cheeks in then, momentarily knocked from his tethered high horse. "What I leave on this earth as an artist will far exceed my moral or physical contributions. I take great comfort in that."

I had then taken my turn to face each man, landing at last on Byron. "Cold comfort," I said.

In the coppice I wrote all of that neatly in my journal, as though I might be given high marks by the tree limbs lording over my shoulders. When I finished, I set down my pen and looked at the broken sky between the branches as I allowed myself to cry. Byron wanted to stop the universe from crumbling and society with it but did not give a damn about my tears.

18

Bitter wind whipped up from the lake, scattering fallen rose petals blown from the cottage walls, kicked up the sandy grains until we, shielding our eyes, followed Fletcher's silent offer—an open door to Diodati's large side room for a banquet of tea and cakes. I cursed Byron for ruining all sweets for me—now when I held a lemon square I thought of his kiss.

A wedge of Bündner Nusstorte with its walnut crunch only made me feel in my belly that he would pull me upstairs and use his hands to make me lose all train of thought. I watched him select a thimble-sized raspberry tart. He caught me looking, and his eyes betrayed his aloofness—with quiet glee I knew his thoughts and mine were a pair.

"Someone say something or else I shall have to write, and the idea fills me with a quiet dread," Byron said. His armchair had lion-clawed feet, which did not match the tigers on the upholstery. The two peacocks—George and Aurelia—joined and were each allowed a tiny tart. Giant FF snored at Byron's feet, where Byron tucked his bad foot underneath the dog's warm neck. Shelley coughed and refused to eat, taking only tea. Polidori looked concerned about the cough and went first towards

Shelley but, fearing he would lose a spot near Byron, stood awkwardly in the middle.

I surveyed the scene and found myself memorializing it in my mind—for part of enjoying myself seemed to be worrying about that enjoyment ending.

"I could tell you the names of plants and flowers at Diodati," I said, emboldened by an earlier interaction. After finding a clump of wild onions near the coppice, I'd cut them with a penknife and brought them to the kitchen. Only the baker, who'd introduced herself as Abigaëlle Elsa to me, had been present. She'd accepted the onions for a savoury tart, which we had eaten. No one knew I had provided them with the onions. I cradled that small secret. With the cold, Elsa the baker had said, the garden struggled. She showed me how to sauté the onions in lard. I thought then that we might become friends.

"What use are plants?" Mary said to us.

"Plants are food," I said. Mary shrugged. I thought of Elsa, who said she would be happy if I found early garlic, wild peas that thrived in cold, and—in the dank of my coppice—wild mushrooms. I told her I would look. She told me morels grew near the rotted trunks of fallen apple trees.

"Never mind Claire's plants," Mary went on. "I shall tell a story. For I saw a bird outside which is my dead mother, and I saw that same bird my entire life, and so I have a story, not of that bird, but of my father whom she left behind."

No one challenged her. She was granted a nonsensical idea, and not a man around questioned her. I knew if I had said the same thing my bubble existence would have been popped.

"My sister's mother—" here she looked at me as though I carried the blame, "allowed a watery vitriol to trickle down to me, even in my father's presence, which was quite worse than if she and I were alone. For then there came into play my father's refusal to leap to my defense."

I listened carefully, for Mary rarely spoke of her father since he had refused her home and still had not spoken to her since the elopement.

"Distracted, you wish to suggest. Above it all. Prone to best outcomes—the ladies will resolve this internally." Mary put on a deep voice. "'Tis not my place to comment, I lord not over these women." She stopped the voice, and Shelley looked sad for her. "I was a girl, father." She took a deep breath. Polidori looked at her, transfixed. "Onward. Regrettably compliant, I spent one afternoon removing all the plates, cups, bowls stacked in wobbly towers, swiping each with a clean cloth—the open shelving made the items collect dust, you see, for not all of us, Lord Byron, have a staff—"

"This was more than regular dirt," I added. "Due to the proximity to the printing press, which cast some fine grime that seemed to coat everything in our house with oil."

Mary silenced me with her eyes. She had her writing face on, serious and determined. "Yes. By the time I'd wiped the last bowl, I felt I ought start again."

She looked out the window, and I thought she was looking for her mother in the red bird that had shown itself in the trees. "Such repetitive actions demonstrate the tediousness of being a person."

"It *is* tedious," Byron said. This stung, but I ignored it.

Mary went on. "Father came in reeking of the oil we used on the wooden screw press, a scent forever mingled with his hair paste and penchant for squares of shortbread, which gave his breath a sugar-puff gentleness that belied his fervour." Mary chewed her lip. "Father bade me join him at the rickety table, whereupon he put in front of me the doll Claire and I had played with, cast aside, and then thought to play with again as though a second burst of childhood would take." She paused. Shelley looked away, blush creeping up his neck. "One cannot go back to that time. Once the doll is put down, it is not picked up again—not really. But my father had changed the doll and offered it."

This Mary demonstrated with her small hands. "He put his hand at the doll's back. He showed me a thin metal wire that made her hands move—first to her face, her mouth, as though she'd heard a rude-funny, then both arms in a good morning stretch. My too-old-for-this smile must have been the accolades father wanted, for he rested a hand on my face—the gentlest of male touches, surely—and showed the mechanisms. *I attached it here*, he said, and *Here's another wire—look, you might make her eyes flutter. Thank you, Father*, I told him. *I will like this very much.*" Mary became very still, remembering. "His voice was so proud and filled with love, and I knew, I simply knew, whatever space was left in him also filled with *sorry*."

"He did not say sorry, though," I said. "And still he does not defend you."

"He did—and does—not."

Stillness overtook the room. I heard the birds outside and felt a deep grief. For all the time Mary had looked out the window as a little girl, she had never told me why. She had carried the birds of grief and love with her and had kept them to herself. No matter how well we thought we knew someone, no matter how much they knew of us, there would always be bits that were missed.

Polidori broke the quiet. "Mary, when you engage in storytelling, you are a clump of joy sheathed in human skin."

"How very disgusting," Byron said.

I turned to Polidori. "You simply cannot refrain from being odd."

"Ah, have you been speaking with my father?" Polidori said. At last, we all laughed.

19

THE LATE NIGHT HOUR could be measured in candle drippings, which pooled on the table in great puddles of wax. Mary again settled William in the next room with not so much as a glance of notice from Shelley. Shelley and Byron, coming more alive the darker the hour, persisted in a loud and intimate exchange of ideas, each whetting the other's appetite with the beauty of the Alps, the labyrinth of the mind.

"*Esse est percipi*," Shelley said.

"To be is to be perceived," I said, and stole from him the act of translation. Shelley shot me a look. I was tired of being locked out of their chatter.

"That is of course what George Berkeley said with immaterialism." Shelley spoke to Byron, but his vantage point at the head of the table allowed him to keep a sharp gaze on me. "Objects are only ideas—they do not exist outside the minds that behold them. So one person's perception is theirs alone."

That idea felt lonely and possibly wrong—for if two people experienced something together yet remembered it differently, that would be such a profound loss I could hardly bear it.

"Yet Shelley, you are godless and Berkeley was a bishop—do you not subscribe as I do to the idea of Matter and Evil?" Byron clasped his hands around his glass but did not drink. Polidori put his elbows on the table, leaning in as though he were part of the back-and-forth and growing more agitated when he was not. It was a pathetic sight to witness his desperation to be Byron's second when Shelley had so quickly become Byron's best and most important person.

Their close friendship gave me feelings of jealousy. For again I felt that if I had been born a man I would have had a chance to be that friend to Byron, even if I had been a man who longed to bed down with him. Without such luck as having been born a man—even one who lusted after Byron—I had to navigate the labyrinth not only of the mind but of the bodies—mine and theirs.

"There is not Supreme Providence," Shelley said. "Property ought to be communal." Shelley cast a glance over the table and settled on me. He was used to impressing me, seeing wonderment on my face at his theories. He thought he knew my mind, thought I was having a perfectly splendid time, content to absorb absorb absorb. He looked at me as though it dawned on him I might spill. "Universal love is the ruling force."

I hoped Shelley would not launch into a diatribe on atheism, for I had sat in that lecture many times and in many countries. Mary caught my eye to tell me she felt the same.

"Shelley was sent down for writing a pamphlet on atheism," she said. Shelley looked at her with more disdain than I had seen. She had interrupted the flow of words between the men, and the silence that followed proved the death of that exchange.

Shelley cleared his throat and tried his best to salvage the conversation. "I've been reading a new poet. Fellow by the name of Keats." Shelley threw Polidori a dog bone. "A medical student *and* poet, so cling to that, friend." Polidori looked wild with the idea. "Keats said poets have the power to bury self-consciousness, dwell in a state of openness to all experience."

"And what is that experience, exactly?" Mary said. She looked at Shelley and then at me, puzzled. Her voice was that of her father, digging for meaning or clues. I busied myself with my napkin, tucking myself into its folds.

"Quite right, Shelley," Byron said. "We must read younger poets to stay current lest we turn into stodgy pudding, so set we are inedible, impenetrable."

The word impenetrable brought a blush to my face that went unseen in the dim candlelight.

"With a physician one wants someone just in the middle—too old and they do not keep up with trends and new practices. Too young and not enough experiences." Polidori stepped in to commandeer the helm of our drunken ship. "Do you know once I did an exam on a fellow who was so thin—perhaps with some sort of condition we do not yet understand—that his skin barely disguised the insides. One could almost see the arteries and muscles underneath without removing the skin."

Mary's eyes widened. "I am revolted entirely. Horrified. And also, please say more."

"Please don't," Shelley said. He pushed his plate away.

"The only thing more tedious than being a vegetarian is hearing about being a vegetarian," Byron said.

"That is why you are so pale, Shelley," Polidori said. He was pugnacious not by nature but by circumstances which roused feelings of inadequacy. "Men need meat."

"I have strength without the flesh of animals," Shelley said.

"I believe my new friend would win a duel, despite his moon-pale face," Byron said.

I had an image then of Shelley's face in the moonlight in Lynmouth, half in shadow and too close, as he'd been in my nightmares. I felt a chill. My own stomach turned.

"I should not duel with another man, for it is a pointless battle better fought in words," Shelley said. Mary took his hand, but he did not squeeze hers, gripped instead by the rising competitive tone.

"You would have the upper hand given your height," Polidori said, "which would make an unfair match."

"Polly Dolly, your jealousy is a form of venom poisonous only to you," Byron said.

Polidori looked to me and to Mary for a defense. As he had only just learnt my name, I successfully fought the urge to rescue him.

"I know not what you mean," the doctor said. "After all, my lord, what power have you that I do not?" This was a silly thing to say, for the men were not equals. Even Fletcher, whose understated presence by the sideboard one might forget, gave a small chuckle.

Byron stood up and placed his hands flat on the table as though he was about to pounce. "As you demand a reply, I shall quickly name three things I am able to do that defy your capabilities."

Polidori's neediness betrayed his handsome face. A man could be fine to look at yet with simpering become a snotty boy one wished to send upstairs. "Name them."

Byron counted as he spoke. "I can swim across that lake in its entirety without pause. I can put out a candle with a pistol shot from twenty paces away—and I can write a poem that sells fourteen thousand copies in one day."

I did not say the number was closer to ten thousand, for Mary and I were not welcome in this one-upping and certainly not with any corrections to fact. Besides, Byron had told me once that he was a man dangerously close to believing in his own mythology. Shelley puffed his chest; that he would lose a duel because of his weakness around blood was another thing I did not say.

Polidori glowered, his breath loud. It seemed he was considering bolting from his seat and attacking Shelley, though Byron was the one who had boasted. Byron saw this and walked to Polidori's place, refilling his cup without asking.

"Remember, Doctor, that though Shelley has some scruples about dueling, *I* have none, and shall be, at all times, ready to take his place."

This was satisfying to watch, for Byron's dexterity with words was unmatched. And yet I felt a pooling sadness in my chest—no one at that table had ever defended me quite so well or so quickly.

Polidori drank his wine in one, swiping at the last red rivulet that trickled down his chin. "I can treat a man with medicine—I understand the body," he said to close the argument.

"And yet you are unable to cure man of his mortality," I said. This awarded me a smirk from both Byron and Shelley.

"I can bring a human into this world and feed it from my own body—can you?" Mary rose from the dinner table and went to fetch William, leaving all of us in the wake of her power.

20

F PANTED, WATCHING OVER our group as we ate belly-deep in fog on a linen sheet over the grass, each corner anchored by lanterns aflame, though it was morning. The sky pressed down. Each dark morning, brutally windy afternoon, or ice-fog night spurred the idea that Diodati was an entire planet and we its only inhabitants.

Byron sat writing with a pot of ink nestled into his empty teacup. Shelley lay with his bilious body crushing the already struggling grass. He had come back to the cottage late. I had listened to Mary scold him—not for drinking too much but for being too loud about it, blustering through the downstairs and tripping on the stairs that led to our bedrooms. "Byron is impossible to keep up with," Shelley had yelled. "Then stop competing with him," Mary had said.

She told me in the morning that Shelley's suggestion was that we all consider sleeping at Diodati when the dinners went long. I did not know what to think about that—for how could I sleep in the same place as Byron yet not next to him? And yet I did not wish to come back to the cottage alone either.

"Sometimes I feel that the only thing that will save me is work," Mary said to Polidori, who sat next to her on the lawn sheet. He had been sensible the night before and abstained, sitting with his medical kit at the ready should Byron drink Shelley to the edge of death.

"Save you from what, exactly?" Polidori saw that Byron wrote and that Shelley, upright, stared at the lake, caught in thought. Polidori, finding neither man presented a challenge, was at ease.

"When I write I understand what it is to truly be alive." She plucked bits of grass and tore them into smaller pieces, littering her lap. William sat wrapped against her body with a shawl.

"My sister is most comfortable when she is writing," I said.

"Relatable," Polidori said. "For when I am in a clinic or with a patient, I find I forget the other—less desirable—aspects of my personality."

Mary pulled a slip of paper from her pocket and read. "The dead breathe inside us. As we have no way of knowing—truly knowing—what fortune or failure comes for us, we piece together the past and it clothes us like some sort of terrible, necessary skin. I wish to be rid of it and yet I know nothing else." She looked at him. "Those are my words."

Byron and Shelley did not speak to each other but rose from the wet grass at the same time and ran to the lake edge. Polidori started to go, too, but Mary took a deep, loud breath and looked over her shoulder at Diodati, which hulked over us at all times when we were outside and seemed to swallow us whole when we were in it. "*Did I request thee, Maker, from my clay to mould me man? Did I solicit thee from darkness to promote me?*" She looked out at the lake, where Byron and Shelley took turns pitching rocks, competing for the most skips. "That is Adam in *Paradise Lost*. I keep pondering that—creation and the self."

I furrowed my brow, for I had written that to Byron in my early letter, *the Creator ought not to destroy his Creature.* Had Mary somehow read it?

"You are a wonderful writer, Mary," Polidori said. "And your voice betrays your size."

Mary did not register his words, instead puzzling over her own thoughts. "I have the themes doing battle in my mind—I know not which will win out. Or if I shall find the time to write a story this summer, for I suppose I anticipated William would happily play or rest outside." She looked around as though the sky had simply misplaced the sun. "Perhaps the only way to cope with the ruinous weather or angry mind is to use it on the page."

When she spoke of writing, my sister's face became a citadel. I wanted that command.

Polidori gazed upon Mary with admiration and let the sun—which had given us a momentary reprieve from gloom—hit his face. Byron and Shelley engaged in a game of who might shove the other into the water without falling in.

I suspected that Byron did not yet know that Shelley was unable to swim. Polidori watched the men. I noticed on his face a familiar look, for I had felt it on my own features back at the Drury Theatre. Likely he felt admiration touched with disbelief—yes, I am here with this man of infamy. Only as I looked more closely, I saw another look on the doctor's face—it was one of focus and desire, and I could not tell if behind Polidori's eyes was a wish to be romping with the men, or lying on the fog-wet grass with Mary, or inside Diodati, kneeling before Byron and taking him in his mouth while looking up at him in gratitude.

Mary put her hand over her brow and looked at me.

The fog lifted and the lake came back into view. I thought about writing and about my conversation with Shelley. "Part of making art appears to be its torturous nature, always wondering if one is expressing on the page the correct turn of phrase," I said. I could not explain what I meant. "Perhaps it's best left to Mary." Mary looked pleased.

Shelley and Byron made their way back towards the villa.

"My lord," Polidori said, "I believe you have been spotted."

I followed his gaze to the lake. Mary looked, too. A boat sailed close to our shore. "A pleasure craft," Polidori said. He reached for the binoculars. "Named the *Liberté*, which is only amusing because they have the freedom and we do not."

The gawkers began to point and shout. Byron and Shelley were safely inside already, leaving only the mark of Shelley's body on the grass. Byron shouted to us, "The gossip-mongers have come to feast on our remains—we shall leave them with nothing."

And with that, we hustled inside.

21

On one of the last early mornings of May, I was awoken with a bang. Frigid-toed, I went downstairs in the hour when night touches day and found someone had left the cottage's side door open, or it had come open of its own accord as though the house had wills and ways.

In the entryway everything had frozen crystalline and shone in tepid sunrise, illuminating and defining each shining bit of ice that had formed on the windowsills and walls. It was nearly June and we had ice and yet I did not scream in surprise. Hoarfrost with shaggy beards covered everything. Amazing how strange and wrong something could be and how quickly used to it one could become.

The sheen of ice would last only a short while until day broke, but it froze the pity I felt for my current situation, and I bore the cold to experience both pains. I pressed my forehead to the coated glass window and squinted when I saw movement by the lake. How confident Byron was, walking through ice slopped on us. It was foolish to wait for blue sky and heat. I needed to embrace whatever weather was given and take action.

Still in my nightclothes, I went out, cautious. For recently as I walked at dawn or at night, I felt a hand of fear on my shoulder, as though I had left something behind or something was on the verge of catching me.

In the scintillating new lemon light, I saw FF. With frost trimming his jowls, the dog patrolled the water line, ready to splash in and rescue his master, who did not appear to need rescuing. Byron's clothing—he had taken the time to fold it—sat at the sandy edge. The sky was not night and not yet day, and in that unknown time, I found the courage to remove my clothing, skin like plucked fowl, and wade in. So strong and lithe was he without the impediment of his bad foot that when he dove he resurfaced far away before the bubbles on the surface had dissipated. He was a man transformed into an elegant seal. I could not have loved him more then, though to be sure he was swimming away from me.

Too cold to feel anything other than shock on my skin, I went to him just as a light chill rain began to fall. On our backs, naked in the water, we floated in the rain. He moved his arms and legs, making the shape of an angel, the shapes instantly disappearing in the water, and, for a moment, I was restored. I floated nearer to him.

"I am not in my right mind," he said.

"I care not," I said, which of course was impossible, for I would always care.

I noted the laudanum slack of his mouth, his legs. Even in that state he was a strong swimmer. With deft strokes he made a circle around me, then came back, suspended next to me. I thought of Mary and her story, all the stories she had in her and how they would pour onto the page and how Shelley would read her words and amend them to his liking and how she would not challenge him. And I thought of my own written words. Was there an age one reached when one stopped asking if this—the place, the event, the moment, the feeling—was all there was?

With the ache of cold water on my hips, on my back, I thought of feelings as movements in the water—there one moment and gone the next. My words on the page were something no one could take away. Byron and I were not angels. We were water bugs, insects that would last until humans were gone. I did not want to be forgotten on this earth, in his life.

I had not realised I had been holding my breath until I felt a long shaky sob escape. It felt so good to let it out I sobbed again. What had

Mary written in our shared journal back in London before I had bought my own? *I separated from my body long ago—how tragic to find we are always in conversation yet never truly one.*

I sobbed again, for not only was I having that same separated conversation with my own body, I was also more and more growing separated from her.

Closer to me in the water, Byron floated his fingertips to mine and only those parts of us touched. It was slight. It was temporary. I felt his touch deep in my body. Yet my body did not feel completely mine. Was that part of being a woman?

I heard Byron swim to shore and felt his absence. I stood, feeling the mucky lake bottom on the soles of my feet. Who knew what lay under the silt? I held my arms over my chest. My body had told a story to me, and I had narrated back a romance—a cheerful one written by An Anonymous Lady.

The lake felt like an empty room. I lifted my head just to catch sight of Byron, who was leaving. We all wanted to have someone enter a vacant room and recognise we had been there, by our scent, by finding words on a page only we could have written. Didn't everyone wish to be known so well? Upon meeting someone we handed them the story of ourselves—how urgently I believed the stories I'd been given.

The sun rose on the lake and urged me back to shore. I could not feel my thighs. I watched FF lift Byron's clothes with his mouth and present them. Byron and his dog walked slowly to Diodati. He gave me a backwards glance but did not bring me with him.

I would go to him tomorrow after I foraged. I would find garlic and mushrooms and share my haul first with Elsa. She had warned me of the stinging nettles, which I had looked up in the library—*Urtica dioica*—plentiful in nutrients, with separate male and female plants. Touched the wrong way, the leaves would pierce and burn the skin. Collected properly, they might be soup, or ease breathing ailments or monthly cramps. Julius Caesar's troops had rubbed themselves with nettles to keep awake. I would cook and share this food with the others. In the frigid snowscape of his icy winter-summer mind, I would find Byron and bring him back to me. I would find that power.

Yet there was more for me than Lord Byron. If I rearranged my story from what I wished it to be to what it truly was, well—what then? What kind of story would it be?

22

THE NEXT MORNING I woke with the night's shadows damp on my body. Determined to find Byron, I dressed quickly, bothered not with my hair or face, snatched a heel of bread to rip apart and eat on my way from the cottage to the villa.

I thought I might find him outside, meet chest to chest. I would act before my nerves got the better of me, pulling his mouth onto mine. Or perhaps I would, like a small and perfect goldfinch, feed him bread. Perhaps then he would choke on it and I would have to save him. I could see myself the hero—yet just as quickly I could imagine failing, Byron spluttering and dying in my arms with only the early morning lake to witness. I chucked the bread and reached the side of the villa, only to see in the peach-coloured light, at a safe distance, Byron climbing into a carriage.

The carriage sped off, spewing sand and pebbles from its large wheels. I did not give chase and stood dumbfounded for a moment. What if I had woken earlier, reached the drive sooner?

"Are you quite all right?"

This question of concern made me burst with a quick, sharp gasp of surprise, which I then tried to make more restained by saying, "I would be fine if you were not prone to lurking and causing me shock." I said this to Polidori, who crouched in the dark growth near the stone steps. He rose up at the centre of the mulberry trees, their unripe, tiny fruits unbothered by the previous frost, casting shadows over his face. A handsome face made more appealing in the setting. Still, I found him off-putting.

We regarded each other the way parents or child minders do their charges. He had caught me rushing up to see Byron. I could find no reason for Polidori's crouched presence other than spying on his employer. As a result, we spoke of plants.

"Marvelous specimens, these." He touched a mulberry branch, which scattered dew and some sort of insect on his palm. He seemed unbothered as he wiped it on the side of his jacket. I wondered if he had grown immune to dirt, bugs, disease in his profession.

I was jealous at the thought of his being unbothered. I had watched Elsa pick slugs off the few lettuces she'd managed to grow in the poor sun, how she had flicked them with ease and not once grimaced. How did one build the layers of not caring? I seemed to care about everything too much.

"Mulberries enjoy the cold, so we're in luck," I said. I had read this in my book recently and found I could recite the knowledge as though I had always possessed it. "They are thought to have healthful properties," I said. Polidori grimaced as he tried an unripe berry. "After all, they've been grown for thousands of years."

I knew things. I could share the things I knew. This would be part of my new Self. Unbothered by disgusting slugs, able to find wild onions, full of useful facts about plants. With the same determination I had felt about rushing to Byron, I strode purposefully towards the kitchen entrance to find Elsa. Polidori followed, unwilling to notice I wished to be rid of him.

He stopped by one of the large urns that flanked the wide doors. If I gave him a task, perhaps he would leave. "Would you be so kind as to collect some wildflowers?" I pointed to the land border between the villa and the cottage. Near the dark orchard a tangle of vines and flowers snaked through the hedgerow.

"Of course—we might make tea with chamomile." He looked at the urn. "Chamomile, too, has medicinal properties. Aids in digestion."

"Like fennel," I said. I could not tell if we were in competition to see who knew the most about subjects other than delicious Byron—and if we were, I vowed I would win by summer's end.

"Perhaps I *will* gather them," he said. "For Shelley does seem to be prone to stomach ailments." He looked at me a moment too long. "Likely you are aware of Shelley's needs." He gripped one of the planted urns as though it were a school chum. It came up to his waist. "You know, my mother went on about the proper way to arrange plants."

"Is there one? My mother gave me no such information." I wished he would leave.

"Any measure of three ought to be arranged for ballast." He touched each plant in the urn, and I could swear I felt his touch on my skin. "A pillar, this tall one here that acts as an anchor and draws the eye up, a filler, a flower or a bushy plant to take up space, and a spiller. This dangles down, trailing like this—whatever this is."

I did not know the name of the dangling flower, purple and small. Some buds were yet to open, others struggled to remain so, a few scattered on the ground because the staff had yet to sweep. I kicked my shoe against my calf, frustrated I did not know the name of the pillar, filler, or spiller.

"I think my mother was correct," Polidori said, "for like the strongest shape in maths and day-to-day, it is a sort of triangle." He methodically plucked the spent or wilted buds and put them in his pocket. Perhaps he had lived his years being misjudged as smart but crude—yet he was a man who kept his mother's wisdom. A man who did not add to the work of others by throwing the detritus on the ground. Then he pointed again to each of the three components of the planter. He threw a knowing glance my way. "Pillar, filler, spiller. I rather think it is the same with people."

With that, he turned, gave a quick glance to the empty driveway—no carriage had returned—and took his leave.

23

I FELT AS THOUGH POLIDORI had kicked me though only his words had touched me. Before I could decide if he meant himself, Byron, and me, or the men, or Mary, Shelley, and myself, Abigaëlle Elsa opened the door.

"Allez-vous bien, mam'selle?" Abigaëlle Elsa said to me.

It was the same question Polidori had asked, yet with so much kindness I felt tears spring to my eyes. So much for being unbothered. "Yes," I said. "Merely hungry."

"Then you must eat." She gave me a firm look as though considering our relationship. "You would join me?" I nodded and smiled and felt like a child. She seemed pleased. "You will call me Elsa."

Her accent was one I could not place. Elsa led me down the hallways, each turn curved so as to allow staff to move quickly and without injury on corners. The downstairs service area was vast, a system of wine tunnels and cheese caves and preparatory rooms.

She showed me into the kitchen. Two long rectangular work surfaces: one with vegetables in various stages of chopping—a mound of sliced turnips, a pile of beets staining the wood—the other with a dead lamb.

This made me stop in my tracks. "Does it concern you?" Elsa moved past the animal, whose head lolled to one side. Worse than being dead, it had been skinned. Polidori would no doubt go right over to it, diagram its vascular paths and muscles, but I stood at a distance. Perhaps Shelley was correct and I ought not eat meat. Then I thought of him as the tall, pointy pillar in the urn and charged right over to the lamb. I held its unmoving head, heavy for a small thing, in my hand.

"How will you serve it?" I asked.

"With preserved lemon and Älplermagronen," she said. We had tried the creamed potato, cheese, and onion dish a few days before—I would have eaten thirds had I not been watched.

I nodded and stared at the small, dead creature. Its life was not for nothing; its meat and wool would go to use. Still, I turned away so its small eyes did not gog out at me.

On tall, open shelving were rows of jars: apricots suspended in syrup, citrus rind, pickled purple cabbage, pickled onions with juniper, hulled oats, brown grain of some kind, yellow grain of another kind, and still another tall crock from which Elsa ladled a mixture of something which landed in a shallow bowl with an audible glop. From a basket on one of the lower shelves she pulled one apple, which she rejected, tossing it a fair distance into a wooden bowl by the door.

"For the pigs," she said. Another apple met her approval. She grated it on top of the gloppy mixture. "Now we need those." With her chin she gestured to a part of the room I had not ventured into. A small hutch with latched wooden doors. Inside was an army of perfectly ordered small tins, each with ornate German letters on the front. *Mehl, Pfeffer, Salz.*

"I keep rice in with the salt to keep it from making clumps," Elsa told me as she watched me snoop. *Mehl, Pfeffer, Salz, Getreide.* A strange poetry.

I picked up the domed lid from a tall, red porcelain vessel. On the bottom it read *Johann Friedrich Böttger.* Elsa brightened. "My mother's favourite, that one. She carried it with her from place to place."

"And the name?" I touched the letters.

"This I know—my mother's tale. Johann was a magician!" She watched my face. "Not the way you are thinking. No rabbit, not like Louis Comte. He made this hard-paste. Porcelain. Before that, we had wood. Chinese porcelain was too costly." She went back to grating. "Bring me the Haselnuss." I searched the shelf for that word. "You know she told me this each time she moved the piece—only nineteen Johann was, she would say." Elsa wiped her hands on her half apron. "Such a young boy to do a thing so great."

Evidence of greatness was all around me. I would never measure up. Still, I found the correct pottery, lifted its lid, and selected a handful of nuts. I brought them to Elsa, who instructed me to dump them on the wooden surface. She set down the apple and grater. From under the counter she pulled two tools and produced them with a grin. "Now, we—how do you say—*écraser*."

We each set about with a wooden mallet—hers smooth-ended and mine rippled. I had seen one before used for tenderizing mutton. Likely the lamb was so tender its meat would not require smashing. Elsa smacked her mallet over the nuts. I whacked the bits that jumped from her pile to mine. I wondered if she imagined she was hitting something other than a nut. As I thought this, a flash of a face looked up at me from the work surface. A ghostly image, only from my night terrors, but there just long enough that I brought the mallet down hard onto Shelley's gaze, shattering the hazelnuts and my vision.

"Now, the sweet," she said, and beckoned me into still another part of the kitchen I had not seen. At the back of the room, far into a long passageway, was another door, this one thick and sturdy. Elsa stepped in, and I followed. A delicious coolness spread over my arms, slipped around my ankles. My eyes adjusted to the lack of light in the larder, and I watched as Elsa moved a few painted enamel bowls. In her hands she held a small crock with a well-fitted lid.

Back in the main kitchen, my limbs felt heavy and hot, my face flushed. Elsa removed the crockery top and dispensed with the glop, which had settled with the grated apple. The crushed nuts went on top. And on top of that, a ladle of what looked to be thick cream from the crockery.

Shafts of light came through the window, illuminating Elsa's face. I saw then she was older than I had thought but not ancient. Perhaps my mother's age. Perhaps she was someone's mother. Someone lucky. She held out a finger under the ladle's stream. I followed suit. We both tasted.

A smile stretched across my face, for the substance was sweet as laughter. The most delectable taste I had ever encountered. "What is it?" I tasted it again.

"I do not know the word in English. Or French."

"German?" I asked.

She shook her head. "*Bubeleh tsuker*," she said. She handed me the mixture of grain, apple, and sweet milk which had become not glop at all, but a perfect mound of softened oat porridge with grated apple and hazelnuts and—"bubeleh tsuker," I said. The words were awkward in my mouth. Elsa laughed.

"Sweetheart sugar," she said, her accent thick. "But when I was a girl, I thought it was Bubbeh Tsuker, which is Grandma Sugar," she said. "Yiddish."

I must have given her a blank look, for at first she flinched as though waiting for me to say something rude. When I only reached for the spoon she offered with the bowl, she gave me a look that flittered between sadness and pity. Elsa said, "Yiddish is like Hebrew in the bowl with German and Aramaic."

"Yiddish." I looked at the concoction Elsa had made and said, "This looks like the mountains here." She nodded. I brought a spoonful to my mouth and could not have been more pleased with the creamy crunchy sweetness, the comfort of cool oats. "Does this have a name?"

Elsa ate hers with brusque efficiency. "Not that I know. My daughter called it pig mush when she was little." So she did have a daughter. As I shoveled another spoonful I felt such envy of Elsa's daughter I could have burst. "What should we call it?"

I studied the eroding mountain. "Mont Blanc."

We ate in quiet comfort as though we were old friends.

"I see you at Diodati," she said. "Looking. Reading." While I did not like the idea of Shelley spying on my whereabouts or Mary's keen eye on my movements, I found comfort in knowing Elsa had been in some way noticing me. Keeping watch. She went on, "You study even the kitchen shelves. You have all the words in your head." She tapped her own temple. "And you choose Mont Blanc?"

"I should find something better," I said.

"You misunderstand—we eat this for years and no one thinks to name it Mont Blanc, though the mountains are right in front of us." She paused. "I think perhaps you see things others overlook."

I bit my lip to keep from grinning. Perhaps my skill of noticing was not something to hide or be embarrassed about. "Do you have the receipt for this dish? I should like to write it down."

She shook her head. "You make it here," she said, and tapped her head, and I was back to being a silly girl, but in a way I found freeing—and safe.

ELSA SET about cleaning the mess we had made together, punctuating the wiping, sweeping, scrubbing with bites of breakfast. I followed her around like a puppy, doing the same, feeling both younger than my age—for who follows their granny around but a young girl—and older, for I had acquired still more knowledge, another skill I could write down and use later.

When we had finished cleaning, the kitchen put back entirely in order and perfectly organised, the mallets swinging from their hooks, Elsa looked at me. She gave me a long, hard stare as though making a decision. "No writing," she said. "All the dishes live in my mind. And the seeds," she pointed to her pocket, "live in here. I come from people who flee. Seeds are freedom, but so often we cannot stay long enough to farm. So we take with us what we need."

"Are you from here?" I asked. "You live here?"

Elsa pursed her lips. "Jews only live in Lengnau and Oberendingen—we could not live anywhere else, you see? Forbidden. And we must only be this thing or that—make hats, or clocks." She watched my face. "Not everyone goes all around being an artist, travelling, being—"

"Like us, you mean?" I blushed. Was I one of them? I wanted to bring up Polidori, who had a profession, to defend Byron's publishing or Shelley's politics, but I felt only small.

"I am not telling you this for blame. You ask, I explain. So those villages had all the Jews. All the bubbehs—"

"And their sugar."

Elsa laughed. "True. Then Napoleon, the Helvetic Republic." This was not information Shelley had given me in France. Nothing I had learnt in school. That was the problem with knowledge—even if you thought you knew enough, there was still more. "France tried to emancipate us. Hah. This only made it worse for us. We had Zwetschgenkrieg. The Plum War."

Her face fell. "Mobs came. Napoleon could not stop the looting. They ruined my father's workshop. He died soon after. Right before the Act of Mediation—no granting of rights for the Jews. In France the Jews were encouraged to be farmers but also told to pick a non-Jewish name. Imagine me as a saint!" Elsa said. She gave an angry laugh. I wanted to say she would be a perfect saint, but she went on. "I left Oberendingen—"

"With your daughter?"

Elsa's face closed quick as a fan. "No." She drew a breath. "She did not—I came here alone." She brushed one hand against the other. "No matter what they take from you, no one can rob your mind of what you know is true. Or how to cook." I tried to catch her eye to convey my sorrow for her, but she would not meet mine. "No one can take away all the wild greens. The herbs." She gave a final wipe of the wooden slab and hung the muslin cloth from her apron and then looked at me. "What I need, I carry with me."

"Women who know plants were often called witches," I said, thinking of a book Mary's father had printed with my mother. The art, meant for children, was terrifying.

"People are afraid of the woods," Elsa said. "Afraid of the nature when they ought be afraid of people."

"I do not wish to be afraid of either," I said. My voice sounded brave, but in truth I was afraid.

She went towards the shelves. On the wall were large wire riddles and smaller sieves. She handed me a riddle. "Take this for the next time you have a poke in the woods. Bring back cress and wild nettles. We will make soup."

I was out the door, past the dead lamb, our delicious breakfast a sunlit memory, before I realised I would not call the dish Elsa had made for me Mont Blanc. I repeated her Yiddish. I would call it Grandma Sugar.

24

The last day of May, Shelley found me on my way to the lawn, where I could see the others sprawled out in a haze of bodies, lemonade, sandwiches. Shelley said my name, and in the odd-feeling air—sticky underlaced with chill—I realised how different it sounded from his lips compared to Byron's. Even when he was dismissive or pointed, Byron said my name with a certain fondness, desirous of an understanding of me, of our connection. When Shelley said *Claire* all I heard was expectation. He had a way of saying such small words—merely my name!—and propping them up with needs.

"I assume your renunciation of the lamb last night was my influence." He gave me a tight-lipped smile of affirmation. I did not respond—distracted by the image of the lolling lamb head, the smashing of Shelley's face with the mallet, and the odious flower in front of me. Shelley put a hand on my shoulder, forcing me to look at him in order to encourage its removal. What he needed, what he expected from me was the overzealous response of the recently converted.

"I helped prepare it, so indeed lost my taste for it," was all I said. Shelley glowered. This was not the correct answer. I would have been better off smiling and saying of course it was he who encouraged such vegetarian heroics.

The flower distracted me again. Elongated, dark purple tongues with a protruding, erect centre, offering all nearby the smell of rotting meat.

"*Dracunculus*," I said. "Smells horrible—what a good job it does beckoning to flies! Robert John Thornton's book, *The Temple of Flora*, is in the library." I pointed to Diodati as though Shelley were a tourist.

Shelley all but glared as a form of punishment. "I have never seen a more sex-forward flower."

I could not bear to look at him. Loathed that he stood too close to me. Byron's deep-throated laugh echoed down from the lawn to where we stood. I looked over that way.

"You know," Shelley said, "not everyone is capable of loving the way you do, Claire. Chasing those with a closed heart is a fool's errand."

I did not reply. Instead I leaned in and took a long whiff of the plant. Shelley grimaced.

"I should say the plant is rather vulgar," Shelley said. He gave a glance to the lawn, where the others were. He meant me. I was vulgar.

"It is *Dracunculus vulgaris*," I said, aiming to prove him unoriginal in his description. "If one stands near it long enough, one can grow ignorant of the smell." I clenched my fists against my thighs. "As you well know, I can tolerate most issues quite well."

I REACHED the lawn in time to overhear Byron saying, "Ah, here comes Claire to suck the fun out of everything."

I was too shocked to respond. Cutting words, and yet his eyes found mine with something more like need. I did not know men. Not really.

"How lonely it is to be the unfun sibling." Polidori added to Byron's dig. "I have a sister—"

"She is fun, then?" Byron said. Polidori gave a regretful nod as though that was all anyone need know about his sister.

Had I not been praised for exactly that trait my entire childhood? Mary, on the lawn in the claustral heat, did not defend my fun nature. William lay looking up at the sky like an overturned bug. Shelley folded himself onto a blanket near Polidori, who immediately fussed over tea.

"Chamomile," Polidori said, looking at Shelley but for my benefit. "For your digestion. I picked the flowers myself."

"Marvelous," Shelley said. "Byron, you've employed a saint. A saint and a physician. The best combination."

"Add prostitute and you have the holy triad," Byron said.

I snickered but only until I remembered I was not fun.

Part of me suspected that Byron's heart had all the complexities of a potato. Still, I could only think that of him when I was not in proximity, for when I was at all near to him I lost logic and felt only love.

I loved him with an all-consuming fire and a gaping openness that I found embarrassing. Or perhaps I was only afraid. Once I had seen a bird that had left its nest too soon—clumsy or kicked from it I could not say—and it lay on the ground stunned but breathing, its new heart visible from the outside. That was my heart, too.

"I wandered lonely as a cloud," Polidori said. It was clear from the confident set of his lips over his teeth that he thought praise would follow his recitation.

Byron groaned. "Lest you foul the day with quoting Wordsworth. The man has sold his soul for commerce sake. He would pen a poem about the water closet if he were offered good money for it. I wandered lonely as a chamber pot. . ."

This settled on Polidori. "So a true gentleman ought never accept a fee for his work?"

"Quite right," said Byron.

"Easy for one who is not in need of income to say," Polidori noted.

Shelley stepped in before Byron could lash out at the doctor. "Art ought to be for art's sake, in service to the sublime." He sounded as though he was prepping for an Oxford lecture as he sipped from his cup. Byron seemed to bring out Shelley's haughtiness. "Few ailments cannot be solved by a cup of weak tea."

"Your statement is an insult to the medical arts," Polidori said, sore from being slighted.

I perked up. "Tea has healing properties, you said so yourself, I thought."

Shelley nodded. "You thought rightly."

"I loathe nightly," Byron said, stretching, all languor and heat. I wondered where he and Shelley had been the night before. If Mary also wondered, she did not say.

"Am I always to be surrounded by fools?" Mary asked, standing up. "Shelley? Take your son. I am going to work."

Who is the unfun one now? I wanted to say, but I refrained, for Shelley looked furious as Byron giggled. Byron did not seem to share his friend's need to calm an argument.

"IT IS quite a lot of setup to eat outside," I said, after Mary had gone back to the cottage.

"I think it quite charming to be in nature yet with the comforts of home," Shelley said, though of course he had done nothing to prepare the ornate service and would leave its cleaning to others, too.

I thought of my coppice, of foraging, of Elsa. "This is not truly nature, is it?" I looked at the lawn, on top of which was a rug, Byron using his dog as a cushion near the gleaming forty piece tea service (I had counted, part out of curiosity, part to look busy), cushions plumped and plenty, folded blankets, uncut loaves of bread, the tiered trays replete with sandwiches in neat triangles and scones the size of infant hands.

If the sky continued to darken and rain slapped the goods, and if time passed and the sun then shone and Byron's staff had not cleared up, still the setting would be lovely. Money had a soft spot for faded grandeur, tolerated a degree of ruin in the form of scruff, damp infiltrating country linen, a few chips on the platters or plates that suggested there was so much money—somewhere—there was nothing to prove.

Debris from a picnic or lawn party encouraged a knowing smile the next morning from revelry-tired eyes. The same rubbish strewn on the street was met with disgust. Had I served tiny scones and butter sandwiches on chipped plates I would be seen as merely poor. I would always need to prove myself.

Byron shielded his eyes from the tea service gleam and looked at the elegant lake as though it judged him. "I ought to slough off my worldly goods," Byron said, eating a watercress and butter sandwich in two bites.

"Is it not often those with too many possessions who wax poetic about a life with none?" Shelley said. Byron thwacked him with a pillow and said, "It is the man born into the most privilege who feels he is owed the most from the world."

Mary reemerged, grim as old winter, mouth drawn down at the corner. "I could not work," she whispered to me. "One might wish to write but cannot always force the words. It is unfair that you write without pause in that journal and I cannot complete more than one line."

Her sourness drew me to her. "It will come," I assured her, "and mine is writing of a different sort."

She humphed as she took a jam sandwich from the tray, wishing everyone to know she would eat but not enjoy it. When she left the last bite on the delicate, gilt-edged plate, I lost patience with her. Everything she did seemed to promote her own temperance, her own restraint, when we both knew full well she was singed at the core with anger. She wanted to eat the last bite yet would refrain from doing so to prove her ability to deny herself. She had retreated before to put Shelley in his place—a quiet slap.

Meanwhile, I ate a biscuit in one bite and took another without counting to see how many were left for others. Mary elbowed me. "I am allowed to eat," I rage-whispered.

"Your nose is coated in sugar," she said.

For a moment I considered asking her to lick it off. We had done this as children, attempting to make the other refuse in revulsion. Shelley glared at us. I pawed at my nose as Byron beckoned us to the tea table. I kept pawing at my nose until I realised Byron either thought I was waving exuberantly at him or being slovenly. Either way, he ignored me.

This would not do.

I went to the table, pressing my belly up against it as I scanned the offerings: jasmine, chamomile, black tea, honey in a pot I recognised from Elsa's kitchen like a tiny secret message, a plate of lemon slices, Byron's hand on the table. His fingers, which had gone over the entire map of my body, crooked in the teapot handle.

"What a man of the people you are, my lord, pouring your own tea," I said, but under my breath so as not to draw glares from Mary.

Byron offered the pitcher of milk to me first without looking directly at me. Not out of politeness, I thought, but because he knew full well I liked the first pour when the cream had risen to the top.

Indeed, I did want the cream and this made me blush for I also wanted to pounce on Byron—prying eyes from the hotel or the picnic companions be damned. I wanted him physically yet did not wish to pay with my heart. I sipped my tea and wondered if it might be simpler to separate heart from body. I pictured this ghastly operation as I smiled and said thank you.

A PLEASANT state of post-tea satiety settled upon us. Mary wrote, using William's belly as a desk as he babbled in her lap. Shelley and Byron wrote side by side, hand-painted porcelain inkpot shared between them, each man entirely focused on his work. Polidori, seeing neither Shelley nor Byron wished to include him, jotted in a notebook I was sure would be sent back to John Murray—*Byron uses his dog as a pillow! Miss Clairmont is unfun!* I had not reckoned with becoming fodder for the scandal sheets when I had first written to Byron.

My journal was already thick with days. I forbid myself rereading for fear I would be dismayed with the discrepancy between how I remembered events and how I wrote about them. Sometimes I felt the others watched me as I wrote.

"I do hope we all come off favourable in your little diary," Shelley said, with a tone bedecked with mockery for Byron's pleasure. To respond would be to admit to a wound, so I stayed silent. Mary lifted her eyebrows but did not react, and when Byron pretended he had not heard, Shelley said no more.

I watched Mary scratch out words time and again. Often she did this before she had completed a full sentence. I felt smug, for I did not edit myself. Then I chewed my own lip, for I did so edit myself, I merely did it before I wrote. Pre-editing. That was a good term. Another might be omission.

25

Wind and songbird and baby babble outside were lullabies that afternoon until Byron shouted, "Fame-fucking maggots!"

The words spat out of his mouth, and FF galumphed immediately to his side on high alert. Out in the lake, two boats approached, gossipers shoulder to shoulder.

"Let them not defeat us," Byron cried, holding a baguette as a bayonet. His taut mouth betrayed his jolly voice.

Instead of dispersing to Diodati and the cottage, Polidori shuttled us away from the main lawn to a glasshouse tucked behind a thick tangle of old-growth pines and Geneva plane trees. It was far too shady to be a useful space for growing things, but a fine shelter from prying eyes with a few wooden chairs, a bench flecked with green arsenic paint. The dirt floor had sprouted sticky pink flowers. Honeysuckle vines had infiltrated the glass sides and roof, giving the entire space the feel of a place left to its own ruin for many years and that appeared to tell us all—nature would win in the end.

"Much better," Shelley said. He settled onto the largest of the wooden chairs, though it would likely have been the most comfortable for Byron with his bad foot.

"I thought it might be a good spot," Polidori said. He had to remind us that he had chosen it. From his tone we were meant to feel he had built it.

Byron still seethed. "I am well aware that Caravaggio was far ahead of me with his louche behaviour, yet I envy him. At that time he did not have to contend with such brutal gossip-mongers—their incessant and insatiable need to know what I am doing, what I am eating, who I am bedding." He gave just the tiniest look my way as he said this and my heart lurched. If I closed my eyes, I could feel the cold lake water, our fingertips touching. "I am surely not the first celebrity pushing at art, debauched or not. Mary, you grew up in the shadow of your famous mother, did you not?"

"How she grew up is none of your concern," Shelley said.

Byron rolled his eyes. "Still, better to be hounded than a panderer selling services—"

Polidori nodded. "Ah, true. You profit not from sex trade, milord."

Byron settled into a corner of the glasshouse, honeysuckle trailing onto his shoulder. "You could do with a romp, Polidori. Frumpy-grumpy such as yourself."

Polidori turned red at the brothel slang and became quite fascinated with the dirt floor near his chair. "Kind offer. I shall pass."

Shelley gave an elaborate smile and jumped at the chance to continue Byron's mission. "Milord, you said there was a *sweetshop* in town, did you not?"

Byron perched his elbows on his thighs. "Indeed. And one girl in the window was lovely to look at. Still, she had the reputation of a best carriage route, far too much in use."

"Beware the Y-shaped woman," Mary said, which made the men guffaw. Shelley looked at her with pride. I did not know how Mary could say such things near him and retain her prim, yet when I stood by a suggestive flower, I became all raunch.

"One does not wish for all pudding and no main," Byron said. "Sweets are nice, but meat sustains."

I was meaty. And sweet. Before I could think of a witty retort to prove my own comfort with suggestive talk, Polidori cleared his throat. Trying to keep up with his employer—beloved, anyone could tell from the gaze, the tilt of head, that the devotion went beyond the role of physician and patient—Polidori spoke.

"I have a joke," Polidori said. The men looked his way. "Hear this. A man comes to the doctor. 'What is the trouble, sir?' the physician asks. 'I cannot discern my current predicament,' says he. The doctor considers this." Polidori, whose affect was quite engaging, with his hand on his chin, used a voice I suspected he used with actual patients. Shelley and

Byron could not take their eyes from him. "'What, pray tell, is wrong with me?' asks the man. 'Let us see,' the doctor says. 'Do you look good *and* feel good?' 'No,' says the patient. 'Do you look bad *and* feel bad?' 'Decidedly not.'" Polidori snapped his fingers. "'You *look* bad, yet you *feel* good—ah, I see, you are a vagina!'"

Shelley chortled. To my surprise, Byron did not. He looked down at his lap and then pierced Polidori's gaze. "You are vulgar-tongued, with neither heart nor mind for ballast," he said, which I took to mean he thought little of his physician and also felt he could have carried the joke better.

Mary chewed her lip. I picked my cuticles. Was I meant to think of my vagina as ugly?

I thought of all I had read. For I sought not only plant and foraging information, but the reference books in the library with their onion-skin pages, each with more and still more facts I imbibed with thirsty roots.

"Did you know," I said, primarily addressing Mary, "prior to the late 1600s, *vagina* did not mean that at all?" Byron paid attention to me. "We had not even a word to refer to the corridors of feminine bodies. Vagina was said in reference to a sword sheath." I could see that my sister was on the verge of snickering. She fought it back.

"And so the pirate mystery of the dark seas began," Shelley said. Mary rolled her eyes.

"I hope that will not be one of your poems," I said to Shelley. Byron laughed. Who was unfun now?

"Claire, where are you learning such things?" Mary asked, face full of scorn. "You might at least try to be more serious."

This sent me inside my own head.

The trait Mary had been most praised for as a child was wisdom, which of course was impossible, merely the word her father had used interchangeably with *beyond her years*. Yet why was that worthy of praise? Why bestow upon a child the compliment that suggests childhood itself is best left to others, less wise and less good?

I looked at Mary and wished she had been praised for something else. Or that I had been praised for laughing so hard I let wee out in my skirts, a not uncommon occurrence for me at age ten, or been commended for my gentle way with anything in the natural world, a wood duck with its wounded webbed foot I had tended to, a sad seedling grown in a teacup after Mary had abandoned our tea parties.

Why dole out coveted approbation to children for traits—high vocabulary, thoughtful pauses, careful listening followed by more considered responses—that would not serve the test of time, becoming characteristics in adulthood that prompted pity or, worse, the disinclination to include her in any gathering other than the serious one-to-one.

"Oh, Claire," Byron said, cupping his hands to his mouth as though calling me inside from playing conkers. "Where have you disappeared to?"

His voice was not unkind. In fact, it was curious. The tone along with his gaze made me miss him, though we were in the same space. "Do we perturb you with our nonsense?"

"I cannot fathom your fascination with . . . sex," Mary said, the last word made her face sour. "All of you." She swept her hand around the glass room as though all of the male population of the world resided in it, William included.

"Still," Polidori said to Mary, as though they had been in intimate conversation, "one does appreciate that erotica—"

"From your mouth that word sounds anything but," Byron said.

"In Pompeii and Herculaneum, long buried under Mount Vesuvius, those on the dig were shocked with what they found," Polidori said. "Large breasts, satyrs with flawless physiques, not *only* couples coupling."

"Seven couples coupling," sang Byron, and though I found him amusing I did not give him the satisfaction of laughing aloud.

"Think of it," Polidori said. "Wind chimes made of phalluses." His tone was matter-of-fact, medical, and because of this, Mary seemed to relax.

"I suppose it has always been this way," Mary said. "A male world filled with sex and creatures who think only of it."

Byron perked up. Likely this was his ideal world. Or perhaps that was too simplistic of me. Shelley noticed my frown and quickly added to Polidori's history lesson. "What the doctor hasn't told you is that quite as soon as the erotics were unearthed, good old King Charlie locked them away again—as though he was above holding his own cock in his hand." Mary put her face in her palms, feigning embarrassment at Shelley's crassness, though her smile told me she was proud.

"And now?" I asked, mainly so I could make sure I could still speak, for I felt only partly there and could not work out why.

"And now all the phalluses and beasts a-laying are hidden away," Byron said. "Lest the women and children go blind in the viewing." He paused and looked right at me, which brought me back to life. "Truly, it is not allowed for women to view the art—and no poor people, either. Only those with money or a title." He shook his head and rested his legs on FF's back, the dog happily acting as footstool.

"Were it not illegal, I should like to see the collection," I said, ignoring Mary's real blush on my behalf. Byron stared with something resembling surprise, and Shelley gave me a questioning look I chose to ignore. "I should like to see how one creates a wind chime from phalluses." No one responded. "With what were they strung together?" Still, no one spoke. "I like knowing things—how a teapot is constructed or a skirt sewn or a political belief formed. My sister is the same, are you not, Mary?" She did not answer. "It is possible we were really quite bored in childhood and had only deconstruction and its opposite to consider."

Polidori crossed his arms. "And what did you learn in this childhood of yours, taking apart teapots and the like?"

His tone suggested we had been on the other side of world where teapots were the size of carriages or could talk so unusual were they. "I learnt to spend time with the parts," I said.

"A handle?" Byron asked, ever suggestive.

"Fine, yes, a handle, if we are continuing with the teapot metaphor. What I mean to say is that we . . ." and here I blushed, for perhaps equal to having shown him my body was showing him the inside of my head, "like to think we understand the whole of something, but we only recognise it in the whole form."

Byron took his legs from FF and stood up. "Yes. Yes, that's correct."

"We better understand the whole if we take it apart and know the bits and pieces of it."

"Of course. Brilliant. This is what I must do with poems." He scratched his neck, puzzling out a piece of writing in his head. "Sometimes in the rebuilding, one must make a poorly constructed teapot."

"Yes." I laughed. "I had a box which never again closed properly, a spinning top that spun only to thrice before lilting to the left, and a disembodied doll that Mary called Bernice."

Mary perched William on her lap and then, thinking better of it, handed him to Shelley who in turn gave him to me. Mary stretched her arms behind her head, her glossy blond hair in rivulets on her shoulders.

"Was Bernice not the doll's name?" Shelley asked.

I laughed again. "Her name was Baby." At the word *baby* William turned, but Mary refused to engage with him.

"A baby doll named Baby. How literal," Byron said. "Charming."

I kept on. "I was a literal child." Byron watched me and then tugged at a honeysuckle vine, his eyes suggestive with desire. "Mary thought Baby was dim as pudding, so she changed it. Point being, after I took Baby apart, I knew the parts but couldn't put her back together."

"That is the risk," Byron said, moving just a tad closer to me. I could picture his cool soft hand on my chin, the drag of it down the length of my throat, pausing on my clavicle and then continuing down. Mary cleared her throat loudly and spoke in an overly enunciated fashion.

"As all siblings do, we have discrepancies in our descriptions of how we view our childhood," Mary said. She made childhood sound so far away, when in fact it had been fewer than a handful of years.

"Mary chooses to pull out of the bag of the past only stories in which are reflected normalcy," I said. "Family dinners, the time her father rescued our brother Charles's fingers from the squish of the printing press."

Mary flipped her hair over her shoulder. "And Claire's stories only serve to highlight the ragtag chaos so she might incite the Greek chorus with wild arms." Mary flung her slim arms around as though in a charade of a gale. "Gesturing to tell the tales of woe and famine."

"Was there famine?" Byron asked.

"Had my belly written in pang-filled song, we would have evidence," I said.

"That was not the way it was at all," Mary said, and regarded me with annoyance and wonder. "You see lunacy and wildness where there were merely moments of disorder."

I darkened. "That isn't so. Disorder sounds as though merely dishes were mismatched."

"Were the dishes mismatched?" Polidori asked.

"Yes. And sometimes not there, for Mary's anarchist father might have gone off to rail against government corrupting society—"

"Government does corrupt society," Shelley said. I feared he would begin a disquisition on faraway politics in order to turn the focus back on himself.

"And yet children need to eat and have water for washing," I said.

"When I was there we always had dinner," Shelley said.

The room was quiet. Perhaps the others had forgotten he lived with us or perhaps they saw my jaw clench. "You always had dinner," I said. "You had a show on for you, Shelley." He turned to face me. "We had years before you arrived. Before you wooed everyone with your attentiveness and staunch beliefs."

Mary looked at her lap. She would lash out at me back at the cottage. She wished to have the kind of background that was just interesting enough to support her creativity yet nothing crude—no vaginas, no hunger.

I turned back and changed my tone. "Before Shelley's dinners there was the time my mother brought home two swans in need of medical care—"

Mary perked up. "Which was the same time my father revealed he would start a printing press for children's books and what better use for the swans . . ."

"Than to be the main characters of a story as two swan parents looking after all five of us children." I looked at my sister. "Which Mary cleverly and quickly wrote—"

"I spoke the story, for my penmanship has never been as clear and precise as Claire's."

I beamed with her praise. Shelley could not hold back. "This is true—Mary makes a mess on the page, and Claire's writing is pristine." He did not say more, yet his encouragements somehow felt like a way of making sure I did not say too much.

His interjection was just enough to puncture the pace of our story. Mary sat there, derailed. I did not want his opinion about the clarity of my pen. I tried to keep going. "It was a wandering circus all within one too-small house."

"That sounds horrible," Polidori said. "Though my own house had no stench, even with eight children—" here he looked at Byron for any signs of interest, "it was quite a relief to leave for Edinburgh at—"

"At fifteen," Byron said. "And a doctor at twenty."

Shelley digested this quickly. "So you've only been a physician less than a year?"

Polidori picked at his thumb. "Yes. Which one might say is your good fortune, for all I learnt is fresh in my mind."

Byron gave him a look of opprobrium for his boast. "Careful, Polly's Dolly, your vulnerability is showing."

Byron did not wish to have a physician with human traits. Polidori resigned himself to crossing his arms, trying to look unphased. I looked at the young doctor in a different way. He was needy for Byron, perhaps in the same way I was. Perhaps I had misread him. I said, "Once our mother left five shillings—a crude amount—as we could not split it evenly—"

"Your mother," Mary corrected. "And a note instructing us to buy toothpicks, which my father chewed quite habitually, and a 'fancy ribbon'—"

"Which could only be found at Harding, Howell & Co., all the way on the Pall Mall—and which I still have." Here I paused, for I could nearly smell the false peach of my mother's hand salve that remained on her note. And I kept the blue ribbon in the pages of my journal. "So we—Mary and I—held hands and walked."

"And walked and walked. I feel sure it was dark by the time we returned."

Byron gazed at us with a sick fascination, as though watching me suture my own leg. "Yet you found the requested items?"

I nodded. "Still, we were unharmed."

"You need not defend your mother," Shelley said. "You were far too young to cross all the corners."

"She did put you in harm's way," Polidori confirmed.

"One does not require a medical degree to know that," Mary said. "Yet we are here. We turned out just fine. Does that not belie the misstep?"

Byron shook his head. "All's well that ends well is not a magic potion that undoes any evil," Byron said. "That is why we have poetry."

"Poetry is politics," Shelley said.

"Poetry is wounds," Byron said. Polidori braced himself for the other two men to argue. He stopped short of rubbing his hands together in glee.

"Is childhood not an accurate predictor of one's life outcome?" Polidori said this not as a question but as a belief. "For my father insisted I become a doctor and I am and thus am here."

"Surely not," Byron said. "For I am entirely otherwise whom and from where I started."

Mary chewed her lip. "There is likely more to the interior of the person than provided only in childhood. This is something I am writing about." Her voice filled with the dew-glitter it always did when she spoke of work. "How we build up from detriment. How we try to shed the garments given to us in our first circumstance."

"Must we trot out all the wrongs that have befallen us?" Shelley said, long and bored.

"I rather enjoy a game of Who Had It Worse," Byron said. He gave me a look. It was a look I knew meant he did not quite believe me. "Even if there is exaggeration involved."

"No exaggeration needed," I said. "In fact, it is only in the telling that it seems bad. At the time, we thought it was a normal childhood. We just got on with it." Something stuck in my throat, a ghost morsel of scone.

"Well, it was real," Mary said. A smile played at her lips. "And what's more, we had a cat named Helen Maria Williams—"

"After the radical abolitionist novelist," I said.

"And Helen Maria Williams the Cat had trousers," Mary said.

"And yet we for a time had only one pair of shoes between us," I said.

We began laughing. The kind of laughter that turned my face deep red. Mary began to shake and snort. I hid my face in my hands with a guffaw and wished I could hold myself there forever—Mary's and my memories twined together, both of us in the present, laughing the way only siblings who have survived the same war can.

PART THREE

JUNE 1816

VILLA DIODATI

1

TO START THE NEW month, I wrote before dawn to my brother Charles, filling a back-front-back with descriptions of our group, the environs, the rooms of Villa Diodati I had seen and how many rooms there had gone unexplored.

Afterwards, I went to fetch William, whose great frantic caws could be heard outside the cottage. With him on my hip I pointed out flowers and shrubs, trying their names on my tongue as we walked past. Everything ought to be blooming but had paused in bud form. We stood on the side of the cottage near a small rack on which fluttered Mary's sanitary strips all washed: the shameful flags of womanhood—that peculiar mix of sorrow and relief that came monthly—each drying in the dark.

Elsa came upon us. She watched me brush William's fine hair from his face while I pulled his hand across the portulaca so he might feel it. "You're very good with him. You wish to be a mother?"

I swallowed and felt how heavy William was, how damp. "I know not—is that a choice?"

"A teacher perhaps," Elsa said. Her hair was swept up in a plait, twisted and held firm on her neck. I tried to imagine her as a girl my age. Had she gotten what she wanted? Elsa watched a bit longer and then asked if I could hand him off.

"Mary has no other help," I said. This did not deter her. She waited.

I went to the cottage, found Shelley asleep in a chair, kicked his foot to rouse him, and set William on a mat on his back with a stuffed toy in the shape of a rat. I did not know how he had come by such a toy and thought it odd considering the plagues and yet left him with his father, chewing on the rat's tail while I joined Elsa.

SHE LED me out the far side of the villa to the kitchen garden; we walked in easy companionship side by side. Worry creased her wide forehead. "Nothing grows that should by now," she said. She shook her head. "Here is meant to be with lamb's lettuce, with courgette, with squash blossom. We need to find other things to make." She rubbed at her face and thought.

"Even in the autumn—this last one I spent in . . ." my voice dropped off. What would she care about Lynmouth? About my lonely days of banishment, of walking alone by the sea, waiting for a letter from Mary, the visit from Shelley a surprise and another secret to keep.

"Tell me," she said.

"I was sent away." I did not look at her. "From my sister's house. And Shelley—the tall one—"

"I know which one is Shelley." She did not look pleased, yet perhaps I looked too long at her. "*Lokshen* legs." She made a gesture of having to look way, way up to see him.

"Yes, lokshen. Too tall." I gave a fake laugh. "He visited me." Here Elsa made a funny sound, and I thought she might not like Shelley. "And in between I was alone and walked and walked. There was good cream from local cows, so nice pastries. And . . ." I looked at the sad crop of vegetables. "Always samphire, rock or marsh."

"Tell me," she said. "More so I can imagine."

"It's a funny plant. It tastes quite nice. Salty. Sea asparagus, you could call it. Glasswort. Mermaid's kiss." She raised her eyebrows. "A mermaid—it's a kind of pretend woman with a fish tail, that lives in the ocean and calls out to sailors and then wrecks their ships."

"Probably they deserved it," Elsa said, and beckoned for me to follow while she worked.

A shed with a steep pitched roof sat next to a small orangerie, both outbuildings kept from view of the villa by a tidy line of miniature pines. I wondered if they would stay short or if were I to return in fifty years they would have grown as tall as the villa. I thought about adding a line to my letter to my brother Charles, *imagine all of us siblings as small plants—new flowers we were, poorly tended.* Though Charles was not quite so. Each child in a house has their own view, their own experience in being brought up, so Charles's childhood was not mine.

"Take this," Elsa said. She gave me a seedling whose roots were wrapped in an old scrap of cloth, with a small bit of earth inside, tied with string taut enough to hold the dirt yet with space at the top for the small plant to emerge. "There are so many."

"We need them for my garden at home. My people need to eat, too," she said. She looked at me; her eyes were lighter blue than Mary's, icy-bright in the pasty chill. "If they knew I used the warming room for this there'd be trouble, so please don't say." I nodded. "Each day I tend to them, say a little hello." She reached into a swill bucket and wet her hands, then flicked water at the seedling sacks. "Strange ways, I know," she said with a smile, "still you can overwater and too little is also doom, so this seems to work."

"How clever."

"You try," she said. She watched as I pushed my sleeves up as far as they would go without unbuttoning them and reached into the bucket. As though casting a spell I sprayed water as she said the plant names. "Lemon balm. That one is primrose—reduces swelling—she'll take over a garden if you're not mindful. Flax, hemp, beetroot, carrot—probably, watercress—"

We had a pleasant rhythm, a water flick and a name, a flick and name. I was sorry when we reached the end of the rows.

She went to the window edge where there were a few more plants in slightly larger bundles made from old granary sacks. "These are bigger, as you can plainly see, so they're ready to go in the ground soon." She moved her hand across the plants, touching their tops, their sides, this and that in soft but intentional movement.

"Does that not disturb them?" I asked as she kept moving them.

"Oh, I am always gentle." She turned to me. "I am pretending to be wind. Over the years I have found the seedlings that do best have preparations for the conditions ahead. Otherwise they get—how to say—windshock. And do not survive or have permanent wilt." She continued her motions and then stopped, letting the leaves settle.

I looked at the plants and then the baker's face and told her, "I wish I had had a mother do the same for me."

2

OUTSIDE BEFORE ANYONE ELSE the next day, the gloom felt like a secret. I woke with resolve to knock on Byron's door, but June's promise of sun gave way to a foreboding autumnal chill. I went into the woods, hoping to find within myself the bravery required.

In the coppice, my eyes adjusted to the dappled softness, all shades of green—emerald from the pincushion, beard moss with its defeat showing, turf moss ample and understated, heath star elegant and wary of touch. Calm took over my body. Never had a place been so soothing. This surprised me, for I had always found comfort in other people—my mother, Mary, the few people I had met in Lynmouth, Shelley, Byron, even Elsa. Here the trees were companions, requiring nothing of me. I took little from them—and the moss tolerated my sitting upon it.

Indeed, I felt sitting there that its gentle weave, the quilting of pattern and shades, had been somehow set out for me. Here, every bit of nature seemed to say to me, be—what was the word? With my palms flat I felt the moss. Light played on the knobby bark of the cembra pines, their dense needles shading the entire area from the world of the villa. Here, I felt neither longing nor expectation. Here, I felt an uncomplicated joy. I neither rushed to forage nor put off the task. I simply began by noticing the purslane's creep and hedge, the way it started small from the ground and quickly expanded at the coppice edge where sunlight shafts came in the afternoon.

With each green I pulled or snipped with the secateurs, I thought of how my mother did not seem to take joy in much at all. She hurried through everything—working, cleaning, shopping, wrapping a book and tying it with a tartan ribbon. This was not because she did not like any of these or that even cleaning dishes was entirely bad (for certainly there was a sense of accomplishment to be found at the sudsy end). Rather, my mother lived in a tense that was not one I could name in English, nor in French or Italian. Not the present tense—in which she was soaping or wrapping or teaching me how to read—and not in the far future, when dishes or book were barely remembered, but rather in the near future, when she had completed everything expected of her. Even her best activities—running the printing press, selling books—she wanted only *to have done them*. Not to *do* them. What had that been like for her? I felt sorry I had never asked.

I felt joy for myself, picking the few elderflowers that had opened in the dash of warmth so I could make a cordial with honey and lemon. And lest I feel guilty for pulling the purslane, the wild dandelion greens, goosefoot, and leeks, Elsa had told me the action was of benefit to the earth—giving more space and light to plants nearby, aggravating the ground just enough to spur more growth.

I walked with arms full of food, pockets jammed with new fennel, the purslane Elsa would serve to the others as a bright, rich salad dressed with pressed olives from one of her jars. I swore if compliments came from the others, I would not take credit for the finding. For there was a lovely secret feeling of providing without needing praise.

I left my foraging wrapped in a kitchen cloth for Elsa by the staff entrance. The day slipped by with ever-increasing cold. I had the feeling of November's dark tug. And in this I felt the sting of future tenses. Where would I be in autumn?

3

After I washed up, I thought about the times I had entered Byron's London home by the back, the dank stone with its slippery potato-peel sludge, how the smell stayed on my boots. Perhaps I had never been fun. Yet I was now the sort of person who could fashion a meal from the woods. I could entertain a child, outwit Byron's friend Scrope Davies, entice a celebrity. I had been brave to do all of those things.

I did not wish to be the sort of girl who would waste my day pining for a man who did not tend to my heart with the care of a gardener. Ink-splotch clouds hovered over the lake. I would not prove myself unworthy of being seen by going in the back door.

I would instead be the sort of person who let herself into a mansion by the front entrance to explore and wander with the sort of abandon a character would have who had stumbled upon the sleeping villa by accident. Rather the way we had the Monster Park of Bomarzo.

Through Diodati's front door I saw first the welcome table, which was too large to live up to its name. In the middle of it, a bough-pot that sprouted from the holes in its ceramic lid a clutch of willow boughs with their gentle grey buds soft as a rabbit's ear, long stalks with a pink flower I vowed to know the name of but did not yet, and the early blue flax cut before the frost had killed the rest. On the far back wall, a large vitrine housed a set of gold-rimmed plates which all faced outward, each with an animal dressed in people clothing at the centre.

As children, Mary and I had snuck downstairs on Boxing Day—a holiday for workers to receive a box of goods from their employer, yes, but Mary's father had instituted this day for us so we would be of the people. This was how I felt at Diodati, the same trickle of tepid fear and excitement as I went room to room. Expectant—that was the word I repeated in my mind as I explored.

In the grand hall, the ballroom, the study with its haughty polished shelves with even more books I might read, all the fireplaces had been prepared for summer. Each one neat as a nun's closet, swept and most blocked by a fireboard to keep out wind or leaves. The music room had no such fireboard, and I was pleased to find evidence of the outside world in the form of a single blue feather. I crouched to pick it up and placed it in my pocket. Outside, it was day but not light, making my body feel the false relaxing pull of late afternoon, the room topsy-turvy with no specific orientation of time.

I preferred the rules of night to the order of day. At night people wore masks at balls, drank too much, said remarks they might regret later but due to the drinking might not even remember. The logic of nighttime allowed me to believe in my own heart I might find Byron in the music room. Perhaps composing a piece of music for me the way he had written me a poem. Never mind that he did not know how to write music.

I surveyed the rest of the music room. It was trying to be circular but had quit halfway through. A cornett shaped like a serpent rested on a stand. A peddle harp so gold and ornate in its carvings one wondered if entry to heaven came with its strumming. Near the windows sat a square grand piano. I went to it and pressed on the keys but not hard enough to make a sound. Was this how I would go through life, leaving no impact, no music?

I pushed off thoughts of nothingness and looked at the object in front of me.

Clementi & Co, black string cover, the entire thing decorated in gilt and cobalt painted flowers. Wood polished to a high sheen.

"Clementi and Mozart had a rather famous piano contest," Byron said. He leaned one hand on the top of the doorframe and kept his eyes on me as he spoke. I could see him clench his jaw as he moved away from the door and came closer to me. I felt that if I flinched he would retreat or evaporate right in front of me, a magic form I had conjured with my own letter so many months ago. Had I been so desperate that I had to write to a famous man?—it was hard to reconcile that Claire with my body standing here in the music room. If I could go back, would I still write it? None of the lot of us would have been there if not for my words.

"Oh?" I feigned nonchalance to buy time to recover from his presence as he moved still closer to me.

"The two men were virtuosos. Clementi was well admired. He toured for years, and when he reached Vienna, he realised Mozart had already claimed the place, in a manner of speaking." Here he turned to face me. Our eyes met, and I could not turn away from his face—the focus of his gaze, the slight tilt of his head, which asked me a question I could not hear, the parting of his lips, inside of which I knew his tongue lived and which I wanted between my legs. "After all, Mozart was held—and held himself—in the highest regard."

"He was perfection," I said. Mozart had died twenty-five years before, longer than any of us had been alive save Byron, who had been a toddler at the time. Surely I knew of his orchestrations. Yet I could not think of a single piece of music the man had composed nor call to mind any chords or sound at all when Byron stepped closer to me. Close enough that he could have touched my neck had he leaned forward with hand outstretched. But he made no motion to do so, and I stood with clenched groin, desperate for his mouth, his teeth, any part of him that would hold, grip, flick, stroke, invade my body the way his being had decamped into my mind since our meeting at the Drury those months before. Desire weighed more heavily on me than coldness or anger. I began to speak. "I miss—"

Byron cut me off. "Emperor Joseph II invites both men to play. A piano duel of sorts at a Christmas ball. Both men compliment the other and yet are in fierce competition." Byron again moved towards me. I could feel his breath as he spoke. "Clementi goes first. He plays a sonata. Mozart improvises on a theme suggested by the guests. With barely a thought the man hears their ideas, creates the notes in his mind, lets those wordless ideas come from mind—" Byron tapped his head, "to hands." He wriggled his fingers in such a way I swear I could feel them slip up my thigh and enter me. "And then days later Mozart is able to write down almost *exactly* what he had improvised. What a cunt. I say this as a jealous man."

He lowered his eyes away from mine. I was glad Byron was jealous. I wanted him to be jealous of anyone or anything near me—Mary for taking any of my time, the woods for calling to me, wild garlic for the time I had spent collecting and cooking it, Shelley for having gotten to me first in some ways.

"And are you—jealous?" I asked. "Of artistic greatness?"

"Yes." He paused. "And I hate myself for it." Byron quickly stepped away from me and I thought my heart would fly out of my body and drown itself in the lake. We would find it washed up on the shore with the odd white shells I had been collecting.

I asked. "Why must it always be a competition with men?"

"Because with men it always *is* a competition, Claire." I felt foolish.

"And what then?" I tried to steady my voice. If Byron was to leave the room, leaving me with the piano and blue feather for company, I would at least know the story. "Who won the duel?"

"They considered it a draw. The emperor gave Mozart fifty ducats, and the grand duchess did the same for Clementi. And both men appeared pleased." Byron stopped by the fireplace and looked at me. "The thing of it was that there had been a bet. A secret between the two royals and, though they professed equality at the ball, in private the duchess had to admit it—the emperor had been correct in his wager. Mozart was simply better. He would always be better."

"Still, they saved Clementi's reputation, if that was the point." I hoped Byron recognised the desire on my face and the sadness in my eyes at his impending departure. "There is a certain grace in that."

"Grace is never the point, Claire. And in fact, after a few weeks passed, Mozart wrote that Clementi had proficiency yet not passion. He called him 'a mere mechanic.'"

"And already we recall one man more than the other," I said. Byron turned to go. "Which would you rather be?" I asked, unable to bear his leaving. "The most skilled mechanic or the passionate genius?"

This stopped Byron. The large windows let in no midday light, casting his face in shadow. "Claire," he said. I knew the tone. His opening notes. I thought I would sprout wings.

I looked at the piano. "I shan't touch it."

"Do."

I shook my head. I knew well how to play. It struck me that I might be similar to this instrument—full of music and ideas that would never come out unless someone orchestrated it, pulled it out of me. Gave me pain. Still, I did nothing.

"If you wait for me to insist, you will wait a lifetime," he said.

I did not sit and play a sonata. I did not settle myself on the small stool and perform.

Instead, I whipped away from the instrument and rushed to him. The surprise worked in my favour, for he gave me barely a glance before reciprocating, his mouth on mine, our bodies pressed together there in shadowy daylight. Anyone could have seen. I imagined us as bass clefs, his fingers on my back dotting me with notes I would carry each day afterwards.

We were still attached at the mouth when a scream broke us apart. It was the sound of a child. The upper register of a girl. Byron held my shoulders with both hands, but we looked around the room. The scream came not from a girl but from a blue-grey bird with stick legs that appeared to have been drawn by the same child whose voice was emanating from its mouth.

"It's a bird," I said, which was a stupid thing to say yet merely what came out due to my surprise. I produced from my pocket the feather I'd collected. "I think it wants to be warm."

Byron did not think this puzzling. He did not tell me—or the bird—that we were ridiculous. Instead, he let go of my shoulders and with his own dragging foot went round the room collecting a throw from one chaise, a deep red woolen wrap that hung on the back of a chair, forgotten. It was not mine nor Mary's, but I could not dwell on that for Byron plucked all of the soft items in the room and swirled them into a floor nest, offered it with aplomb to the bird, who accepted readily. Thus satisfied, Byron turned back to me, offered me his hand with the same aplomb, and pulled me upstairs.

"YOU RESISTED for so long—"

He pulled the bedcover off. "Admirable, I think." He mounted me. I gripped his back, his buttocks, could not control my hands as they went from his body to his face.

"I have longed for this," I said. He thrusted.

"I resisted." Another thrust. "Yet when a girl of eighteen presents herself at night—"

"It is day," I said and cried out. No embarrassment. Only pleasure.

"Well, a man is a man and can only do so much."

"I did not present myself to you—" I felt the need to correct him. He had found me in the music room. He had initiated the reunion—hadn't he?

"Everything you do is a presentation to me."

His body felt every movement, each breath, the way I remembered. I would never be able to accomplish anything if I spent my days aching with desire, with lust. I tried to see Byron's face in the dim bedroom light, his eyes that held mine with a mixture of care and curiosity. He wanted to know I was with him in this moment.

And I was, but only partly.

For I knew the world to be bigger than only he. I thought of the agapanthus seed heads, tall and regal. I thought of dank green moss under my bare feet in the coppice. I thought of my own body. I thought of piano dueling men, who had laid claim to what first, who commanded ownership of the body I called mine. I willed away the days of drudgery with their cloth nappies, the one stubborn hook on my boot that needed to be repaired, the thought I might have a bit of ginger stuck in my back teeth. I kissed him and he put his lips on mine as he pushed deeper into me. I thought of Mr. Darcy—that line, *I was in the middle before I knew that I had begun*.

After the fervour, I tucked myself near him. "I feel sometimes I am too soft."

Byron put his hand on my face, pulled it down my neck, onto my chest. I thought he would grip harder but he refrained. "The wind might hurt you, Claire," he teased.

"I feel that way from time to time," I said, and willed myself not to cry, for I had wished for this moment for so long and then it was upon me and I knew not quite what to do with myself. "Would that I had some of my sister's steely nature. Mary is more even-tempered."

"She is more than even-tempered. She has no temperature at all. Butter would not melt in her mouth."

I sat up, unafraid of my nakedness, the fullness of my breasts, the slight plump of belly and hips, and reached for his hand. He regarded me with care. "I am moved by your tenderness, Claire."

Byron dozed, and I looked at each of his eyelashes to commit them to memory like a song of notes on a page. I wondered if what he found compelling was less my tenderness than my newness in the world. If what he desired was my youth. The parts of me he perceived to be unscarred.

Being eighteen was to wish never to age and also to wish at every moment to jump ahead. Often I felt both conflicting ideas at once. When Byron opened his eyes and looked at me, I felt he understood this—that he could slip a shadow form of himself in my mouth so that he inhabited my body. A sort of magic I found alluring, though I also knew it to be an elaborate form of narcissism. If he inhabited my body he could then be gazing upon himself, both younger and older at the same time.

Afterwards we talked long and low in the sheets and then had another round near the desk. Byron's ink stained the edge of my hand, my forearm as he laid me over the desk. I put my cheek on the writing surface and reached for him behind me. When he simultaneously gripped my hand and groaned I felt all powerful. I knew when he next sat down at that desk, no matter what words he wrote, that I would be everywhere in evidence.

4

MY THIGHS ACHED WITH the memory of the couple of nights before. How did my body come to relish such an odd concoction of pleasure and soreness? Each stair I descended brought Byron cupping my face, my hands on the smooth swim muscles of his legs, the constellation of freckles on his flank, his mouth on my ear asking *do you like this?* With a satisfied step, I picked up the post in the hanging basket and went out the door with a smile jam-coating my face as I went back to the cottage to change.

"Aren't you cheerful for such a dark day," Shelley said, his words kind while his gaze wandered over me. "I trust you slept well."

"I did, thank you," I said. The words came naturally, though I had never been a liar. He took another look at me. My wild hair could be blamed on the fine cold mist coming in from the water. Yet I was in the same dress as the day before. This was not entirely uncommon, but the morning was cold and this my lightest dress.

I stumbled to cover my tracks before Shelley could put the details together—surely I had come from Diodati. Surely, too, I wore the same dress. Therefore, I had spent the night.

"I chose the wrong dress for today," I said, tone overly bright. I gestured with the letters. "I reached the mail basket only to realise the chill—so here I am, back again. Silly me!"

Shelley held a pen over a page. The ink chose just then to drip. I pointed to it. "Yes, yes, silly you. You must go and wear something warm." He paused. "You know, Claire, men worry most about losing their abilities. A waning of talent." He looked at the blotched page. "The fear that each bit of work, each line, might be the last."

I knew what he needed, and I felt I had to give it. "You are far too powerful a writer to have the flood of words dry up," I said. "Do not worry about such things, Shelley."

"Oh, Claire. I am so grateful for you," he said. "What truly plagues me—in my darkest hours—is the thought of anything happening to those I care for." His look was a mix of tender and expectant.

"You are too kind," I said, and gestured with the letters again before rushing up the crooked staircase to my room to change.

HEADING OUT the cottage's side door to avoid Shelley, I could hear Mary pleading, "Take him lest I forget my words," and Shelley clomping his large frame around the too-small sitting room in objection.

By the edge of the drive, I felt in equal parts the desire to retrace every bit of my nights with Byron and the desire to read everyone's letters. I checked around. No one watched, but it was too risky. Out the gate I went, hurrying away from the imposing iron posts.

I clutched the letters and my thickest shawl, a deep-red knitted thing

I had made in Lynmouth. It did nothing for my complexion and little for the cold. The weather seemed to have woken from its sunny slumberous day and remembered it was furious with the world. I was glad I had decided against the boots Shelley had given me back in London. In fact, when I thought of their thin calfskin, the calf whose body had gone into the making of them, the gift—Shelley seeking out a present, watching a shopkeeper perform its fine wrapping and ribbon, how he had presented it to me in the London half-dark—I felt as though my brain itched. I could not scratch at the concern—had the boots been an apology? A barter?

As I walked, I grew more uncomfortable. A stinging in my folds. Too much pleasure with Byron and thus punishment. Truly there seemed so many variations one might make of two bodies—rather like flour and water and butter, I had told Byron, pastry crust and pound cake and crumble topping and kneaded bread, all with the same ingredients. I had learnt so much already from Elsa in the kitchen and more from Byron besides, and yet with pride I realised I had taught myself even more. The easy tug of wild garlic's slim roots, purslane salad, nettle tea and nettle cake. I made a list of flowers and plants spotted and studied, and I had begun folding over pages in the reference book as though it were mine.

The walk was thick with ivy and beautyberry winking at me as though it knew what I had got up to the night before. I thought about Byron. Not in his present-day state but as a child. How he had told me about having to drink curdled milk, sieving it through cheesecloth or muslin. I thought of his foot. Of his mother plied with drink and his nanny visiting his bed—this he had whispered to me with his face turned away. I thought of rancid bedclothes he had laundered himself. Surely this kind of hardship was meant to make one more compassionate to the plight of others. Others potentially weaker. I saw how, at his best, Byron would shield me to the marrow, a substance I had only learnt of from Polidori, who had crunched so hard on the lamb he was able to suck out the inside he deemed filled with iron necessary for us to survive. Byron had been born into misery, that was true. Shelley, too, had suffered at the hands of classmates.

Somehow both men felt this gave them permission to inflict similar pain on others as adults, using cutting remarks to prove their strength. Cows along the side of the road lowed and signaled I was nearly at the mail carriage. How startling the beauty of every day, even on the cold days. Perhaps part of my discomfort was not only the sting between my legs but the reconciliation needed; I was meant to revile the men who stood up against slavery and yet treated the everyday woman—I was the woman—as nothing more than curdled milk meant to be gulped down or filtered out.

I could hear myself telling these thoughts to Mary, waiting for her measured response. She would feel it was not a male issue but rather a woman's duty to adjust. I passed more cows, a row of cold-worn poppies that had half opened and then ducked back into their buds. I passed a small dog that looked like a fox and wondered if it was a small fox that was truly a dog. In each field I looked for my sister. I looked for my sister, for I felt a part of me wishing to break open—I could imagine her in the field, beckoning to me. We would admit to keeping secrets from each other.

Still, I also kept secrets from myself.

I looked for Mary in the field, though I knew her to be hunched over William, willing him to quiet while she made a messy attempt to write, quill tip dripping on the page, resentment and guilt building in her chest. I read her letter as I walked.

Dear Fanny:
I fear with weather turning we will be entirely confined to the house. This will not help my spirits which are in continuous need of bolstering. Still, when the weather is poor one does feel justification at tucking up inside. Here, the great windows face the lake, affording a view of impending storm.

I must work, Fanny. I fear, even at eighteen years, a part of me is withering. Has withered. Which tense to use in motherhood for one feels always caught part in the past, reflecting because the child changes so readily each day that one comes upon a new person each morning. And yet still one is always thinking of what stage is next—when will he crawl, speak, call for me with whatever name he uses. Mother, mama, mummy, ma. All words I never said.

Oh, Fanny—this place holds us all in a swathe of pre-storm. You ask how I am and my inclination is to give a rundown of how others are, as though I cannot discern completely my own state from theirs. I shall tell you this: CC's newfound outdoorsman skills give us a boost in food and, rather selfishly I confess, make her less of a problem for me. Shelley is most in his work—urged to the charge by Byron, who is able to make anything, even art, a sport of competition. And the doctor—he is uncouth, well-groomed, and quite dashing, though likely I find him thus primarily due to his competency around William. I try only to focus on this part of him for truly he has held, bathed, gotten the baby to sleep during ruinous thunder—and yet one must not reveal too much to him for it may well wind up in the gossip pages he sends to Murray.

One realises the imbalances in relationships. So many women are far prettier than their husbands are striking. Is this because the world is teeming with beautiful women? I think rather it is women lack the confidence to pursue the most handsome. Or perhaps this is catty of me and women have such depth they look beyond the surface and it is men who are shallow and care more for the exterior. Shelley the exception, I hope, for though I am guilty of looking-glass gazing on occasion, I wish I were not. He does not waste his time with hair irons or powders. I ought to be more manlike in this regard for I am at my happiest in two ways:

My First happiness is when William is first awake; his calm demeanor overtakes his whole body. His eyes focus on mine with such love. Such gratitude for fetching and feeding him. When he is in my arms this way and I am in charge of his nourishment I feel—how might I say it? I feel I have won. I feel I have succeeded. Then I feel the tiniest bitterness for this is what nature intended of me and not a skill or talent of my own making. I am merely a mother and no one receives a prize for that other than the well-being of the child.

My Second happiness is on side four of the page, after the start of a story (so many beginnings written with no followings) and before the terror which grips when one understands there is something trying to be said and feels panic about writing the story to completion.

Perhaps this is also like love. O Fanny all I know is that I am better when I write. One would assume I would remember this and see to my own care. Still the task or talent (both are true) falls by the wayside if there is anything else which needs attention. This thing which brings me joy and satisfaction is the last and hardest to come by. I pay in minutes and I am poor of time.

So why then spend time writing this letter instead of choosing time for the story I wish to write? For starters, I am quick with my pen. Shelley insists good writing takes more time. I do not disagree aloud. Yet I feel I write just as well with quick words as with slow. And more the reason to write to you, I crave friendship. Sometimes bitterly so. Claire is only useful in this regard when I can keep her nearby. She is drawn so to the woods, to the lake, to the villa, and I fear my arms are not long enough to bring her back to me. Do not scold me for my selfishness! For a girl can get lost—or worse—in the woods and Claire is as open to the world as a wound ready for lemon. Alas, William requires me just now so all love until later days. Affectionately Yours, Mary

So I was useful in Mary's eyes, and yet she would not give me the gift of saying so to my face. If she ever asked me directly, *What secrets do you keep, Claire?* perhaps I could tell her. Perhaps we would decide an agreed-upon truth.

The rumble from mail carriage dispersed these thoughts, and I gave a nod to the driver, who knew to wait for me to complete my task. I quickly read one from Shelley to Thomas Jefferson Hogg, compelled to take my mind from the stinging sensation in my Area of Distinction.

> *Hogg, dear Friend—*
> *You jest in your latest about my "two wives"—*

Here I paused and furrowed my brow. A cold wind picked up, swirling the road dust. The carriage driver leaned towards me with the fish glue. "Je ne peux pas attendre longtemps aujourd'hui, chère fille. Une tempête arrive." The driver grew already impatient. I presented a few scones I had secreted away and wrapped in a serviette I did not think anyone would miss.

Near the carriage wheel, a rabbit straight from a children's book like the ones my mother printed, with a bouquet of dandelions jaunty in its mouth. Our eyes met as I climbed into the carriage. I wanted to be that rabbit with delicious things to look forward to, Byron's mouth and body, a good hunk of bread and soft cheese onto which I would drizzle honey.

I wished I had not begun to read the letter, for it was a kind of poison.

> *You jest in your latest about my 'two wives.' Mary has seen your note and this caused a row the likes of which you have not seen. Hers is a temper best suited for ill weather, so perhaps this is the perfect setting for her as the bluster and rain torrents come out of nowhere. Still, her outburst could have been prevented had you been more of a gentleman in your letter. You carry bitterness, I think, that Mary never melded with you and your intentions.*

Shelley had been the one to push Mary towards Hogg. Hogg had been so sympathetic with Mary's mood following the death of the baby and the bloody aftermath that Shelley could not stomach. Hogg had been a gentleman then. What had he said in the letter? And had Shelley left it out in plain view, or had Mary scrounged and found it, suspecting something?

> *I realise I encouraged that failed liaison between you both but please, now refrain from a comment of wives, for I have only one, and that is Mary. That you suggest her sister to be the other wife was most disruptive. I shall not write her name here, but the girl is none of your concern.*

A fat rain droplet fell upon the open letter, causing the ink to run, Shelley's words partially ruined. Panic rose up in me. With great haste, I ducked into the mail carriage, used the hem of my dress in an attempt to dry the letter, which caused more mess. Using the fish glue to reseal Shelley and Mary's letters, I felt upset I could not speak to Mary about her own letter, nor had I the time to read Byron's and Polidori's, which promised—on the back—*headline enclosed*.

I jumped out of the carriage, the sting of shame in my groin and on my mind as I imagined Hogg receiving the letter and writing back with a quip about Shelley writing in the bath and causing more confusion.

The carriage sped away as the rain picked up, cold and heavy and unexpected. Shelley had been correct in his description of my sister's moods—changeable, their unpredictable nature leaving one exposed to sorrow or stabbing, which was the sensation I had then in my belly. As I walked in the ever-colder air, I began to shake.

How much went unsaid, unreported between all of us. I felt ill inside and out, my skin rippling with the treachery of Shelley's letter. And I would not know what Polidori's headline, now swiftly on its way to the publisher, contained.

My toes ached with cold. Rain slopped onto me. I was hit with recalling a night in Lynmouth: a storm, Shelley showing up at night with a currant cake, the sight of it slumped had sickened me. The chill increased. I felt such fatigue I thought I might lie down in the road and be none the worse for it, when quite suddenly Byron's ornate carriage appeared beside me.

5

"YOU'LL CATCH YOUR DEATH," Mary said, as she swung the door open for me. She had a way of expressing love in such a critical way I wondered if my mother had undue influence on her. Shelley held his hand out, which I refused, using the woven gold rope on the left side of the step instead, though it was soaked through.

I thought of Marianne Dashwood and quoted *Sense and Sensibility*. "*Though heavy and feverish, with a pain in her limbs, a cough, and a sore throat, a good night's rest was to cure her entirely*". Still, the characters in that novel hadn't been contending with vaginal woes in addition to being caught in a rainstorm.

"Do not speak of yourself in the third person, Claire," Mary said. "And also, rest is not the cure for everything—is that not correct, Dr. Polidori?" She said doctor as though it was synonymous with God.

Polidori was wedged between Byron and Mary, and when he responded to her in a not-quite but almost whisper, she tilted her head as though only the two of them were in the carriage. Byron and I shared a quick eyebrow raising. If Shelley noticed, he did not say. He looked mainly out at the passing landscape to avoid travel illness.

"There is always bloodletting, too," Polidori said. "Rest will not power over miasma nor over all infection. We do not know entirely how certain illnesses go from one person to the next, but I can assure you, Mary, your sister having been caught in the deluge poses no threat to you or your child."

I thought Mary would fling herself at the doctor. Instead she looked to Shelley to share her relief but found no willing receptacle from him.

"Claire is soaked through. She looks a fright," Shelley said.

I could imagine him writing about his ghastly sister-by-law in his next letter or poem—hair frumped into lazy waves, fabric sheer to my shoulders, the swell of my breasts easily visible through diaphanous muslin. His attention to my details was repellant.

"I am hideous, and I apologise," I said. Mary stared at me. Her mouth repeated the word *hideous* without sound.

Byron offered me a blanket, which only accelerated my heart. The wet dress stuck to my thighs. I wanted to leave the carriage. To walk in the rain alone or with Byron; better yet to have Mary cast William aside and look at me. Truly look at me and tell me what she saw.

Instead, I pushed my ill feelings all the way down to my sogged boots and used my knowledge as a deflector for my discomfort.

"Tell me, Polidori, do you know of Marcus Antonius von Plenciz? I read his book *Opera medico-physica* in the library." I looked at Byron as I spoke. He looked amused. "The book is old, yet he espouses a theory of *contagion*." I said that word carefully, for I had not said it before and Mary's father had made fun of us for mispronouncing words we had read but not yet said aloud. She had said *dem*-on rather than demon, and my mother had called her a little devil. "Contagion." Perhaps I would become a physician! I would take my place amongst the men and stethoscopes.

"Practitioners such as myself have our *own* bible," Polidori said, trussed with pride as he recited. "It is called *Domestic medicine; or, The family physician: being an attempt to render the medical art more generally useful, by shewing people what is in their own power both with respect to the prevention and cure of diseases, chiefly calculated to recommend a proper attention to regimen and simple medicines, by William Buchan, M.D.*"

"Has there ever been a more tediously named book?" Byron wondered.

Polidori gave me a pandering look and addressed the carriage. "Regardless of Claire's enthusiasm," he said the word as though it were a child's lolly, "those theories von Plenciz put forth have not been accepted by the scientific community."

"Still, we ought to have arranged transport for you, Claire," Byron said, casting a skein of kindness to me.

"We would have been here sooner had Byron not delayed our departure," Shelley said.

"Only due to working," Byron said. "The heavens opened, and I bled on the page."

"And you mixed metaphors," Shelley said.

"Still, headway with the third canto of *Childe Harold*," Byron said. He looked at me. "One never knows where inspiration will unfold."

I stung, I shivered, and yet I felt aglow with pride.

6

THE RAIN ABATED, REPLACED by an air of November, which did not help me stay in the moment, worried as I was about where we might be then, if Mary would have again grown tired of me, if perhaps I might be here alone with Byron and the menagerie.

We walked over cobblestones past Swain's Stationers, drapers, gilders with their hand mirrors to purchase as a summer souvenir, furriers doing brisk business what with the chill. Outside the modiste, Shelley paused in front of the large front window. He gave a furtive look inside that no one seemed to notice save for myself. I stepped into the doorway to peer closer.

"Do you require an article?" Byron asked. "Gloves?" He said the word which such familiarity and desire I thought everyone would know he had recently undressed me, leaving only my gloves on. And what then? What if they were to find out?

I shook my head. Behind the polished wood measuring table stood a young woman with thick auburn hair, her gaze intent upon us. The seller had made no attempt at covering the heavy freckles sprayed across her nose and cheeks—*Sommersprossen*, Elsa had told me, pointing to her own—but did look away when she saw Shelley focus on her. I looked at Mary, but my sister had her attention on Polidori, who appeared to be palpating William's head. Mary reveled in the medical attention. Shelley abruptly marched a few paces away from the modiste at the same time Byron was spotted; tourists began to point and giggle and inch ever closer to our group to try and hear us.

A steady line of curricles leading people away from town to their warm hotels or homes provided cover enough, and we ducked down a narrow passage through which the artist studio could be reached.

I felt sorry for my sister, who had chosen a man to love whose gaze would always be partly elsewhere. Not because I thought this wholly unnatural, for perhaps it is only in Netherfield one might find an exclusive devotion, but because Mary had told herself a different story as it pertained to her, as though she alone could claim Shelley's divided heart, his body.

She was wrong. I thought of Mary's letter, her need to write. How it might save her.

"Mary, are you working on something in particular?" I could ask this without giving away any ideas I had read her letter.

"I am," Mary said, brightening. To the others she said, "Claire provided a bit of fire for me." This caught me off guard, and I smiled, despite feeling unwell.

"Have you produced it?" Byron overlapped her.

"It is primarily in my mind," she said.

"Ah," Byron said, "the place where all writing is at its best."

"Still," Mary said, "I should like to try. I need time."

"We all need time, Mary. We also all need money," Shelley said, "and I believe this latest of mine will bring it."

"Time is currency," Mary said.

"Are you suggesting I take away your time?" Shelley asked. His tone was particularly male—pointed towards Mary yet jocular to everyone else.

As though understanding his mother's wish to write rather than be with him, William began to wail. Shelley gave a dramatic sigh, which Byron thwacked him for—a gentle punch on the shoulder, but it was enough to stop Shelley in his tracks. "I am allowed to sigh."

"He is a baby," Byron said.

"William or Shelley?" I asked. The joke slipped out and everyone laughed. Shelley fumed. William laughed and then screamed.

"He is hungry," Mary said. "Always hungry."

Polidori stepped in, ever her saviour. "Mary, I have seen a specialty pharmacy. Let us go together and purchase a bottle. That is my solution for you. Then any of us might feed him for you."

"Is it not more natural for a mother to feed her own child?" Shelley asked.

"That is one view," Polidori said in his office visit voice. "Yet the contraptions—the porcelain bottles—are small works of art and efficiency. For Mary's sake—I think useful in this instance."

I nodded encouragement. "Elsa has shown me where the cold storage is—I can warm milk for you."

"You do spend a good deal of time with the staff," Shelley said, and rubbed his shoulder from the thwack and crossed his arms, though it could not have hurt much.

"Is Polidori not also staff?" I asked. I had not meant it as an insult, rather more for my own armour. My teeth began to chatter slightly.

Polidori reddened but could not protest. I wondered if he filed away my words for more gossip reportage.

"After the artist studio, I should be more than happy to help you, Mary," Polidori said.

A grateful smile from her. "I should wish very much to have an hour—"

"She means two—" I said. My cheeks flushed with love for my sister and her determination to work. "And she ought to have it."

AT THE studio we saw slashes of first light on canvas, fruit in decline the artist had painted with such beauty it took a moment to realise the rot, women with cats and women nude but for gleaming sashes arranged just so, and a canvas longer than it was wide, filled so full of flower petals, whorls, and buds they reached around the edges of the frame. We were all drawn to it, my skin bristling with fever pricks. Were they only flowers? No. Underneath the flowers was a girl I had not seen upon first glance.

"It's rather a trick of the eye," the artist said.

"Beauty is a great distractor," Byron said.

I felt unduly sick at missing what had been right in front of me: a young woman stretched out in a puddle, limbs dotted with flowers. Byron bought the work and arranged to have it shipped to the villa. As I stood staring at the painted lady, I suddenly wondered if she was dead or merely asleep. Then I was falling, saying a sudden hello to the ground.

7

AFTER TOWN, I WAS too ill to move from Diodati to Maison Chapuis. Byron stationed me upstairs, tended to me—half man of lust, half nursemaid with henbane for aches, coriander broth for fever reduction. I cannot say I minded his dual form.

Fever had its grip on me. Byron brought me hot tea with too much honey, Elsa sent up a currant cake with cream I knew was hard to come by as the fields were not as green for the cows. Also nearby was a bouquet of flowers too neat to be only wild, and I thought someone had bought them from the luxe place in town. I woke once with my sister next to me. Her arm draped over me the way we had slept as children during storms. I turned to face her. Our noses pressed as she said, "I could not survive if you should succumb—"

I squeezed her hand. "I will be well, Mary. I promise."

"Very well," Mary said. "Then don't be stupid." Or perhaps I dreamt that, for I wanted to remind her she was not in the best position to give advice but could not form the words.

I dreamt of my coppice of trees, the calm cool dank of moss and dapple, the way my skin—even my scalp and toes—relaxed in the private realm. I longed for that safe soothe.

My journal appeared next to me. I knew not who had put it by my bedside with one of Byron's good pots of ink and fancy pens. I wrote in the missing hours and then slept.

8

A DELICATE TOUCH ON MY ankle. Another on my forearm. My neck. I lifted my head in a sleep haze and saw Byron, face clear in the moonlight. With a studious grace he plucked flower petals from the fancy bouquet and placed them on my body, which was unclothed though made modest by one of his silken robes—one sleeve across my breasts, another across my pelvis as though the robe itself were reaching for me.

I moved the fabric, and Byron held his gaze on mine. With tantalizing slowness he kept placing flowers all over me. This required a great stillness on my part—both because the blooms did not want to stay put and because all of his touching roused in me a desire for him to cover my body with his. Another on my belly. My hips. All along my collarbone as though I wore a gown sewn from fullest summer. He knelt on the bed next to me to reach the spaces between my fingers, and I kept entirely still except for my hand, which went to him. I began to stroke him, which dislodged some of the flowers and he gripped my breast. I was not entirely better from fever but so close I could not hold off my desire any longer.

I was half in, half out of the odd haze of not-quite-slumber that accompanies fever. Not enough to deny myself or Byron the leisure of the encounter, but not fully in it either. In the back of my mind I was writing about the moment as it was occurring. It was possible women were never fully in their bodies, always feeling them looked upon by others, evaluated for meatiness or beauty; even upon joining with another body there was the sense of being elsewhere. Not far off, but not there on the bed.

Afterwards, he slept. I cleaned myself off but not before seeing in his looking glass my body still flower-covered, hair long and a mess. I thought I looked beautiful. The trick perhaps was to see oneself at the exact point of someone else's desire and hold it. Someone who was honest in their adoration.

I allowed myself to stand in the moonlight regarding my physique and Byron's decorating of me. Then I thought of the painting he had purchased. Byron liked art and had made me into it. I wondered if I would have a permanent place in his writing, in his world, the way he wished the world to always know him. As I picked out petals from my hair, I wondered about Ophelia and whether if someone had come upon me in the bed covered in blossoms I would have looked gorgeous or dead.

9

I COULD FEEL THE FEVER still had slight hold of me. Still, I could not bear being stuck in the room a minute longer. A note on the pillow: *Gone on an excursion to Castle Chillon—back soon. X LB*

With shaking hand I held the brass candle plate, the slim light guiding me down the side staircase to the housekeeping staircase and then to the music room. One of the housemaids was already at work, scrubbing the grate, which meant there had been a fire, life continuing on without me. I was glad Byron and I had rescued the large blue bird before it met its singed death. The maid doused a rag with oil and then used emery paper for a full clean. When she reached into her bucket for brick dust, she saw me and gave a head bow.

"Do not trouble yourself," I told her. My voice was different. Perhaps illness and knowledge of my own body gave me wisdom. Still, I felt fairly floating as I watched her continue her work, brushing the pieces with black lead, washing the deeply veined marble hearth with such tenderness I thought I might cry. At last she pulled from her pinafore a clean linen cloth and used it to sop up the water. She rose and gave a quick curtsy. The show was over.

I felt a further chill. I knew I ought to go back to bed yet did not have the strength to climb the stairs and—worse—worried I would lie in bed all day without Mary slipping a note under the door to say hello. I worried Byron would cease checking on me, would not tend to me the way the housemaid had gone over each part of the fireplace so carefully.

So I tucked myself on the velvet settee, pulled a fur over my lap, and rested my head on my hand and my hand on the arm of the furniture. My feet touched something warm and soft. I picked up my head, at first astonished and then happy to find the blue bird and its puffed out belly roosting on the other end. I admit I bid it good morning.

"Shall I remove him for you, miss?" asked another housemaid. From her wrist swung a short-handled tinderbox, the linen tongue darting out like a jester. I must have given her a look of confusion. "The bird, miss."

"Oh, no," I managed in an odd whisper. "Please leave him." The bird and I exchanged a look. I was glad he was not a fever dream. Glad, too, that I still had his blue feather in my dress pocket. The dress draped over the chair in the bedroom. The bedroom with the bed that had consumed me and Byron so recently our shadows and imprints seemed housed there. "This is . . ." I paused. "Gerald."

The maid did not introduce herself to the bird, and I could not fault her for that. Instead, she struck flint against steel and lit the fabric tongue on fire. Gerald and I watched in fascination as she dipped a match in sulphur and used the light to ignite it all. Everything seemed gorgeous and nested with feather sheen and velvet, perfectly clean marble and a flower petal still slicked to my bare ankle, Gerald's large eyes liquid amber and the whole room feeling to me as though it were about to be set on fire.

Byron appeared at the door. "Shelley ruined the outing," he said, and did not elaborate. Instead, he shepherded me upstairs to bed.

10

I AWOKE, FEVER FREE, TO a changed world. Dark at noon and nightswill by two, everyone hunkered over pages in the study, each either not registering my presence or giving me a finger-shake that meant do not disturb lest they lose their words. I wafted room to room, a spectator ghost in the midst of geniuses.

I settled in front of the largest fireplace at Diodati with a slab of bread thick with butter that Elsa had brought up herself. With warm flames and full belly, I must have nodded off again. When I lifted my head, the others had taken places in the room with me. Shelley sealed a letter and put it with one from Mary into the post basket, which only made me curious as the fairy Puck.

Polidori took Byron's pulse; I wondered if he had been ill, too.

A figure came into the room—I recognised the ruddy-cheeked, auburn-headed girl from the shop in town—and displayed to Mary a sleeping William in the crook of one arm and an elaborate blue-and-white porcelain bottle in the other. The object was the key to Mary's freedom. The girl had a pleasant and competent affect.

"Thank you, Elise," Mary said, and accepted her sleeping baby like a pile of laundry on her lap. I raised my eyebrows to Mary. "This is Louise Duvillard," Mary said. "Called Elise. Shelley hired her." A kindness on his part, I thought, and yet could not help but notice the girl's attractiveness. With a wave of Mary's hand, Elise was dismissed. Mary went back to work.

The sound of pen nibs on paper accompanied the wind and side-slanting rain.

"A symphony of poor weather," Polidori said. He looked pleased with his choice of words and jotted them down.

Byron looked up from his pages, gave brief notice to the world outside as candles flickered on his desk. "We have all we need at Diodati, do we not?" He looked at me as he said this, and my whole chest felt full as though he were the lake and I had been immersed in him. I put my hand to my heart so nothing would leak out.

And then Mary screamed, which made William wake and cackle like a demon baby.

Mary clutched William to her chest. "Why is there a bird on the sofa?"

I looked. "Gerald?"

"You've named him?" Byron asked, amused and pleased. "Of course you have." Byron sprung to action. "He's cold, Mary, and so we will warm him."

Mary glared at Shelley. "Wildlife does not belong inside," Shelley said.

"And this from Sir Vegetarian," Byron said.

"Birds do harbour diseases," Polidori said, backing not so much Shelley but Mary, who hunched over William.

"I shall take you to town tomorrow," Polidori said to Mary in his dulcet doctor tone—decisive and pandering both. "We shall get William inoculations."

"Against birds?" I asked, and fought back laughter. Byron gave in, guffawing.

"Against illnesses," Polidori said. He reached out to touch William's head. Mary could not have looked more grateful if Polidori had pulled her from the guillotine. I lifted Gerald and put him on my own lap, away from Mary. This settled her a bit.

"Have you interest in things medical, Claire?" Polidori asked. It was clear he could not fathom such.

"We did rather enjoy odd scientific experiments as children," Mary offered.

"Shocking frogs," I explained. "Yet truly I found my first suggestions in novels—have you read Fanny Burney's *Camilla or a Picture of Youth*?"

"More of your drivel, Claire," Mary jabbed. "For it is the same category as *Sense and Sensibility*."

It was a novel of sisters, one sweet natured, another lovely, one heady in affairs of the heart and Lavinia, terribly scarred from smallpox. I recalled reading the book in a day while Mary had been out with Shelley. A thought crept in that perhaps Shelley had given it to me, and I wondered if it had been a consolation for being told to stay in our room while he and Mary went to her mother's grave for their first consummation.

"Is that not the novel with characters called Indiana Lynmere and Edgar Mandlebert?" Byron asked.

Mary turned to him. "I am surprised you know of it."

Byron set his quill aside. "I know it only because it was popular and ridiculous, perhaps not in that order."

"And yet you remember it well," I said, "which is the point."

Byron stood and came to pet Gerald, which brought him close enough I could feel his breath on my chin. I looked up at him and wondered if Byron would make an excuse for us to take our leave. He did not.

Everyone turned back to their pages, with Mary's hand flying. The more Mary wrote the more the air around her crackled with energy. To be near her was to experience a frenetic dance of pen on paper; she was happier then than at any other time I looked to see if Shelley noticed this—either he did not or did not wish to admit it.

Luncheon was set out—limp greens between fresh bread, marmalade I knew to be from the year before, all of the food scrounged and scarce. I would need to forage to keep us well-fed. The men went to tuck into their plates, half-heartedly interested.

Mary and I were left with dwindling embers and desultory conversation, the combination of which made me colder than truly warranted.

11

An oddly gorgeous day of creamy June light upon us, I stood in the window of Byron's bedroom and flung open the drapes only to hear him moan—a shiver of dread went through me as I worried he would discard me again. But no. Not a sound of dismissal. Not passion. Only regret for having had more than his share of wine the night before. We took tea quietly and went downstairs with ten minutes between us so as to give the appearance of coming from separate rooms.

Downstairs, Polidori had his hands on Shelley's chest with the stethoscope: medical and yet so intimate I had to look away, for there was nothing Shelley enjoyed more than being tended to, fussed over. Mary looked pleased as punch, posture be damned as she hunched over her pages, William and Elise nowhere to be seen. Byron wrote.

All felt peaceful, and I thought perhaps I might try my hand at writing a story, not revisiting *The Idiot,* but something new. I moved to the desk by the window, staring out and wondering if I might make an excuse to wrap up in a heavy cloak and visit my trees and write there. I could trace the path there with my eyes and longed for it. I needed the envelopment of dappled light, the sweet scent of stone pine and damp needles and old bark. I was so taken with the idea of my coppice as a haven that I had not looked at the lake, but when I did, I gasped.

"A most peculiar thing," was all I could say, for the lake had sucked up its own water, and the skies went dark. Byron came to my side.

"I'll be damned," he said, so softly it was as though his voice had been swirled up in the lake, which was roiling in its water tunnel.

The window glass shook. The doors between the entryway, sitting room, and living rooms all slammed one after the next in an angry round of applause. Something smashed, and a muffled grunt followed. Another door slammed. Mary gave a yelp, which alerted William. His high-pitched howl from the next room mixed with another burst of wind that rattled the windowpanes with so much force I thought they might shatter.

I moved quickly to help close any open windows. Shelley followed. Polidori pushed a snaked velvet coil under the front door to block the seam as though the air outside were poison. Elise came in, her pretty face confused, her round form all in a dither, and handed the baby off.

Mary unwrapped William's swaddle, whereupon his arms and legs stretched out in surprise, a tiny sea creature on land, unsure until she rewrapped him and carried him away, leaving Elise.

Amidst all this clatter and banging and scurrying breakage, Byron sat unmoving in the quickly diminishing light. Outside the sky went darker still, seemingly black in an instant. Still Byron did not rise to help nor seem moved by the noises or clatter.

I ran from one place to another, securing papers under the weight of the blotter or the heavy-handled knife-sharp letter opener. Polidori's face went red with effort as he traversed the wide rooms closing each door. Shelley's pale chest heaved as he used old newspaper to sweep and collect shattered glass. All the while Byron perched on a footstool, either knowing his bad foot would make him of little use rushing or—it seemed to me—enjoying being the calm, unmoving thing in the centre of the storm.

He regarded us with a strange curiosity. His beautiful face might as well have been carved of marble. The room quieted quickly as the lake sank back into its own belly and again became water. Total darkness outside. Byron stood, methodical in lighting the many candles in the room before taking a spot on the scroll-armed couch. He gave a quick glance at me, and I went to sit by him. Mary came back in and put her hands in prayer under her cheek to show she—not Elise—had gotten the baby to sleep. Elise seemed to take note of everyone's comings and goings, a quiet figure in the corner.

I felt choked on the sudden silence.

"One cannot underestimate the effect of weather on mood," Polidori said, as though anyone had asked.

Byron ignored him. "I have completed my *Childe Harold* canto." He gave my thigh a surreptitious stroke—we would celebrate later. "It is a mess of scratches and cross-outs, but it is complete."

Shelley stuck out his hand to offer congratulations, but to me he looked bereft. "Lucky you to have been caught by the muse." He flicked his eyes my way.

Byron did not take his bait. "There is no such thing as a muse, only an *a-mused bouche*."

"SO NOW that my work is finished," Byron said, "We shall play a game." He clapped his hands. The lack of our response made it appear that we knew not what a game was. This peeved him. "Fine. I shall begin. Life Raft."

Elise furrowed her brow, confused. Byron rushed through the rules. "Dark waters. Boat. Each player must explain whom they select to shove off."

"But why?" Elise's voice was clear but soft. I wondered if she had used the same voice as a couturière, if Shelley had approached her because of her pretty face or because he had wanted to buy Mary a gift.

Polidori, attempting a manly rescue, nodded. "Yes, what purpose has Life Raft? Are there insufficient cork vests for floating? Food rations? Why are we throwing people overboard?"

Byron sneered. "You do have a way of making everything deconstructingly dull, Polly."

The doctor deflated, but in a demure way as though Byron had given him a shy compliment. It seemed the crueler Byron was to Polidori, the more Polidori hunched his shoulders, sank in on himself, which then made Byron in his elegant suit and perfectly tousled hair even sharper—slick oil portraiture come to life.

Elise tucked a thick swathe of dark-red hair behind her ears and nodded, taking instructions seriously, studying all of us. Perhaps she did the same when she wasn't observed.

Mary gave more consideration than I would have thought to a silly game and said, "Of course I choose Shelley to remain first, but Byron's legacy requires him to be saved, and Polidori can—in theory—keep William safe." She paused, beaming at the doctor. "He says he is not by any means an expert in matters of infancy, but he has a gift." And then, matter-of-fact, she said, "Which leaves Claire. Sorry, dearest." She brightened. "Still you're a fine swimmer."

I went cold as my limbs hit the fake water. I recalled the waves on the ship crossing from England. The murky wet of sweat-soaked night terrors. I would be cast out again.

Byron, seeing my dismay, offered a veiled support. "Your sister seems to have a soft spot for curmudgeons," he said to me.

"Let me be clear: A man who is curmudgeonly is granted that name, whereas a woman with the same tendencies is called ill-tempered," I said. No matter what, I was unable to forgo defending my sister. Mary allowed a smirk, and with that, I forgave her as I always did. And then loathed myself for it.

Polidori spoke up. "I should think we need to be practical in the life raft. As such, my employer remains," he turned a sycophantic gaze to Byron. "Shelley is a father, Mary has a child, so Claire—you're overboard again, I'm afraid."

"You sound a little too happy with that pronouncement," Shelley said. "I shan't participate in this folly." He set his eyes on mine. In them I read *I will not abandon you. I shall keep you in the boat, night-churning waves be damned.* I looked away, wishing he would do me no favours.

"It is ungentlemanly to sit out the game," Byron said.

Shelley sighed. "I should not wish to choose." Mary stabbed him through the face with her eyes, and he reneged. "Mary, of course, it's always been Mary I should save. I shall say no more."

"I should say you're all trapped," Byron announced. "I would save myself and jump in, for I have swum great distances before and wish not to be indebted to anyone."

"Other than the banks," Shelley said. Byron flicked his fingers at him in mock hurt.

I must have sighed or made a sound, for Byron cleared his throat and looked at the still-dark sky outside. "If the weather brightens in the next day or two, I shall journey to the brilliant Madame de Staël's estate—and bring Claire with me." He had not asked if I should want to meet the famous *salonnière*. Still, I jumped at being asked. When would I stop being agreeable?

The game seemed finished, attentions fading.

"Ought I join your outing, too?" Polidori asked.

Byron brushed him off. "You have said you will take Mary and the child for inoculations."

Polidori grumped, for he could not have both loves in his sights. I ought to have been pleased about Madame de Staël-Holstein, famous for her writing, her fine mind, her famous salons. But I felt deflated from Life Raft.

Shelley stood, towering over me. "And you, Claire? Who remains in your life raft?"

This caused everyone to stop their chatter. In the firelight, they turned to me, suddenly interested. For while I might be swimming around alone, they all wore shawls woven from self-centredness. Though they would never admit it, they wanted to know where they stood with me. A surprise burst of anger filled me, and I clutched my belly.

I did not give them the satisfaction. "I should keep only FF," I said, and held the dog's big, dumb, sweet face. FF licked my cheek in gratitude. Let them all swim, I thought. Though I suddenly remembered Shelley knew not how to swim. He would drown.

12

In the morning's dawn, Mary met me outside my room with William asleep in her arms. I'd had a night without Byron, wound in my own sheets tracing back over the game—no one would save me. My sister and I stood in the soft quiet. "Shelley is desperate to keep up with his lordship," Mary said.

I whispered, "What is less compelling than men racing to keep up with other men—and in poetry of all things!"

Mary put her arms around me. "You mustn't feel bereft about the life raft, Claire. You know in my heart I should throw everyone over and keep you by my side." I sighed into her hair. "And if I did have to throw you over," she whispered, as Shelley coughed from his bedroom,

"I should always offer you my hand." She paused and pulled back. "So long as you would allow me to pull you up rather than tugging me into the water with you."

~

THE WALK to my coppice in the mist-dark had been eerie in the lantern light, but once I had spread folded hessian on the cold ground and sat in the stillness, I relaxed. It was an odd home but one I had made for myself. I scrounged and went to Elsa with wild celery and fennel bulbs.

"Early morning is my most favourite hour—before the day has disappointed me," Elsa said. "It might surprise you how many folks are awake and about at all hours."

The truth was that I did not know who went where or when. I felt myself watched, yet knew not whose eyes I felt upon me. Byron tended to be awake all night, Polidori chased after Mary, Shelley lurked, and Elise appeared with William around any corner at any hour, helping to quell Mary's heavy moods.

Elsa accepted the celery. "Ah, good. Salad for dinner. I've skinned a rabbit, so perhaps a stew."

After I helped her wash the stalks, she regarded my dirt-streaked dress and sent me to change, for she knew I was headed to Madame de Staël's and thought I ought to put myself together. "Am I not enough like this?" I asked in order to make her *tsk tsk*, which she did.

"Ah, if only the world would welcome a useful girl," she said. "Go—and I promise something for your bathing efforts."

~

CLEANING DID feel effortful, even in Byron's familiar bath: washing face and ankles, each dirt-rimmed nail, tepid grimy water sluicing until my skin was free from muck. My naked body was the same and not the same. For I had lived inside it my whole life, and yet there was a tremendous loneliness within the body, its functions that were either necessary or shameful, the feeling that no one would know my body the way Byron had, and yet anyone seeing or touching my body also felt like a betrayal, as though I'd revealed too much.

From the few items that had migrated from cottage to villa, I chose my cleanest dress. When I returned to Elsa, I set about chopping the celery into thin and even pieces. From my position near Elsa's work station, I could hear rumblings from outside and—when Elsa made a motion for me to stop my chatter—could hear conversation. Polidori and Mary. William babbling intermittently.

"After all, he will need them to travel," Polidori said.

Elsa gave me her hands as a question. I pretended to jab her arm. She nodded.

Polidori went on. "Napoleon's sister mandated vaccination for all newborns and adults—clever woman."

"And I?" Mary asked. "Am I, too, a clever woman, doctor?"

We could not hear his answer, for horses clomped and into town they went.

"She is so different from you," Elsa said without specifying. I nodded, sad for the part of myself who still wished to be like my sister. "She lives inside—you are out in the world?"

This cheered me—for here I was, cutting food I had found, about to meet a strong and powerful woman, who would see me with Lord Byron and consider me his equal, though I was so young. "Are you in the world?" I asked her. She nodded, a flash of sorrow on her face as I sliced fennel.

"I will be. I should like to have everything in order before summer ends." She paused. "Never you mind my departure."

Lucky for my fingers, I had set down my knife. I did not wish to show that her words pained me. We stood with a plate of warm ginger biscuits between us and, upon her urging, I told Elsa about Life Raft "Truly," I said, "I am a foolish girl to complain about such trivial matters."

"If I had played, I should have kept you in the boat." She quelled my skepticism. "For you can forage—"

"In the ocean?"

"You have a heart the size of the lake," Elsa said. I thought perhaps I had never known such kindness. How I wished she would embrace me and let me cry, though I was not quite sure of what I would say when she asked what made me so upset.

I opened my mouth to tell her how grateful I was, how hers were words I needed, but the biscuits had given me a bellyache.

I SAT with Elsa until Byron found us, scolded me for hiding in the service rooms, ignored Elsa, and took two biscuits. He studied my dress. "Did you wish to change?"

"I have done so already," I told him. "I have no others."

He frowned. "You will not fit into your sister's clothes—"

"Shall I dress in yours?" I asked, recalling one night in London when I had donned a man's suit and he had been ravenous with desire.

"Touché," he said. "Still, go trade frocks with Elise." As though she had been conjured, the girl appeared. Byron snapped his fingers. "We must leave if we are to arrive before dark—it is already and always dark. Make haste, Claire." Byron waved his hands between her dress and mine, and off we went to trade without query.

I TWISTED out of my frock and handed it to her. Elise gave me the courtesy of not being offended at the intimacy of donning an item still warm from another person's body.

"We are not exactly the same true size," I said, "but close enough." Her dress was lime-coloured with elegant vandyked edges which distracted from the garment being a bit too short. She looked different without William to hold and in my maroon dress. We looked cousinly.

"Miss Clairmont, I never said whom I should choose in that horrid game," she said, with her back to me so I would close her buttons. "I should choose you, I think, for you have the most life ahead of you." She turned to face me.

"Thank you for that—I was only just eighteen in April."

Elise's face brightened. "I am also in April, but three years on from you. April 28th." That our birthdays were so close ought not to have meant anything, yet somehow it made us look even more similar.

"Thank you," I said to her. "For the dress. Byron ought to have asked you without presuming."

"No," she shook her head. "He ought not to have told you what to do in the first place."

13

THE OPULENCE OF BYRON'S carriage did not quell my stomach rolling about in anxiety. I felt I ought to have with me a passport to leave Diodati. The longer we stayed in the villa, the more it became a country inhabited only by us and with no precise government. To leave the environs gave me a sense of freedom I was not sure I wanted.

In the first hour, Byron dozed. I looked out the window and then used the ornate bourdaloue. In the second hour, his hand lolled on my lap, I felt stirrings of desire, and we engaged in a decidedly uncommon use of the interior handrails. Before the third hour, we approached the high-walled grand entrance and fierce gate of Chateau Coppet.

Madame de Staël's manor house was painted pink and was entirely symmetrical, with an arched doorway in the centre surrounded by window after window, left wing and right wing stretching the building out in elegant fashion. We passed informal gardens, and when we walked up the steps—Elise's dress rustling on the stairs—we were greeted by a large staff.

As we entered a space as big as my coppice of trees and with ceilings just as tall, Byron whispered, "She is brilliant of mind, average of face, and she will not be fond of my carriage, for she detests Napoleon and is approximately a hundred years old."

I thought back to what I knew of her. "Was she not born in 1766?" I did the maths of ageing; women seemed to become decrepit sooner than men of equal years.

Anne Louise Germaine de Staël-Holstein, philosopher, political progressive, was a popular *salonnière.* I knew she had hosted everyone from Thomas Jefferson to Lafayette to Thomas Paine. She was famous for serving far too much food to foreign dignitaries, heavy wine to liberals, engaging noblemen in philosophical theory they could hardly keep up with.

Byron pulled me back towards his chest before the door opened. "I am glad of you, Claire."

My heart soared.

MADAME DE Staël's formidable face betrayed no emotion. She had wide-set eyes, a tall forehead and taller hair, and a beauty that at its peak would have been described as handsome—and likely she would not have shown emotion about that, either. Her reputation—wit, gravitas, and ferocity of intellect—assured that she would be remembered for her writing rather than her looks. I had no idea how a person built that sort of reputation, for it seemed as though adults arrived in their adulthood fully formed and I had only just begun to acquire bricks.

"You have outdone yourself," Byron said when the last of the dishes was set before us at the table. "This is a magnificent feast." She responded only with her eyes—a flick to say *eat.*

"As you know," she said, "Napoleon prefers boiled beef and chicken fricassee, which he ate for breakfast." This made my stomach turn. I took a mint leaf to chew to quell the discomfort. "So I give you the opposite."

She gestured to the array on offer. Wine, coffee with cream, trout with tomato sauce, stewed cardoons, watercress in aspic, snipes in savoury jelly, braided bread dotted with currants, sliced bread neatly upright on silver racks, prunes in brandy, heaps of mushrooms from which rose a garlic and shallot scent, and roast woodcocks with the head attached so they appeared to be roosting on the platter.

I did not think I could eat for the shock of such a mass for three people. Who had foraged for the watercress, for the mushrooms?

"Miss Clairmont," Madame de Staël said, "help yourself, for no one ought make a plate for a woman except herself."

Her voice was smooth and lilting, and I wondered if she had managed to say and write so many daring things in her life precisely because she carried herself so perfectly. Tone, posture, collar, hair—not a thing out of place. Still, she had managed to anger Napoleon enough that he'd banished her, and she had not backed down. I admired her strength. She arranged a good-sized portion of fish and mushrooms. Byron took notice.

"I like a woman who is not afraid of a good meal," he said.

"I like a man who keeps no opinion of what or how much a woman eats," she said in French, which I understood but Byron did not. I bit my lip to keep from laughing.

I said, "Byron knows Latin, Greek, Italian, and Armenian—"

"Ah, only the Italian provides any jolly—if only you knew French, my lord, perhaps you would have better humour," Madame said.

"Never have I had complaints about my *humour*," Byron said, "in any language."

Byron tucked into his plate. I saw how quickly he devoured his mushrooms. I still had not managed a bite but said, "I see you are fond of the champignons. I shall try to recreate this dish."

"Are you . . . do you enjoy cooking?" Madame de Staël asked. "I have never known my way around a game bird or a receipt."

Byron chewed and washed his mouthfuls down with wine. "Cla—Miss Clairmont is a keen learner," he said. "She is curious, and this alone makes for a wonderful student."

"And just what are you teaching her, my lord?"

AFTER LUNCH, Byron and our host discussed his work at length, and then Byron excused himself to read and respond to a letter Madame had received from François-René, vicomte de Chateaubriand, whom he greatly admired.

Madame's staff presented a thick wedge of cream cake dotted with candied violets and dusted with sugar crystals dyed blue. I could not take my eyes from the sight—how had they dyed the sugar? I would have to ask Elsa.

How adult I felt, being engaged in conversation with her. "Shelley preaches free love, and Byron believes in it wholeheartedly. Indeed it is a concept not unfamiliar to me, as my childhood home was filled with it."

"Free love is a farce," Madame said, as she touched only the tines of the tiny fork to the cake. "Women will ultimately pay the wages for the 'sin' of free love." She spelt sin with her fork. I had been so excited to be included in the radical concept of free love that I had never once stopped and thought about the divide that existed within it.

I had spent so much time foraging, alone in my coppice, conversing with Elsa about seedlings and Grandma Sugar, defending myself to the group of writers far more skilled than I, that I had turned quite wild. I had forgotten the human girl I was supposed to be.

"May I ask . . . when is the age one feels a becoming has happened?" I swallowed hard. I was neither the girl I had been on Skinner Street nor the one on the elopement or in Lynmouth, not even the one I had been when first I went to the Drury Theatre. A girl and a half. I lived in the netherworld of in-between.

"Ah," Madame said. "We wish so fiercely to abandon the girls we used to be. Impossible." She touched her thick Jacquard dress. "Quite a heavy burden. For how might a girl know who she is to be whilst being judged the whole time?"

She did not answer her own question.

"If one looks closely one finds signatures attached to more than treatises." She cast a glance to where Byron had sat at lunch. "Or poems. Marks on the floor from the chairs, a scar on the body, the carriage track—each room I have entered, book I have held and folded a corner. Each mouth I have kissed. *Personne n'a contrefait ma signature, j'ai signé moi-même*. There is no forgery. Even as a young person, one leaves a true mark—or is written upon."

She turned her watery blue eyes to me and cocked her head as she studied me and I took another piece of cake. "My dear," she said. "Perhaps you've had enough cakes."

"I disappoint you with my appetite," I said.

Madame cocked her head. "There is great freedom to be found when one has disappointed everyone around them."

"I'm afraid no one has any expectations of me," I said.

"Then the only person you will disappoint is yourself." She moved my cake plate out of my hands.

I took it back. "I think Byron likes me as I am."

"Byron likes everyone as they are for a short period of time."

My heart bled on the silk settee. "And then?"

She did not respond to my question but posed one of her own. "Is he your first?"

I did not know quite how to respond. My mouth stitched itself shut like the doll Mary's father had made us.

"I see," Madame said, and gave me a look of such great pity that my stomach soured as we stood up. She motioned for someone to fetch Byron and his carriage. "It is growing late. Let me give you a piece of advice I do so hope you find useful." I gave her my best listening face. "Men do not change, Miss Clairmont. "They merely unmask themselves."

14

On the way back, a soft rain thrummed the carriage windows. I felt surprisingly sick from the twisting roads. This made me feel girlish and weak, so I kept my discomfort to myself. I was so good at hiding any poor feelings.

Madame's estate was only outshone by the salons she had hosted over the years. She had poise and the sharpest mind, was admired by all—save Napoleon—and yet I did not envy her. For it seemed exhausting. All around me I had examples of what—whom—I might be. I could toil in obscurity as an artist or revel in infamy as a writer or find employment or study though I would not be allowed a degree. Or I could be like Mary, not quite one thing or another. If she desired fame she did not show it. Perhaps Elsa's position was best, though I thought if I said this to her she would tell me hers was not a life based on choice. To which I replied—in my imagination—do I have a choice? For it seemed as though I had been raised to think I did and told that I did, but when it came right down to it, I did not feel I had any say. I had so many voices telling me how I ought to be I could barely hear my own.

In the carriage, Byron's pale face came alive in the plummy night. I thought of the girl who had journeyed to the Drury, how all she had wanted was to meet him, and then to have him. I had done both. And I had even won him back. As we approached Diodati my success faded, for I realised I was indeed a foolish girl—I knew not what might come after the winning.

The teeth of the gate against the last remains of light in the sky marked our return. The chimneys sprouting from Diodati looked like horns. The entrance was illuminated by lanterns Fletcher had set out for our late return; Diodati seemed to welcome us into its mouth.

"Come inside with me," Byron said, his voice warm. "The day has worn me down—and you, too, from the looks of it." He gave a gentle, loving sweep of his palm on my cheek and led the way to the staircase.

Only, just as we began to climb, Shelley's hulking form appeared on the stairway landing. "Look what the night dragged in," he said.

"Shelley." Byron's voice was flat—he did not scold Shelley for being in Byron's private space, but his usual jocular tone was absent.

"You were gone a long time," Shelley said. He took one stair, then the next, moving awkwardly as though controlled by marionette strings. He got closer to me. Close enough to jab one of his long pale fingers to my breast bone as he said, "One would think you had deserted us, so long did we wait for the sounds of carriage wheels on the drive."

Byron took the steps as fast as his bad foot would allow, interrupting the space between Shelley's body and mine.

"I can see you are not yourself," Byron said. For the first time I looked at Shelley's eyes. They were unfocused and meandering. I recognised the look from Byron's house in London.

"You know laudanum doesn't agree with you," I said, though I knew no such thing. All I knew was that Shelley expected me to tend to him, to show I cared more for his well-being than whatever hours I had given to my excursion today. Shelley's lingering gaze on my face was the same one I had known since first he'd appeared in my doorway at Skinner Street—an unspoken question on his lips. I cowered behind Byron as a chill crept over my skin.

Out the large window the clouds gave way to an odd blue sliver of moon, the three of us held in its light. Shelley pushed his upper body towards me while Byron tried to lead me away. I felt I had no choice but to acquiesce as I'd always done.

"Come, Shelley, let me settle you," I said. Byron raised his eyebrows, surprised and displeased. "We shall return to Maison Chapuis, and I shall make a brew of chamomile and fennel dust to ease you to sleep."

Shelley rested a big hand on Byron's shoulder. Byron's face remained fixed.

"You always did know just how to settle me, Claire," Shelley said. He loped down the stairs, and I had no choice but to follow.

15

IN THE BARE SLIP of morning, everyone else asleep, I read Mary's letter first.

Dear Fanny,

I trust this letter finds you well. Likely you have heard by now about the nursemaid Elise. It is a common enough name, I suppose, yet I think of the French, 'eglise' and wonder if she is in some ways my church. I ought pray to her and give thanks for the hours she affords me. Yet now as I try to mend the broken parts of myself on the page, nothing comes. When his printing press was damaged, Father had to put the pieces back together and felt this had made the machine work better than before. Is that merely the story we tell ourselves? That we somehow benefit from being shattered? Indeed, I ought to have thanked Claire when we were still back in London. Did I thank her? I scarce remember who we all were then—this place has pulled us in, enraptured us. Perhaps I might be reading too much Milton.

Is it so wrong of me to want my sister to fill in for me the parts I cannot get right, to have her make up for the too-dark parts of me? To be sure, Claire can be annoying and intrusive—even her sweetness if she tries to help with the baby pokes at me. Not to mention she seems unable to predict outcomes. Sad to watch her at eighteen unable to comprehend she is entranced with flame, umber and plum, and with those sticks burning yellow in the moonlight she puts her hand into the fire. Oh, she will yelp when her flesh sears, shocked by pain. Or am I envious of her insistence she will not be burned? She embodies languor, hours seem to stretch out in her yawning body, arms up to the sky like a terrifying creature, only of course, not terrifying, as she somehow beams sunlight as she stretches in the morning.

I flit with inefficiency of movement; if I need three items from one room, I remember only one before I turn round to retrace my steps and gather the others I have forgotten. My body and mind seem disconnected. My brain has taken up the bulk of the space, and my body struggles to keep up, so it is always given marching orders. Where Claire glides across a room, no hurry, no hour in which the task must be completed, I am collecting minutes, hoarding them to what end?

It is not as though there is a jar filled with unused seconds, to which I have access at the end of each day or year. Merely, I have hurried and somehow over-busied the same act of making tea

that Claire has made equivalent to spreading butter softened on bread still warm so that little effort is required for the slather. I am left feeling rather mousy. We should have been better served with my head on her shoulders. Still, I am fond of her.
Be well, Your loving sister Mary

She was fond of me. A moment of pleasure until I recalled Mary's mother. Mary Wollstonecraft had written: *Fondness is a poor substitute for friendship.*

I went on to Shelley's next.

Hogg, I start by admonishing you, though perhaps you think I have no right in so doing. I urge you to reconsider your lack of vegetarianism. For years you were soldier alongside me in this way of treating the world's animals, those with no voices, as worthy of saving. And now I fear you will further fall into the realm of Ordinary Man complete with drumsticks or lamb shank, barely cooked flesh on the plate. It is enough to turn this man's stomach—and yet I should not impose my will over you for that is not the man I wish to be.

Tirade finished, I tell you—Never have I imagined scenery such as this alpine world. We are situated on the Lake and yet I look not here but rather forward to the mountains. I have read Julie ou la nouvelle Héloïse *and determined that being in the place where a novel is set provides an altogether new experience. Rather brilliantly, Mary's mother wrote that Rousseau made women into a fanciful kind of half being. I conclude that Rousseau is the greatest man the world has produced since Milton.*

Hogg, I am only half as bewildered by the changing weather as I am by CC. Her friendship is inconsistent. The feelings occasioned by this discovery prevent me from maintaining any measure in security. Where before I was convinced of her devotion, now I am untucked. Her coldness provokes in me a fearful spark. I had thought our connection ineluctable. Ought I content myself with one great affection? It is a weak man who gives way to trivial sympathies. One must strive for wide benevolence, which is my daily tonic. Nothing should shake the truly great spirit which is not sufficiently mighty to destroy it. Still, the contemplation of female excellence is the favourite food of the imagination.

You ask if I am impressed or burdened by Byron's progress. I am loathe to admit to either. The blessing of a typical summer is the lack of accountability to get anything done. With morosity here one feels an ever-pressing need of work—so I must go see to it. Most affectionately, PBS

Devotion. That was what Shelley wished from me. I did not wish to give it. I looked quickly at the first of Byron's two letters.

. . . after so many years it is my belief that people partner for only two reasons: when they have found someone who calms their anxiety or someone who inspires them.

I waited for the part that would say something about how I, Claire, was the inspirational sort. No such line existed. I scanned the page to see if there was evidence of any of the rest of us, and sure enough I came upon a line which referenced his earlier thought.

. . . Mary is quite an anxious sort, as is Shelley in matters of health. He looks to her for inspiration and so they become a single rat eating its own tail. There is a loneliness in every marriage, even the happy ones; we are always imagining more than the other might ever know and thus they are unable to give it. Further, two people being of similar minds requires a modicum of distance which folds within an aloneness.

The weight of this settled on my shoulders. Even if he committed himself to me I would not be able to unknow this theory. We would always be somehow apart.

The dark deepened, as did the cold. A heft of cloud brought shocking snow, so heavy in the mountains I could not see their peaks. Snow fell on my boots, froze my toes, winter flabbergasting summer and my mind. I saw the letter from Polidori, oddly addressed to himself.

Some days it is madness being human—finding I need both toast to keep the machinations of my body going ever forward and also must swat away the persistent thoughts—like gnats—of what I ought do with my humanness and in what is surely a short time. Is documenting LB's life truly living? I fear he sucks the life out of me.

My mind is an apothecary—vial of crushed tarragon to increase appetite, tincture of laudanum to address the pains that come nearly always at night and nearly always in the presence of a particular person—and think of the glass cylinder filled with Anthemis tinctoria, given for hysteria. Yet no medicine is there to combat a strong-scented bouquet of fear.

Is it from fear we understand ourselves? Of course we must dig in, gardeners all. Top layer of crusted ash from the volcano covering the next more vulnerable layer with its black. He fears he is being drained, sucked dry by fame and by his own need. So the succubus is vulnerable, too. Yet not so much as their subject, first horrified and scared by night shadows and fangs and then, with not a little hint of sadness, the giving way.

Oh, let this note recall my shame: looking forward to mistreatment for it feels in a way desirous. The bite comes and no one is more privy to it than I. For where else on the body is more hidden than the inner thigh, more tender than the neck veins. To offer up such softness is to submit fully to being in partnership with someone else. I do not think I have the heart for it.

I ought to have left then, lest I find myself ill again from cold exposure, but I could not resist the temptation of Byron's other letter. I was greedy to find myself mentioned.

> *Peregrinatio in Terram Sanctam. The first travel guide in 1486. Bernhard von Breydenbach on his travels with Reiwich. Perhaps I seek a guidebook, for there is not one to be found here. Days and nights blend into each other. I am a tourist in my own bed—I understand the concept of the bed, yet there is always that grasping for language, wondering if one is in fact in the place at which one was told to meet, if in fact, the person or persons (!) one is next to in the sheets know anything useful (where is the bakery? where might a man find a drink?). I feel sometimes I am but passing through—unsure where I am off to next—and there is no such guidebook for someone such as myself to follow . . .*

The wind picked up as I skipped ahead.

> *Shelley waxes as though one were to receive emoluments for the natural rigours of this landscape, which perhaps he will one day, having navigated the emotional rivers of this place. Still, I go on—there may be a torrent one day, there might prove respite and sun the next . . .*

I kept scanning, desperate to find myself in his pages before posting everyone's letters. And there, finally:

> *. . . she is all beauty in the physical and also the relief, the curing of one's hard edges—this is a potency unlike any other, a kindling of such force—*

Satisfied, I turned back.

16

In the grey chill of the next morning the starlings gossiped as I walked the outskirts of the drive. Mornings when I had slept at Diodati, I made a showing of being outside lest Shelley or Mary rose early and wondered at my whereabouts, though most days they had taken to staying tucked away until later. I pulled a too-thin shawl close, about to turn back for Diodati when movement in the brush caused me to stop.

There, peeking out suddenly in front of me was a great horned beast of a creature. It looked more centaur than real. I pinched the skin at my exposed wrist. I was awake.

The animal stared at me. Its horns were the size of harps, elegant in curvature. I felt as though I were already looking back on the morning, the peculiar blue-tinged air and the animal's sad, knowing eyes, its soft fur I would never touch. I pressed my boots into the hard near-frozen ground for proof I was really there.

I knew right then that no matter what I felt—despair at the growing distance between me and Mary, worry over what would happen to me at the end of a summer without sun, what would emerge from connections to both Byron and Shelley—I would look back on being eighteen with a sense of wonder, of longing. I knew more of what I wasn't than what I was.

Even with the animal staring at me, I could close my eyes and smell the inside of the Drury Theatre, the sticky sweet stage face paint, the iced cakes already going stale. Yet before any pleasure could root in my mind, Shelley's slack wet mouth from the night before appeared in my mind and my chest pounded. Rather like a night terror but during the day.

The animal's hooves on the dirt broke the spell, and I was back in the Now.

So grateful was I to this beautiful beast that I bowed. The animal bolted away.

Before I reached Diodati's door, I again stopped short.

For down by the lake edge, I saw myself. There I was, standing at the lake's lip and then hunched down, picking up a shell—one of the white ones I had been collecting and had in a bowl in my room. A pile of found beauty, a collection of moments I could hold. Yet of course I was at the door and could not be also at the lake.

The figure turned. I had to grip my own arms for strength. For the figure looked so much like myself I wondered if I had turned ghostly overnight and now watched myself hold William. Yet as the figure turned, her auburn hair came into view, and I saw it was Elise wearing my dress. She gave a small wave and I waved back, as though we were in a looking glass.

17

BACK IN THE STUDY, everyone huddled under blankets of their own choosing: Mary under a fur, which Shelley somehow did not mind, though it was made of animal, Shelley under a quilt, Polidori without a blanket and warming himself with layer upon layer of clothing so he appeared a stuffed man and quite ridiculous. Byron held out to me a silk and wool throw I recognised from his bed and I felt aglow—it was a message between us. I thought of his words in his letter: *She is all beauty in the physical and also the relief . . .*

I gave him a warm smile. When he met my eyes I saw his were glazed, nearly runny with drug.

"Such relief I feel," he said, "knowing we are safe inside."

Polidori spoke. "My lord, perhaps sit down." A conspirator's look to us. "He is in an altered state."

Byron paused, doubling back over his words. "She is all beauty in the physical and also the relief, the curing of one's hard edges—this is a potency unlike any other, a kindling . . ."

My cheeks went hot and red. The letter had not been about me. It was a love letter to a drug.

I tried to regain composure as I handed out the post. Byron took a letter opener to his parcel. Still wielding the dagger of it in his hands, he let out a roar.

The room stilled.

Byron showed us the newspaper in his hand and then smacked it hard on the mantel edge.

"It is about us," he said. Shelley rose and went to see. Mary turned her small face towards the men. Byron went on. He read in an overenunciated way that terrified me. "'*The whole Swiss setup of that group is a sordid league of incest.*'"

Byron drew our attention—his nostrils flared, his jaw jutted forward. I stole a furtive look at Mary. Impenetrable. How I wished I knew her thoughts.

Byron spat at Polidori, "You realise you are no better than the hotel guests." He gestured towards the lake. "Worse, in fact. For they pay for their boat trips in the hopes of seeing me. Doctor, you are paid to take care of me. And this is how you show your loyalty."

Polidori uttered noises that were not words. Byron took a step closer to him. "All they will see is this story. Should gossip take the place of true art? Of writing?" He drew a sharp breath.

Polidori cowered in his seat. "It is only a story."

"Said the man to a group who engages daily with the act of making stories." Byron grabbed at his hair, his throat splotched red. "It is not only the story that matters, you fool. It is the dissemination of information. At the butcher perhaps a told tale would not be believed. Yet in here?" He held the paper above his head. "People will believe anything because it is in the paper. There is no story so absurd that cannot be invented at my cost." He breathed hard, turned to face Polidori. "The glasses used by the mongers on the lake must afford very distorted optics."

He still held the letter opener in his hand as he approached Polidori.

Polidori hunched but did not flee. "I can explain, my lord." He looked at the rest of us. "That is not how I wrote it. That is not what I meant—"

I could not defend Polidori, for I knew him to be a gossip. Yet I also knew he had not used precisely those words in his reports and letters. Still, he could have crafted a lurid tale that had gone beyond his contract or this could be hearsay, entirely based on reports from the hotel guests. And still further, I could not puzzle out if the papers were entirely wrong. For when I looked from face to mouth in the room, I could not say we were not oddly, intimately connected.

I opened my mouth to say something on his behalf, but I was too late. Byron lunged at him, striking him in the chest with the letter opener. Polidori yelped. FF, who had been in furry sleep, chose that moment to rise, bark, and go to Byron. The paper went out of Byron's hand and caught flame.

Mary rushed to put it out before the room went up in smoke, at which point Shelley grabbed the letter opener and said, "Enough!" And settled Byron back on the couch.

"Are you bleeding?" I asked Polidori.

A flitting grateful glance. He checked the wound. "No—he's pierced the first two shirts but not the skin." He had been saved by the cold weather.

18

I HELPED ELSA LADLE SOUP into shallow bowls, which were far too elegant for the country soup of carrots and fennel. With some of the staff home in the dark cold, she was shorthanded and gave me her appreciation for serving with her.

The wind, the slurping, the rustling of newspaper. I had a section on which was a headline: *1816 The Year Many Will Starve to Death*. I felt guilty for the food we had and a pinprick of pride in having helped to find it. Gerald sat on my section. He liked to peck at the words, perhaps thinking they were insects and he could taste them. If Mary objected to the bird being at the table she did not say. She had a faraway look to her face, and I suspected she was only half here, delivering a mind-only monologue, a story taking shape in her head as she said, "You cannot possibly know what it is to live your life constantly underestimated."

I did not say how wrong she was.

Along with our sordidness, the paper brought news of hail in London, snow in Boston. Shelley had a drip of soup in the corner of his mouth. The broth had been made with chicken bones: the quietest insult I could manage.

I could not stop staring at the disgusting rivulet as he spoke. "It says here that John Quincy Adams is confined to his home in London due to freezing rain and hail."

"Likely sunspots," Byron said.

"That may well be," Polidori said. "Still, for the common man, weather is not merely atmospheric.

LATER, BYRON had settled and took my hand under the table. I knew not if he had forgotten we were in public view or cared not about the others being nearby, each with a section of newspaper fanned in front. He turned to me and spoke softly. "I write and the poetry sells yet not because of the writing. They think me lacking depth." He did not sound bitter, only sad. In my mind I sifted through the paper's words. *Sordid*, bad. *League*, good. *Incest*—untrue.

Polidori tried to engage Shelley. "Oat prices are unmanageable, so feeding horses is exorbitant, causing travel prices to increase—"

Shelley kept on. "Farm animals are dying, we're lighting fires in the height of summer—the world is topsy-turvy."

I knew Shelley was correct. I knew his heart to be in the right place and his passions well-spent as he gestured with the paper. Yet the way he could be so astute and protective of the masses he knew not and see not the impact he had on those in front of him caused my chest to ache. A great wave of anger swelled in me.

"I think when tens of thousands of people are dying it is more than *topsy-turvy*," I said. How good it felt to pick on him. My anger singed the ends of my hair, the hem of my dress. I would go up in flames. In the doorway, Elise stood listening, soaking up our words, waiting for an appropriate time to interrupt. Her face was impassive, but she watched mine.

Puncturing his political bubble made Shelley glare. "You pick a word then, Claire."

I wanted to express myself fully, to unravel the skeins of fact and fear inside myself. What had Byron urged me? *Say the thing, Claire.* But I could not.

IN THE depths of that afternoon, the men slept, snoring and snuffling one to the next. Ugly beasts with bellies full of soup. Elise had William in the music room. I could hear notes on the piano, William's laugh. Outside, the darkness seemed to intensify. This made the soft noises eerie rather than prettily distant.

I looked out the window towards the lake.

"It is dangerous," Mary said when she stopped next to me.

"How so?"

"Shelley says—"

I turned her shoulders so we looked at each other. "Shelley says, Shelley says. This is the same lawn. The same view. The same lake. We are not swimming in it, Mary. It is not dangerous to look upon the dark afternoon."

She twisted her mouth. "It would be dangerous to go out."

I went to the study, took the two closest blankets—the fur and the quilt—and wrapped us up as I pulled her out the front door, yanked her along the lawn to the water's edge. Truly, it was dark as night.

"It is not dangerous here. You mustn't let fear get the better of you," I said. I softened then. "You were always so brave. You were the one shushing me in thunder. Now look at you."

Mary looked at the wet, cold sand. "And now I am full of it. Of fear. That is what happens when one becomes a mother. To be a parent means to live always with the fear of heartbreak."

"I think you held hands with grief for so long you might never let go of her fingers." Mary nodded. I crouched. The blanket touched the ground, and I knew I would bring cold grit back inside with me. I dug through the sand and found one. "See?" I said.

Mary crouched next to me, a tiny animal with the fur blanket around her. "What is it?"

"I have been collecting the most marvelous shells. I saw them when first we arrived but hadn't allowed myself to collect them until recently. Why do I put such rules on myself?" I asked. I looked to my sister as though she held all the answers to my life.

"Because you are loyal and do not wish to upset the world?" Mary found a shell, rubbed it with her slim thumb to get the sand off. She handed it to me.

"Perhaps." Yet as I said this I knew it only partly true. The other reason I did not allow myself to enjoy, to hold, to keep the shells—my mother's voice in my head, *whatever is the point, Claire, for you will leave here and have one more thing to discard. You can't very well take everything with you.* Would I have my mother's voice in my head for the rest of my life? Even after she was gone and I as old as she was now?

This I could not ask Mary.

Mary found another shell. Cleaned it, handed it to me. This was what I lived for, my sister and myself in the lake tide, wet feet and whipped hair sticking to our faces in the falling icy rain.

She looked at me and then tilted her head to the darkening sky. "We ought to go inside before this gets worse."

I ought to have stayed quiet. I ought to have appreciated the shells and those moments. But I did not. So excited was I to have my sister with me that I blathered on, aware that when I grew excited, I spoke too fast and my words bled together. I told her about the giant animal I had seen, sure it was a mountain animal come down due to hunger and that I had not known the name of the animal. We stopped by the front door, my pockets filled with the shells.

"Is that not an incredible sight to have had?" I asked her. "I felt so lucky. It was as though the creature had come to see me personally."

Here her face was a book slammed shut. I knew her silence. Her frown. She did not believe me.

Tears pricked at my eyes in the rain that froze on my scalp. I said, "When you refuse to believe me, Mary, I have a disinclination to tell you anything."

Mary charged ahead and spat back. "Has that not always been the case?"

She held out her sandy hand to me to display a pile of the small shells. I took each one and held them. She offered her hand, and without us having to say it, I knew how fiercely we loved each other, how she had a piece of my heart older and more solid than the shells, vaster than the lake. Yet as I watched Mary retreat to the cottage, it occurred to me that some of my best times with my sister, the times I felt closest to her, were ones in which we did not speak at all.

INSIDE, I wished only to be upstairs, in bed with Byron. Instead, I sat writing my accounts of the days, even Mary's cruelty—for if we truly love someone, we must love also the ugly insides of them. The others read or wrote or listened as Shelley prattled on.

He spoke sentences as though the thoughts had only just occurred to him, but I had heard him say as much before. It was a rather elaborate form of performance—and for whose benefit?

"Language shows man's ability to wrestle chaos into harmony. Which in turn lends itself to our understanding of or at least our gratitude for beauty." Here he looked my way. I would normally have looked away, for I did not wish to be the subject of his gaze, but the lumps of anger from being with Mary on the beach forced me to look upon his features. "As poets we must endeavor to put human nature into form. Poetry is the looking glass into which we find ourselves."

It sickened me that no one else found him intolerable in that moment. The room felt smaller, or perhaps I felt larger. I sat up straighter the way I always did when my brain latched to an idea. Mary did not believe I'd seen a majestic creature, locked eyes with it. Fine. She would still have to listen to me speak. And she could not forbid me writing of it. "Surely we cannot expect art, even the most important work, to be forever relevant," I said.

Shelley blanched. How dare I suggest he might not one day matter? Byron scowled.

Mary tried to button me up. "I find themes repeating over years and decades."

"Consider the Bible," Polidori said from his preferred corner seat.

Byron latched onto him. "Polly Dolly's correct—for of course we had *Paradise Lost* on the shelf there." He pointed to the far left shelf. A gap in the leather bindings made the books look like teeth.

"I've had it with me," Mary said.

Byron went on. "Which is itself a play on Mankind's demise. So yes, Bible, repetition, and so on." He crossed his arms in a blanket made of carefully procured smug.

I shook my head. "I misrepresent myself, then. What I mean to say is that words change." I thought back to school, to a nasty note one girl had passed to another, a quote from *Much Ado About Nothing*. "Think of Shakespeare. *She knows the heat of a luxurious bed. Her blush is guiltiness, not modesty.*" I waited and then repeated. "We think of a luxury bed as fine quality featherbed and bolsters," I looked at Byron. "Or silk if one prefers." He looked away. "Yet at that time, luxurious did not mean such."

Mary held *Paradise Lost* in her arms the way she held baby William. "Claire means language is fluid."

I nodded. "What once meant lechery—" Here I chose to look directly at Shelley, which surprised even myself. I would have to muddle over that choice my brain had made. "Became interchangeable with lust and then—now, I mean to say—means nothing of the sort. So when one writes, it must be with the knowledge that all we hold fixed at this moment is mere illusion."

I went to the window. The sky with its chunky clouds hulked over the lake, making even the water dark. "In fact, everything we take for solid is truly liquid." Here, the men became quiet and Mary, book in arms, came to stand by me. "We thought we knew the world," I said. "And yet. No one knew such darkness upon darkness."

Byron broke his stance and went to the desk, quickly scribbling something with the quill. I made a silent reminder to snoop on it later.

"We expect too much of the world," Mary said. She gripped my shoulder. "Each day upon waking, we create a play, a palatable pantomime whereupon we believe the myth that all will be calm, safe, and good." She turned away from the window, and I followed so we faced the men. "Language changes over time, and so we must do as Claire suggests, write and accept our words will be interpreted in ways that suit the reader of whichever day or decade." She fiddled with the blond curls at the side of her head. "This is self-centred to begin with, of course, assuming we will be read at all."

Byron opened his bird-beak mouth but with a sharp look from Mary shut it before self-promotional song came out. Mary went on. "Perhaps we write only for ourselves. Perhaps for audience current. Perhaps luck will find us—and years will pass and we will be long disintegrated in our graves—" She paused, and I knew she thought of her mother and the grave Mary had visited often. "And yet still read by others who might have no knowledge of this dark world, this summer, this room. This is the best case scenario, you understand?" She addressed the room. "That we will be forgotten but our work will not."

19

So dark was it still the next morning that I had lit many candles. On my lap I held a thick heavy book that had a broken spine. Byron and I had already taken our tea and toast. He slumbered next to me, wrapped in silk and crumbs. The quiet was a secret place and we its only inhabitants, passing back and forth the lemon marmalade, bright as hope. We were close to the longest day of the year, yet with the low slung sun of winter it felt we were Decembering.

I turned page after page looking. Animals of the forest. Of the grasslands. Of the mountain. I needed to find it, to know the name of what I had seen.

There. An ibex. I said the word aloud, unsure if I pronounced it correctly. Yet no one was there to hear or correct me, for how would they know the pronunciation of an animal they had never seen? I had been face-to-face with a mountain creature. Yet it had been so cold, so much snow atop the ridges, it must have come down to forage the way I had. "Ibex Ibex Ibex Ibex." I said the word like prayer. The way Mary had whispered her first baby's name over and over, needing proof she had been real, had been held, had been loved.

I needed proof of what I had seen. Even if no one believed me, I would know.

The candle next to me slumped. "Morning came and went, bringing with it no daylight," I said to Byron. "Without sun there is nothing to let us know the time."

"Claire," he said. "Yes." And then he dashed to the desk. He wrote with frantic pace, going back to pages he had clearly written in the days past, pulling sheets from a drawer, another from in between two books. I busied myself with more toast, jam thick on top, a blop of it falling on the nature book. I swooped in with my finger and ate it. Whoever read the book after me would find a sludge of orange and perhaps wonder how it got there.

At last Byron stretched his arms. "You may read it," he said without looking at me.

DARKNESS

I had a dream, which was not all a dream.
The bright sun was extinguish'd, and the stars
Did wander darkling in the eternal space,
Rayless, and pathless, and the icy earth
Swung blind and blackening in the moonless air;
Morn came and went—and came, and brought no day,

Here I stopped. He had listened to me and kept me in mind as he wrote. My hands shook then, so I had to stop lest the writing become smudged. *Seasonless, herbless, treeless, manless, lifeless*—True. We were seasonless here. The disorientating nature of those broken cycles had brought me and Byron back together and brought this poem to life amidst the death on the page.

I felt this poem deep in my body. In my bones. Yet his penmanship was so poor I struggled.

The waves were dead; the tides were in their grave,
The moon, their mistress, had expir'd before;
The winds were wither'd in the stagnant air,
And the clouds perish'd; Darkness had no need
Of aid from them—She was the Universe.

So moved was I that I found myself writing out some of his phrases, making his illegible letters into neat words, each which struck my heart as gorgeous and indelible.

He had captured the atmosphere, the feelings, the everythingness of all of us here. I read more lines. *She was the universe*—the weather, nature, and, possibly, me.

Byron was in only his shirt and put his hands on my shoulders, leaning down to see what words I'd written.

"I thought you were adding to your journal—I do sometimes worry about how I appear in there," he said. When I shook my head, I received a nod of approval. And with that, he shed his robe, donned proper clothing, and came closer to me. He took the bulk of my hair in his hand and pulled my head back so my lips faced him. He put his mouth on mine for a moment and left the room.

Being the first reader of his poem, having his words come from my mouth, was such an intimate task and of such import I had to set my quill down and take a breath to steady my hands a moment. My stomach's quease settled, and once more I picked up the pen.

My eyes lingered on the pages, my fingers hovered over the words. I felt as though my body danced with *universe*, with *moon*, with *mistress*.

When I finished making sense of his words, I pressed my thumbs into my palms, fingers stiff. I took the long corridor from Byron's rooms to the far end of the wing. From the guest wing, I heard low voices and went to investigate.

I had not been down this far and realised, when I saw Polidori's doctor cases, that this was where his bedroom was. My instinct was to turn away, but my nosiness was stronger than my pride. I peered through the crack in the open door.

~

I COULD make out Byron's form in a chair, though Polidori's body blocked him. Polidori had his back to me. He leaned forward, close to Byron. I struggled to get a better look without making noise. What were they doing? Byron's face was near Polidori's waist. Polidori reached his hands round and seemed to cup Byron's jaw. An intimate action which sent my heart rolling into my knees.

"Invigourating." Byron's voice was choked. Polidori was at such an odd angle. I peered closer. Polidori's face on Byron's. Were they kissing? And what of it—ought I scream? Be offended? Jealous? Join them?

"I see you there," Byron said. "Come here, Claire."

I knew then that I would kiss them both. I would find myself swathed in their different maleness. Byron peered around Polidori's body so I could see him as I came forward.

"Do you want some?" Byron asked.

Some what? What did I want? I had so little been asked this that I struggled to know the answer. Byron smiled, his teeth white from a mix of dried basil and mustard oil I'd made. "Go on, Claire, have a bit of tooth string—it's marvelous stuff."

"Milord." Polidori's voice gave no sign of minding I had found them. "My lord, you are bleeding."

I approached them, the three of us oddly close together. Byron put his fingers to the side of his mouth, catching a small drip of blood. Polidori instantly dabbed at Byron's mouth with a white handkerchief splotched with red. Byron shooed him away. Polidori kept the linen, and I watched with furrowed brow as he put it in his pocket as though saving it for later.

I did not like this feeling—but what was it? Not quite jealousy, more a feeling of being left out.

Byron held out his hands, and I had no recourse but to show him the page I'd finished. His eyes went wide as he read my words. I worried he would object to the neatness, to the small alterations. He could banish me from reading his work, from his room, from his heart.

"What is floss?" I asked. Polidori was a doctor. Surely his touch was professional on his employer's chin. Yet it was more. The hook of his palm on Byron's jaw. The rise and fall of Polidori's chest so near to Byron's chest. I knew the look in Polidori's eyes. It was the look I had when I first went to Byron's house. When I could not wait to be with him.

"Floss is a string to clean your teeth, or between them," Polidori said. He leaned closer. "An idea less than a year old—but seems to be effective in preventing rotting. Which leads to infection which—"

Byron stood up. Pushed Polidori away. Polidori pulled in his desire in a great inhale.

"Now you've gone and bored me again, Polly Dolly." Byron licked the last bit of blood from his teeth and grinned at me. "Let us all go downstairs so I might crow about my poem—Claire was the first to read it, you know."

No, I was not jealous. I was thrilled.

20

"IS IT NOT A small miracle," Byron said, after announcing he'd completed "Darkness," "to have a young girl's admiring gaze—on one's writing when first it appears?" Byron selected his words, relished them slow and sweet as pulled taffy, as an odd quiet outside drew us each to the windows. Green-hued sky. Burst of birds speeding from the lake over the villa towards town. Byron went on. "Claire's eyes are kind to poetry, and her pen—for she did show her penmanship—is like no other."

A faint blush on Mary's cheeks. Polidori coughed. Shelley fixed his gaze on the odd green light, the sudden churn of lake water. "Isn't that so, Claire?" Byron said. "The time and care you take reading my words is unparalleled."

Shelley clenched and unclenched his fists. A great unsettled feeling in my abdomen like Gerald the bird had roosted there and then flown off, leaving a trail of feathers and muck. If Shelley had had suspicions in London, or had seen me going to Diodati from the cottage and wondered, or if he had caught a whiff of Byron's lingering gaze on me, Shelley had also told himself a story. A story about a smitten girl who had not any hope of requited feeling.

Yet here, from Byron's tender tone—supposedly about my reading his work—Shelley seemed poised to fathom what had occurred. He squinted out at the lake as though Byron and I were on a boat and he struggled for a better view of just what the goings-on entailed. A sharp inhale at the pale-lime light.

Shelley turned from the window, his large form illuminated by green.

He stared at me. "Jane—" he corrected himself, yet I felt again fourteen. "Claire?"

What would he ask of me? His voice was too probing, too needy. I did not want to be near him. Did not want to contend with Mary, whose face crumpled like a discarded draft and then smoothed itself out immediately.

Byron's fists on his hips, ready for battle. Shelley met him at the window, the haunting stillness pulling us all to look at the lake and sky, which met in a thin-lipped kiss.

I wanted to break the tension, but Polidori tried first. "I have been pondering how to help the gossiping. I could send materials to Murray and have him hold them to be used at a later date." Byron tore at his hair. "Or hidden away and not published at all." Polidori tried again. "Or, should you require me to do so, I should return the money to Murray. Cancel the contract."

"It is far too late for that," Mary said. "For you've sent news quite regularly. Isn't that so, Claire?" She looked at me in such a way that I saw she both wanted the information I had and also blamed me for keeping it from the group.

I nodded. "Yes, however—"

Byron spoke over me. "We ought to be determined to prove the headlines wrong. Yes, that's the way forward—if we write, if we do so well enough, create work which lasts, it should not matter what the paper printed. We shall claim victory."

Shelley was distracted, looking at me. "I had not realised we were at war."

"Then you live up your own asshole," Byron said. Shelley flinched. "You are not entirely known yet, Shelley. To some, perhaps. Yet think of this: If you perished today—" Here Mary's mouth became a tiny O—"Your name would likely be forgotten." A wrinkle of bother on Shelley's face. "So we have a charge. To take the weather, our 'league,' the vicious gossip—and turn it back on itself. Write more, write better, and one shall be remembered for what one accomplishes here." He turned to the windows.

What had I accomplished? What would I be remembered for?

A great surge of self-loathing came towards me at the same time the odd stillness outside reached its peak and the sky seemed to shatter with torrents of wind and rain.

At that moment, William gave a howl that caused FF to begin a rapid succession of deep barks. Gerald screeched. The peacocks fanned. Fletcher appeared with Byron's monkey on his shoulder and beckoned us. "Come quickly, my lord. A tunnel cloud approaches."

With only five of us I would have thought an orderly procession possible. Indeed all I wanted was the safety of Byron's bed, the approachable task of reading his work and making it neater. Instead, we were a group of guinea fowl unleashed on a bed of crickets—this way and that as a great howling from outside threatened to come in.

Disorder ruled: pages in the air, quilt on the ground far too close to the fire, Byron barking orders at us all, FF barking dog things at no one, Gerald and Byron's monkey wrestling, Shelley looping Mary into his long arms, someone's elbow catching me in the face. A shock of blood from my nose. A hand pulling me into another room, downstairs, catching my blood in their hand just as thick hail hit the windows.

21

"QUICKLY," POLIDORI SAID TO me, when it was clear the others had deserted us.

He pulled me through the kitchen, past Elsa, who crouched under the prepping block. Our eyes met—I assured her with mine I was quite well, despite the bleeding. She chucked a damp kitchen cloth up to me. I held it to my nose as Polidori secured us behind the heavy door of the larder, where the barest trickle of light came through a single arrow-slit window long glassed over.

"I ought to get Elsa," I said, voice muffled.

"She is under heavy furniture—she will be fine," Polidori said. "Mind you tip your head back, Claire." His doctor voice soothed me, though when I followed his instructions the blood ran down the back of my throat. I gagged. "Come here."

I obeyed. He held the cloth tight against my nostrils and with his other hand pinched the bridge of my nose. It would have hurt had I not been shocked by the sudden fluster, thinking of the needy look in Shelley's eyes—*all this time it's been going on*, I imagined him saying—and the odd churning of shame I felt suddenly. Perhaps he did not know. Perhaps if he did he would realise he could not protest.

I pulled the doctor's hand away. "I think it's stopped." I squinted at the cloth, just able to make out the bloody shadows on it and my hands. On Polidori's, too. "You are a good doctor," I said. I knew then I could easily give men the praise they required. "Have you practised long?"

"I have not practised at all," he said. "One must be twenty-six. Another five years—my birthday is not until September."

I nodded, though he likely could not see the motion. "It is easy to forget just how young we are, isn't it?"

In the odd dark the quiet opened up between us, the same way I felt expanded in the coppice. Polidori's voice was hushed, conspiratorial. "Sometimes I think I was born ancient," he said. He was next to dried onions, cornichons, pots of marmalades. "Byron said that. Not I."

"Byron is an ancient man trapped in the body of a young one." I paused. "Some days I feel quite old." I thought about what Madame had said: *Men do not change. They merely unmask themselves.* "And other times I feel so terribly young."

I heard clinking, Polidori touching the jams and relishes as he said, "I believe you will look back on this summer and wonder if you ought to have known better."

My mouth fell open, and I was grateful for the dim light. "I know not what you mean."

"I think you do. What are you exactly to Shelley?"

That he asked this in the dark was a small blessing, for I could feel the blush on my cheeks and a quick sickening in my belly. How to possibly answer that? I stayed silent.

Polidori's exhale through his nose made a whistling noise that made me want to laugh, but only in the way I had done at the kitchen table on Skinner Street, caught trying to break into the political conversation. Here I was again being scolded.

"You seem to distract those around you," he said.

This was not as cruel as it might have been. I stoked the damp courage in my belly.

"Did you pull me into the safety of the larder only to lash out at me?" Another nasal whistle. "What might I possibly distract *you* from, Doctor? For you have only two jobs—to look after Lord Byron and write gossip—I seem to help with both."

He cleared his throat the way men do when caught out without the benefit of other men nearby to muscle in as protection. "I stand corrected."

My standing up to him seemed to make him gentler. There were two sorts of men—those who grew monstrous when a woman stood up to them and those who realised their rudeness and softened. No, that wasn't quite right. There was a third kind, those men who used their gentleness in order to dominate.

Polidori was not that sort. He settled, and I, too, relaxed.

"The men," he said, gesturing to the villa above, a world away from us. "I find I come back time and again to their conflict."

"Byron and Shelley?" I asked. "Do they not get on famously?"

Polidori crossed his arms over his chest. It was odd to picture him thinking about the men as other than himself. "I mean to say they conflict within themselves. At first I believed it to be a discrepancy in money matters; with Shelley's title and promise of funds, squalor and hunger are an artistic idyll. A hobby." He waited for me to object. "Yet that is only the surface." He leaned closer, his words hovering near me. "For a man who believes wholeheartedly that he is good and moral, and yet possesses the desire to get what he wants—that can be a poor combination."

I sat with his words. Held them in my hands. Tucked them up my sleeves, whereupon they took on a life and ant-crawled over my skin. After a bit I asked, "Is it safe up there in the villa? I worry for the others. Is this the sort of storm that might kill someone?"

I could see it. A downed tree limb on Byron's shoulders. Shelley's body crushing Mary's, with panes of glass piercing them both. My own body exposed up there, clawed at and ragged.

"Fletcher will attend to them." Polidori seemed to choose his next words carefully. "After all, they did not seem terribly concerned about our well-being."

"True," I said, but it pained me to say it aloud.

A heavy, damp quiet crept in. I thought of the jams and jellies, the pickled eggs floating in brine looking out at us. "Now that we are alone, perhaps you would like to ask a medical question, Claire." He came closer.

He needed to feel useful. He needed me to make him feel useful. I thought—of female skeletons, of boggling monthly bleeding maths, of Mary's ill baby, of the tremor my mother had in her right hand. I thought of my night terrors, which no doctor ever understood.

"Is there a condition, a sickness in which one . . ." I hesitated. "I do not know how to think of my body as belonging to me." I thought of Mary's words. Perhaps the words of all girls. "I don't know when precisely I became separated from my body, for we have remained forever in conversation but we are not one." I stopped, wishing I could bury my words. Honesty had led me to Byron, but it would get me into trouble with others.

"Never you mind me!" I said. "I shall understand myself tomorrow or in five years' time or never."

"You know there are times," Polidori had told me, "the dead needed to be unearthed. Examined. Learnt from. Understood." He reached for my wrist. "You, however, are very much alive, as we know from your pulse, and so your body tells its own story."

Here my shame rushed out at me, pulling me under until Polidori counted the pulsations on my wrist and placed the back of his dry, knuckle-protruding hand on my forehead and sighed. "Yours is a terminal case, I believe."

My eyes widened, for I had never thought of myself as prone to illness or to complaints. Rather, I saw my body as living nearby yet not fully connected to my personhood. Indeed, all that had happened with Byron only reinforced this feeling, as though I were the caretaker of a complicated, fertile land plot on which I might grow anything and so tended lovingly yet with not a small degree of detachment—thrive or fail, the crops were not me, only the shell of me. Yet there was Polidori. A doctor holding my wrist, demanding I look up at him.

"By terminal you mean—"

"Oh, Claire. You realise there is no cure for you. This particular form of disease—"

"I am dying then?"

He dropped my wrist and laughed. "No." He peered closer in the half-light, regarding me as one might a petulant child. "You have what Johannes Hofer discovered."

I gave him a blank look. My fingers wished to fiddle with a seat tassel, to worry the edge of an elegant piece of furniture, but there was nothing in the cool larder to distract me.

"Claire, you must try to be at ease," Polidori said, and moved towards me in the dark. He put his bony hands on my shoulders, which did not help the cause. "Johannes Hofer was a medical student." He swept his hands, enjoying his lecture. "North of here, in Basel." He paused, as though I might invite the man for tea. "This was long ago, of course—" This settled the matter of tea. "Yet what he noticed is today mightily relevant."

Polidori crouched down to deliver this matter of import to me. "He noticed soldiers, others far from home, who became inconsolable. These people were at great risk for death due to missing home badly. He called the disease *nostalgia*, Claire. And I believe you to have Nostalgia Proneness as a core trait."

I smirked and crossed my arms over my chest. "Ah, you see, Doctor—" I stretched the word like taffy in my mouth, "I have not a home to miss and have not had one for such time I believe this to be a misdiagnosis."

My eyes had adjusted to the dim, and I saw his look: equal parts knowing and pity. "You mistake home for being a place," he said. "For you, it is a person." He paused. "I watch you carefully." What else had he seen? "Mary is your home. I believe your body feels pain at your sister's absence. Your mind follows," he paused.

"Perhaps the body knows before the mind," I said. I could not bring myself to explain how I knew this. I could see it, my mind walking ahead, dragging its sagging self, its small mind feet, leading my pathetic body as though it was an injured horse being led behind the barn to be put down out of earshot of any children. I did not like what Polidori had to say. I felt myself fold up against his words. I did not like his diagnosis. I did not particularly like him studying me, for who knew what he might discover.

"And you, good doctor? What is your ailment?"

He began busying himself with the jam, twisting each pot so each faced outward in an organised army. "I have no complaints."

In the dark, courage was easy. "Oh, but you do—for tooth silk is a poor substitute for—"

"Stop there, Miss Clairmont."

"Remember when you could not get my name—how long ago that seems. Yet we *all* watch each other too closely now to forget names or what we've seen." I went to him. In the candlelight he looked like a boy. He was a boy, really. "I think you have love in your heart—"

He stepped back. "Not love."

"Desire then?"

"In all my reporting back to the publisher, never have I made mention of his lordship's darkness." Polidori crept closer to me; side by side we sat on the cold floor. "Do you not think that if he were horrid to look at—some clawed creature or man of ugly face—we would not afford him the same admiration?" He would not continue without my words.

"If a man with no resources acted that way, he would be a bum rather than a scoundrel." I did not say Byron's name, as though he could hear through the walls, which was ridiculous. "A gorgeous face when combined with title grants one certain leverage—"

"Claire, my employer is the embodiment of all weather—such coldness my hands have never known, then that sudden warmth, that glow . . ."

"I understand the situation more than you realise."

Polidori went on his knees. Close enough to kiss me. Or put his hands around my neck. "Some days I wonder if it is you who stands in the way of any meaningful connection with him."

My mind gave me two options: He would kiss me or harm me. I willed myself to find another. I would befriend Polidori, show him he might confide in me—so he wanted Byron? I did not mind. I, of all people, understood. "You see me as competitor, when I am compatriot. Byron shone upon me, and I needed no garments, no food. Only his adoration. That is some of what I write in my journal."

Polidori put his face close to mine. "The man threatens my very sense of life—his cruelty. His—"

"Mouth?" I asked.

Polidori's eyes on mine. Then quickly he pulled back. "What else do you write in that book of yours?"

I shut my face the way I would the journal—for I felt then he would rip out pages and read them, giving no respect to privacy if given the chance. "Nothing of import. My own thoughts." I paused, trying to throw him off the scent. "I am only a silly girl, am I not?"

He moved away. Crossed his arms over his chest. "I do not like thinking of my name in those pages."

"With a contract for £500, I hardly think you've the right to object."

"Still, you cannot write about me in such a way—"

"One cannot control what another person writes about," I said. But I felt horrid because Shelley had been the one to tell me that all the way back on the elopement, when I'd read a shared journal entry and Mary had been ungenerous about my intellect. A clatter outside the door. I pried it open and heard jumbled voices from down the hall or upstairs. *Come out, come out.* "Admiration might be just as uncomfortable as a disparaging remark. Either way, the quill is out of your reach."

He gripped my shoulder as I went to leave. "I know more about you than you might think, Claire."

I spun round to meet his fierce look. I would not be undone by him. "Does it not bother you, how he treats you? He never uses your proper name."

Polidori blushed, for in the larder doorway we could see each other properly. "I wish I minded, but the truth is I will take whatever fondness I can from the man." He looked away. "Your sister told me I am like a girl who behaves as one far prettier than she truly is."

"Above one's station, you mean?" I thought of Mary's letter. "Friendship is a poor substitute for love."

"Indeed. And yet I tolerate his bites." He looked at me. "Something we have in common, I think. Tolerating more than we ought."

Just for a moment, I felt a remove from the outside world. Then I thought of the others upstairs. "I am so skilled at tolerating," I said. I began to cry. Polidori did not insult me by offering a pat on the shoulder. He was beautiful and sad and altogether smaller and less full of himself in the doorway than he had been. "I love too fiercely," I said. I wanted him to tell me I was wrong.

"Sometimes I believe I love no one at all," he said. "Other times my heart tells me I love only those I cannot have." Polidori arranged his collar and sleeves as though we had been intimate in the larder. "Love is not a cure-all, Claire. In fact, I have come to suspect love is a disease uncurable and—sometimes—fatal."

22

IN THE KITCHEN, I saw evidence of Elsa's handiwork—a lattice crust on a what looked to be a carrot pie. She had left a note for me. *Little miss—no meat so only roots for dinner.* I took the note with me as I dragged my feet towards the upstairs world. I did not want to see the others, for Polidori had made me feel I was only a hindrance for them. Mary was my home yet likely an inhospitable one. Byron, changeable as the weather and, as Polidori had said, possibly every bit as destructive. Shelley. His name felt like a sentence. Heavy in my mouth and only making me feel like crawling back into bed.

I did not. Let the others stay indoors and write about nature. I went out into it.

It was too wet to sit in my coppice, so instead I gathered mushrooms. Most I did not know the names of: rippled fawn-coloured ones from the logs on the darkest side of the area. A clutch of gold and orange ones, close together like parents and children in elegant skirting. A patch of brown and white champignons sprouting from an old pile of horse manure. Byron had liked them at Madame de Staël's so I ripped them out for him. Another group, these with small, thin stems. I held them in my palms, their tops like tiny cloche bonnets, and when I had too many, I lifted my skirt hem and used the material as a pouch.

I gathered as though picking was an apology for every wrong I'd ever done. I was sorry for being young. For being naive. For agreeing to follow Mary on her elopement and for the part of me that wished I had remained with my mother and Charles on Skinner Street. For feeling stronger than I truly was. For the female circumstances of my birth, of coming into a world that seemed hell-bent on my extinction and with no one forming a preservation society upon my behalf. I was sorry for thinking Mary cared about me as her equal, when clearly she was the writer and I was merely the sister, and even that only by law. I was sorry for my past self's comprehension of what knocking on Byron's door back then would mean for me in the present day.

I looked down. An enormous pile of unsorted mushrooms in a heap.

"I am sorry for many things," I said aloud to my trees, whose wet, sagging branches were silent in reproach or love, and I could not say which.

THE DAY still would not brighten. I stood looking at the frigid lake, wondering at the skim of ice on top. I had to remind myself of the month. Say the word aloud. June.

I went inside the staff entrance, flooded with relief and warmth when I saw Elsa.

"See here," Elsa said, when I gave her my bounty. "Chanterelles smell of earth and apricots. Gold like yolk." She held some to her nose. "These, no." I had picked puffballs, and she picked them up and tossed them in a scullery bin. "I am your Pilzkontrolle. So see here . . ." She gestured but did not touch their skulls. "These have a fakery—they look too much like death caps—and those will kill you. Wash your hands now, Claire." She gave me a hard look. She watched me lift the rest of my skirts and dump the mushrooms onto her prep table and scrub my fingers. "Your skirt is a good basket. You did a good job."

I wanted to be at an age when I might have built a self solid enough I could do without praise.

~

WE TOOK dinner on our laps. The carrot pie in neat latticed wedges. Chopped endive. A pithier tart I had made all by myself from mushrooms and cold butter after Elsa left early due to impassable roads. She had left me another note, this time in the form of a biscuit dipped in chocolate, which I ate and which had filled me too much for the tart, so I sat picking at the endive and wishing it was chocolate while the others tucked in. Fletcher stood watch with his back to the wall.

"This smells quite good, Claire," Mary said, as she took a bite. She offered me a smile with her words. She gave me a pat on the knee. "Clever girl." She wolfed down her tart and had a rare second helping, which filled me with pride. And when part of the crust fell from her fork, she caught it in her small hand and ate right from it.

This struck me as peculiar. "Are you quite well?" I whispered to her, for she loathed poor table manners and thought they were the easiest way to spot inferiority. Even more peculiar was when she placed both palms—one still dotted with pastry flakes—on the table and tilted her head to peer at Byron. "You say you think highly of women." Byron kept eating, pushing his fork into his luscious mouth with an amused look on his face. How he liked a challenge. "Yet I believe you do not think of them at all, only of yourself in relation to them. You have a sort of woman in mind—witty, lush, without class and therefore free in some way—and then another sort, mousy and sweet and ever so requiring of you the hero, such a fine swimmer you are!"

These were more words directed at Byron than she had spoken perhaps ever—and I thought he would rise from his chair and tower over her, grip the arms of her chair and bring his face so close to her neck he would see, as I could, her pulse under the pale skin. A blue vein ticking the nervousness I knew she felt.

Instead, Byron began laughing. Small at first. Almost a child's giggle. And then it grew. He inhaled a deep, ragged breath, laughing so hard he began to cough. Fletcher brought him a goblet filled with water, and by the time he had swilled it back, Shelley, too, began laughing.

I wanted Mary to protest this joviality. I wanted her to challenge Byron more. To turn her quick words and keen mind on Shelley, demand he account for his treatment of women, query his whereabouts at night. To joust with him and win. How I admired her start with Byron.

Yet she did not, for she, too, was overtaken by laughter.

"I feel most peculiar," Polidori said, with his hands in his lap. Quite without warning, his arms went over his head. "See here! My hands are pigeons refusing to roost. Am I a bird?"

"You are not," Mary said, with her face fixed in seriousness. "You are a baby." And then she guffawed.

I looked at Fletcher. "What, may I ask, is happening here?"

Fletcher and I held a conference by the door as the others acted in a strange stageplay for which there did not appear to be a script, and yet they moved as though choreographed.

"Did you give them medicine?" Fletcher asked Polidori, who tended to his pigeons, patting one hand with the other and cooing.

Polidori snapped to. "Not medicine." He pointed to me. "Claire. This is your doing."

A wave of nausea from the smell of the food I'd made, from the feeling I had caused this oddness, that I was responsible for any wrongdoing. Polidori's hands flew in circles around his head. "Mushrooms."

"Sorry?" I said, so fluent was I in the assuming of apologies.

"Fungus," Polidori said. His eyes grew wide. "*The Medical and Physical Journal* had an article." Polidori's eyes skittered around as he spoke. "Everard Brande, a physician. He treated a man whose family ingested fungus in Green Park. Plant intoxication." He went to Byron, touched his neck, and Byron did not fling him off. Indeed, Polidori lingered on Byron's skin. "Fluttered pulse." He tilted Byron's face up, and I thought he would put his mouth on Byron's. "Dilated pupils."

Shelley spoke. "I feel well. I feel. Feel I well. Well, I feel."

I ran to the library and returned with Linnaeus's *Species Plantarum*, an updated volume of his taxonomy of plants. Fletcher and I pored over the pages. "*Psilocybe semilanceata*," I said, when I finally found the drawing which matched the slim-stalked mushrooms I had gathered. "*Freiheitskappe*. Liberty cap."

Polidori would not leave Byron's side, but Fletcher intervened, moving the physician closer to me. "You ought to look for more illustrations," Polidori said. "I shall accompany you."

We held hands—for I feared he would fly off—on the way to the library, and when we returned with James Sowerby's book, full of gorgeous coloured fungi, we showed the others, who were not quite as interested in it as they were in listening to the wind howling in the chimney and Gerald's warbled throat song.

"We ought to be productive," Byron said, and set about to work ripping pieces of paper into smaller bits as though called to do so by a greater force.

Mary wrote easily, but when I read over her shoulder, I saw the words were strange: *Come & look; here's a cat eating roses; she'll turn into a woman; when beasts eat these roses they turn into men & women.*

Fletcher and I threw our hands up at each other—what could we do?

"Will you die?" I asked Polidori, while staring at Byron. What would I do if I lost everyone in the room—and at my fault? "How likely are you to remain this way?" All the freedom to have pigeon hands and laugh uncontrollably and for Byron to sing softly to himself, looking pleased as punch, yet he did not rush to me and hold me in his arms. I felt a fool.

Polidori was transfixed by Mary. Shelley focused on me as I watched Byron who was intent on Mary who only watched her hand on the page. A carousel of unmet desire.

As each of them became entranced with their work, I felt myself recede as though watching through a long telescope.

No matter how bizarre their actions, they held such focus on their work. Surely everything Byron wrote would be published and if Shelley completed poems they, too, would find an audience one day and Mary—I looked at her then, furrowed brow and teeth clamped onto the end of a quill each time she paused her writing—she would persist and find a story and even Polidori with his pigeon hands and gossip managed to write and be paid for it.

"I write not for any grand purpose," Mary said to no one and to everyone.

"I write for it clears the mind," Polidori said.

"Do you not write to be remembered?" Byron asked.

"I write so as not to forget," Shelley said.

"When I write, I forget myself," Mary said. "Which is a blessing I accept whether the pages be published or burned or forgotten."

No one asked me why I wrote. And I did not know the answer anyway.

23

A MOST UNGENIAL MORNING. Rain sloppy on the trees, whose shoulders sagged under the wet weight. Candles lighted everywhere. Sky a pressing lurid grey. Everything felt to me out of control, doom seeping in under the doors and window sashes, keeping us inside, yet even that did not feel safe. Who knew what would be next? Daily order broke, and we ate at odd times, one person with a fish fork in the pickles early this morning, another with a nub of cheese without a plate at the in-between of first tea and midday. One by one the others had appeared, no worse for wear from their fungal adventures. I had gone to the kitchen and warned Elsa, who gave a smirk and told me perhaps she was not such a good Pilzkontrolle after all.

Polidori and I sat close to each other in the dining room. This was not because I wished to be close to him but because it was off-putting and formal to sit at opposite ends of the long table. He had regaled me at length with his dream from the night before in which he drank from a lady's skull. It ought to have been scary, yet it was only boring, for he told it in a clinical way.

"What will you do about it?" I asked Polidori, as he began to fret about Byron, who was still sore from the papers. He pecked at his toast, eating around the edges and leaving the middle, which was sogged with butter.

I thought of Polidori patting my back by the larder. His private kindness made me sad for him, for men were not lauded for their kindness and therefore did not work to keep it growing. Yet I found I was angry about this, too, for denying of such a nature made him like all men—one thing alone and another when others were present.

He put his thumb and forefinger on either side of his pretty mouth as though clearing crumbs. "I know not. What I do know is I shall no longer write to John Murray. I cannot betray all of us again."

"You had a contract," I said. "I should not wish to judge betrayal when I myself have been—" My hand flew to my mouth before I'd finished the whole statement, and before Polidori could opine, Fletcher showed the others into the dining room.

The rain slashed against the windows with such ferocity it seemed the lake was heaving itself upon us.

"I fear the windows shall crack," Shelley said.

"Steady on," Byron said. He had been sitting with a new page, writing, but seeing that Shelley was unraveling, slipped the pages into a leather case at his feet, exasperation on his mouth. For all their mutual admiration, Byron had no patience for Shelley's fears. In fact, as he locked eyes on me, I realised one of the qualities he admired in me was my lack of fuss.

"The windows are strong," Mary said. This calmed Shelley, as though Mary were a glazier or had any expertise in this area.

Polidori gazed upon my sister and Byron. "How I enjoy a woman who does not complain and a man who worries silently," he said, upon which Shelley removed himself from the room. I thought this was to deal with his stomach or bowels, as both had a habit of acting up when he fretted, but when he returned, he did not pat his stomach with relief.

"Ah, you've taken a tincture," Byron said, and gave me a wink.

"More potent than a theriac," he said. "Polidori's gift to me." Polidori tucked his chin to his chest as Shelley fairly swayed in the doorway, long arms reaching for either side of the frame before he bolted out.

"That is one way to keep someone silent," I said. I thought of Shelley giving Mary Godfrey's Cordial back in London, when he asked me to convince him to make the journey to Lake Geneva all those months before. There had been snow on the spring flowers—I ought to have known the world was coming undone. Minutes ticked by.

Elise appeared at the door. Half her hair had slipped from its bun. The hem of her dress was torn, though when I saw this I wondered if it was yet another thing I noticed that no one—aside from Elise—had seen. Without a word she marched over and handed William to Mary, turned on her heel, and left.

Fletcher rushed into the room, guiding Shelley. "Apologies, my lord, for Mr. Shelley has been to the lake thinking a dragon rose from its waters—too much of God's own medicine."

"Anaesthesia for the soul," Shelley said. "And for dragons." He went to sit by Mary and turned her face so she would look at him. "It had wings!"

Mary pursed her lips and tugged William away when he lunged for her breasts. Shelley leaned over to the baby, and Mary yanked him away. "You'll crush his feet," she said, though her face suggested what she meant was *you are an idiot*.

Shelley's mouth was slack as old lettuce and just as wet. I had to look away. I focused on FF's loose jowls, also wet but somehow not repulsive. This comforted me. I buried my face in his great neck and only raised it when a great smash of thunder shook us all.

There was no lightning, no great burst illuminating the sky.

"My, how calm you are now, Shelley." Byron gave him a look of approval and, seeing me still ensconced with his dog, lauded me with the same.

"How pure is Claire's love for the beast," Byron said, and raised his eyebrows so I would know he meant FF and Byron himself.

"I do love this dog," I said. "We never afforded dogs, but I find—"

"Oh please, let us not traipse down the road of beloved pets we never had nor places we never saw," Mary said. Her look challenged me not to wince at her words. I succeeded. She looked to the doorway to see if Elise would reappear or explain why she had run off so, but when the nurse did not return, Mary stood to bounce William on her hip. When she appeared tired with this, Polidori moved to her and wordlessly took over the task, and I thought they may as well fuck on the fire hearth for all the gratitude passing from each to each, though I also knew he would rather have had Byron on him than Mary.

Shelley, still loose in the body, opened his mouth to say something, but it came out slurred. Mary went to him and pressed a pale finger to his mouth. Without removing it, she turned to me and said, "Dark days require levity. Tell a story, Claire. You're good for a laugh."

This did not come out as a compliment.

How I resented that Mary kept portraying me as capable only of providing amusement and Byron had said I sucked the fun from any room. Which was I?

"She is not a writer, so perhaps a story start to finish is not natural for her," Polidori said.

"She is just here in front of you and needn't be referred to as she," I said.

Mary and I said aloud in unison, "She the cat."

Mary explained, "That is what Claire's mother said if we should ever refer to her as *she* in front of her."

"Very well," Polidori said. "Tell us something."

It was a challenge he thought I was doomed to fail. I looked at Byron. He neither encouraged nor discouraged me, though I thought of him swimming, stroke after strong stroke across the Hellespont. Shelley's nod was most reassuring, yet I resented it. He saw me as serious and fun, which was how I wished to see myself, and this conflict in my nature was partly to blame for my confusion over Shelley all this time.

The wind was so loud I had to speak as though addressing an audience at court.

Just as I began with "I knew a girl—" Polidori piped up.

"I'll have a go," he said, and sounded foolishly loud, for just then the noise outside hit a lull. "First it starts as heartbreak—"

"The only thing more tiring than hearing details of other people's heartaches is hearing their dreams," Byron said.

"I quite like to hear dreams, if they're filled with illogic and mayhem," Mary said. This was true and quite a redeeming facet of her character—she had infinite patience for dreams and distorted imaginings.

"I imagine the good doctor would love nothing more than to regale you with his dreams of lady skulls bare of skin," I said.

"Well, I prefer a proper story," Byron said.

"Ah, the lord wishes a bedtime tale," Shelley said.

"It is day, my love," Mary said, her voice laced with sadness, the kind she'd had all winter and spring, as though she could barely muster strength to speak at all. Instantly I worried for her.

"Mary—" I started.

"Heartache it is," Polidori spoke over me. "Here's a story—"

"Quick, one hopes," Mary said.

"Yes." Polidori gave her a glance of admiration. "A story of a friend who loved a girl who had promised to run away with him . . ." Mary looked at Shelley, sadness replaced by a small smugness on her lips. "And on the night in question, by a busy shopping street at the night market—hawkers and vendors by the carriage road, that sort of thing—where they had arranged to meet to avoid suspicion, she never shows. And only when the market is over and the man is brokenhearted at being made to play the fool does he hear the vendors talking about an accident: A girl was trampled by a team of draft horses." Everyone was quiet. "'Can you imagine,' one of them says, 'the ill fate of being in the wrong place at the wrong time.'"

"Not even true love might stop misfortune's timing," Shelley said. His voice was slow and lugubrious, a rope tightening around my ankles.

I could not cope with him. "When I was at Miss Cunliffe's," I started.

Mary stepped in. "Claire went to the ladies boarding academy of Walham Green—such good fortune to study music and French there."

"I was already fluent," I said, but did not allow my voice to rise. "For that was my mother's native language. And anyway, I was a pupil-teacher to reduce the fees and even so only stayed a brief time." I took a long, deep breath. They had stories. I, too, had stories.

"As I was saying, I knew a girl at school," I said, my voice clear and with just the right breeziness, "whose brother had very nearly the same thing happen to him—not at a night market but rather at the girl's family estate."

"Whereabouts?" asked Polidori.

"Somerset, though that's hardly the point."

"Well, I should wish to picture it."

"Go on, Claire," said Shelley. He gave me a look I had come to loathe—one of love, of encouragement, of ownership.

I looked away from him and kept my voice steady. So I was not a *real* writer. Who was in charge of deciding such things? "Very well. My friend's brother is decidedly in love—"

I moved about the room, my skirts swishing, gesticulating with dramatic flair as though I were onstage at the Drury. "The girl is lovely to look at, devoted entirely, clever and amenable to quiet walks, reading, ever open to his political diatribes." I did not look at my sister, for I did not wish to wound her, and so near to her was my description. "So my friend's brother goes round to the Somerset estate, determined at last to plead for the girl's hand in marriage."

Here I saw my audience, even Mary, captivated. "The brother arrives to the grandeur of the place. The staff show him inside the grand halls." Byron laced his hands together. Polidori leaned forward. "He has tea." I paused. "Possibly directly under a portrait of the girl."

"That would be a good touch," Byron said.

"He states his reason for the visit—beaming at the butler, at the footmen—so great is his love he cannot keep quiet. Only, when the girl's father comes into the study, he's ashen and shaken—my friend's brother couldn't possibly have his daughter's hand in marriage. Well, my friend's brother is irate! He is of good standing, has ten thousand a year and so forth and says as much until the father puts a hand on his shoulder and says, 'My dear boy, my daughter has been dead for nearly twelve years.'"

Byron stood and beamed. "A round of applause for Claire!"

Everyone clapped, even Fletcher and Elise and Elsa, who had crept up and stood back from the doorway, listening. I looked at my sister for her approval, but she did not meet my gaze.

24

IN THE GLASSHOUSE LATER, I pinched centre leaves from the seedlings to encourage side shoots. I felt a sense of relief amidst the plants, despite the heavy wool darkness outside that made me feel less like I was surrounded by windows and more that I was submerged in the lake.

I looked down at the burgeoning tomato plants, the fennel bulbs, and found myself unwound. Let the others have their stories. I would follow Elsa's way, knowing about the natural world rather than separating myself from it. I looked up only when a sharp rap on the glass startled me.

Mary's face at the window gave me a fright. I beckoned her inside. "It's far too cold and dark for you to be out there," I said. "You know you're prone to chill."

"There is not much of me for warmth," she said. She did not highlight my larger frame near her. She did not have to, for standing this close to her I felt for the first time not as a giant oaf, but as an oak—solid and grounded and ample—next to her petite self. For the first time, I did not feel ugly near her. I moved my dirt-covered hands over the seedlings the way Elsa did, preparing them for the harsher world outside.

"Your story," Mary said. I waited for the compliment to come. "It won't be worth writing."

I kept moving my hands. I wished the plants could speak. And speak up for me. "Why not?"

"Well, it wasn't yours. So to make it seem as such is deceitful. Plagiaristic. That is simply not what real writers do, Claire."

"Is it not?" I kept puttering with the plants—old fish stock to feed the roots of the licorice plant, dividing the straggly rocket slowly. Byron always moved slowly and held people captive in his movements. Shelley, too, lumbered and seemed to control a room with his deliberate unhurriedness. Only Polidori, the working man, scurried.

Mary, however, took power from my slowness. "Claire, you held them captive for a few moments on a stormy day. Can you not be satisfied with that? Why must you always push so?"

"Why must I always be satisfied?" I moved faster now, trying to think what would be helpful to Elsa.

"If you want to steal your friend's story for your pages, go ahead. But a publisher would hesitate to offer on such. Not to mention your friend would be hurt."

"First of all, I have not said I wish to approach a publisher about my writing." I crossed my arms and faced her. "This might come as a shock, Mary, but I do not always seek to monetize my thoughts."

"Good thing—for it is unrealistic to think a journal would be profitable." She paused. "And perhaps you feel no need to rush for income because you have me to feed you. You should know you cannot have Shelley's good name and credit providing for you forever."

Her words stung, so I lurched back. "And you should know I had no friend at school from whom to take this tale. So busy was I writing to you, trying to go back home to support you as you asked, I had not a single friend. But neither did I steal another's story to tell my tale. I made it all up—right then, by the fire." Mary looked truly shocked. "And everyone loved it."

Whatever surprise my sister felt quickly turned to anger. "You embarrass yourself, Claire."

"It is not I who is embarrassed by my story—they were captivated—it is you, Mary. There is a difference between embarrassment and shame, sister. Shame is what one feels after an immoral act—it implies regret—whereas embarrassment comes with the judgement of others."

Here I began moving each seedling to the wooden shelf nearest the door. Elsa would be taking them with her as soon as there was a clear day. I thought of the small plants as chicks about to fly the coop and felt a pang.

I went to Mary. "I ought to be angry, yet instead I know only sorrow. I accept you, Mary. Loving someone—truly loving them—requires loving all of the parts of them. The people they were before great consequence and the people they became afterwards."

I paused. I would say it. I would dip my toe into dark water and see if she came in after me. "I am a before and after."

Mary touched her small palms to the window glass, leaving her handprints. "Have I not always known you, Claire?"

She would not ask what I meant. She would not come into the water with me. "No," I said. "I do not think you have."

Say the thing, Claire—I could hear Byron's voice, his insistence. The way his eyes tried to pry open my mind so the thing would spill out.

"You wear your vulnerability like a gown," Mary said, "when the truth is, your lack of virtue is appalling."

I wanted to ask why that had one meaning for her and another for me. Yet I did not wish to argue with her over her virtue, and when she'd given it—and my own, which had been taken.

Instead, I looked at the greenery. The plants with known names and seeds saved one year to the next, how known the growing world could be and yet with the shade of my coppice, how mysterious, too.

"The *truth* is," I began. A disturbance on Mary's face. "The truth is . . . a thing." I looked to the twisting vines, the struggling orange and yellow nasturtium as though they had answers for me. "I know not how to hold truth, but it is solid, is it not?"

She did not answer at first. Just when I thought she would leave the glasshouse without a word, Mary's long tucked-away petulance came spitting out. "Oh, what is the truth, anyway?"

This worried me. For if people—sisters—could not agree on what Truth was, how might we agree on anything?

"Is the truth not one thing?" I asked. "The thing that happened?" I would start from the beginning, back on Skinner Street and wind up here in the glasshouse. I would tell her everything.

Mary wandered the glasshouse, a tiny elegant fairy amidst the food that nourished her day after day, though she knew not how to grow it. "There is *your* truth and there is *my* truth and they may not match." She leaned and smelt the mint, breaking off a leaf and chewing it whole.

"A story changes," she said, with a confidence I admired. "At the time, it is one story. Upon retelling the day after it is another and then years on—it is still quite another story altogether."

"So which is the truth, then?" I needed her to acknowledge me.

I thought back to how excited Mary had been upon her return from Scotland, so taken with Shelley that she barely remembered I had been in the house with him those months whilst she was away. How Mary had begged me travel with them. How Shelley had visited me that first night. How he told me I should not return with my mother, who had come to fetch me and yet slept soundly in the room next door.

How my night terrors began on that trip. How Mary had never asked me what brought them on—only how she wished they would go away. That is what she said to the doctor when I screamed and screamed: *How might we get her to stop carrying on?*

Mary's voice was a hiss, competing with the scraping wind. "I feel sometimes you adore me—and I adore you. And yet you have no life of your own, so you attempt to take mine."

"I have assembled a life out of the scraps I have been given. In fact, I tried my best to protect you, Mary, from some of the harsh parts of the world, from our circumstances, from your own—"

"Oh, yes," Mary broke in, "you are young and vain and poor—"

Hearing her say my words was a slap. She must have read my letter to Byron before the Drury. Had she found it in my pocket? Read it on my desk whilst I nipped to the outhouse?

She had known all along what I was up to, what he was up to. What a fool I had been to introduce them, thinking she knew nothing of our contact.

What a fool I was to think I had any secrets from her.

Mary gave a quick puff of air to warm her hands and stood very straight near the lantern. She looked like a paper doll about to catch flame. I felt a chill. For if she had known about my interactions with Byron, it was possible her silence was to encourage it, so she—and Shelley—might benefit from meeting him.

"Mary." My voice was soft, the way it had been when we were children, and I thought Mary heard this. I went closer. Took both of her hands in mine. I was cold and she was warm or perhaps it was the other way round, just as when we had held hands in the dark between our small beds I sometimes forgot whose hand was whose when we squeezed so tightly.

"I do so love you, Mary," I said. "And I wish you only good. But there are things you must know—"

"And I love you, Clara," she said.

She stared at me with what I first thought was pity. Long and hard she looked at me as though we were each on one side of a looking glass, waiting for the other to move. I held still. Mary looked away for just one blink.

And then I understood. Mary did not pity me. She was afraid of me.

25

SNAP SPLOSH SNAP BRANCHES, wind chill and cold sweat, bellyache eyelash drip wet leather dry mouth.

Words appeared in my mind as I stomped at night from the cottage—where I had fairly ransacked my room in search of anything warm. Why had I been so unprepared for this world? Why had no one warned me of chill, of water funnel clouds, of snow in June, of the dangerous pull of desire for love. I was a seedling poorly tended to. Or no, I was a dog desperate to please, who would not dare whimper in the day for any cruelty experienced the night before.

Ankle deep in ice-scrimmed puddle. In the woods I stood still with only the tree branch creak and wind whip circling around me. Was that what it felt like to be a witch? As a woman, would I need to choose between docile dog and too-powerful witch? Or I could be like Mary, whose quiet was her power. She would pour it onto the page. I could do the same—yet I was too hungry. Too angry. Too raw. Exhausted from being turned this way and that and being convinced the confusion was something I had brought on myself.

A motion to my right side and I pounced.

"MY GOD, Claire—what on earth?" Mary rose and hurried to me. Small warm hands on my face.

I could not speak. I gestured instead with the slack body in my hands.

How I must have looked—bedraggled hair, cheeks flushed bright cold-red, gripping the dead hare.

"Claire—" Byron strode towards me, but Shelley held him back.

"She is chilled through, let me—" Shelley brought a throw and went to wrap me in it, his parcel. I flinched. Polidori cast his eyes over me, assessing. I was everyone else's. I was not myself.

"I have dinner," I said. No one seemed to understand what I had done. They stared back at me, the ugly creature in the midst of the sumptuous library, rich navy silks and gold threads, flickering candlelight casting just the right shadows on the formal rugs. I sloshed the outside onto the inside. Dampened the fabrics.

No one complimented me—how I had caught the animal myself, found dinner for us all.

Mary rang the staff bell. Elsa appeared with a new girl, shy as a finch, who wordlessly took the limp body from my hands. Her gentleness felt like an apology, the kind gesture one girl can give to another and never speak of afterwards.

"Claire, let us find you dry clothing," Mary said. "You must get warm."

I allowed Elsa to lead me out of the room, but stopped in the doorway. I addressed them with Mary Wollstonecraft's words. *"If we revert to history, we shall find that the women who have distinguished themselves have neither been the most beautiful nor the most gentle of their sex."*

26

OUTSIDE WAS RAIN-SOAKED CHAOS and always dark, and inside no better, for the damp wood hissed and smoked, William cried, and Elise sang to him a song that threatened to make us all mad. *Es wollt' gut Jäger jagen, wollt' jagen von Himmelshöhn; was begegn't ihm auf der Heiden? Maria, die Jungfrau schön.* Elise's voice was light and clear, cheerful as coins in a pocket. Given the topic of the song, this struck me as funny and odd.

I translated as she sang. "A good hunter wished to go hunting—to go hunting from the heights of heaven; what should he come across upon the heath? Mary, the lovely Virgin." Here I looked at my sister, for how could I not?

Elise sang again. *Der Jäger, den ich meine, der ist uns wohlbekannt.*

I translated. "The hunter that I mean is well known to us—"

"Elise, I must ask you to stop. Please." Mary held her hands to her head.

"He does like when I sing," Elise said. It was unclear which "he" she meant—for while she held William in both arms, heavy sack of potatoes that he was—she looked at the other men in the room. I swallowed too loud. Mary blanched.

I took William from Elise, marveled at his angelic hair and slightly open mouth, and brought him to Mary. Her gratitude came in the form of a hand squeeze as we performed the baby-passing ritual we had perfected in London.

Byron spoke in an odd lullaby voice. "*I sung of chaos and eternal night.*"

"I recognise that," Mary said. "*Paradise Lost.* Such a good companion that has been."

Mary's proprietary tone annoyed me.

"*Neither man nor angel can discern hypocrisy,*" I said, for I had also read Milton. I looked at Shelley. "*The only evil that walks invisible . . .*"

Shelley pursed his lips. "I live not a life of hypocrisy," he said.

"I was quoting. Mary quoted."

He clenched his jaw. "Very well. I shall quote myself. *The earth was grey with phantoms, and the air was peopled with dim forms as when there hovers a flock of vampire bats before the glare . . .*" When Mary flicked a question at him with her eyes, he said, "Lines I am working on."

Shelley cough-cough-coughed to fill the space, enough that I wanted to smack the side of his head, but Mary patted his back while still holding the baby and Byron shifted in his seat, unable to get comfortable, and Polidori cupped his hands to the window and said, for surely the fourth time, "How brutal—aren't we lucky to be safe inside?"

I ought to have felt safe, but I felt instead annoyed. I missed just for a moment the quiet of Lynmouth. It had been a lonely time, I knew, but if there was a noise from a drawer being closed, I was the one who had made that noise, and if there was a crumb-covered plate left out overnight and a mouse hind-legged on it in the morning, I was to blame.

There was a sort of peace to be found at the centre of loneliness, a quiet aloneness I missed. It was difficult to know what I wanted, what I needed, when I was around so many others far better at stating and having their needs met. Even William was better at this than I.

Mary's silence encroached upon the room. I kept replaying our conversation. How might there be anything other than a single truth? My sister's silence ate at me.

"Mary, you smother me," I said, and as the words flew out of my mouth, their sharp sparrow beaks were a surprise. For it was not only Mary, it was Shelley with his gawking eyes, yet I addressed only my sister. Byron folded his hands as though this were a play and he happily in attendance. "You are a woolen throw doused with water and flung over us all."

"My sister feels sorry for herself," Mary said. "To be surrounded by those who know their place in the world must be a burden for her."

"*She* is here," I said of myself. The others all had their professions. What was I? A girl. What had I heard from each—writing required a light to be shone into darkness. Writing needed to contain truth-telling. Writing demanded that one *say the thing.*

"Perhaps I might tell a story," I said. I chewed my lip until I thought it might bleed. "Like so many stories, it begins with an innocent girl—"

Byron raised his eyebrows, and Shelley did his audible nose gasp. Mary's head snapped up with the quick jolted motion of a marionette. Her eyes locked onto mine. Polidori stared at me, took in my entire form, looked at the others and furrowed his brow.

Before I could continue, the doctor spoke over me.

"This night calls to mind one of your poems, my lord." He swept his arms towards Byron but kept his focus on me. "Surely we all recall *The Giaour.* For I read that time and again, as everyone did. Who would not be captivated by a vampire who returns to destroy those he loved?"

Byron gripped the edge of the mantel. "I find it difficult to look back on earlier work—for one always notices bits to change, yet it is too late."

"I should not wish to change a single word of yours. For once something is published it does seem finalised." Polidori went on. "*But first, on earth as vampire sent, / Thy corse shall from its tomb be rent: / Then ghastly haunt thy native place, / And suck the blood of all thy race; / There from thy daughter, sister, wife, / At midnight drain the stream of life.*"

Mary clapped her hands. "You are quite good at recitation, Pols. And I agree—what is written in draft might be changed, but once brought to a larger audience ought not to be."

Shelley shook his head. "I think one ought to have a chance to revisit work. A later edition made better by the passage of time. The author might see their work differently."

I looked at Mary. "The truth—the story—is one thing when first written and yet changes over time. As does our understanding of it, is that not what you said?"

Mary flashed a look at Shelley, who lurched up, grabbed a book from the mantel and waved it round. "Polidori is onto something. This night calls for something horrid."

I could have given them something horrid. I could have given the truth. But fear gnawed at my belly. For Mary had said that there was no single truth. A familiar retreat coursed through me and my posture flagged.

Shelley cleared his throat and read aloud. "*The Juniper Tree* by Jacob and Wilhelm Grimm. Quite good names, I must say."

His voice had melodic fortepiano tones. He pushed his wide shoulders back and held the book in front of him as though giving a public reading, and I recalled how easily one found oneself captivated by him.

"*Long ago, at least two thousand years, there was a rich man who had a beautiful and pious wife, and they loved each other dearly. Though they wished, they had no children. The woman prayed for them day and night, but they didn't get any. In front of their house stood a juniper tree. One day in winter the woman was standing beneath it, peeling herself an apple, and while she was thus peeling the apple, she cut her finger, and the blood fell into the snow.*"

"Indeed," Polidori said, "it is a marvelous structure, for it allures with words such as *rich* and *beautiful* and *pious*."

"And yet it is at once foreboding," I said, "for they want something they cannot have—"

"Yes," Mary said, "and there's the specificity of a juniper tree for no good reason—"

"And blood for a very good reason," Byron said.

Shelley nodded. "The trick is making the good thing bad and the bad thing seem good."

Byron trailed his fingers along the spines of the books as he walked the length of the vast shelves. "What about this?" he held a volume out. Shelley accepted it. "*Fantasmagoriana.*" Shelley frowned. Byron snatched it back. "German ghost stories translated into French." Byron tried to read the subtitle."*Recueil d'histoires, d'apparition—*"

"Before you butcher the language, give it to Claire." Shelley took it from him and walked it to me, dropping it in my lap.

"*Recueil d'histoires, d'apparitions, de spectres, revenans, fantômes, etc.; Traduit de l'allemand, par un Amateur,*" I read. "An anthology of apparitions and ghost stories, translated from German into French by . . . an amateur." Perhaps there was hope for me. "Anonymous."

Byron scoffed. "Hardly. Jean-Baptiste Benoît Eyriès."

"How might you know that?" I asked. It came out more stringent than I'd intended.

Byron lost his patience with me. "The literary world is quite small, Claire. If one publishes anything, at some point word gets out."

There were eight stories in the slim volume. I read the contents. "*The Grey Room. The Black Room. The Fatal Hour. Death's Head. Family Portraits. The Revenant. The Death Bride. Silent Love.*" Each word seemed too potent. Too relevant. Too puncturing.

"Shall I read one aloud?" I asked.

Quiet draped the room. My sister spoke. "Claire has a lovely voice for narration."

I blushed from the compliment and set about flipping through the pages. Which to choose? A ghostly barber. A family painting that falls and kills those standing underneath, and a ghost who is trapped in the painting and kills children.

"Are you reading them only to yourself?" Polidori asked. He was bitter at not having been asked to read. I kept my eyes on the page.

"Ah," I said. "Here is one. 'The Grey Room.'"

The wind and rain tormented the windowpanes. Gerald alternated between quiet feathery snuffles and screeching. FF snored as though being smothered with a pillow. Mary sat so straightly upright she appeared stuffed. Polidori's mouth was sour, his whole being defining the word *sullen*. Byron watched me, waiting for me to deliver anything to amuse him.

I read as though the headmistress at the worst and strangest small school.

It was an odd story. A man travelling, offered a bed in a grey chamber, yet there is an issue—the man has forgotten from an earlier visit that the room is haunted. No matter, the man is "dead tired"—here I accentuated *dead*, which Byron approved—and thus would not, could not be bothered by the spirit. However, the room is indeed inhabited by a ghost. The damsel of the castle, whose name is Gertrude.

"Ugly name," Shelley said.

"Irrelevant," Byron said, and elbowed him.

I stared at them. "Gertrude had every intention of remaining a virgin. She wished to take her vows and enter a nunnery."

"Guessing that is not what happened," Polidori said.

Mary looked uncomfortable but said nothing. I read forward. Why had I chosen this story? I licked a finger and turned back some. "Here, let us try another one—the ghostly barber?"

"Do press on, Claire," Byron said. "You've begun and I'm intrigued."

I closed the book.

Byron stood, came forward. His body was close to mine. Chest to chest nearly. I tipped my head up out of habit and desire—for I wished a kiss and also wished not to have to say anything further.

Byron took the book and stepped away. I tucked myself into the corner of the room under one of the heavy furs, with my feet slipped under FF's giant head.

Byron could not read the pages so asked Shelley to do so. As Shelley folded one long leg over the over, he told about Gertrude being raped in the grey room by Count Hugo the Black with subdued drama. How she could not become a nun. The curse laid upon her three hundred years of agony, in light of which Gertrude poisons herself. "Only nineteen," Shelley said. "Such a pity."

Mary coughed and held her hands out. Once she had the volume she kept reading. How Gertrude haunted the grey room, holding a crucifix in one hand and a dagger in the other.

"She is a very successful hauntress," Mary concluded. "For she does not actually kill the man, she merely scares him."

I stood and went to warm myself by the fire. "Perhaps that is enough."

Byron clapped his hands. "Very well. We shall do the same."

Polidori's eyebrows went high up his forehead. "Meaning?"

It was Byron's turn to be the instructor. Dutifully, he fetched paper, pen, ink and handed them out. "I suggest we each write something. A story which might scare the others."

The silence was steady. Each shift of a body in a chair or a foot on the floor caused a collective flinch of fear.

"Are these ghost stories only to amuse you, my lord?" asked Polidori.

"Possibly," Byron said. "Or perhaps we have power to quiet the storm's mind."

Shelley said, "You have a head start, Byron. Will you not pick up from where *The Giaour* left off, a bloodsucking, hunched creature?"

Byron thought. Put his pen on the page. Shelley took this as a challenge and began. Polidori chewed the quill tip, leaving the feather sogged. After the larder I did not want to be repulsed by him so sent him my pity instead. Mary did not move. She sat and stared at the fire. So long did she gaze without shifting I thought her in a trance of warmth.

"I wish to make people afraid," she said finally. "What gives one the most dread?"

An answer came and left my mouth before I'd had a moment to consider if I wanted to hold it or let it go. "The most deeply chilling is thinking one is safe—in a place, with a particular person—when truly in peril. Thinking one has done the necessary thing, the righteous thing, only to realise one has given life to the most treacherous thing of all, deceit."

27

I KNEW I OUGHT NOT go upstairs. I knew my own room back at the cottage behind its solid door with its bolt lock and empty bed would welcome me back: cold at first, wet perhaps from the run required from the villa through the orchard with its tree limbs scratching one against the other, reaching out to me. I knew the cottage to be in my best interest this night, and yet when I stood at the door about to leave Diodati, I could not face that dash by myself.

Instead, I turned to go find the others in the room where we had been sitting for the ghost stories. When I arrived, it was empty. The fire's last crackles offered little heat. I could see my breath as I reached out to touch my own lips. My fingers were cool and shaking. I was alone, so why the fear? A swishing noise from the corner caused me to swivel, this way and then that, trying to see which corner, what caused it. "Hello?" No one answered.

I had no notion where to go. Elsa had gone for the night, and I imagined the scullery with its knives and syrups, its unlit corridor. I stood at the base of the grand staircase and knew I should not climb and yet watched my feet begin to do so. Here I could not tell truth from imagination: up the first flight I became so fearful with fatigue I might have been an ancient lady, a skeleton dragging my own bones up the last flight until I reached the wide hallway. The candles had blown out. I swallowed saliva and fear, feeling my way along the wall and hoping to see a warm and welcoming light. The corridors stretched on and on, dark and darker still. To where had everyone disappeared? I heard then a cry and stopped to listen harder—William? Or no, an animal of some kind. I wished to sink onto the floor, bury myself in my own skirts and cover my head until first light of morning, yet fool that I was, I kept on. Heart pounding, a fine line of perspiration on my upper lip, though the air was chilled. I did not call out for fear of what might find me. As I thought I would faint from terror, a slim shaft of light appeared in front of me.

Half in darkness, Byron stepped out. I could not see him well, only enough to see he beckoned me to the doorway. Once I scuttled to him I dared not breathe before he grabbed my hand and I shrieked. "Why Claire, you're frozen through," he said. "Do come in and get warm."

Relieved and nearly panting, I stuttered a thank you and stood by the fire. Only then, once I had begun to warm myself, did he speak again.

"You look as though you've had a terrible fright."

I stared at the fire licking the logs, relished the warmth. "My nerves,"

I said. "A bit frayed from the evening, I suspect." I allowed myself a deep breath. Before my lungs could fill, Byron's hand gripped my shoulder. He spun me round.

When I faced him, his eyes took the glow of the fire, his mouth in a snarl, "Oh Claire, you truly are made of such young flesh."

I felt my stomach lurch. My breath returned fast and I stepped back, too close to the fire and worried my hem would catch. What a peculiar thing to say.

I wriggled out from his grasp, only to dash to the other side of the room, whereupon I saw my own reflection in the looking glass. I seemed young, younger than ever and scared. My own fire raged in me—I loathed the fear that coursed through my limbs. I turned to yell at Byron.

But he was not there. I was alone. Again. Yet when I turned back to the looking glass for comfort in my own reflection, I saw behind me a tall, dark figure and screamed.

"Did you think you were alone, Claire?" Shelley's voice was so low and slim it sounded like a whisper, but one dipped in arsenic.

"Shelley—I must go now," I said, and shouldered my way towards the door.

He laid his long fingers in a grip on my forearm, tight and still tighter. There would be a mark in the morning. "You are never really alone, are you, Claire?"

I pushed past him, down the stairs, past the dark sitting rooms, out the door so fast I could not be sure I shut it at all, ran with skirts gathered through the orchard and wished the trees would protect me as I bolted that last distance to the cottage and in that door, up the narrow set of stairs to my small room, where I made the frantic movements of a caught animal—no one under bed, nor in the wardrobe, nor behind the door. I closed it, bolted it, and buried myself under the covers. I fought and fought to stay awake, to keep myself safe.

A storm raged outside and I clutched still with diminishing horror. I awoke and lay against the mattress for a few minutes, remembering. In the lamplight I checked my arm for a grapevine of Shelley's fingertip bruises—my skin was bare.

28

IN THE MORNING THERE was fog heavy and damp, like something almost being said. After my nightmare, I felt scared. I also felt hungry. And both of those feelings fought each other in my stomach and mind. I knew the only thing that would quiet my racing heart was to be in the coppice with my palms on the moss and the damp air circling around me as protection.

I was halfway between the cottage and villa when without warning the sun burst out. It shone on the lake and coated everything equally, the squelchy ground, the struggling orchard limbs, my face. It seemed to promise it would remain unclouded.

Still, I felt uneasy, but as I took steps towards the familiar path to my coppice, hunger got the better of me and I turned to the villa. I could see that the maid had pinned sheets and clothing to the lines; each item fluttered like a small apparition confused to be in the daylight, small reminders of the nights that had occurred, ones we could never get back. Out from behind one of the hanging sheets popped Shelley. I clutched at my chest, recalling my nightmare.

"Where is it you've scurried to all these days?" Shelley asked. He scanned the path, and I hoped he would not follow.

"I do not scurry," I said. I sounded defensive, like a child caught taking swipes of icing from a cake meant for an adult party. "Mary is the scurrying one. You've confused us again."

He did not seem to like this. "You sound tired, Claire," he said. "Mind you do not let your tone take on your fatigue." I hated when he told me I felt something—as though he knew me better than I knew myself. He studied me and started to say something but could not finish, for Elise called from the doorway.

"Mrs. Shelley needs you," Elise said. "We both do, come to think of it."

This was all it took for Shelley to leave me with the ghostly garments.

I HOISTED myself up onto the prep table and ate a wedge of hard cheese, alternating between bites of that and bits of stale buttered bread Elsa softened in a bowl of hot chocolate. The salt and sweet were the perfect salve for my mood. She finished chopping carrots, wiped her hands on her apron, and took a piece of the bread and dipped it into the bowl. How I relished sharing food with her, watching the quiet efficiency she had in the kitchen, the glasshouse, the garden.

"You always know what to do," I said.

She took another piece. "Maybe this is from necessity." She looked around for her next task as she chewed. "You have a good appetite."

"I always have," I said. I was about to apologise for it, but she gave me a look and shook her head.

"This is a good thing, for in the bad times the scrawny ones feel famine first," she said. "Now, you must take leave, scurry off—for I need to keep writing." She hefted large ledger books from the other side of the room over to where I was sitting. A drop of hot chocolate dripped from my bread onto the pages. She wiped it with her sleeve and gave me a fake rap on my hand.

Each page had list upon list of food items, dishes, columns for cutlery and candles. "What's all that?"

"The house ledgers. So much required to run this kitchen. And now . . ." she gave me a quick look and then turned away, "I must prepare for my own departure. So I write everything down for the next person."

I could not eat the last piece of bread. Elsa would leave. I would never know her in winter. I would never see her in other houses. I wanted to cry with the agony I felt, yet out of fairness to her I did not.

"I understand you must leave," I said, and when my voice did not waiver I thought—this is what it means to be an adult. I was becoming an expert at further hiding my pain. "It's very good of you to leave so much information for the next person."

She nodded. Made a note. My heart ached. My belly ached. I felt altogether constricted. "I should let you work," I said. "I'll find some wild nettles for you—we might make soup of them. Fear not, for I will not return with mushrooms!" I laughed and she joined me. Then I paused. "You say scurry."

"Is that not a good word?"

"It's a mouse word," I said. "Shelley—Mr. Shelley used it today. I do not think I move that way . . . I am slower. More like this." I showed her my lumbering gait.

"Scurry to me is useful, for there is so much work to always be done here." She paused, furrowed her brow. and looked at me. Then she came forward and took my hands. "I worry for you, my dear."

I ought to have been glad for her care. Instead I flinched and pulled my hands away. She wrote in her ledger. Still, I did not leave. After a few moments she said, "Di sheps lernt zikh moyreh tsu hobn farn volf nor lsuf frest zay oyf . . . der pastekh."

"What does that mean?" I asked.

She shook her head. "One day you will know."

29

ON THE WAY TO my coppice I wrote in my head, something about the day and those late-night chats Shelley had established long ago. That first one, when my mother came to fetch me in Calais. How he'd sat up with me. How he listened and offered solace. *You need tending to,* he had said. *And I shall be the one to do it.* Over those weeks, months slipping into years, he had inched his way into every nook, and, as of April—the night of the Great Convincing—into my body. He had never hurt me. Each time, he had told me a story of devotion, of caretaking. And I had listened.

As my feet took the familiar path, I breathed in the soft air. My long hair grew damp with mist. I would lie on the ground, caring not about my dress. Taking a pot of ink from my pocket, I sat down, bottom instantly chilled, but happy to settle into the woody darkness I had come to love, and I wrote.

A rustle, not of leaves but of air.

He did not creep out of the shadows. He did not suddenly appear and make me jump.

He had been sitting there all along, part of the dark air of my calm, safe coppice, the entire time I had been sitting writing. The darkness around us reminded me of all of the other dark places I had been with him. Liquid leaked from my nose, and I had naught but my sleeve to wipe it with. I cried and knew from their sting my eyes were red, my cheeks, too, from rubbing and disbelief. I was ugly then and embraced my ugliness.

He held out one long arm. I could see the pale skin of his wrist, the buttons undone. His veins glowed green-blue like mould on cheese. He pushed his hand at me, brushing through a stray patch of wild nettles. *Urtica dioica* is what I thought, as though naming the plant would keep me from flinching as he held his hand closer.

Shelley waited for me in silence.

I remembered buying the journal in London, how the bright blue cover had called to me. How I'd kept the silky hair ribbon bought with Mary in the pages to mark the day I'd gone to meet Byron for the first time, as though that was when my life had changed. That was the odd, sad trick of life—it was always changing; we were too distracted to notice.

I clutched the book so hard I thought I might pierce the cover with my grubby nails. "It's mine, Shelley. That's what I told Mary, too." I stuttered with fear. "I know we used to share . . . a journal. All of us . . . but this is only for me. So I would prefer it remain only in my view."

I heard a voice in my head but could not understand the words as though they were in a language I had never studied, the plants and trees around me trying to warn me, to inform me, whose tone urged me to shout but I could not.

"Claire."

He was not angry. He did not rip it from my hands. He merely waited. He knew I would give in. I always had done. No matter that I knew plants. Could forage and feed others. No matter that I did not feel I was the young girl he'd met whilst Mary was in Scotland, was not the banished soul in Lynmouth. I'd sought out Byron, claimed his heart, and yet I became, alone with Shelley, the same girl I'd been from the start. The girl he'd taken.

And with a creeping blush on my cheeks and shame burning in my belly, I handed everything over.

30

ONCE MY JOURNAL WAS safely back in my hands, I bathed at the cottage. I tried to rid myself of any of the dark interaction with Shelley. If I spoke of it, he would say he'd done nothing wrong. Land was for everyone; my coppice was not truly mine. I had convinced myself I had found the dank fecundity of pines and moss and solitude, but as I scrubbed my body clean, I understood it was merely a place that belonged not at all to me. I had nothing to call my own.

How long had he been in the coppice? I had lost a sense of time. The more unspooled my clothing, the more unraveled my skin, my insides, the more distance I felt from my actual body. A relief to pull back. A slipping away of the self. That was a line for a poem.

As I scrubbed and dried myself, I thought I would remember it as a poem, one I would never write, for I had thought I could die there, with the pines and sky as witnesses. Had I prayed in all the moments with Shelley? Byron had no faith and Shelley was an atheist but perhaps women had no such luxury—for we were always praying, *please let me be safe, please let no harm come to my children, I would do anything if—*.

I had closed my eyes in the dark so often I learnt to rid myself of bones, becoming water. I was the lake, my body open for swimmers, reflected in sky.

And my journal? Also somehow communal, for that was part of

being a writer—giving up a sense of privacy. I would not speak of it, for I did not wish to debate whose truth was *the* truth. I took my time bathing, brushing my hair, spreading honey-milk balm on my wide hips.

UP AT Diodati, the music room was drenched in pale sunlight, an elaborate tea set out on rolling carts as everyone sat and wrote. I fidgeted with pouring, with a sugar cube, with a tiny lemon scone, only to realise I wanted none of it.

Mary sat scribbling. She'd barely stopped since Byron's ghost story decree.

She wrote with immunity to the world around her—when she'd held William on her lap she dribbled ink on his head and had not noticed. I thought he looked like devil spawn as Elise held him. I patted myself on the back for keeping this to myself.

"I am writing of a bare-skulled lady," Polidori said. "She is punished for spying through a keyhole."

"That sounds pointless," Byron said, yet Polidori wrote on.

Shelley scratched at the skin on his wrist, where sure enough the nettle welts appeared—*Urtica* meant burn—yet unlike his stomach pains or blood issues, he did not garner attention for this ailment. He scratched and scratched, which would only inflame the skin more. I felt that the plants had tried to protect me. It hadn't worked. Yet I thanked them silently.

Shelley took up his pen. I wondered if he was continuing his poetry or if he was recalling lines from my journal, revisiting my coppice in his mind. How he had taken what was not his. He had been a champion of my writing, and I was embarrassed to realise I wished to know his thoughts about the pages he'd read, and yet I also did not wish to know anything and also I was too ashamed to tell Mary or Byron or Polidori, for then they, too, would want to read—if they hadn't done so already without my knowing.

I tried to calm myself by watching the others.

To anyone else it might have appeared that Byron made headway in the challenge he had set forth—he wrote and paused, wrote again—yet I knew his patterns and thought it half-hearted. He seemed distracted. Anxiety pecked at my feet under the table—was it self-centred of me to think his distraction was because of something I had done?

In an attempt to placate any possible tensions, I recited some of Coleridge's *Christabel*. "After all," I said, "it is filled with fear."

Byron perked up. "And the supernatural. Well done, Claire." He recited the first part from memory and skipped ahead to the second and asked, "*What ails then my belovèd child*?" He looked at me.

I could not recall much of the verse save one line. "*She had no power to tell . . . so mighty was the spell.*"

The words hovered mothlike by my mouth. I could have held them. Cupped them. For perhaps silence was a spell that needed to be split open.

Yet before I could speak further, Shelley screamed. He clutched his head as he'd done once with toothache, eyes wild and wide. He snatched the candelabra from the centre of the table and bolted up. "I am haunted! I am remembering a woman from long ago who is said to have had eyes on her breasts—oh, I am in pain. My mind is all horror."

He left the room, tearing at his skin.

Polidori gave an exasperated sigh, set down his pen, and followed.

LATER, WE regrouped, yet Byron was not with us. With a light ether, Shelley had settled. Mary wrote. I made a list of receipts I needed to copy from Elsa, who would speak the instructions. Writing each dish and the ingredients required to make it gave me a sense of purpose, a feeling of neatness and calm.

Elise came with William. "I feel unwell," she said, one hand on her stomach.

Mary seethed. "I am in the middle of an idea."

"Claire? Shell?" Mary begged. Shelley spun round, reentered the room from the recesses of his mind, and took his child but only as a gesture to me—his acquiescence was troubling.

I could not bear to be near him so went to find solace with Byron. I climbed the stairs, opening Byron's door only to find his bed empty. I crept on. Another door, another empty bed.

As I went down the hallway, I wondered if I might find him with someone else. He could be with Elise if she were well. With Fletcher—had he loved him all along? What might I do? Would I lash out at Elise if she were there, auburn hair splayed on the mattress? Or would I yell at Byron? I had to accept that to keep Byron I would need to embrace free love, be at his whims.

I kept going. Finally, there were no more bedrooms. Baffled, I turned to retrace my steps and heard a cough. I recalled finding him hidden in London. When I opened the linen closet door, there was Byron on the floor, with his back to a pile of folded bedclothes.

The small space smelt of lavender. On each shelf were small sachets cinched with a bow. I stood for a moment, and he tugged on the hem of my dress. His was not the form of a hunched bloodsucker. He looked up at me and was not even a man but a boy.

I knelt before him.

We kissed and kissed, yet instead of passion, I felt each lip touch, each tongue trace was filled with sorrow. I focused on the space between our mouths rather than the connecting parts.

He whispered, "I wonder sometimes if I will run out of ideas."

"Is that why you suggested the ghosts?"

"I gave the prompt to match the weather. And my mood." He pushed away, wedging himself in the corner, with his arms over his knees. "I wrote a fragment—but I won't continue." He put his forehead to his knees. "Did you write anything?"

I nodded. I hadn't put all of it down, but I didn't want to lose his attention and thought I might keep it by being engaging. By being—if not fun—then creative. "It's a love story."

"How boring."

I glared, but the only light came from the cracked-open door, so it was possible he did not see. "It's a love story in the afterlife."

He sat up straight, interest piqued. "Continue."

"A girl. A man. Their bodies becoming . . . " I paused. "One." He groaned in excitement. "And then she kills him."

"Bloody hell, Claire."

"Exactly," I said. "Quite . . . Or perhaps he kills her. I haven't worked that bit out yet. Regardless of the killing, one of them is dead. But it is only then that they realise they are truly in love and must proceed as a strange couple—"

"A ghost and a killer?"

"Or . . ." My mind raced. I could feel the story. I reached for his hand. He did not pull away. His touch urged me on. "Or they can still somehow be intimate—"

"You make the story, you make the rules."

True. My words sped up, so caught up in the story was I. "So they are intimate and secretive and all proceeds apace until after several months she is at market."

"Has she no staff to go for her?"

"She must take action lest she only sit round with a ghost playing Whist, which is not gripping. So she markets and is gripped with a craving."

"For blood?"

"For milk. She goes to the barrel and ladles it into her carrying pot, but when she looks into the liquid, she has no reflection."

Byron leant towards me. "Are you saying she herself is an apparition?"

"Possibly. Or would you find it more compelling if she were a person still, yet perhaps had fallen pregnant—"

"By the ghost?"

"Of course by the ghost—whom else?" I glared again.

"And because she is with ghost-child her reflection is gone?"

I felt the frantic pace of words and plot leave me. "I don't quite know. It's possible none of it makes sense."

His voice tightened. "Of course it doesn't make sense, Claire," he said. Did he mean the story? Or us also? "Yet if you write it properly, it will be believable."

Believable. That was a word I wanted. "Do you think I should keep writing the ghost story?" I wished I didn't want his approval, yet I knew I did.

He moved towards me. "I think if you find yourself unable to think of anything else, you ought to write it down. For that is the writing spirit tapping your scalp, and it is not something to turn from."

In one smooth motion, he pulled me towards him and, with his good foot, closed the closet door, leaving us in complete darkness.

I could barely breathe, for since I followed Mary I had a fear of dark rooms. Without the distraction of looking at him, Byron's voice was deep and clear. "On the highest shelf in the library of my mind, there is a book in which we are together. It is true that a part of me, albeit small, could imagine this, Claire."

My heart rose as our hands pressed together. "I, too, could imagine this."

"Still, Claire, it is a book on a very high shelf, the sort one might only find incidentally when on that rolling ladder—which I must rarely use with my foot. Despite myself, I did come to a fondness for you." He spoke in the past tense, the language of love lost.

I reached for him, and his arms around me felt lithe and warm, and when we kissed, I tasted that sorrow again. We were close in that dark room, skin to skin, mouth on mouth, mouth on neck, teeth on neck. Such a loving and intimate movement. Yet it felt like a goodbye.

31

In the kitchen while forming dough into small boules or in the library scratching pen nib onto journal pages while the others wrote, my chest ached for Byron. I was aware of my heart in the way of a muscle sore after an arduous walk. The notion that I had a muscle right in the centre of my chest, unnoticed until it beat fast with desire or felt punctured in my own body, was curious. As humans, did we not notice what we had until it was broken or aching?

I went to check on the bread rounds after Elsa slipped them into the oven. They were plump and perfect, and I could not resist snatching one. I put it in my pocket, and it nearly burned my thigh but I did not mind. Outside, I went to the lake and stood at its lip. To balance the heat from the roll, I took off my boots and stockings, caring not a whiff about propriety—for that is what a broken heart will do to a person—I put my feet into the cold water and pinched off bits of hot bread.

Mary fairly floated on the lawn and made her way down to me. I handed her a bite of bread, and she nibbled it, looking out at the mountains. "I should not have thought how majestic the view would be," she said. "After all this time here still one cannot overstate the sublime. How small one feels."

"I rarely feel small," I said. But then I thought of the coppice invasion, the closet sorrow, my own dwindling prospects.

Mary reached for my hand. Feeling her dainty cold touch made tears come. She thumbed one of the teardrops and did what we had as children and ate it. That was also siblings, trying to take the tears for the other.

Mary sighed. "Oh, Claire, one cannot be angry at a dog for behaving exactly as one expects a dog to behave."

I had not told her of our ending, yet she recited Byron's own words at me because she knew. I clenched my jaw in anger. Everyone seemed to know everything about me before I knew it myself: a humiliating part of youth. "So how a man behaves is also a fault of mine rather than a character deficit in him?"

Why had I thought myself doglike? For truly a dog is loyal, yet perhaps they have no other option. A dog chooses not when or what it eats, when it might run outside, where it sleeps. A dog cannot decide even when it might shit. I had looked to others for praise for my loyalty. I had to forget that and be not doglike but like the ibex, alone and mystified but fighting for my survival. The ache I'd felt for Byron would recede daily, as though I watched it from a great distance.

"You seek knowledge and wisdom," Mary said. "As I once did. All one might hope is that when it arrives it is without the serpent's sting."

She was correct. She was eloquent. I hated her words. "You have been reading too much Milton," I said, and chucked the last of the bread into the lake, where it was swallowed in one beaky gulp by a grebe.

32

THE LONGEST DAY OF the year.

Try as I might to keep my spirits up, after my conversation with Mary, I felt I was coming apart. Losing the haven of my coppice had broken something in me—a much larger part of me than I might have anticipated. Those feelings of doubt, of pain, only intensified as I understood the kiss in the dark, warm closet with Byron to be our last.

I splintered on the page. Everything felt shorter—the daylight hours, our time at Diodati, even my words felt they ought to give over to terseness.

The day's hot breeze felt nice at first. Only in the corners where the terrace met the villa exterior or in the craggy shaded bits of stone wall by the orchard did I see icy bits, cold runoff, the last vestiges of the dark chill. Without those, one would think I'd imagined the whole thing.

Finally, summer.

At last the sweet swipe of warmth over my ankles, around my neck as I stood looking first at the lake and then at the front of the villa. The water contained within it stories of boat trips from the hotel, a bottle of ginger beer dropped over the side, branches and algae and green scum and the bones of what had once been living things. And in the villa were all the nights and conversations captured in the walls. People held memories, but places did, too. I thought of my room in Lynmouth, which grew tighter, the bed narrower in each recall. I thought of the wobbly house in London, my tiny writing nook, which was cast in sinister candlelight, Shelley lurking in the hallway whilst Mary slept the heavy hours of a new mother plagued by the morbs.

I tried to recreate in my mind the room in the inn where first we went on their elopement. Had the walls been peach or lightest blue? It bothered me that I could not exactly remember. As though not remembering was a betrayal of myself.

Mary wrote her story with such fervour I envied her. Polidori had taken up Byron's fragment of story and seemed caught up in that. Renewed by sun, Elsa stretched the meager fruit harvest with mashed swede to make more jams and put those up. Shelley had disappeared into town for some untold business. Byron, giving me as much attention as the wallpaper, had laid out his gear for an upcoming boat trip, on which I was most definitely not invited.

Everyone seemed to be preparing for the future, and I knew I needed to do the same.

The air was a parenthesis of things I could not say. The flowers burst open, all sending their scent out at the same time so it was impossible to discern what one was smelling. My nose was confused. My body felt heavy. I wanted to be alone with my trees and moss for comfort. Wanting also company, but if not Byron's then whose?

I wrote all of this down, for perhaps I, too, would be a writer. Was one already. At what point did one declare what one was? Polidori was a doctor who could not practise. Was he still a doctor? When might I allow myself to announce myself as something?

It was my own company I longed for.

Not the me of now but the one I would have been had I never gone with Mary on the elopement, never met Shelley, never written to Byron and thus never received his invitations, never brought everyone here. Never never never never.

Who was that girl? We each sat writing, haunted by the ghosts of the people we could have been.

33

"IF YOU'RE NOT MINDFUL you'll slice a finger right off," Elsa said. Still, I did not slow down, for I had only moments—the sun's cape on the lawn gave me a chance to regain my footing with Byron. I set out cold gravenche Shelley had caught side by side with Byron that morning, the two men with shoulders touching and lips moving, saying what I did not know.

I had filleted the fish myself, sat with the tangled bloody innards in my lap. I had skills and knew they would save me. I did not retch as the guts sluiced into a bucket.

"Bring these," Elsa said, as she waved a pile of almond biscuits. She'd wrapped the sweets in a blue linen cloth. It was an eye-catching blue, not far off from the blue of my journal, and that gave me a moment of pause.

I wiped my hands on my apron, and I flicked back through the journal—nothing missing, nothing torn. And yet. The ribbon I used to keep my place was not where I kept it, at the Drury Theatre meeting. A marker of sorts. Had I carelessly tucked it in near to that date but not exactly there? I puzzled over this as I packed more items.

"Do you have what you need, Claire?" Elsa said.

I did not know what to answer, for I had thought what I needed was Byron. Or Shelley's praise. I did not truly wish for either of those. "You are so good to me."

She handed me the heavy basket. "Someone ought to be."

DOWN BY the lake, Byron and Shelley stood as though posing for a nautical oil painting. Each wore loose-fitting slop trousers made of thick canvas and an osnaburg shirt, leather packs and jugs of water at the ready. Elise watched from a distance, holding William on her hip and encouraging him to wave. Polidori watched from the terrace.

I brought the basket of biscuits, breads, and fish and knew they would eat it giving no thought to the efforts that went into its making. Shelley slung his arm round Byron's shoulder as they surveyed the accoutrements required for their journey. Their smiles showed their delight, for it seemed there was nothing men enjoyed more than the acquiring of items for manly outings. How envious I was of their impenetrable male bond, an allegiance as strong as the church buttresses in town.

Byron handed me a letter. "Be a good Claire-y and post this?"

What could I do but nod? I did not think about refusing or throwing it in the lake until much later.

Mary fretted over Shelley—did he know to drink enough water, would his stomach survive? Byron could not hide his annoyance with her. "We shall sail around the lake. Not the world."

"And we have Maurice," Shelley said. A hefty man with tree-trunk arms stacked more gear. "A boatman well-versed in the ways of the water."

Byron cast a glance at the lake. "See the little boat I bought? A chaloupe. We shall call to various ports around the lake—" Here Shelley raised his eyebrows, for Byron might have just announced there would be fucking at each port, "to see what Rousseau described in Heloise."

"We shall dine on wild honey and chestnuts," Shelley said. Even the lake seemed to roll its great eye at this.

"And I shall continue to add more to *Childe Harold*."

Shelley nodded, ever-entranced by his friend and competitive to boot. "And I shall begin—something, I am sure of it. A hymn. To the beauty of the lake, to the environs . . ."

"To the wild honey and Byron's chestnuts?" I offered.

Mary snickered. Not once had they asked what we would be working on. I studied Byron's otherworldly beauty as he set about loading the boat in the shallows before heading to the deep. He was so close to being human, which was sadder than not being human at all. Mary paused, a sudden look of panic on her as she shouted.

"Mind you remember Shelley cannot swim!" They either did not hear or ignored her.

34

I POSTED BYRON'S LETTER BUT not before reading it. He'd written to Scrope Davies.

Come visit my v. pretty villa on the Lake. Alps behind and. Mt Jura and water in front. Diodati. Pls bring with you Waite's red (only red) tooth powder & brushes & tell Murray I have much of the 3rd Canto of Childe Harolde completed. Ought to be finished by the time you arrive. Will be on Lake Leman shortly in open boat and v. much looking forward to change of scenery.

Yrs ever most truly, B.

PS I left Dr Pollydolly at Diodati with a sprained ankle acquired by successfully tumbling from a stone wall—the man cannot jump. Add that to his list of faults.

Byron had written Polidori's injury as an insult, as though he had been a jester performing for the court and fallen. That was untrue.

On the way back from the coppice that day with Shelley, my spirits in tatters, my dress also, I had sobbed so loudly I scared myself. And only the fillers, pillars, spillers to hear me. Shame vined up my legs. I had to get away, start a life on my own. And then, in the midst of my tears, "Claire!" Polidori had waved to me from the stone wall, "I shall help you—poor Claire." His hands on his hips in his best pirate impression, yet before he could prove himself the hero and tend to me, he fell. Any chance of him asking about my tears or my torn dress trotted away because he held his ankle and moaned so much eventually Fletcher came. Fletcher gripped Polidori under the arms but his eyes roamed my dress. "We had better get you cleaned up," he had said to Polidori, but again he looked at me. I took this as instruction and had gone into the cottage to do so.

Reading Byron's letter only confirmed that he was writing me out of his life. No mention of me. No matter what story was told there would always be bits left out. I was guilty of this, too.

I wondered if Scrope would come to Diodati. They were old friends, so a visit would not be unexpected. Yet, too, Byron had told me how Scrope's biggest worth as a friend was being there to clean up a mess.

35

I FORAGED. ONIONS AND PILES of nettles collected using the thick edges of my skirts so I would not sting my skin, bilberries and beach roses, garlic and dandelion buds. I added them to the list I had of each item I had found or foraged or cooked since arriving.

Each time I copied Elsa's instructions about when to strain beets for red spätzle, how to knead for better chew, the correct amount of chives for knödel, I felt more accomplished, better prepared for a future. I would be an explorer, able to survive on my own in the woods or field, mountain or streamside. I quieted my mind by imagining I would discover a new place the way Captain Cook had mapped the east coast of Australia. I had learnt of Cook's bravery. His rise from poverty to apprenticeship to maths and navigation reminded me of Byron, that somehow rising above one's birth circumstance became reason for cheering.

I hefted the woven willow basket onto the prep table. A few bilberries escaped.

"We have enough," Elsa said. "Too much."

"I thought we might never have too much." I wiped my brow on my forearm.

"We have only a smaller group now, and your sister barely touches her food."

I had the skill of being able to find food, and yet what good was it if I had no one other than myself to feed?

"DO YOU think writing matters if you are the only one to read it?" I asked Mary. She had set up a makeshift desk in the shade of a poplar tree. Only the tree was narrow and she had to keep shifting the desk each time the sun moved. She ought to have chosen an umbrella pine.

"I wish to be left alone, to work," Mary said. "I have not even been to bed."

"So you abandon me, too, then—" I hated my own neediness, yet I did not feel useful.

"You have the power to vex even the grass, Claire." Mary's small hands clenched, tiny fists like an infant. I felt giant and awkward. Any grace I had once held—entering the Drury Theatre or unclothed in the lake—had gone. Only in my coppice had I felt beautiful. And since Shelley's invasion there, not even there. "You make my work about you. It is not."

"All of you focus so on writing when the world is here—in front of you." I stretched my arms wide.

"You are the world then?"

"No—the lake, that clutch of trees—" I pointed to the coppice. I ought to tell her Shelley had been there. Taken my journal. Read it. Yet I refrained from doing so because I did not want to hurt her—why should he have gone there to seek me out specifically, demand to have my book, how could I ever convince him to leave me be? Those were questions I could not bring myself to answer. "I feel I am most myself outside. The skylarks and grebes, flowers, the insects—"

Mary looked up. Swatted something away. "They are ugly."

"I am ugly," I said. I was her little sister again. Powerless and sad.

Mary's face became a statue of itself. Stone. "You are not ugly. Impetuous and perhaps fickle—"

"Fickle?" Here I mustered strength. "I am more loyal than you might ever know."

"Is that how you see yourself?" Mary glared at me.

"You can be cruel, Mary. Is that what you write? A ghost story of a girl whose heart is stone?"

"If I am coldhearted, then I am the ugly one, am I not?" She stood, ready to move the desk again. Her skirts billowed in the breeze, a flag of a country with a population of one. "If we truly love someone, we must love even the ugly insides of them, did you not say that?"

Her words struck me into silence. For I had not said them. I had only written them in my journal.

36

MARY BECKONED ME TO stand by her outdoor desk as she wrote, hair in a swathe over her face. At her urging, I read over her shoulder. I had been foolish to think of my privacy as anything other than an illusion. For though we had not shared pages for months, the groundwork had been laid so long ago that both she and Shelley assumed they had rights to my words, my days, my everything.

Mary wrote: *Who is responsible for creating? The pursuit of knowledge could lead to answers or to ruin—for we might learn too much. Still, we are made by those we love only to be undone by them only to again be rebuilt. No matter our creations, they will blame their creator for negligence.*

Mary wrote that the creature—her creature—brought only torment. I retreated to the lake edge to watch a pair of swans, a mother and her fluffy grey cygnet, their graceful necks nuzzling. Did my sister mean science? Or the way she and her mother had been wrecked by pregnancy, loss, birth? I turned back and saw Mary stare at me with a mix of fatigue, dismay, and caring.

I wondered if perhaps I, too, was her sad creation.

I SPENT the afternoon helping Elise fill out her papers, trying again for her passport.

"I will come with you when you depart," she said, taking her time to make sure her printing was neat. "I must go with you, that is what your sister tells me."

Afterwards, Mary was thankful to me. "Come," she said. "Let us celebrate the possibility of further help—and my progress on the page."

She and Polidori and I sat in the library, revisiting ideas of ghost stories. Polidori, at Byron's desk, said, "Claire, read *Christabel* again."

"*The lovely lady, Christabel, / Whom her father loves so well, / What makes her in the wood so late, / A furlong from the castle gate?*"

Polidori furrowed his brow. "Geraldine is a she-vampire."

"A vampire, you mean." I read on and stopped. "Christabel praying in the woods, the night she spent with Geraldine. Must we hear another round of two maidens punished for their sins of being together?"

Polidori looked away lest he be guilty by association. Mary shut me down with a look and spoke as though giving instructions for a cake.

"Things not being what they seem, evil lurking under goodness," Mary said.

My chest ached. My belly felt full, though I had not wanted the salad lunch Elsa prepared. I would ask her for an elbow of bread and a plop of jam.

"Still," I said, my voice small and distant, as though I spoke from inside a cave. "What is most important is that Christabel cannot say what happened to her."

Mary shrugged. "Ah yes, the use of spells in otherworldly works can be useful."

There the silence moved in like fog. Mary took up her pen, and Polidori hunched over Byron's desk, took a quill, touched it to his tongue, and began to write on Byron's pages.

Polidori wrote each word as he said it. "A vampire is a creature of thirst."

POLIDORI HAD written his doctoral thesis on somnambulism and took to demonstrating his familiarity with the subject by roaming the halls at night while the men were still off boating. William slept through, the easy sleep of the unhaunted young, Elise near him. I found Mary awake at all hours, churning out pages, line after line as though spinning wool.

When I told her this she nodded, eyes wild, "Yes, Claire, yes. That is the thing of it—I make a whole thing of its parts."

I could not *say the thing* to her. Not even with Byron and Shelley away.

POLIDORI WROTE of the art of being a gentleman. One with fangs. Mary kept writing. I tried to write. Yet each time I set about trying to make a story, I found what I was really doing was trying to keep from writing certain parts of the story. As a result I kept balling paper and tossing it into the fire.

"That's quite enough, Claire," Mary said without looking up. "Are we made of paper?"

"I do not mean to be wasteful," I said. "I could write in between your lines if you prefer."

She moved her page closer to her chest. "I should prefer to keep this for myself," she said. "Still, if you haven't an idea, take one of your walks."

This was solid advice, for I did not want to write something hollow. I would have to accept that writing demanded an admission.

37

A MOONSHAFT PIERCED THROUGH THE curtains and found my eyes with such targeted aim I had no choice but to awaken. The villa was quiet. No Polidori clomping. No Elise in the rocker, holding William as she gave him another bottle.

I slung my bare feet onto the cold floor. A gut-tug forced me up. I needed to find my sister. There was no apparent distress when I reached her. She had fallen asleep on but not in the bed, pages under her like leaves in my coppice. An ink bottle had spilt and darkened the waist of her dress, spread, gotten on her hands, which had found her face, and she had stains all over. I ought to have woken her. Cleaned her up. But I found myself still. Staring.

She had not come into my room those many months ago. Had not awoken in similar fashion on her elopement and found me—unalone—in my bed. Perhaps that was why she did not, could not, wake up. I took a small breath, ready to leave her, when her eyes shot open. In the moonlight they glowed, her small, sharp teeth visible. I gave a gasp, expecting her to say my name. She did not.

In the morning, she appeared at my door. The only remnant of the night was a slight shadow of ink on her palm.

"Listen," she said. "This is what I have written: *He sleeps but he is awakened; opens his eyes, behold the horrid thing stands at his bedside, opening curtains, and looking on him with yellow, watery, but speculative eyes.*" She drew a breath. "Thank you, Claire."

Without asking why I had come to her room, she turned and left.

38

A FEW DAYS LATER, THE post brought with it a card from Shelley addressed to Mary, so of course I read it:

> *Byron has written a poem, The Prisoner of Chillon. I am an atheist and yet have found belief. How wrong I was not to have seen what was before me until now—the peaks, white-tipped and aching upwards, vast water here before me and long after—this is prayer.*
>
> *I began Hymn to Intellectual Beauty as we walked and found Edward Gibbon's house and garden. All in ruins now. Quite fitting as the man penned Decline and Fall of the Roman Empire.*
>
> *We traipsed round the grounds. I helped Byron collect rose petals and acacia stems (glorious scent).*

Here my heart leapt for a moment as I thought of Byron sending petals to me the way he had placed them on my naked body when I raged with fever.

> *Byron had the petals packaged up and sent to John Murray to remind his publisher of Gibbon's last lines. Byron in foul state after word from Mme de Stael that Lamb's novel has succeeded, he is widely considered to be Glenarvon, "mad, bad, and dangerous to know." Make no mistake, no matter what is truth, people will believe what they wish.*

Mad, bad, and dangerous to know—and yet unpunished for it, for men could behave as monsters and suffer little consequence, where my life was built on consequences.

BUGS LITTERED the lawn. I tried to put the cockchafers right side up. They skittered on my palms, and no matter how much I helped them, wound up upside down again.

Mary appeared, watched me, and said it was a waste of time. An odd rose, tiny, the lightest pink right before it goes white had grown on branches and arched over another tree, creating the shape of a turtle, which I pointed out to Mary. "I don't see it," she said.

I tried again. "Claire, you see things that aren't there and do not see what is right in front of you. It's very young of you."

"Mary, if you lack the eyes to see it, that does not mean it isn't there." I loathed that I saw so much. Felt sick about being the translator and cartographer for everyone around me. My most recent library learnings: Epiphytic plants are plants that grow harmlessly on other plants and derive their nutrition and water from air. They do not cause any harm to the host. While in the case of parasitic plants, they derive their nutrition from the host, adversely affecting the host plant. I could no longer separate the science of what I was reading from our group—who amongst us was host, who the one draining life?

39

BEFORE DAWN I AWOKE. Dressed at the cottage. Folded or hung my clothing. Wiped the desk and made my bed. A sense of order felt good. I coiled my hair in a taut bun at the nape of my neck and went with schoolmarm steps to the villa.

In the kitchen, Elsa was already at work setting sprigs of tarragon into crocks of olive oil. She gave me a once over. "Aren't you tidy today?"

"Will the oil take up the taste of the herb?"

"Yes. By autumn."

"Where will you be then?" I asked.

"The New World." She slipped another sprig into another cruet.

"Is it safe to be there?"

She shrugged. "Each day a woman—a girl!—must ask that, no?" I nodded, but it was a slow response. Elsa swiped her hair back from her face with her arm. "And you, where will you be?"

"This is the point for today," I said. "I should like to propose—"

Elsa looked up, gave me a look of such sorrow I thought I might melt and slip through a crack in the stone floor. "I wish you—"

"Oh, no—not with you. I should not impose myself on your travels—I mean to stay on my own completely." I started again. "I should like to propose I gain employment as a cook. I might work in the kitchen . . ." Another look from her. "Not at Diodati." I knew it would be backbreaking work, tiring and subservient, yet I would control the food, the heart of a house.

I needed to go somewhere new. A place where I was not known. Possibly would not be known at all. I should not be known as a girl who followed her talented sister. Not seen as the lesser of two wives of a famous poet. Not the lover of the most famous writer. Not herself a failed writer. "I should like to go off on my own—and be free of . . ." I did not say more.

Elsa nodded. "You have many fine traits. Useful skills."

I smoothed my dress down. I ought to learn better to hot iron. I had ideas of how I would make my way. Elsa hummed to herself as she kept at her task. I helped ferry each cruet to the shelf and took each happy exchange as a measure of her support.

I would wrap up my time at Diodati. I would pack my few belongings in a case I might manage on my own. I would take my journal, dresses, and a clean apron, say my adieus and start fresh. A new world.

I helped Elsa clean everything up. She hadn't said I was foolish to consider pushing off on my own, had not scoffed at my youth. Rows of cruets each with sprigs, all I had foraged, washed, dried, chopped, put up for a season at Diodati neither of us would experience. Elsa faced me and gave a tight-lipped smile that could not cover her concern—as though she knew something I did not.

PART FOUR

JULY & AUGUST 1816

VILLA DIODATI & CHAMONIX

1

I CREPT INTO BYRON'S CHAMBER, where the emptiness was a soft song of soured love. I no longer longed to give him my body, rather I wanted to take something.

A clean sheet. A perfect new quill all the way from the Kingdom of Norway. The good pot of iron gall ink shaped like a monk's hood. I took what I wanted and left. He was still away with Shelley. Had he been there and heard me in the room, he would have pretended otherwise.

I set my treasures on Byron's large desk in the library so I might face the water and begin my own ghost story. I ought to be able to tell a tale the way I had by the fire. I sat. Pen daggered before the blank page. The lake was flat and refused to reflect anything other than the plain sky, which was the colour of laundry water and entirely uninspiring.

Polidori's clomp announced his arrival.

"Forgive my intrusion," he said. "I am meant to send another round of . . . pages to John Murray."

"No bother," I said. "I sit with perfect paper and a new pen—and cannot write a lick."

Polidori took a seat in the tufted armchair. He splayed his leather notebook and readied his pen. He did not write. Instead he closed his book, tossed it on the floor by the fire. "I should not wish to send anything to Murray. I remain committed, finished with all of the gossip. I should prefer to write of a more . . . substantial subject." Yet he did not write. He rested his hands in his lap like a schoolboy finished with his exams.

We sat for a long time just like that.

"It is as though we are posing for a portrait," I said.

"One which shall never be painted," he said.

I turned to face him. We did not *say the thing* yet we knew it to be true: Of our group, we were the ones of least consequence. The ones most likely to be forgotten.

2

I MEMORIZED THE DAYS WHILST Mary wrote her story. She set the words in a large notebook in which she had already begun to number the pages. I watched her write the word *creature.*

The fangs of the creature already grasping my neck.

I read her sentence aloud. As soon as the words were out, Mary heard the problem, for fangs do not grasp. From the doorway, Polidori said, "Is that not terrifying—the idea of being killed by the mouth of another? I might use that myself."

"Victor Frankenstein is not killed then," Mary said. "He is in the midst of a nightmare."

I watched her rewrite the sentence. Gone was the word *creature.*

I felt the fingers of the monster already grasping my neck,
and screamed aloud with agony and terror.

I leaned forward, sneaking more of her words.

Sleep did not afford me respite from thought and misery;
my dreams presented a thousand objects that scared me.
Towards morning I was possessed by a kind of nightmare;
I felt the fiend's grasp in my neck and could not free
myself from it; groans and cries rang in my ears.

I stuck my finger to the page. "That sounds terribly like me in my night terrors," I said.

Mary shut her notebook so quickly I knew the ink would smudge and render some words illegible. "This story has nothing to do with you, Claire."

LATER, WE heard revelry from across the lake. Distant music from a hotel lunch party. A warm wind wafted over our knees—mine bare, for with no one nearby I had pulled up my skirts and relished the feel of air on the small hairs on my thighs.

"You are quite hairy," Mary said.

"You are pale as milk," I told her. These were words of love because we were alone and the day was sunny. In this spirit I went on. "You seem taken by your work—isn't it funny that an offhand suggestion from Byron brings you such inspiration." Mary dug her fingers in the dry sand until she came upon one of the shells I had been collecting. She handed it to me. "You have such speed with words—I have no doubt you will make something of this latest piece."

"Your spirit is indeed a generous one." She gave enough pause that I let my heart soar with this small compliment. What could be better than sitting in warm sand with one's dear sister on a sunny day, trading niceties?

Mary cleared her throat. "Yet, Claire, your incessant emotional giving builds in the receiver a festering ingratitude—yours is the sort of giving in which the other person will always disappoint. They will not ever give enough in return."

I did not wish to hear her words. I also knew immediately they were true. "So I must go against my nature, then?"

Mary shook her head, her mouth pinched. "I can offer no advice. For I give so differently from you."

"Yes. Yours is a frugal sort of giving." I wanted to hand the shell back to her. I also knew she didn't want it, so this would only serve to punish myself.

"I am not poor in love, Claire."

"No, yet you behave as a miser," I said. "I have more feelings than I know what to do with and no control over them, and you have vast control yet suffer from a dearth of feeling to the point of being manufactured."

Mary did not protest. She perched her chin on her forearms and looked out at the lake and pointed so I would turn, too. There in the centre two cygnets shy-necked with their swan faces, so near each other they formed a heart.

"Between the two of us is the balance of giving," she said.

We sat in quiet—both of us wishing just for that moment to be a little more like the other, until the swans glided away and the light went with them.

3

AFTER TEN DAYS, THE boat was close to shore. The best weather of the summer had been saved for their trip. The men had started their return to shore while I had been picking mulberries. I had a half-filled basket swinging from my arm. I left them with Elsa, who would prove alchemist by turning them into jam we—well, likely not us—could enjoy years later, a strange sort of travel through time.

I scrubbed my stained fingers, but to no avail. Still, I felt Elsa studying me—her mindfulness was not unpleasant, only curious.

FF's loud bark and the peacocks' screams signaled the boat was back.

Their laughter and dirty feet told of their closeness and shared experiences. I would never know what they had seen or spoken of. The way Byron regarded Shelley's gait, the way Shelley fawned over Byron's easy stroke in the water as he swam to fetch the oar Shelley had let go. Byron dove down and resurfaced again and again like the slippery seals I had seen in Lynmouth.

Shelley announced his devotion to Byron with a toweling robe that he presented as a gift-wrapped parcel and then tucked around Byron—their tenderness made me seethe.

How gentle they were with each other. How they anticipated the other's needs—surely you must be frantic with hunger, Shelley. You must set your foot up, come in by the fire, my lord.

Polidori and Mary and Elise and William and I stood there as though made only of ideas, as the men went inside.

We followed them in, as it seemed the polite thing to do. Both men lounged by the fire as Fletcher brought Byron a thick stack of letters that Byron immediately ignored. "There is the pressing matter of—" Fletcher showed a few letters that bore the word *urgent*, a few more with *due upon receipt*.

Shelley took it upon himself to relieve Byron of any concern. "My travel companion and I have both made use of our time," he said. "Byron's canto—complete. 'The Prisoner of Chillon,' also finished. François Bonivard and the plight of solitary confinement at last explored."

"And this one," Byron thumbed to Shelley. "Show them."

Shelley fished a paper from his jacket. Without being asked, he read "*A Hymn to Intellectual Beauty.*" Polidori could not help himself and clapped. Mary had tears in her eyes, either from pride or because they had not asked after her own work. I thought about slugs. How banal they seemed. Slow and harmless. How they decimated entire crops. How Elsa told me the Germans were eating them as food. I could think about slugs and yet make my face and eyes look fully engaged; I was a woman of remarkable talents.

Shelley gave me a warm smile. "Now this goes off to Leigh Hunt—for I have no doubts he will see fit to publish it in *The Examiner*."

I did not want to be amongst them any longer. "Would you like me to post that for you?"

Shelley held the poem out to me for a moment and then, searching my face for congratulations I had not given, seemed to reconsider. "Perhaps I shall post it myself."

SO SHELLEY did not trust me with his work. A slight which surely would free me further. I would be going off on my own soon anyway, so I did not worry too much about his judgement as I went to Elsa. The kitchen was light and hot. Too hot. I immediately felt a prickle of sweat on my scalp and fought the urge to scratch—Elsa did not want hairs in her food.

She beckoned me over with a floury hand to the prep table, where she stood kneading dough—knead knead and then a turn of the dough. As she went she sang a song. *Bim-bam, bim-bim-bim-bam*, she sang. I asked what the song was. "It would not make sense to you, I'm afraid."

I hid my hurt—I would always be able to find hurt, always feel locked out of other people's conversations or language—by gathering all the dough bits still in the rising bowl and on the table and making the tiniest ball of dough. Without warning I popped it into my mouth raw. Chew chew and turn. I knew Elsa saw me do this, but she did not scold me.

"It is only a song that goes *bim-bam, bim-bim-bim-bam* . . ." She laughed. "Only sounds. It's Friday, so I make challot, double-braided." Before I could ask more she said, "Lord Byron likes bread. You like bread. Everyone likes it, even if they don't know this kind of bread."

She showed me the double braiding, the laying of one on top of the other, the double rising. "This is shlissel challah."

"*Shlissel* is key," I said. I thought about how I would make this bread when I was on my own, how good it would feel to have the memory of her as I found employment somewhere far away.

Elsa nodded. "It is a key bread—a secret baked into a loaf. A kind of language. Sweet, soft, shared by a family and then only a memory of itself." She took a brass key from her pocket. "We press it inside the dough, and someone finds it when they rip a piece."

"I will miss you when you leave," I told her. "Unless I leave first."

She raised her eyebrows in a question, but said, "And I you. That is the way of life, coming going." She reached for one of the already baked loaves and pinched off a piece of a braid, hot and warm. "That is the purpose of memory."

"Then I should like to keep this memory nearby."

She gave me a hard look. "Try to make the good memories take up more room on the shelf. When I lost my daughter, I thought so many times of the last nights, the last looks I had of her—well, they were not good sights. I try now to make those smaller, keep the better days bigger. How her hand felt in mine in the bath. How her laugh sounded like rain."

My eyes filled with tears too heavy to swallow back in their sockets, and a few slipped down my face onto the bread I held. I ate, chewing the sweet salt. Elsa did not look away from me. Her eyes were a kind of key which opened the door inside my chest, my belly, where I had locked away all sorts of other memories. Not all of them pleasant. Some of them terrifying and worse still for the loneliness a bad memory entails because it swirls in the mind and we cannot share it with another, not truly.

"I was taught to keep things private," I told her.

"There is a difference between privacy and a secret, yes?"

I did not know what to say.

"You crave the bread, yes?" Elsa said. I nodded. She held my shoulders. "And you have not bled?"

All I thought at first was—she rhymed! Bread and bled. A poet in the kitchen! An unfortunate snort-laugh escaped my mouth. Elsa's wide firm hands gripped my shoulders harder.

"Claire." Elsa took my hand and put it on my own belly. "You understand?"

"Oh." It was such a tiny word.

The only one I could make come out. It had been a long time since I had done the maths of mess, of moons and blood and muslin strips. "But I had some—"

"Spots?" Elsa made a motion as though flicking water droplets from her fingers. I nodded. "Not *niddah*. The beginning."

She held the loaf to me. The bread was warm and smelt sweet but felt heavy in my arms. Inside was a real key. A lucky thing to find.

"Come," she said, and took my hand. "I will make Grandma Sugar. It won't fix the problem, but will ease the ache."

4

DARKNESS FILLED THE SKY, the air, my lungs, as though I had fallen into an inkpot.

I ran to the coppice with no lantern, trusting my feet to know the way and trusting the trees and woods not to send out an animal to rip me apart. Or perhaps I wished for that. Let me be eaten alive, I thought.

But then I reached the dip in the ground, the easy softness. Perhaps it was possible to reclaim the gentle green dewy space there.

I lay flat on my back and cried.

I cried because I was in shock and I cried because I missed my mother and harder because I understood then that a part of me would miss my mother for the rest of my life.

Missing her echoed from pine to pine, a lonely throbbing ache in my chest that was not founded in truth, for if she had been there I thought she might have slapped me—stupid Claire.

Yet I fought the logic, preferring the mother in my mind who looked like my mother, smelt like my mother, had my mother's watery green-hazel eyes, yet acted not like my mother, spoke more kindly—*sweet Claire, fret not*—and held me.

Only the earth held me. Buoyed my big body on its soft, tender moss.

I had another secret. And I knew I had to keep it for as long as possible—which also meant keeping my journal with me, for I trusted no one to keep their eyes from it.

~~MARCH,~~ APRIL?, MAY ?, JUNE—. I spent the day flipping pages, counting. Trying to reconcile numbers and dates and the insides of my body, which I would never see. Had Mary been happy to learn she had fallen pregnant with Shelley's baby? I thought back—she wasn't unhappy but perhaps was not joyful, merely accepting it as an inevitable outcome. I felt nothing but fear.

In my mind I could see the stack of rags, feel their coarseness in my hands, the chafing on my waist from the odd belt I fastened to secure one.

𝍸 𝍸 𝍸 𝍸 scratches for days, dots, dashes, the lost language of my girlhood. No matter how many times I counted, I came up with confusion. I wished to confide in someone—but knew Byron and Shelley would have their doubts about me, Mary would find only horror, and Polidori would only nod in the quiet, grim way of doctors who think of new life as only miraculous rather than ruinous.

I ATTENDED my own funeral today. A pall of mourning for the girl I used to be and was no longer. There lies Claire, who was unfun. Who was devoted. Who was like any ordinary girl—for what is jovial in a man is taken for compliance in a woman, and I had done no better than to succumb to ordinariness.

I lay part of myself to rest, wondering if I always would grieve the selves sunk in the lake, buried in the field on which the cows grazed the meager grass.

Come back, I wished to shout to her, yet feared she had receded already to the netherworld of shadow and unmade poems.

5

JULY CONTINUED TO UNEARTH itself from the freeze. Dusty sunlight. A near-continuous dripping of frost runoff, crusty ice wedges leaking down the roof pitch to one's hair in a surprising and chilly alarm. Great crested grebes with their wing-slap on the water's surface.

Everywhere, everything appeared to be waking from a sick slumber. With my hands on my belly, I ought to have felt some sort of hope. A renewed vibrance. Instead, I felt trapped inside my own body. Skin flushed. Hair thicker. Belly and hips bigger—not wildly, yet enough that I could tell. My whole being carrying ornaments of shame.

Shelley and Byron never tired of congratulating each other about the work they'd completed, and engaged in a game of Pale-maille, content with mallets and balls. On the lawn, Polidori fretted over his story. Elise sat with William. Mary broke her writing practice only to say to Elise, "How would I ever do without you?" which pleased Elise.

"Shelley says I am one of the family now, so I will come back with you," Elise said. Mary's face crumbled a moment until she rebuilt herself. "Your sister sent off for my papers."

"Wonderful, of course," Mary said.

Elise nodded, not seeing my sister's gratitude had turned to doubt."What happens if my passport does not come through in time?"

I watched this as though watching a West End show—enjoying myself in a passive way in the sunshine, all the while knowing what I knew.

Any dreams I had of building a life somewhere else had been dashed in a single moment with Elsa. And of course I felt a fool for not knowing. So many bread ends had I gnawed on. So many queasy days, feeling I wore a body that was not mine and yet, my body was not ever truly mine, so how was I to know the difference?

I fetched four stones to anchor a coarse linen sheet to the ground. Byron sat with Shelley next to him as though they were the betrothed couple.

"I find I cannot write, having been so long cooped up here," Shelley said. "I come back again to themes of change, of metamorphosis. Should you mind terribly if I had a change of pace? A few days in Chamonix?" Shelley asked. Mary opened her mouth to respond, yet Byron beat her to it, for the question had been meant for him.

"Clever man, splendid idea," Byron said. I hoped they would leave and not come back.

"And Claire?" Byron said, without looking at me. It was not a question so much as a command.

Of course Shelley agreed. Mary said nothing on my behalf. Did she wish me to come along with her as I always had done? Or did she not wish to leave me—desperation on display—with Byron to have Polidori again take up his gossip pen?

"We can see the mountains perfectly well from here," I said. "No need to go to Chamonix to do that."

Byron crossed his arms. "Her intensity is rather contrary to a good time, is it not?" The silence that followed was everyone's agreement.

I went to fuss with the foodstuffs. Elise stood by me with William. "You have a way with a table," she said, with a tenderness that seemed to have nothing to do with the way I splayed pats of butter onto a plate.

"I mind not the tasks," I said, for what else might I say without screaming—what would I do with my life? How had I fallen into this mess? Why did I repel people so? Why did my sister value the life she'd created over defending me? "I do not mind the tasks, for they are easy to do compared with bigger problems."

"And you write everything in your book, I hear," Elise said.

"Where did you hear that?" I asked, though of course she had become the air of the villa, everywhere and in each room at all times. And perhaps had been in Shelley's confidence. I looked to make sure my journal was where I had left it on the picnic cloth. It was.

Mary said to no one in particular, "Progress is being made."

"You say that as though you are not the one making it," I said. I brought her cheese she would not eat in a gesture of kindness she did not need. I refused to treat my body gingerly, to give myself over to the news.

Mary nodded, "That is how the best writing feels, as though it comes through my hand but from somewhere else."

Polidori's eyes flitted from one person to the next. His hand did not. "I am stuck, for I have taken Byron's idea and made it my own—it is mine, is it not?"

"A story becomes yours if you make it so," Mary said.

Elise held William, who gummed a crust of bread and spat it on the lawn. I ate nothing. I wished to leave, to start my life anew, and yet could not. I did not rest my hands on my belly for fear of drawing attention to its new protrusion. I tilted my head to my chest lest my doubling chin suggest I had rounded. How public it was to be a woman with a body, how humiliating to understand someone might know more about me than I knew about myself.

For the first time, I felt lucky Mary's powers of observation did not match mine. That she overlooked me constantly was in my favour.

A gust of wind swept through and dislodged a stack of toasts. They tumbled to the sheet, which caused FF to rise on his back legs and leap in his blundering heft to consume them, a great and gentle beast, but not in possession of coordination, so he wound up mainly on Shelley.

"He has bruised my organs," Shelley said.

"Bruised your manhood is more apt," Byron said. Polidori fussed over Shelley, which was just what was required.

"The water is far too placid," I said. The chill from June returned into my skin. Dread slipped its gloves over my hands.

"If you find the scene all too calm, perhaps you ought take your leave," Byron said, just as the lake spewed wind so powerful it shook the plates.

Of course it was ridiculous: the clatter of cutlery and disaster of sandwiches flying as FF snuffed up every available morsel as Byron still lay on his side, amused, and Mary scowled at ink splatter on her pages, while Shelley and Polidori played hospital picnic.

Byron continued to lounge. His languor infuriated Mary. Her small body tensed as she glared at him while trying to clean up her ink mess. Yet she did not raise her voice. Did not directly confront him.

"How still you remain in a storm," she said. Byron drank the praise. "As though Prometheus and Epimetheus have been to visit you and, finding nothing in their satchel, decided rather than fire they would give you—"

"Calm?" Byron interrupted.

"Emptiness," Mary said. "Come Shelley." How I admired her control.

The small daggers of her personhood. Her insult ought to have come with translation services, for what she meant was *Shelley is mine*. Shelley went right to Mary's side.

I thought Byron might pounce. If not physically then trounce Mary verbally.

"The lake," I cried, trying to distract Byron. "Look at the lake." The water was still oddly placid. I wished to be that lake, that water.

"Oh, Claire!" Mary said. "What now?" She would never admit to needing saving.

"Yes. Oh, Claire," I said. It felt oddly freeing to think of myself in the third person. "Claire has noticed something."

Byron put on his dramaturgy voice. "Claire noticed how she spoke of herself as a young royal." He bit into the corner of a sandwich and chewed it in a way that suggested I was the bread—completely consumed and helpless in his hands.

I wanted to tell Byron he was the devil, yet I had never said such a thing about him when we were together, and to say it aloud when we surely would never be together again—well, that would have been too much. I had nothing to lose, I had already lost everything. And I ought to say the same for Shelley, for his deviousness was altogether worse. My secrets sat like poisonous stones in my belly. My mouth opened of its own accord, a drawbridge over which I had no control, "You men—"

But the loudest clap of thunder changed everything. A flock of birds in a great cluster flew too low over us.

"I hate birds," Polidori cried. He cowered as the sky broke apart with rain.

"Look," I said as I stood up. And finally everyone did. The lake was calm no longer. In its middle a tunnel of water rose up, larger than the one in June, gathering girth and making a loud sucking noise.

Mary screamed, her high-pitched wail blending with the wind howl. Elise ran with the baby towards the cottage. Polidori abandoned his employer and followed Elise. Shelley, the slowest to respond, gripped his belly, saying he was convinced he suffered internal blood issues. He grasped Mary's hand when she offered it, and off they hobbled, clutching her pages. FF sunk his teeth into Byron's collar and helped him up.

He and I stood wordless in the craze of sandwich ends flying, ducks squawking, the water heaving towards us in the nearly black sky. He flicked his eyes, and I knew not to follow him and his dog into the villa as he moved in the fastest way he was able, a limbering run yet still making haste. I took one last look at the mess outside and went to find solace in the kitchen.

I was not the lake. I was the weather—unpredictable, powerful, out of anyone's control.

6

WHILE I WROTE IN my journal, they played a game of Shadows—each positioned just so in order that their shadow became elongated, temporary sculptures on the clipped grass. Shelley dipped his head.

"Now my shadow is kissing yours," he said to Mary, who had not joined in. I set my journal down to watch. He could not cajole her from her work, even with his singsong shadow kiss. Polidori dipped his own shoulders just enough to the side that his shadow head leaned on Byron's. I caught Polidori's eyes, and he immediately stood upright.

"We played a game like this, Postman and Pennies," Elise said.

"How jovial," Byron said.

"I shall be postman," Polidori said, and rushed inside. He returned with a cap and convinced everyone to play a round. "When I knock at the door, a pretend door, each of you must ask me if I have a letter for you—"

"And how many pennies it will cost to have it," Elise said. "The number of coins is the number of kisses."

Byron looked intrigued—he would kiss everyone there, perhaps with the exception of Polidori, who had engineered the game purely to kiss

Byron. Shelley's shadow loomed large, though he said nothing. I inched closer to Elise.

Mary looked up. "Elise, you mean to say you play this game and men give pennies to kiss you? Indeed they decide the amount each kiss is worth?" Blush took over Elise's cheeks. To have Mary explain the rules was to understand. "This is not a game," Mary said. "It is an excuse."

She said nothing else as she settled herself back down with her work.

"Something is missing," Shelley said, in the voice of a bad actor.

"Oh," Polidori said, and clapped his hands. "Forfeits!"

Any relief I felt at having not been the focus of the fun or unfun of the Shadow game went away, for when I crossed my arms I realised I held nothing.

It was gone.

"My journal," I said. Really, it was a shout.

Shelley went on. "Now, we must make Claire perform a stunt or answer a question in order to have her something returned—Claire, you're a good sport, are you not?"

I was not.

I had never wanted to be a good sport. And yet was that not what amiability and being an agreeable girl demanded? "So I am to have a punishment— " My voice shook with rage.

"An amusement," Shelley said.

"Is this something embarrassing?" Elise asked.

"Embarrassment is over quite quickly, that is its blessing," Byron said, though he did not look at me when he said it.

Who had my journal? And where had they put it? Usually with Forfeits one was blindfolded. I understood I hadn't needed to have my eyes covered—for I had been distracted enough to set the journal down just for a moment.

Had they read it?

Learnt my secrets?

"I want my book back," I said.

"It is not a book," Mary said. "It is a diary. A journal."

I stood my ground. I did not need to be agreeable any longer. The damage was done. "I should like to have my belongings returned to me at once." Byron snickered. "You call it a diary, it is more. It could be . . ." I thought quickly. "A novel itself. Like Heloise. A novel of a girl—"

From underneath her skirts Mary produced the journal.

"Who wishes to read of an ordinary girl?" Mary asked. "It is tiresome enough being one."

7

I HID OUT IN THE cottage, eating a loaf of bread I made myself, dipping bits into a pot of raspberry jam so dark it looked like blood when it fell onto my skirt. It would stain. I cared not. I spent the rest of the day reading through my journal since I had it back. It felt half my story and half as though it were someone else's. I added details I'd forgotten—a plant name, the way Shelley appeared in my writing nook always just as I wished to be alone, the taste of Byron's blue tea. I tried not to cross out anything, for that felt cruel to the me of March, of April, of before.

ELSA STIRRED carrot soup with one hand and copied one of her receipts for me with the other as I washed dishes. Polidori had informed us Shelley had gone into town to sign papers of some sort, but I thought perhaps Polidori had it wrong and Shelley was procuring items for the trip to Chamonix.

I hoped he and Mary would go and leave me here, and I would be left in peace to sort out the muddle of what to do. There were herbs, Elsa had told me, ones which lent themselves to choosing a different path forward. To real blood. Perhaps this was the answer. If Shelley and Mary took William and Elise, I could gather the herbs, steep them in hot water, drink the brew. Sit with Elsa until. Until. A future.

Byron's life. Shelley's life. Mary's life. All would continue as planned. I was the only one interrupted. How was it that a girl carried the burden for everyone?

On the way from the kitchen I passed Polidori. He wrote in the near dark, continuing Byron's vampire fragment, determined to make something of the story, the bloodsucking monied gentlemen whose immortal beauty was as undeniable as his manipulation.

I WAS under the tarpaulin of half sleep when tiny claws gripped my forearms. "Wake up!"

My eyes opened. My body stiffened. "Claire." It was Mary. My body unclenched. "Please say you've not decided against our tour in Chamonix. I couldn't bear the journey without you."

8

I PACKED A HEAVY WOOLEN shawl the colour of rotten apple flesh. The air would be cold again in the mountains, but the life growing inside me offered its own heat. Items into a small case. One which—despite my belly, whose bulge I could no longer ignore—I could manage myself. The one I had imagined taking with me as I left. I laughed out loud at my own ignorance—how would I have gotten anywhere? Walking in the moonlight for hours. Oh no—I could have asked the postal man for a ride. Could have settled in a small French village over the border. Could have been like my mother and found someone to lend me their name.

In her room, Mary had a neat stack: chemise, stays, the corset, which had given her permanent bruises but which she minded not, for it improved her bust. From the hallway I watched her pack, almost went to her, but then realised at some point soon she would count the cotton strips we'd brought from London. She would realise they had not been used, sullied, washed, dried. Not nearly enough. She would have proof. She would ask me. I grabbed a handful of them and hid them under my mattress.

9

ON THE WAY TO Chamonix, Shelley slept. His great head lolled side to side with each curve in the road. I looked out at the formidable mountains. Tried not to lose my breath at the sheer cliff face and the feeling we would at any moment careen off. They would find our bodies. We would again be a headline. But what would the words read?

I read over Mary's shoulder as she wrote with a tiny travel quill Shelley had given to her. *Effulgent trees having been sheltered from the torrents and ice these past weeks. Sudden elevations with Mt Blanc always in sight—a watcher over us all. Snow aches the skin—the pines descend on either side as we traverse up and up and over and each time I think we will fall to our deaths we survive and yet that threat of violence is still violence.*

I stopped reading. Where I always had the strong stomach, now I did not. I was sick in my own wrist bag. Shelley did not see, but Mary did, and as though we were children hiding evidence, she took the revolting thing from me and chucked it out the window.

"I do hope, Claire, that you haven't put too much of yourself into your journal." She reached for my hand in a welcome show of love. "Elise mentioned you are up at all hours, and I wish you to know . . ." She would tell me she knew my secret. "You mustn't feel competitive about writing in it—" she gestured to my book, which I held on my lap lest it go missing. "For the men are used to the work and I am somehow inspired, which is a good thing. Truly, Claire. It is for the best that I have an idea and stick with it."

"I have never done anything other than encourage you, Mary," I said.

I was relieved. Also annoyed. "And should I not also find a subject worth writing?"

"Oh, Claire, you always strove for unconventionality—"

I slumped. "Me? You're the one who ran away at sixteen and dragged me with you."

"I hardly dragged you—"

"You begged me, Mary. Begged. 'Oh, please Jane,' you said." My old name was a stone in my mouth.

"I brought you out of loyalty," Mary said. "I was saving you."

"Is that what you really think?"

"You were more amiable then." She drew a long breath. "Easier."

We stared at each other. If she'd thought she was saving me, then she'd acted out of love. Yet the look on her face was unsure. She clamped her mouth shut, and I thought she might be fighting the urge to admit the truth.

"I think you brought me on this trip and perhaps the elopement for your own sake—and for his." I pointed to the sleeping mass of Shelley's folded limbs, awkward in the calèche. "His silence is also a demand."

Mary's face burst into a raged red. "You so love the artist life, this foraging wild woman you've become—jumping into bed with a lord, befriending the staff. For you, a tidy home and a solid career and marriage and a baby—it probably feels like defeat. To me, after our childhood, it feels like victory."

"You mocked me yet here you are, admitting you want Netherfield after all."

"No. I wish not for a grand house and a ball—" she spat the words. "I wished only for the simplicity of having a life to call my own." She drew a breath. "I never thought you would try to take it."

The slap of that idea hit with such force I could not speak. Panic rose in my chest as the carriage came to a stop outside the modest hotel. The mountains with their ecclesiastical peaks surrounded us.

"He means you no harm, Claire."

Harm. I nearly choked on that word. Harm. "How might we know just what is harmful?" I asked.

She said nothing. Just kept holding his hand. And I thought we were not the only sisters in the carriage. For complicity and egotism were also siblings.

Shelley awoke, stretched his too-long arms and swiveled his head to take in the scenery, settling his gaze on Mary, who gave him a loving smile.

I thought of how my mother had mended a broken vase and how Elsa stuck pieces from a smashed ginger pot around the edge of a seedling pot, how women had to make do, strove to make beautiful something ruined. I thought of my body. "It is only in being broken we might be remade."

Mary turned to me. "Say that again."

I said it again with the intention of going on, of telling her *the thing* but stopped when Mary suddenly gripped my shoulder. "Yes, Claire. You truly see me for all that I am." She gave me one of her rare, wide, grateful smiles. She thought I meant it about her. I had meant it about myself.

FATIGUED TO the point of near ruin, we arrived Chamonix at seven o'clock, having left the house just after eight in the morning. Carriage, mules, walking, all familiar to the three of us. Rooms at Hôtel de Ville de Londres. Mary went up the hotel's stone stairs holding Shelley's hand. She turned back to see if I followed—which I had to. I could not stay in the carriage, for where might I go? I caught up to her as Shelley signed the guest log.

Mary immediately hunched over her pages, with Shelley gazing upon Mont Blanc. Besotted by glaciers. Ignoring us. Shelley went off for a wander in the blue evening light.

I sat with sugared milk and missed Elsa and mourned my current state.

Shelley returned to the hotel all a dither. "I saw it!" he said. "A *bouquetin* . . . a large goat with massive horns."

"How marvelous," Mary said.

"You believe him?" I asked.

"Of course I do," she said. "I trust Shelley with my life."

IT TOOK my sister and Shelley a full day to recover from the act of travelling. I pitied their weaknesses. This gave me an entire day to roam, which I did, and feel lost, which I also did but would not admit to over watery potato soup for luncheon, which I ate alone for my companions were too tired to eat. That statement alone made me rageful, for I would never be the sort to be too tired to eat.

I looked in the register of Hôtel de Londres, where Shelley had signed us in. He listed himself as *lover of humanity* and *democrat*. In the column where one was meant to write occupation, he had not written poet, not even political agitator. Instead he had jotted *atheist*, yet written this in Greek. I knew this was only to shock people. Next to his name was Mary Shelley. I added mine. Claire Clairmont. I underlined it to make up for it not being there in the first place.

At midday, Shelley forced us onward, determined to ascend Montanvert. "We shall not be defeated," he said, as though an army awaited his word. Then he tripped and fell, skinning his knee. Of course he fainted and Mary grew apoplectic with worry and only then were we allowed to abandon the climb. I could have kept going but was forbidden to do so by the guide, who while watching Shelley lean on his tiny betrothed said to me, "A woman cannot wander alone in the snow."

10

"SO WHAT DO THE men do?" Mary asked the tour guide, who led us around the ruins of Chateau de St. Michel.

"The women do the work—reaping, making the hay, and in the

autumn they will do—how do you say?" He mimed killing an animal. "Peel it?"

"Skin it," I said.

"The women skin the marmot, the foxes, and sell them."

Shelley looked as though he was about to be sick. "Whyever would they do that?"

"For twelve francs," the guide said, and looked at Shelley with great pity for such an uninformed man. I wanted to skin, to hunt, to provide. I wanted to confide in my sister, tell her my secrets, though I knew the risks—she would banish me again. I would have no home.

"I can scarce think of anything other than my work," she said when I had dismounted, purple under her eyes revealing her sleeplessness. "There is a fine line between inspiration and obsession."

Her devotion to the page protected me, for afternoons and evenings after touring, Mary scribbled more and bade Shelley sit next to her for warmth and to have him read over her shoulder what she'd written the night before.

It took work to decipher her words through hurry and smudge. I took to leafing through her work in the mornings, weak coffee in hand, while the sun nosed out between the peaks as Mary and Shelley slept. Shelley had a heavy hand in her notebook. First, a word misspelt that he had corrected (*iggmatic*, she had written rather than enigmatic—my too-clever sister could never spell). Her choice of *smallness* did not meet his satisfaction, so he struck it through and put *minuteness* in its place. He was not subtle.

Each time Mary had written *have*, Shelley struck it through and put *possess*.

When she wrote *wish* he penned *desire* or *purpose*. *Hope* was *confidence*, *add to* was *augment*, the simple truth of *ghost story* became *a tale of superstition*.

We were all equal, Mary had written.

Shelley slashed through the words and put *neither of us possessed the slightest pre-eminence over the other*.

I wanted to smack him. Mary had written *I do not wish to hate you* and he had made an *x* over it, replacing it with *will not be tempted to set myself in opposition to thee.* When first the monster appears on the page, Mary had written it had black hair. This would not do, Shelley had clearly decided, and made a mess on the page by adding *lustrous black and flowing.*

Like mine.

Mary wrote: *If I cannot inspire love, I will cause fear.*

I felt she had written this not about herself, but about me.

"YOUR FLUENCY is unmatched," Shelley said the next day, as my sister ignored breakfast and ate only ink and paper.

"It is only a story," Mary said. "Byron asked for one, and so I make one."

"I am glad to see you happy," I said to her.

"It is more than a story," Shelley said. "It should be a novel."

Mary set the quill down. Cracked her knuckles, which had been my mother's nasty habit. Mary looked not at her work but the street and view. "Yes, Shelley. Quite right."

Shelley seemed pleased. He took up his own pen and began a poem entitled "Mont Blanc."

I felt useless sitting there. I longed for wild onions. For stews made of found bits. I squashed any remnants of longing for Byron.

"And you, Claire?" Shelley said. "Will you deny the world your work?"

His knack for always making me feel capable of more was a stone I felt I would carry forever. He pushed a piece of paper towards me. "Perhaps set down the journal and try something new?"

11

Again, porridge with a sort of unidentifiable dried fruit confit. No butter. Food also short here. Outside an expanse of cold misery Mary found inspiring, wandering in a shawl whilst Shelley managed to injure himself almost immediately. The porter had to be summoned, and Shelley waited out the day, working from the safe confines of the hotel's finely appointed front room with its fire and settee. He wrote of the mountains best while apart from them.

Mary and I mounted mules. I wished Byron could see me, unsure if he would find me amusing or be impressed by the ease with which I rode. "I have never been so chilled," Mary said. Before us the white sheet of ice and packed snow. "This is most—"

"Stunning," I said.

"Desolate." Mary ate my word with her own. Same view, same feel in our limbs. Two entirely different experiences. I sighed.

When the sun dared shine, even the iridescence fought back, hurting to look at. And when the clouds moved in, we were forced to turn back for fear of freezing to death. Each vista was empty and desolate. After she went back to Shelley, I kept walking. In between cobblestones were blue flowers, and far off at the end of town a shaggy bush of rose de alps. When I came back flushed to tell Mary I had indeed found life amidst the cold, she had left a note at the desk. *C—Have gone to tend to S & write. Will not be down til morn.*

I asked for a sheet of paper, which would be billed to the room, and took my dinner by the fire. I had begun writing an odd fairy tale. I would try again.

Some time ago, a girl was given three gifts—a spinning top, a small cat, and a plant with tendrils that took the form of questions. Each morning she would ask the plant a question, and each afternoon the plant would have transformed its leaves into an answer. On the morning in question, the girl was so entranced with the spinning top and the sweet warmth of the cat nearby that she forgot to ask the plant a question, and the next morning she found it was shriveled and quite dead.

No, that would not do. I crossed that out with a large X.

I did not wish to write about questions, for I had no answers.

I thought a bit and reread what I had crossed out, hoping to salvage a word or two so it wasn't for naught.

Not so long ago, in the dead heart of winter, a girl sat with her cat. They were hungry and the fire had gone out, so they had no choice but to venture outside together. For the girl would never leave the cat, and the cat needed the girl for her human virtues. It was a brutal winter; the girl's toes ached with chill and the cat's breath was white ash, but still they kept on, side by side as they always were until—

Here I paused, for until what?

I thought of all of the dark places I had been: the back room on Skinner Street where I slept when Mary was in Scotland and Shelley had come to stay, the boot room at the inn that first night of the elopement, where I had stayed up till all hours alone with Shelley, my nook this past winter and spring, where in the barest flame I first set nib to this journal, the coppice. How Shelley lurked in all those spaces. I could not bear to think of the coppice with Shelley in it. I pressed my eyes until I saw spots and went to bed.

12

THE NEXT DAY, SHELLEY wrote in the men's lounge. Mary and I wrote in the common area. I finished my fairy tale. Mary held out her hand as a question. I gave the story to her.

Not so long ago, in the dead heart of winter, a girl sat with her cat. They were hungry and the fire had gone out, so they had no choice but to venture outside together. For the girl would never leave the cat, and the cat needed the girl for her human virtues. It was a brutal winter; the girl's toes ached with chill and the cat's breath was white ash, but still they kept on, side by side as always until the dark orchard at the edge of the town. The girl turned round, for she had been told not to venture into the woods and was ready to go home with the cat and make a thin bowl of soup from a limp carrot and an old potato, but the cat had gone ahead. Once the cat's paws touched the inky shadow, the cat disappeared. The girl had no choice but to follow.

In the orchard, it was not winter. The cat stretched in the warm sun, the happy apples were asleep on the trees, each shinier and more ruby-coloured than the last. While the cat went ahead, the girl stared at the trees for a long time and from a distance as though she were shy—which she was not—or scared—which she realised she was, for the apples seemed too many and too bright, beckoning. As the girl approached the apples she remembered her mother waxing on about their sweetness, their tart perfection, and how each time her mother described such a perfect fruit the girl had voiced a desire to try one, only to have her mother warn her. Apples had choked the mother's other child and given everyone such a fright that they never had them in the house, even when times were lean and the fruitmongers giving them away.

"I can make them talk," said a man. He kept his eye on the cat but addressed the girl. With his big hand he cupped an apple on a nearby branch. "Do you require anything?" he asked the fruit.

"Only sunshine and rainfall and your attention," the apple said.

"If they are thirsty, I give them water," the man said to the girl. "If the sun is too hot, I hold up an old sail for shade." There was no water nearby, so the girl did not know where the apple man would have got a sail, but she did not object.

The cat circled the man's legs, for she was drawn to his words.

"What would you give me?" the cat asked, and the man was not at all surprised to find the cat could speak, although the girl was disappointed, for she believed the cat would speak only ever to her. The orchard was so quiet the girl became uneasy.

"If you are hungry," the man said to the cat, "I should grant you all the apples you wish. I am loyal to my apples, and they are loyal to me," he said.

He turned to his trees—each apple he regarded put forth a scent of sweetness and sang to him, PICK ME FOR I AM THE SWEETEST, PICK ME AND FEED ME TO YOUR CAT.

My cat, the girl thought but did not say, for she felt her voice growing softer and softer until no words could come out.

As the cat grew ever fonder of the man, rubbing against his calves, the man selected the ripest of the fruit and, from his belt, wielded a knife which, until then, the girl had not noticed. When he drew it across the apple he appeared fierce and the orchard air darker.

The blade entered the apple, making a perfect slice, which the man threw. The cat went to eat it. The next slice the man threw even farther away and the next all the way on the other side of the orchard, and the cat dashed off, leaving the man alone with the girl.

"Do you like apples?" the man asked her, but the tone was not really a question, for it came out in such a way to suggest there was no response

other than yes. The girl's mouth was a perfect O shape, but no sound came, for her voice seemed to be sliced from her altogether.

"I shall put my knife away," the man said, which put the girl at ease for a moment. "Here," he said, "let us sit for a spell."

He showed her a quiet space between the dark trees, whereupon they arranged themselves on a woolen blanket. The man told her of each kind of apple—Blenheim Orange, Bramley, Snow Fameuse—and how he had collected the seeds and planted them at just the correct time, and when they were ready for harvest, he gave so much away to the people of the land, yet he did not wish to be lauded as a hero for he was but a humble apple man.

All the while he spoke, the man's voice was soft and tender and his hands large and nimble, flitting all around like birds before a storm. He did not wield his knife, yet she felt his tenderness as another kind of blade all the same.

Each time he explained the apples or the orchard or the ways of love and loyalty, a bit more of her skin broke, as though he had sent his blade right through the core of her. Still the apple man kept telling her all about the land and its history and how grateful the hungry townspeople were when he tithed his harvest for their benefit. He told her the orchard would take care of her, and the cat would know the girl loved her by bringing her back to the orchard time and again.

By the time the cat came pawing back to them, a satisfied smile on its whiskered face for she was full of apple slices, the girl had put herself back together.

"Is this not the most delightful place?" the cat asked. She leapt into the girl's arms and gave a grateful purr which filled the girl with happiness.

All around them the dark trees seemed to multiply with heavy bark and bursting fruit, and the girl wished only to turn away and run back to her bed and forget they had ever ventured out of the house. The cat showed the girl its yellow eyes and asked a silent question that caused the girl pain in her stomach as though the apple knife came through it.

And though the man had not used a knife, he had sliced the girl perfectly open. Each drop of her deep-red blood became an apple, and as she lay back on the orchard ground, she looked up to see all of the other beautiful apples, each made from the blood of other girls.

THE END

I thought Mary would object to the lack of science. How could one thing become another, a liquid become a fruit? Or she would critique the talking cat.

Instead, she said nothing. I ought to have left well enough alone, but instead I asked, "Have you nothing to say about it?"

Mary fixed me with a pitying look. "The girl is very foolish to have gone into the orchard in the first place."

"She did it for the cat," I said, wounded. "It is a story of love."

"Did she?" Mary did not stop writing and did not stop looking at me. How she could control her hand on the page and her eyes on mine was a small miracle. "For a fairy tale to work, it needs a moral, Claire."

"Can it not leave it up to the reader to decide right and wrong?"

"Of course you might, but some readers do not want to choose—"

"It is a love story, for the girl loves the cat, and any confusion over love and evil is because the girl wishes to please the cat and thus—"

"Do you know your problem, Sister?"

"I feel sure you will tell me, Mary."

"You cannot think ahead. That is the problem in the story. You must know what is going to happen to the people on the page."

"So you've plotted it all out then—this Prometheus myth of yours?"

"I should not like surprises," Mary said. "One must think of the eventualities." She gave me a long, hard look, her cheeks bright as apples. "Even a hungry, poor girl ought to know nothing good might come of following her cat."

13

RIGHT BEFORE LEAVING CHAMONIX, I reread the fairy tale. Like all of its kind, the story was odd and set me on edge, though I could not quite parse out why. I could not placate my upset stomach and further distraught mind—for what would become of me? What on earth would happen to me?

Once more I took in the astonishing view. Ought I climb those mountains, lose myself in the heft of snow, the vastness of cold? I was too scared. Too big. Too female.

I went to the hotel desk to ask for my room key. Splayed open was the hotel log. I traced my finger over names of strangers who had arrived since we'd checked in. And then to our date of arrival three days prior. Shelley's name. Mary's name. Nothing else. Where my name had been—plain as day—there was an inkswell of black. I was being erased. But by whom?

OUR DEPARTURE from Chamonix was the last day of July, a cloudless Saturday. Mary said she longed to kiss William and turned that longing into sleep. We passed by the Great Waterfall, which played with the strong wind and sprayed a fine mist as we rode past. Shelley stared at me. I rearranged my shawl under my chin and leaned against the seat.

"What were you writing back there?" Shelley asked, though he knew I tried to rest.

"A story."

"You seem fond of stories," he said.

I stared out the window, demanding of my mind not to wind up back in the coppice. "My daily accounts are not stories."

From the corner of my eye I could see him lace his long fingers together on his lap. For once he was not ill on the carriage, did not complain of wooziness nor headache.

He found his power in slow, sotto voce speech. "You have always observed quite keenly. Yours is an uncanny ability to recall and put onto paper all your fine mind has seen during the day." I wished I did not relish his compliments, yet I did. I loathed myself for this. "Still," he went on, "your mind is only that of a young girl, who appears to misunderstand the ways of the world."

He unlaced his fingers. He remained still. Too still. "Your little book . . . one must realise the great duty of a writer, that without exception something once written will be taken as Gospel."

He did not touch me with anything except his gaze, which he forced upon my eyes until I had no choice but to look at him full-on as I spoke. "Polidori was paid a hefty sum to write his accounts and send them back to John Murray." I took a long, shaky breath. "I have no such contract." I feared he would take my journal and throw it out the carriage window. I tried to divert him—I was always good at that. "Your advice is taken. In fact, I wrote a small story when we were in the mountains."

He sighed. I had not succeeded. "To what end?"

"Did you ask Mary the same question? You encourage her to write a novel, and yet for me—"

"You are different creatures."

"We are both women who like to write."

"Mary is working on a *novel*, Claire." He said *novel* as though it was synonymous with *life raft*, which perhaps it was.

I stared out the window. The open field rolled out before us in the settling dusk. The lake at last appeared, listening in. "What if I should wish to write a book?" I asked. "A novel."

Shelley coughed. "Have you not already done so?" he asked.

"That was before—in Europe—and it was lost, you know that," I said.

"Well, it seems you write fiction well enough," he said, and shut his blubby lips as though they were sewn together.

Not another word was uttered, even when finally we alighted at

Diodati. Mary looked girlish as she rubbed her eyes. "You know what tomorrow is, Shelley?"

He still did not answer. She accepted his silence as a form of devotion. The next day was the anniversary of their elopement. Fletcher held a lantern, while Byron came to greet us. He asked us inside to talk, though it was already gone so late. Mary, seeing Elise, went inside to kiss William.

Byron lingered outside on the steps with me.

"Good trip, I trust?" he asked, with the politeness of the newly acquainted. His manners once lured me. Now they crushed me, for how quickly intimacy may be erased and given to coldness. How we look to others to be the answer, when in truth they are the questions we ought to ask ourselves.

Shelley hovered in the doorway. He regarded my form, brow wrinkled. Had he noticed I was bigger? Byron looked up the drive towards the gate. "We shall leave the lanterns on, for we await another."

He called to Shelley. "You've yet to meet Scrope Davies." And then glanced at me. "A man skilled at cleaning up a mess."

14

If I pressed my forehead to the glass above my desk, I could train my eyes to the right, towards the shadowy coppice path, or to the left at the gleaming lake, whose light cast upwards as though sending a signal to the heavens. The lawn, orchard, grounds tidied of people as though they'd been swept up. Until a bell clanged.

I opened the window, craned my top half out to afford a view, and tried to listen. Byron stood with a hand bell, the others gathering round as a man in a ridiculous hat—which sought to outdo my bird Gerald and the nearby peacocks—gave a deep bow of greeting.

I went out to meet Scrope Davies before dinner. In London, I had impressed him. Now I had no such illusions, for when at last I reached the terrace where the others stood, already having made their introductions, I was short of breath and, I knew from Mary's expression, looking worse for the exertion.

"Miss Clairmont," Scrope said, with the serious enthusiasm of a gambler, which I knew he was. Indeed, I knew he'd sorted issues for Byron in the past, settled his affairs, took up with women Byron had cast aside. He studied the lake as though calculating what he could get for it.

"I keep your letters safe," he said to Byron. "In a Bible of all places."

There had been more letters. Ones I had not posted. This made me again feel foolish—I had thought I had known everything, when in truth we can only ever know a part of anything.

Had Scrope not found me intelligent, fetching—possibly brilliant? Or had I only remembered it that way? He was both shorter and more gruff than my mind had made him since London. I'd wanted him to hold me in high esteem, when in fact any praise he'd given was directed at Byron—how clever his lordship for finding a girl as amiable, smart, and large-breasted. Elise brought William out to Mary, who held him a moment and then handed him to me.

"I don't suppose we can rustle up a few hands of Macao this evening?" Scrope said.

Byron tutted but didn't say no. "Is it not similar to Baccarat?" Polidori said. "Perhaps at Fogel's Tavern?"

"Davies needs no such wagers this evening, Polly Lolly," Byron said. "He's up £6,000 by gambling at Watier's—"

"A large sum, £6,000, as you well know," Scrope said to Shelley.

Mary furrowed her brow. What was the meaning of that sum? Shelley ignored her look.

"Fine, keep me from my fun," Scrope said, with a big smile that showed he cared not.

"I hear you've had only fun," Byron said. He shook a finger in Scrope's face. "You've been spotted with Lady Caroline Lamb—how quite like you to dip your pen in the same pot."

"Don't be ridiculous," Scrope said, with so much enthusiasm we all knew he had been seen with her.

"Careful, for you might well end up in her next book," Byron said. Scrope clapped his hands and laughed, which startled the baby. Only Shelley's laugh continued, though he hadn't been part of the joke.

"You know," Byron said, "I've had a change of plans. I believe Scrope and I will have dinner in town this evening—sorry to miss you all."

15

AUGUST'S LANGUOR. MIDNIGHT SO warm it could be afternoon, first light the feel of noon. I felt only panic and regret. I ought not to have gone on the elopement. Should have resisted every chat with Shelley, each devotional action towards Mary. Did I regret the letter to Byron? I ought to entirely. Yet I adored the version of him I had created in my mind.

I ought to have spoken out at the meetings with the publishers and Shelley in London which I'd gone to at Mary's insistence. She had stayed home, bedridden. She had asked, and I had complied.

And I'd told myself I was doing what she could not, accompanying Shelley on his tasks.

Yet that was only part of it. I had wanted to see myself in the light in which I had always put Mary. Smart. Needed. Praised. Desired. Such dangerous words.

I ought to have been a bestselling author, truly. For while the men had each spun a story I had believed without question, I had also told myself a tale so glossy, so engaging, and so perfectly portrayed that I did not understand I was writing my own demise.

And now, pregnant. No family money. No employment that might bring funds. Foraging skills not likely to build me a wooden home or gain me passage on a ship to the New World. Barred from returning to the home I could barely count as having once been mine.

16

At sunrise, a note under my bedroom door at Maison Chapuis. Byron's hand.

Please come to Diodati for 1 o'clock.

As a plum sun nosed its way up, shone first light on the water, I bathed. Took my time with my lotions. Smoothed bergamot crème onto my elbows, all the less-touched parts of myself. I touched the roundness of my belly. Considered it from the side in the looking glass.

All this time I had believed I was integral to those around me. Mary's father thought I buoyed his daughter's darkness. Kept my brother Charles in line.

"I need you, Jane," Shelley had said that first night of the elopement, my mother in a room down the hall at the inn. He'd needed me then and many nights since, the integral nature of his need would bring me closer to my sister.

And then Byron, such a whirlwind out of my control and yet perhaps more truthful to say I brought the storm on myself, my adoring letter, the Drury, my refusal to see I was not Elizabeth Bennet. I will disappoint you, he'd told me right away. Yet I was resolute in my disbelief.

Men do not change, they merely unmask themselves.

Still, as I went to the front door, I thought: Byron has come to his senses. He wishes to get back together. Or, Scrope Davies would have told him an agreement was for the best. Whatever complications there might be, Byron rejoining with me would smooth them out.

Inside, the bough-pot was filled with pussy willows and rose mallow, the sort of flower that appears delicate yet may induce vomiting. I stood admiring its contradiction to avoid the ache of feeling I had and then walked to the library.

Words I overheard: *frivolity*, *foolishness*, *paternity*, *mendacity*, *Mary* or *martyrdom* I could not discern.

These pierced my skin, settled into my chest the way the bees had made a nest in the corner of the glasshouse. I heard Byron clearly say, "She is at best a parenthetical."

They knew. I had not kept a secret. I had not been asked to the villa for a proposal. I had been tasked with coming here to find out my fate.

I entered the room as Scrope patted FF's great head and said, "It is possible to be ruined by loyalty."

Three men stood before me. "All of you—" I was at a loss for words. Behind them were all those books filled with words, information, ideas, art. "You think you are heroes—"

"Everyone is a hero right up to the point where they might inconvenience themselves," Byron said.

They turned over and over my situation the way one might fold meringue, carefully at first and then, finding they could not settle, shoveling ideas over forcefully, as though preparing the earth for a grave.

In my mind I was singing a song of dirt and hope and lust and ruin—and not in that order.

I worried I would never be able to parent this child—not because of any innate lacking but because of a blockade everyone else was building. I worried I held this not-yet-fully-formed person inside my also-not-yet-formed self. Too late.

"A child wants a parent's care," I said. I was barely there. My body had left itself and hovered by the windows looking in.

"I shall claim the child as my own," Byron said, with the passion of a man purchasing a cow. "It could be brought up by Augusta Leigh."

"Your half sister?" Shelley queried. He did not hide his scorn. I recalled the rumours about Byron and Augusta.

"Fine—it shall live with me, then."

"It?" I asked.

"The brat."

I rose and screamed. Shelley stood before me, pressed my shoulders as though attempting to root me to the floor. Byron appeared before me, impassive but in charge.

"I promise to look after it, at least until seven years, at which point going away to school is reasonable. You—" he pointed to me "might be the child's auntie." I opened my mouth to object. "This would afford you to retain your character and see the child without injury to anyone's—" and here he looked at Shelley, "reputation."

The stormbirds settled outside the windows, all in a row as though spectating.

Shelley spoke up. "Fear not, dear Claire." He held me in his gaze as he had always done. "I went to town ages ago—and made provisions in my will for you and the babe."

"Let me guess," I said. "Six thousand pounds?"

Shelley had known. He had gone to town to change his will, made provisions for me—because he'd known what was happening to me before I had. That he understood my body and its processes better than I was the ultimate humiliation.

Scrope went to make a fuss until Byron held him by the shoulder. "Claire—there is something else." I did not let hope catch spark. "You have a talent—"

I raised my eyebrows. Perhaps he had read my journal but came away not only with my secrets but with understanding that I, too, could write. And well.

"You shall be my amanuensis," he said. "For you have proven yourself worthy with your neat pen and fine eyes. Make fair copies of all the drafts I've done here." He gave me his famous smile. "You'll do that for me, won't you?"

17

The remedy for a troubled mind is a task. That was what Elsa had told me back when she'd first shown me the new seedlings that were in the ground and growing life as I was. With the sharp efficiency of a butcher, I set my tools in front of me: New paper. Quills. Best quality ink. Byron's pages, their ink smudge and furious words a torrent of weather on the page.

The waves were dead; the tides were in their grave,

I tried not to linger too long on *grave*. My whole chest felt heavy. My entire body. As though now that everyone knew of my pregnancy, I was suddenly enormous.

The waves were dead; the tides were in their graves.
The moon, their mistress, had expir'd before;
The winds were wither'd in the stagnant air,
And the clouds perish'd; Darkness had no need
Of aid from them—She was the Universe.

He had made the grave plural. I paused. I paused so long an ink droplet fell, and I started over. There were many waves and, I supposed, likely only one grave, the same body of water or shore holding them. I did not change his words even by removing a lone *s*—though I doubted he would notice. But I could have.

Rubbing my palms with my thumbs, I looked up. Byron and Shelley fished at the lake edge. They might catch anything. Might choose to eat it or throw it back or feed it to FF. Men had so many choices.

I went back to the poem. Started over.

I barely paused. I removed the *s*. *The waves were dead; the tides were in their grave*. Better.

18

Mary paused her writing for the day and disappeared into the cottage, only to emerge on the lawn in the afternoon.

"Here," she said, and held out a cake. Shelley gave her a boat-sized smile, though the cake was misshapen and most unappealing. I could see she had forgotten to add something—eggs, perhaps, for she would not have wanted to fetch them from the coop, reaching into the warmth of the feathery undersides. As a result the cake looked to be made by a child.

"How perfect," Shelley said. "Shall we all go inside for tea?"

Scrope coughed. "Byron and I are going fishing, I'm afraid. Do enjoy. And happy birthday, Shelley. Twenty-four, and many more, as they say."

"Do they say that?" Polidori asked. "In a month's time I shall be twenty-one." He paused. "Lots of fun?"

Scrope steered Byron away from the cake no one wanted, while Mary and Shelley, arm in arm, went to eat it.

"A second piece?" Elsa asked the next day. She pushed the plate towards me with a knowing look. Zuger Kirschtorte, layers of sponge with nut-meringue and buttercream, which tasted so good it only made me feel worse.

"I feel pain that you're leaving," I said. "Which is a selfish thing to say."

"It would be selfish to make me stay," she said. "Not selfish to feel—I feel it, too."

We sat grim-faced, with the deliciousness in front of us. I thought about bringing a piece to Mary, who sat alone working, yet the thought of her taking careful forkfuls—just her teeth on the fork tines—was too much.

I contemplated a second piece. I was a glutton for pastry and regret, and there was naught I could do about either.

"Here," Elsa said. "We shall share one."

I had written a list for her—all of the dishes I'd learnt to make, all the names of wild flowers, of how to tend to seedlings. "It's everything you've taught me."

Her eyes filled with tears. I had to look away, for I thought I would break apart. "Time is cruel to parents," she said. "So often we try and fail, and even on the best day, the most golden, it is gone by night."

I nodded. I knew the power of naming things—how I'd absorbed her techniques for kneading, for the lightest eggs and the heaviest of creams, for Bubbeh Tsuker. "Grandma Sugar," I said. Elsa reached for my hands. Hers were warm and soft as new dough.

I knew so many words, so much more than I had known months ago, yet I did not know words for what had happened to me. It was most unsettling to know of a wrongdoing, and yet not have the means to say it.

"I would not have survived this summer without you," I said. She would leave in a week.

"You must survive," she said. "That is the job of ordinary girls."

19

WITH EACH DAY, MORE transcription. Two weeks passed. I copied *Childe Harold* in triplicate. Painstakingly rewrote "Darkness," each draft neater than the one before. The more time I spent on Byron's work, the less patience I had for my own. I apologised to my journal, with its filled pages and blue cover gone wrinkled from love and rain. I wanted to do better. I ought to rest the journal on my belly, whose protrusion was undeniable, and write outside. Perhaps tomorrow when Shelley and Byron returned from another boat trip. I would leave my copied pages for Byron to find. Oh, such praise he would lavish upon them, even more so when he would realise I was not there to soak up the froth.

There was power in not needing to hear I had done a good job.

GRANTED ACCESS, I made Byron's desk my own. Polidori did not like this, as I had pride of place in the library, yet he did not complain too much, for his continuation of Byron's story fragment proceeded apace. "The Vampyre," he said. I read with great interest his pages about Aubrey, who befriends mysterious and seductive Lord Ruthven, only to discover during their European sojourn that the lord is more than alluring, he is a predator—and undead at that. Aubrey must contend with this knowledge as he witnesses the manipulation, seduction, and ruin of young girls Ruthven leaves in his wake.

"His aristocracy is a clever cover for his killing," I said. That Byron was Ruthven was so obvious I did not need to mention it.

"This is it, Claire. I feel it—this is a story people will want to read. Who does not wish for that concoction of romance and fear? This will garner a deal."

"You already have a publishing deal," I said.

Polidori blushed. "A real one. Not gossip."

"I should like one also," I said. "Perhaps when I—"

"You think writers are in the business of truth or explanation," Polidori cut me off. "That is not so. We are in the magic business, Claire. For people wish to be carried away, spellbound and awestruck to make an hour of being alive easier. Decide why you write, and then I believe you shall know what to write."

20

ALL MORNING I HAD worked. Copied. Deciphered words, lines, stanzas.

I rubbed my tired hands. The tree branches in the coppice above my head were an intricate map of wood and space, a place I would not ever go, the way one branch halts its growth so the neighbouring tree might find light.

So many offshoots of smaller branches, twigs, they looked like the sketches of lungs Polidori made next to a skeleton. So much housed inside us we never see. So much in the library we might never know. So much sunk in the lake, hidden away until—if—it is dredged years on.

I looked up, tilted my head to the sky, my palms on the thick soft moss. An entire trunk bending, twisting itself in service to survival, to stretching for sun.

Mary had said to me this morning, "Part of loving someone is suffering so they might be happy."

"THIS CANNOT be true." Shelley slammed the letter onto the dining room table that night. The strength of his hand shook the boiled eggs in their cups. We had not so much been invited to dine at Diodati as happened to be nearby when the food was set out. Shelley pounded his fist. "Leigh Hunt has lost the bloody poem."

Byron looked outraged for his friend and said, "Did you not make a copy?"

Shelley shook his head. "After our boat trip I sent it off—he'd said he'd take care of it."

"Hunt lost it himself? Or might the postal process be to blame?" I asked. All those times I had walked the path to the postal carriage in dust, in rain, in cold. Shelley had not wanted to trust me with that letter. Perhaps he'd been punished by the postal gods he did not believe in.

Shelley let out a noise that merged scream and moan.

Unpleasant enough that I focused on my egg. Tapped its head to crack the shell, sliced off the top, added salt and pepper, and ate without looking up.

Shelley's writing was not my problem. I had enough of my own. All the time I felt an urge to feed myself yet understood I was not truly feeding myself, more the thing inside me. I knew it to be a child, a baby, yet because it turned and swam in the darkness of my body and I could not see it, I felt its foreignness, even as I hand-fed it an ordinary boiled egg.

"You must recreate the poem at once," Byron said. "That is the only way forward, Shell."

Mary paused writing long enough to add, "'Tis true—there is but one way to deal with the devastation of loss," she said. I was reminded of encouraging her to write her pain. "You must find your notes, search the snowy expanse of your mind, and try again."

SHELLEY SAT. Plain paper. Ink. Title on the top. "Hymn to Intellectual Beauty." He began. Stopped. Hand to head, remembering. He wrote his memory of words, his recreation of his own work.

After a while he pushed the paper at me. "Yes?"

I sat then with new plain paper, half-gone pot of ink, old quill. With great care, I copied it for him not once but twice.

It was always important to have an extra thing for safekeeping.

21

DAYS LATER, WITH STEADY hand, I presented "Darkness"—in neatest form—to Byron. He read it through. I did not need his words to tell me it exceeded his expectation, though he did say so.

"We shall carry the copy back to London when we leave in two weeks' time," Shelley said.

I opened my mouth to say something—what? That I wanted to stay. That I wished to live in my coppice, grow moss on my limbs and become the forest. That I wished to go to the New World with Elsa, though I had not been asked and had no papers nor passage.

"And good news," Shelley said. Mary perked up. "Claire will copy all of *my* pages." He looked at Byron. "Our personal amanuensis."

How well I had served both men. How much silent power I gained from controlling their words.

"How lovely for you," Mary said, "to have something purposeful to keep you busy. If one cannot write oneself, one may give the world the gift of legibility."

22

I SMOOTHED SHELLEY'S PAGES OUT on the desk. In front of the window was the lake watching me with its great placid eye as I transcribed. Just the title first. I did not like how my *s* curved too dramatically, so I tore up the page and began again.

Got one line in, and this I struck through. Messy. Yet it did not have to be. I relished the chance to start over. Begin again. It would be perfect. If a word was indecipherable, I spoke it aloud and found the cadence. I had no control over my body. My life. But each word on each page? Mine to decipher and transcribe, transpose.

All those nights, the late-night chats, Shelley's face touching mine as he whispered into my ears, those days following him around. How Byron moved, his dragging walk, the ease of his naked body, I found the words. I wrote the words.

What had I seen at the artist studio. One of Shakespeare's plays in painting form. *The Death of Cardinal Beaufort* by Sir Joshua Reynolds. A fanged creature, a demon, lurid near the body. In 1789 when it had shown, viewers protested. And so the painting was changed, the monster erased from view with layers of oils, varnish, time. One day, someone might restore it, find the demon again. "Monsters may stay hidden only as long as we allow," the artist had said. And in the library I'd found another example. A palimpsest.

A story scroll that hid underneath it an entire other story. Reused with the original text underneath. Hidden. My body was a palimpsest.

The work I was doing for the men, too. In each word of theirs, I was present. Polidori was correct—writing was magic, a way for me to disappear on the page and take my secrets with me.

23

ELSA HAD A KERCHIEF over her hair but tilted her face up to catch the sun. The light had turned from that early summer hopeful brightness to the dullness of a spoon half-dipped in honey, a reminder of autumn's approach.

We sat watching the apiarists extract honey from the skeps woven from sedge. "See? They'll strain it to clean it, then put it in the ironstone jars or boxes—maybe that jug we have near the milk?" She described the process, but what I heard was *we*. What we had. As though I had become part of the kitchen, lived in her space. "The trick with honey extraction is to save the wax for candles—those they'll take to market. You know, hives often come with a will."

I had not inherited hives. Nor money. And though Shelley had provided for me, for my child, there was not a hive in the world big enough to contain the buzzing in my chest. Elsa went to fetch a piece of honeycomb for us to chew. Off on the terrace I saw Elise bouncing with joy, heard her singsong voice. Her passport had arrived. She would leave with us.

"Here." Elsa and I bit into the honeycomb, not caring that honey dripped down our wrists, stuck between our fingers, slipped down my chin. Sweet as fading sunlight. Honey could last for hundreds of years.

Anyone who tasted it would know nothing of our summer, these particular bees, this moment with its architecture and warm wind and my helplessness. Still, in that tasting would be traces of us, and in that I took solace.

24

"KEEP GOING, CLAIRE, FOR truly yours is near-perfect penmanship," Byron said. He had his fishing rod under his arm like a rifle. "All the better for the publisher—he will have no queries, and if I have blundered surely you will correct me." He went outside. I stayed at the desk.

Days ruled by the order of transcription. More than a task. Not a chore. A job. The men granted me this opportunity, and I had no other option but to embrace it, making use of my neatness, my keen eyes, my strong and capable hands.

My sister wrote and wrote, her own novel, *A Modern Prometheus or Frankenstein*. So caught up was she in the whirlwind of her mind, the story gushing onto the pages, that her hands were ink-stained and when she stopped for bread the bread itself became blackened. She ate it regardless, and then her mouth was ringed with ink.

"Do you wish to add lightning to the storm scene?" I asked her, proud of my idea. "Would it not lend the atmosphere?"

Mary shook her head. "No, Claire. That is too much." She pinched her lips. "Too much indeed."

Her job, my job—both consuming us. My words were not entirely my own. Byron's. Shelley's. A dash—for breath. For pause. For extension. A full stop where perhaps there was a comma. I changed or edited as I saw fit.

Who was to say I had transgressed? Did Shelley not show the way in Mary's book—this word rather than that? Did Byron not praise me for my attention to detail?

This was not my task. This was my power.

25

DAYBREAK. A MORNING I had dreaded. Elsa pressed a folded note into my hand, my heart tight as a fist. She faced me in the kitchen, had to rush out for her journey.

"Goodbye feels like you're dying," I said to her.

"It is, in a way, for we shall never again meet," she said.

I could see myself in the years to come: a baby growing into a child, disappointment and years showing in my skin, and always the smell of bread and sugar bringing me back to her.

She cleaned the prep table as though she would be there tomorrow, efficiently beheading the carrots. I did the same, though I would not be allowed in the kitchen after she left. "There are three deaths in Judaism. The first is when the body no longer works. The second is when the soul leaves the body—maybe this is burial, when the body goes back to the earth."

"And the third?"

Elsa set her rag down. Took mine. "When your name is spoken for the last time—"

"When no one remembers you—"

"So until that time, I am alive—" She put a single finger to the side of my head. "In there." She paused. "And probably elsewhere, too, unless sea illness gets the better of me."

I wanted my words to come out smooth, poised, grown-up. Instead I cried and choked on them. I felt I might truly disappear.

A long embrace and she was gone.

I could not bear to hear her footsteps as she walked away from Diodati, from me. Yet I could not face the aloneness anywhere, so I went to the lake. With my feet in the sand, I thought the water would swallow me whole, pin me underneath, where I would live my days as a siren. It did not. Firmly rooted on land, I remained a girl. A girl with a note in my pocket.

She had written the receipt for Grandma Sugar. *Just in case you forget!* I would never.

And then something not in English.

ךעטסאַפּ רעד—ףיוא יז טסערפֿ ףוסל ראָנ ,ףלאָוו ןראַפֿ ןבאָה וצ ארומ ךיז טנרעל ספעש יד

I did not know what that meant. And then I turned the note over, where she had translated it into English, which was difficult for her; her wobbly penmanship made me even sadder.

> *The sheep is taught to fear the wolf, only to find itself eaten by the shepherd.*

26

All of us lined up in the drive. Scrope with his silly hat on his smug head. I handed over some of the work I'd done. Feeling the papers leave my hands, I felt as though I was giving a part of myself, so much effort for someone else's benefit. "The Dream," "Darkness," and "Prometheus," with that line I admired, *What was thy pity's recompense*?

"Rest assured," Scrope said, not to me but to Byron. "These will make the journey without leaving my hands."

"Make sure John Murray receives them himself," Byron said.

Shelley stepped forward. A furtive glace to me. "I believe I speak for us all when I say we are grateful for your hospitality."

My words, my commas and dashes, any changes I had made were on the page. They would travel. So much was out of my hands.

PREPARATIONS FOR our departure. Passports. Trunks. Sandwiches. Written work.

It would be impossible to discern whose words were whose. Each page of Polidori's story, of Mary's novel, of the poems the men had penned—all had everyone's fingerprints on them.

And impossible to reconcile the maths of my pregnancy.

I had no control over my body. Over my fate. I would not have devoted love, would not own a home, ever stop saving scraps of fabric, of food. I would be in some ways poor forever. And yet. I would not be forgotten.

I wove myself into the fecund earth of the poems, cast my shadow and sun gleam on each page, slipped each word between my fingers and turned it this way and that until I had in some way claimed it as my own. All of that art. All of those pages. None of it brought into the world without me.

To be a woman in the world was to make sense of men's words. I had been given this job and found I was quite good at it, for another part of being a woman was to get on with the task at hand and bury some of the feelings that went with it.

And I would bring something else into the world. An entire person. As the sun sank itself into the horizon, the lake capitulated into a honeyed fervour I found sad only because I knew it was one of the last sunsets I would see here. I would go to England. Have a child there, be hidden in another rented room.

I searched the sand for one more shell as I saw Mary, oddly lit up as though she'd been made by one of the sun's rays and might disappear at any moment. This instilled in me a clutch of panic, and I went to her, brushing sand on my thighs as I walked.

"Do you believe we shall forever be as close as we are now?" I asked.

"We will always be sisters," she said.

"That is not what I asked." I tried to keep up with her, but she pitter-patted to the driveway in such haste I was forced into an awkward run-walk to keep at her side. "Do you wish me to be banished from your sight?"

She stopped so abruptly a great cloud of dust rose from her boots. "I have not asked for that." The silence that followed registered in my body as pain. "Yet in truth I do not know if I might be able to give you what it is you seek."

"Which is—"

"Which is my eternal devotion."

I swallowed. "Are sisters not naturally devoted?"

"We share no blood."

I tried my best to soften the anxiety in my voice. If I did not have Mary, then everything I had sacrificed was for nothing. "We share a childhood, and our young adulthood and now—"

She turned and slapped her hand over my mouth. "No. Do not."

My breath was so fast and shallow I was near panting. The heat coated both of us, yet Mary remained pale and calm, her small hand over my lips as we stared at each other. Carefully, as though she expected me to keep talking or to scream upon its removal, she took her hand away.

"Promise me, Claire."

I looked at her again.

"Promise me, Claire, that you will—"

"I am wary of dealing in promises," I said. "They create a debt."

"There will always be a price to pay," she said, and took both of my hands in hers. "Silence affords no explanation."

My mouth shut. I gave her the nod and the silence she wanted.

27

"ARE YOU NOT DINING with us?" Mary asked.

"Byron has gone ahead to town and waits for me," Shelley said.

"Very well, then." Mary pecked his cheek. "Claire will sit with me, will you not?"

"I will," I said. "Yet I have work to do."

"Ah, yes, the women work while the men dine out. Now that is the title of an altogether different novel," Mary said. I snickered. Us against them.

"Claire, walk me to the carriage?"

August's buggy moonlight created a rippled light on the ground as we walked. Shelley stared ahead. "Did we not feel joy together?"

"The two of us or the three of us?"

"All of that."

"I don't know, Shelley. It is all so clouded now."

"Joy, once lost, is pain," he said.

"That is dramatic."

We reached the carriage. He pressed his gaze on me. "I've written a poem."

I sighed. More work. "Another one?"

He held a folded paper to me and went off to town.

I worked next to Mary. When she tired she put her head on her arm and slept at the table as the candles slumped. I read Shelley's poem, "To

C__, Singing." I could not measure the discomfort in my belly from the baby, the poem, the night itch. My skin. I left the poem on the table while I went to rummage the drawer for more candles.

Upon my return, the poem was not quite where I had left it, though Mary was still asleep. I unfolded it, read it again. Where the poem had been "To C__" she had amended it. This I knew was because I was the *C*. And that would not do. Now the poem was called,

TO CONSTANTIA, SINGING

In thy dark eyes a power like light doth lie,
Even though the sounds which were thy voice, which burn
Between thy lips, are laid to sleep;
Within thy breath, and on thy hair, like odour, it is yet,
And from thy touch like fire doth leap.
Even while I write, my burning cheeks are wet.
Alas, that the torn heart can bleed, but not forget!

It went on. I folded it and slipped it in my pages before bed.

A GREAT shouting before dawn. From my cottage bedroom I could see a single lantern light, make out a small chaise, one summoned from town. Still lake, lawn quiet of people. By nine o'clock, William and Elise had not yet emerged. By ten, Byron and Shelley stood with their backs to me, where I sat with an outside desk, writing or pretending to do so whilst eavesdropping.

Polidori had been dismissed. No time for goodbyes.

Byron made a hissing noise. "My veins filled with ice, truly," he said.

"I never cared for him," Shelley said. "And from what you've told me—indeed, that story he recounted in the dark hours of yesterday . . ."

"The man has no scruples," Byron said. "None."

Neither Mary nor I could prise out any details. And when she summoned me in the evening, she handed back to me all the shells we had gathered. Triumph shone on her face. "I am well on my way with a plan," she said. She meant *Frankenstein*, yet I also felt she meant me.

28

DAY OF DEPARTURE. I packed. Cleaned the room. Part of growing older, it seemed, was living with a certain degree of not knowing, coming to accept a degree of uncertainty.

My belly was like a walnut tree's burl as I moved round the room, sweeping, leaving this book there, and folding again my chemise. Slips of paper. *Court not yesterday for it is a love unrequited, Claim not tomorrow's hours with their fickle fortune, Hold fast to today for your wealth is shown in being alive now.*

The penmanship was unfamiliar. I knew not whose hand had written these words, nor if they had left the bits of paper in hopes they might be found by me or someone else. That was the thing with discarded words, they could be picked up and held, kept for years and then released. I put them in the leather case with the rest of the pages.

I looked round the room. How many shells might I take with me? I imagined holding them, examining them years or decades hence. Perhaps there would still be grains of sand from the damp day of collecting with my sister. Perhaps I would never hold them again. Perhaps someone from a faraway country would find them and wonder about their provenance.

A knock startled me.

Fletcher appeared at the doorway to fetch my trunk as I held the bowl of shells.

"You can't take those with you," he said.

All summer I had collected the delicate white shells, washed them, kept them. I was tired of men telling me what I could or could not keep. "I may take with me whatever I wish," I said.

"You would draw suspicion when you cross borders."

I furrowed my brow. "Why might that be?" I asked. "They are shells—I would be a girl travelling with souvenirs."

"No," he said. "You would be a girl travelling with a collection of bones."

ON MY final visit to the library, I found he was correct. The lucky stones, the luckiest with what appeared to be letters on them, came from the ear bones of a certain kind of fish. All this time I'd collected them as things of beauty, when in fact I'd been a gravedigger in the sand. Still, I slipped one into my pocket—a gift for Mary the next day, on what would be her nineteenth birthday.

"WE SHALL cross the Channel to Portsmouth and head via the West Country to avoid the Godwins—" Shelley said at breakfast.

Mary's pinched mouth made me wish to force her to taste the honey from the pot on the table. "No one ought know about any of this." Her hand winged at my belly. "Our parents have no notion of your condition, and I do not wish any speculation."

"I've found a place for us," Shelley said from under his piece of toast. "Number five Abbey Churchyard in Bath."

I nodded. Everything I did was with acceptance. I was still young and poor, though no longer vain.

"Not for you," Shelley said to me. "You shall be at—" He consulted a paper pulled from his pocket. "Twelve New Bond Street in Bath, where you might wait for the birth. Under the name of *Mrs.* Clairmont."

I had never felt more like my mother.

Though I'd given Scrope some work, I had with me other manuscripts: the third canto of "Childe Harold," "Mont Blanc," "Hymn to Intellectual Beauty," and Mary had part of *Frankenstein*, plus some shorter poems by Byron.

My letter in March opened a door I hadn't known existed. I'd walked through it, found myself in another land, and pulled everyone into it. Had it not been for me, the parcel would be empty, and Mary would not have her manuscript. The world would remember them and would hold the door open for them to walk back into the world.

"DO HURRY up, Claire," Shelley said, near the carriage in the Diodati drive.

Frantic, I tore back to the cottage, upstairs and back down. Peered under the table, cushions. Back out to the drive, panting. "I am still searching."

"For what?" Mary said, as she studied Elise, who had on a new dress and whose auburn hair shone down her back as she climbed into the carriage with William.

"My journal," I told her. "I've looked everywhere."

"We must get on with it, Claire. We've a long journey ahead, and you're in no state to—"

"I know what state I'm in," I said. "However, I need the book—it has everything in it." I gave a furious rummage in the last open trunk. Nothing. Defeated, I slumped. Tears came to my eyes. "I wrote so much—and now. I've lost it all—just like my first novel."

I did not have my journal. A part of myself gone with it. I had only stray pages. Some notes, including Elsa's. My own self in disarray in the loss of the book I'd held, written in, loved in all the months leading me up to this very moment. Details that would sink into the lake.

Mary pressed me towards the carriage. "Fret not, dear sister," Mary said. "I am quite sure it will turn up. Probably when you least expect it."

WE ARE pulled away.

I write this now on the back of a receipt from Elsa, one for shlissel challah.

I look at the place we are leaving, not at Mary. Not at Shelley. Elise with William in her arms. I do not look at my own belly, for it feels only part belonging to me. I hear crunch-grit under the carriage wheels. Layers of earth, sand, mud, all making ruts in which the next carriage will ride and the next, until there is no choice other than to slip into those craters.

Away from Diodati I see the devastation from food shortages, failed harvests, distress everywhere in evidence amidst the labouring classes. All the while we were sheltered in the dark and cold, the fabric of society was set aflame.

Out the carriage window is a series of goodbyes, my own cantos to the months here. The lake with its ode to calm and churn, villa and cottage in sisterly conversation—anchored by land together yet forever at a distance. I see myself running round the grounds. I wedge ink between forearm and carriage side, risking ink spillage as I lift myself up to see: the coppice, just the tops of the very tops of trees huddled together as though they are protecting the dark moss.

All this time looking at the coppice trees with their sure trunks, their elegant branches, limbs outstretched in gentle simplicity as they seek sunlight. The cleverness of trees is what we do not see, that system of roots underground, as though Medusa has been turned upside down.

The average walker in the woods thinks only of what is in front of them, above them. Does not give pause to the underneath. Is it too much to hope others after me will do this, think of their feet pressing into the ground, under that a whole world of movement and time and roots?

Enough ink left for barely a line or two—what should I write?

I will be forever in the pages I transcribed, yet no one will know it.

No one will see the palimpsest of my work, the undergrowth of my life—woven into the words. Still, even if no one wonders about me, parts of me will be there—just an ordinary girl, alive.

EPILOGUE

FLORENCE, 1879

I CLOSE MY JOURNAL. Keep it on my lap. Its weight makes me ache. So much of ageing is trying to be rid of discomfort. Knees, knuckles, all stiff. The heart, too. It is less about feeling well and more about the cessation of ache—so what do I feel having read my journal?

Not pain, exactly. More the memory of pain, the wish to undo it while knowing this is impossible. Hours, days, and years are plaited in just the way they always have been. Does understanding ease pain or increase it?

The truth: We are always trying to piece together the past, to reconstruct it to the best of our ability in the hopes of explanation, or, in my case, trying to resurrect what had been there as record and then taken. That is what I tried always to impress upon the children I taught and acted as governess to all those years after that summer—to label everything in the clearest of terms, not only for the sake of posterity, but for one's own clarity of mind.

Had Shelley survived longer, perhaps he, too, would have reflected back on the coppice, on the elopement, on Skinner Street, and understood that given the way he had cleverly pulled me into his praise, his arms, his work and family, anything he demanded was impossible to resist. I am sure he would see this differently.

This is the pain of storytelling. One person remembers it one way, and another remembers it otherwise, and still another different from that, and so on until there is nothing that quite matches and we are left with a crazy-quilt of beauty and ruin from each remembered or misremembered or repainted version, the demon or flower underneath each layer.

Yet Shelley did not survive and so cannot tell that story to himself nor to anyone else. Nor did Mary. Not for long enough. I did survive—the longest of everyone—and these words on the page tell the story. I call it mine. I did not understand the fairy tale when I wrote it—the curse of all writers, being so deep in story they cannot always find the meaning underneath.

Who took the journal is a puzzle I will never solve—for they each had motivation, each had powers of deception, distraction—Byron, Shelley, Mary, Polidori, Elise, Fletcher, even Scrope. Any one of them might be the thief who stole my book, hid it at John Murray's until some assistant found it, tracked me down, had it sent on decades later. No matter. I retrace the steps and find on any given day it is a different culprit. And they are all gone, so there is no one to ask.

The cottage, too, is no longer. Razed or burned I know not. I know only the space where once it looked out on the lake. So, too, are these spaces one holds in the heart. Where once stood this parent or that sibling, that lover or this friend, now there is only space. Time removes some of the pain yet cannot erase the emptiness.

I find in ageing, my memories undergo a peaceful sort of erosion, slipping the way Mary and I once stood tall on the dunes of some beach—I think it was a beach, could it have been a great mound of dirt?—and without warning, sank and tumbled. We screeched in surprise, in youthful pleasure, and also fear—for we knew of children digging holes on beaches, only to be trapped by sudden waves. Or we knew of men, soldiers, caught under building ruins and buried alive. Yet being buried alive is the act of Memory itself. In those careful or careless pits, plop goes the memory, where it is preserved in darkness.

Like the gentleman-monster modeled on him, Byron became immortal—that is what fame and infamy provides. Elsa told me we stay alive as long as someone speaks our name. I suspect Byron's name will be uttered forever, even without fangs.

Let us each write a ghost story, Byron said that night in that summer's wild weather. All too obediently we carried out his command. What is a ghost story? Not what we are afraid of, rather more the sadness we carry with us. For truly we haunt ourselves. Who might I have loved yet never told? That is a ghost. Who are the children we might have held before we lost the chance? Who is the person I longed to be and could not become in this lifetime? All ghosts we carry.

The others left their marks, their pages, while I copied other people's words, each black ant of squidged letters proof to the group I had not the capabilities to write my own novel. Still, a smile on my face now. For though they are all dead and cannot bear witness to the journal in my hands, I did write a story. Not the one thrown in the fire. The ghost story I wrote was my journal.

A FARMER tends to a flock of Valais sheep. Feeds them, moves them field to field, shaves their thick fleece. The local spinner washes the wool three times, dyes it with black walnut, cards the wool into fine strands, winds it round wooden spools made from poplar by a local carver. Warp, weft, weave. Partway through weaving the weaver develops an ailment or perhaps is a mother and cannot devote the time to her process. Another weaver finds the abandoned dark threads and perhaps adds red strands dyed from madder. And still another, having travelled and brought back indigo, adds that. The cloth is made, bought, worn by others.

One person begins something, but the other writes the majority of it, or finishes the story. Who is the author? Who owns the beginning, middle, and endings of our stories? Or someone tells you a tale. A fragment. Two sisters. Dissimilar. No shared blood.

What is my story and what is Mary's? Impossible to know whom I would have been without her. And she can never know whom she might've been without me, without the ghosts that clung to her from birth. Is my lack of singularity my great tragedy or great fortune? Does a woman have to be extraordinary to be remembered?

Mary told me in letters that when she dreamt of Diodati, always it was filled with people dressed bright as pieces in a fruit bowl on the lawn—some party we never had but could have, and always, she said, always someone's baby needed to be held, yet it was not William nor any of the others she lost afterwards. Not mine, either.

I, too, have dreamt of the place, those houses of the past that are the place yet also not. And in this version my body is the way of water—smooth and muscled and yet also the body I wear now, with its velvety soft sag and stomach flounce. Even in the dream I wonder how I can be both the girl I was and the old woman I am now. We are always both.

This is the way of all past, alive and dead both.

This used to alarm me. Now I find great comfort in knowing everything remains. Alba, my sweet daughter. Such pain in losing my girl. The questions in her eyes I would never be able to answer, the tiny plum of her mouth as she rested in my arms. You have a child and never know the last day you will pick them up, hold them to your chest. I wish I had memorized the date. And more pain that Mary and I were not united in our grief. Could not comfort each other and instead grieved alone, which only intensified the pain. Alba did not live to be six. The rest of them—Shelley, Polidori, and Byron—all dead in quick succession after that summer, and Mary, my sweet Mary, with her pale hand and arched looks, wrapped forever in devotion and loss.

No, on mornings such as this, I lie in bed and hold onto my body, feeling my bones. I cannot quite grasp the way my physical form is now, nor quite remember how it was when I was young.

I wish I had known that I contained wonder and beauty and strength.

I wish I had better explained what had happened to me and what I thought and felt about it.

Still, I think of all the art produced that summer that has lasted these many years. I think of the record I tried to make: my own book that was lost. I suppose by putting it down on paper, I told my story to my trees in the coppice, to the corners of the pantry, to the slim lip line of lake onto sand, and to the people and ghosts and creatures formed that summer, wherever they may live or haunt. As I wrote then, I was an ordinary girl. Like so many before me, mistreated—overlooked or hurt or manipulated or ruined by the all-too-female trait of compliance, of amiability. All along the men talked of political uprising. Will there one day be an insurrection of women rising up? I like to think so.

I like to think of joining in, at least in spirit form. And I would ask the ghost of my sister to hold my hand as we go with the throngs. It can take a long time to figure out the truth. This does not make it any less the truth.

ONE WOULD think the more time passes the less I might miss Mary. I have not found this to be true. For I miss the sister in my memories—often bathed in that early morning light, when everyone else slept and we sat on the stoop at Skinner Street, or that same light my brain fashions in Lake Geneva, with Mary sometimes holding baby William, the entity of the three of us and the lake and the burgeoning sunshine wrapped in possibility.

I miss also the sister I did not have. This is what one learns as the years slip by: When we grieve someone we grieve the person we knew and also the person they were not. And this missing fades but does not disappear. I can touch the scars of my younger years, examine them as though they belong to someone else, and I tend to her with care I could not show myself then.

Part of the bravery I have attempted is the act of letting go. Not only of the loss of my Alba, whom Byron took, renaming her Allegra. I cannot bear to linger too long in her short life, the warmth of her face in the space between my neck and collarbone, her unnecessary death in a convent after he had blocked me from seeing her, with no protest from Shelley.

I do not let memory control me, I wrote to my sister just before her death. She's been gone nearly thirty years and yet is with me in each hair clip, every morose rain, any sunbeam slinking hours away across the shining wood floor or sad afternoon with its grey cloak, in each evening when I understand—again—I am alone.

Still, the crowds of memories jostle for pride of place in the mind, and I allow myself to sort through the ragpicker's bin of them for a treasure. I tend to my memories as a curator. A strange collector of the most personal items. Yet still there are those surprises: underneath the memory another story. The true story hidden from view all these years.

There is an exquisite pain in poring over old conversations, finding old insults, imagining what one might have done differently. I know better now than to berate myself over what I ought to have done. For when we look back, we must remember those were words and actions built on the understanding one had at that moment. I did not have then the knowledge I have now. For I was at the beginning or middle of the mystery, and it is only at the finish one comprehends.

What I mean to say is I accept what I did not say. What I did not—or could not—do. What I mean to say is I forgive myself.

I allow the memories to come to me, try to enjoy them or study the ones which hurt or betray my sense of well-being, but I do not give myself fully into them. Especially, I say them aloud. I tell them to a friend or acquaintance, in letters, in conversation, even with myself.

I write the truth down, and then it does not have power over me. I am free.

AFTERWORD

JOHN POLIDORI DIED only five years after The Year Without Summer, likely by his own hand with prussic acid. The following year Shelley drowned in a boat accident off the coast of Italy. Lord Byron, having left behind a sea of affairs with women and men, joined the rebel army fighting for Greece against Turkey, and died in 1824 at thirty-six. Mary succeeded with *Frankenstein* and died at fifty-three. Claire Clairmont lived to be eighty.

John Polidori sent his gossipy travel journal to London and went to Italy to expand on "The Vampyre." The story was accepted, but upon publication was misattributed to Byron. Eventually this was corrected, and Polidori was listed as the author of this genre-changing work, forming the basis for all modern vampires.

Lord Byron continued to write poetry and satire, publishing until his death. He was considered a major part of the Romantic movement, but his reputation as a poet and a libertine was eclipsed by his affairs and sexual exploits.

Percy Shelley wrote poems for the rest of his short life. Despite some criticism of his personal life, he is regarded as one of the major Romantic poets, focusing on themes of freedom for the individual, pushing against societal norms, appreciating nature, and looking for a utopia. Though his body is buried in Italy—next to Keats—Mary asked to have Shelley's heart sent to her so she could be buried with it. Posthumous editions of his poems were altered by Mary to edit out references to Claire Clairmont.

Mary Shelley's *Frankenstein* is considered the first literary work of science fiction. It still sells forty thousand copies annually. In 2021, a first edition sold for $1.17 million, the highest recorded price for a printed work by a woman. Mary first published *Frankenstein; or the Modern Prometheus* anonymously in 1818. It sold hundreds of copies. In 1831 she revised the novel and published it under her own name to great acclaim. In the introduction she detailed the night of the ghost stories, how her book came to be in that dark summer. She wrote of Diodati and everyone there. Except Claire Clairmont.

Mary left a last letter for Claire: "I look back on our whole affair that bleak summer with such fondness, so much affection for my creation, my Frankenstein, and for our offspring of happy days, when I was not alone."

Elise left Lake Geneva with the Shelleys and stayed with them as they moved to Italy. She thought Shelley impregnated Claire. So did Godwin, Mary's father.

Claire Clairmont outlived the others. After the death of her daughter, she became a governess, taking care of other people's children, living all over the world. Though she kept many journals, the one from 1816 is curiously missing, as is the story—or stories—she wrote that summer. She decided not to pursue writing of her own and to lead a "regular" life. She wrote to Mary, "I prefer a quiet life." In her unpublished "Reminiscences" she wrote, "I have trodden life alone without a guide and without a companion and before I depart forever I would willingly leave with another what my tongue has never yet ventured to tell. I would willingly think that my memory may not be lost in oblivion as my life has been." No one remembers her.

When Scrope Davies left London for good due to gambling debts, he stored a trunk filled with his papers at a bank. In 1976, the bank opened the trunk and found original manuscripts from the summer of 1816. Perhaps one day a similar trunk will be found and opened, and we might find Claire Clairmont's stories and journals from 1816. Until then, I have tried to give voice to her memory in this book.

AUTHOR'S NOTE

IN ONE OF Claire Clairmont's real letters to Lord Byron with unknown date, either from March or April of 1816, she wrote, "My feet are on the edge of a precipice."

This novel is about that precipice.

Claire's letter goes on to say, "If you feel your indignation rising, if you feel tempted to read no more, or to cast with levity into the fire, what has been written by me with so much fearful inquietude, check your hand: my folly may be great, but the Creator ought not to destroy his Creature."

Do we know that Mary read this letter? We do not. Maybe she did, maybe she didn't. We know the sisters lived in a cramped household in which no one had much privacy and that Claire was undervalued as a person and not valued at all as a writer. Claire's language was so precise, and since that letter still exists today, I believe it played a part in the creation of *Frankenstein*.

Fiona Sampson's *LitHub* article "The Treacherous Start to Mary and Percy Shelley's Marriage" (May 31, 2018) had the following line that haunted me: "Percy has two equally powerful needs: to believe himself to be good, and to get what he wants." That conflict is at the core of this novel.

I have compressed certain timelines for the benefit of the story. While the climate disasters caused by Mount Tambora's eruption are documented—thick ash clouds blocked the sun, which caused food shortages, and there was snow in July in New England and parts of Europe—it was not known that the eruption was the cause until the

1970s. Another example of this happens with Shelley's poem for Claire, "To Constantia, Singing," which was written in 1817. I chose to have the novel end when Claire leaves Lake Geneva. Had I kept the novel going, I would have had the poem surface in 1817, but given the short span of the book, I moved the writing of it to demonstrate the sort of emotion Shelley expressed about his fiancé's stepsister. Often, the ideas for stories or poems exist in the writer's mind well before they make it to the page, and I do not think the Romantics were any different in this regard. Eventually, Mary had a hand in editing that poem and removed Claire's initials from the dedication.

In Polidori's travelogue that Claire reads, I have included one line from Polidori's real journal: "He keeps two daughters of Godwin who practice his theories; one is LB's."

The letters are my own creation, with the exception of a few lines or ideas: "I had ten times rather be your male companion than your mistress." "Remember that I have confided to you the most important secrets. I have withheld nothing—can I help therefore feeling utmost anxiety with regard to your sentiments & opinions of me." "An utter stranger take the liberty of addressing you." "I know pride often destroys our own happiness & that of others" (letters from Claire to Byron).

"An eighteen-year-old plump girl who scrambled 800 miles to unphilosophize," "an addiction to poetry is very generally the result of 'an uneasy mind in an uneasy body,'" "man-monster" (from Byron's letters).

In a letter to Mary from the summer of 1816, Fanny Imlay wrote of Byron: "I cannot think, from his writings, that he can be such a detestable being. Do answer me these questions, for where I love the poet I should like to respect the man."

Shelley's letter about the menagerie and lifestyle at Diodati was based on a diary entry he wrote in 1822 while visiting Byron in Italy:

> Lord Byron gets up at two. I get up, quite contrary to my usual custom . . . at 12. After breakfast we sit talking till six. From six to eight we gallop through the pine forests . . . we then come home and dine,

> and sit up gossiping till six in the morning. I don't suppose this will kill me in a week or fortnight, but I shall not try it longer. Lord B's establishment consists, besides servants, of ten horses, eight enormous dogs, three monkeys, five cats, an eagle, a crow, and a falcon; and all these, except the horses, walk about the house, which every now and then resounds with their unarbitrated quarrels, as if they were the masters of it . . . P.S. I find that my enumeration of the animals in this Circean Palace was defective . . . I have just met on the grand staircase five peacocks, two guinea hens, and an Egyptian crane.

In one of the letters I wrote to Hogg in Shelley's voice, I quote one of his real lines from a letter he wrote to Hogg in 1814: "The contemplation of female excellence is the favourite food of my imagination."

The rest of the line reads as follows: "Here was ample scope for admiration: novelty added a peculiar charm to the intrinsic merit of the objects: I had been unaccustomed to the mildness the intelligence the delicacy of a cultivated female." This letter also details his first meeting with Mary.

Byron's letters provided the basis for his language throughout the novel. I did not have to exaggerate. An example from one of his real letters (not about Claire): "fucked her twice a day for the last six—today is the seventh—but no Sabbath day—for we meet at Midnight."

In the scene in which he finds out about Lady Caroline Lamb's novel, the "fuck and publish" line is Byron's. Also his is the line about the "sordid League of Incest." Byron wrote, in a letter to Medwin, "There is no story so absurd that they did not invent it at my cost. I was watched by the glasses on the opposite side of the Lake, and by glasses too that must have had very distorted optics."

In a few instances, I have used a line from Mary's journal or Byron's letters in their dialogue. For example, when Claire and Byron discuss Joanna Baillie, Byron says, "The composition of a tragedy requires testicles—If this be true Lord knows what Joanna Baillie does—I suppose she borrows them." This is from a letter Byron wrote to Annabella

Milbanke on September 6, 1813. Byron's line "I am subject to casual giddiness and [faintnesses], which is so like a fine lady, that I am rather ashamed of the disorder" is from a letter. Looking back on her time in Lynmouth, Claire did write, "A life of sixteen years is already too much to bear."

During the mushroom scene, Mary's nonsense is from her real journal entry dated October 6, 1816: "Come & look; here's a cat eating roses; she'll turn into a woman; when beasts eat these roses they turn into men & women."

Also in that scene, Claire recalls Shelley's counterpoint to Baillie's play *Orra* in his play *The Cenci*. This play was not written until 1820, yet Shelley's words relate so much to Claire's journey and my view of Shelley's treatment of her that I chose to have it appear here, with her remembering his actual words.

An interesting follow-up to this is a review that appeared in *The Literary Gazette and Journal of Belles Lettres, Arts, Sciences* (April 1, 1820). It detailed the horrors of the play:

> We have heard of Mr. Shelley's genius; and were it exercised upon any subject not utterly revolting to human nature, we might acknowledge it. But there are topics so disgusting . . . and this is one of them; there are themes so vile . . . as this is; there are descriptions so abhorrent to mankind . . . and this drama is full of them; there are crimes so beastly and demoniac . . . in which The Cenci riots and luxuriates, that no feelings can be excited by their obtrusion but those of detestation at the choice, and horror at the elaboration. We protest most solemnly, that when we reached the last page of this play, our minds were so impressed with its odious and infernal character, that we could not believe it to be written by a mortal being for the gratification of his fellow-creatures on this earth: it seemed to be the production of a fiend, and calculated for the entertainment of devils in hell . . . That monsters of wickedness have been seen in the world, is too true.

When I wrote about the "two Claires," I borrowed from Shelley's exact words, which were "there are two Claire Clairmonts. One who can be irritable for she is prone to nervousness and though you have not had an episode recently one assumes the terror still lurks. This Claire can be quiet and withdrawn and with good reason for the world seems to defeat you when really the world offers its embrace to you. The Good Claire is gentle and kind and cheerful the most engaging of creatures." I paraphrase there a real letter Claire wrote to Byron in April 1816.

The dialogue during one of the early Diodati dinners is based on one from Moore's account in his compiled book of Byron's letters and diaries.

Shelley did write to Hogg in the summer of 1816 and reference reading *Heloise.* His one line that appears in the letter is "I conclude that Rousseau is the greatest man the world has produced since Milton." This letter is available in the New York Public Library Digital Archives. Also in that letter, I quote some of Shelley's real words from an October 14 journal entry:

> Jane's insensibility and incapacity for the slightest degree of friendship. The feelings occasioned by this discovery prevent me from maintaining any measure in security. This highly incorrect; subversion of the first principles of true philosophy; characters, particularly those which are unformed, may change. Beware of weakly giving way to trivial sympathies. Content yourself with one great affection—with a single mighty hope; let the rest of mankind be the subjects of your benevolence, your justice, and, as human beings, of your sensibility; but, as you value many hours of peace, never suffer more than one even to approach the hallowed circle. Nothing should shake the truly great spirit which is not sufficiently mighty to destroy it.

As I explored the stories of each character and the inspiration they might have taken from their environment and interactions, I also wove in details or observations from their poems or stories. An example of this is the scene after Byron ends things with Claire (again), when she and Mary are by the lake eating bread. In Mary's novel, Frankenstein warns his companion, "You seek for knowledge and wisdom, as I once did; and I ardently hope that the gratification of your wishes may not be a serpent to sting you, as mine has been." I felt Mary would have said those words, likely inspired by *Paradise Lost*, to Claire.

I believe Claire Clairmont was a writer, a journal-poet whose work was never fully realised. Here is an example of her writing from a letter to Fanny during her time away from Mary and Shelley in 1815.

> I wish I had a more amiable and romantic picture to present to you, such as shepherds and shepherdesses, flocks and madrigals; but this is the truth, and the truth is best at all times. I live in a little cottage, with jasmine and honeysuckle twining over the window; a little downhill garden full of roses, with a sweet arbour. There are only two gentlemen's seats here, and they are both absent. The walks and shrubberies are quite open, and are very delightful. Mr. Foote's stands at top of the hill, and commands distant views of the whole country. A green tottering bridge, flung from rock to rock, joins his garden to his house, and his side of the bridge is a waterfall. One tumbles directly down, and then flows gently onward, while the other falls successively down five rocks, and seems like water running down stone steps. I will tell you, so far, that it is a valley I live in, and perhaps one you may have seen. Two ridges of mountains enclose the village, which is situated at the west end. A river, which you may step over, runs at the foot of the mountains, and trees hang so closely over, that when on a high eminence you sometimes lose sight of it for a quarter of a mile. One ridge of hills is entirely covered with luxuriant trees, the opposite line is entirely bare, with long pathways of slate and gray rocks, so that you might almost fancy they had once been volcanic. Well, enough of the valleys and the mountains.
>
> You told me you did not think I should ever be able to live alone. If you knew my constant tranquility, how cheerful and gay I am, perhaps you would alter your opinion. I am perfectly happy. After so much discontent, such violent scenes, such a turmoil of passion and

hatred, you will hardly believe how enraptured I am with this dear little quiet spot. I am as happy when I go to bed as when I rise. I am never disappointed, for I know the extent of my pleasures; and let it rain or let it be fair weather, it does not disturb my serene mood. This is happiness; this is that serene and uninterrupted rest I have long wished for. It is in solitude that the powers concentre round the soul, and teach it the calm, determined path of virtue and wisdom. Did you not find this—did you not find that the majestic and tranquil mountains impressed deep and tranquil thoughts, and that everything conspired to give a sober temperature of mind, more truly delightful and satisfying than the gayest ebullitions of mirth?

> The foaming cataract and tall rock
> Haunt me like a passion.

In this novel, I tried to stay true to the timeline of Claire's life, including her time in Lynmouth, in London, meeting Byron, and her departure to Geneva; even the snowstorm in London that keeps Claire overnight actually occurred—on April 12, 1816.

There are numerous references in this novel to the writing that was created during this time period. One example in which I take liberties would be when Shelley, on Monster Night, speaks of vampire bats he had seen at a museum exhibition. He attended the exhibit and used a line from the catalogue in the last long poem he wrote, "The Triumph of Life." Of course, we do not know if he uttered this line during the summer at Diodati. It is true that everyone's hands were all over everyone else's work. Claire was transcribing and making small edits and tweaks of both Byron and Shelley's work, Shelley was editing Mary's *Frankenstein* pages, Polidori borrowed Byron's story and Byron then took it back until he gave up and handed it back over to Polidori (Byron was initially credited with writing "The Vampyre"). And Mary edited Shelley's poems posthumously, including changing dates and making it appear that a poem he'd written about Claire was actually about Mary.

When they first arrive at Diodati, the words Claire recalls from her own journal are hers from 1814. "Alps peaked and broken, wondering forward, another retreating now, the light, airy clouds arrested a few moments on their aspiring France, and then fled away, but we might better behold the sublimity of the scene."

For those wishing to read another fictional account from a different angle, I suggest *The Aspern Papers* by Henry James, which is based on Percy Shelley's (and possibly Byron's) letters to Claire.

In his book about Shelley, biographer Richard Holmes moves away from the "long-established Victorian picture of Shelley as a blandly ethereal character" and reveals Shelley instead as "a darker and more earthly, crueler and more capable figure."

I also recommend *In Defense of Harriet Shelley* by Mark Twain. A line that sticks with me: "Shelley had found this child [Mary] of sixteen to his liking, and had wooed her in the graveyard. But that is nothing; it was better than wooing her in her nursery, at any rate, where it might have disturbed the other children." And this line, about Claire Clairmont, struck me: "She was very young and pretty and accommodating, and always ready to do what she could to make things pleasant."

I am grateful for the books, articles, and insights of many researchers, writers, and scholars, in particular Daisy Hay and Nora Crook. Crook's article "Mary Shelley's Concealing 'To—': (Re)addressing Poems" closes in the following way:

> I did not expect this paper to end up being "about" Claire Clairmont, but this brief exploration into the theme of "re-addressing" poems led me that way. It has been known since 1878 that she was the addressee of Shelley's two Constantia poems (the ones known as "To Constantia, Singing" and "To Constantia") and, since 1940, it has been accepted that she [Claire] is the "Comet" of Epipsychidion (White, Shelley, 2: 266). The part she plays in Shelley's poetry (not just in his biography) may be greater than has been recognized or, where recognized, agreed upon. But, looking beyond biography, re-addressing the poems discussed here adjusts our map of Shelley's poetic development, and the poems come out rather better for such

scrutiny. Understanding advances in such small incremental steps.

Art must, sometimes, have to do with puzzles.

This is my version of the relationships and art of 1816, my version of the answers to those puzzles.

In her preface to the 1831 edition of *Frankenstein*, Mary wrote of Byron's challenge: "'We will each write a ghost story,' said Lord Byron; and his proposition was acceded to. There were four of us."

Claire was there—she was the fifth. Her erasure from the stories created is part of the story of that summer. This novel seeks to examine some of the possibilities of her story.

READING LIST & PARTIAL WORKS CONSULTED

"200 years of Frankenstein" by Darren Slade (*Daily Echo*)
"7 Strange Facts about Lord Byron" by Yasser Kayani (*The Culture Trip*)
"Byron in Context/The Poet-Heroin the Work of Byron and Shelley" by Alexander Grammatikos (European Romantic Review)
"The Ambiguous Heritage of *Frankenstein*" *The Endurance of Frankenstein: Essays on Mary Shelley's Novel* by George Levine
The Aspern Papers by Henry James
"Beethoven, Byron, and Bonaparte" by John Clubbe (Napoleon.org)
"Beginning Life" by Richard Lansdown
Bread or Blood by Alfred James Peacock
"A Brief History of Homeopathy" by I. Loudon
"A Bundle of 18th-Century Love Letters Is Unsealed at Last" by Jenny Gross (*New York Times*)
Byron and the Forms of Thought by Anthony Howe
Byron and the Romantics in Switzerland by Elma Dangerfield
Byron, Life and Legend by Fiona MacCarthy
"Byron's 'The Giaour'" by Adam Roberts (*Medium*)
Byron's Letters and Journals, edited by Leslie Marchand
"Byron's Lover Takes Revenge from the Grave" by Dalya Alberge (*The Guardian*)
Camilla by Fanny Burney, edited by Edward A. Bloom and Lillian D. Bloom
"*The Cenci*: A Tragedy in Five Acts" (*The Literary Gazette, and Journal of Belles Lettres, Arts, Sciences*, review date 1 April 1820)
"Claire Clairmont and Mary Shelley" by Deirdre Coleman (*Women's Writing*)
Claire Clairmont and the Shelleys by R. Gittings and J. Manton
"Claire Clairmont on Her Letters and Journals" by Lesley McDowell (Wordsworth.org)
"Claire Clairmont's Fair Copy of Shelley's 'Ode to Naples'" by M. Rossington (*The Review of English Studies*)
The Clairmont Correspondence, edited by Marion Kingston Stocking
A Classical Dictionary of the Vulgar Tongue by Francis Grose
The Climate of London by Luke Howard
"Climatic, Environmental and Human Consequences of the Largest Known Historic Eruption" by Clive Oppenheimer (*Physical Geography*)

"Cooking the Books" by Simon Fanshawe (*The Guardian*)
"Copies of Mary Shelley's Original *Frankenstein* Text to Be Published" by Alison Flood (*The Guardian*)
The Development of Byron's Philosophy of Knowledge by Emily A. Bernhard Jackson
The Diary of Dr. John William Polidori, edited by William Michael Rossetti
"Did Mary Shelley Actually Lose her Virginity to Percy on Top of Her Mother's Grave?" by Olivia Rutigliano (*LitHub*)
"Documenting Revision" by Robert Brinkley (*Keats-Shelley Journal*)
"Does it Matter if Mary Shelley was Bisexual?" by Fern Riddell (*The Guardian*)
"Dr. Stephanie Forward Explains the Key Ideas and Influences of Romanticism" (British Library)
"Dr. Polidori and the Genesis of *Frankenstein*" by James Rieger (*Studies in English Literature 1500–1900)*
"The Eerie Gravestone Where Frankenstein's Story Began" by Flora Carr (*Time*)
"The Encouragement I Received": Emma and the Language of Sexual Assault; https://jasna.org/publications-2/persuasions-online/vol37no1/easton/ (Jane Austin Society of North America)
The Endurance of Frankenstein, edited by George Levine and U. C. Knoepflmacher
"An Epic Poet As Mary Shelley's Co-Author" by Nick Owchar (*Los Angeles Times*)
"An Essay on the Shaking Palsy" by James Parkinson
"Every Cloud" by Eleanor Fitzsimons (*Beside Every Man*)
Fantasmagoriana by Jean-Baptiste Benoît Eyriès
"Fleeting Gestures and Changing Styles of Greeting" by Penelope J. Corfield (*Urban History*)
"The Forgotten Drug Trips of the Nineteenth Century" by Clare Bucknell (*The New Yorker*)
"Frankenstein at 200" by Fiona Sampson (*The Guardian*)
The French Cook by Louis Eustache Ude (Katherine Golden Bitting Collection on Gastronomy)
The Gay Subculture in Georgian England by Rictor Norton
"Georgian Attitudes Towards Homosexuality were More Tolerant than Previously Thought" by Ian Randall (*Daily Mail*)
"A Giant of Painting Sheds New Light on Darkness" by Seph Rodney (*New York Times*)
"The Gruesome History of Making Human Skeletons" by Sarah Laskow (*Atlas Obscura*)
Hebrew Melodies by J. Braham and I. Nathan
"Hidden Demon Uncovered in 18th-Century Painting" by Amanda Holpuch (*New York Times*)
Hidden Labor and the Naked Body by Joshua Nguyen
"The History of Pediatric Infectious Diseases" by Stanford T. Shulman (*Pediatric Research*)

Denlinger, Elizabeth. "Horrid Mysteries of Cl Cl 26: A Tale of Mothers and Daughters." 19: Interdisciplinary Studies in the Long Nineteenth Century, 2018. doi:10.16995/NTN.817. (New York Public Library)
"A Hospital Visit Reveals Medieval Secrets Hidden in Books" by Katherine Kornei (*New York Times*)
"How I Made a Remarkable Discovery in LGBT History" *by Eamonn O'Keeffe*
"How Not to F*ck Up Your Face" by Valerie Monroe (*The Cut*)
"How to Stay Sane in Brutalizing Times" by David Brooks (*New York Times*)
"How Twitching Frog Legs Helped Inspire *Frankenstein*" by Erin Blakemore (*Smithsonian Magazine*)
http://hibiscus-sinensis.com/regency/skincare.htm
http://knarf.english.upenn.edu/Gifs/shelhse.html
http://knarf.english.upenn.edu/Places/cologny.html
http://www.katetattersall.com/early-victorian-era-make-up/
http://www.newsteadabbeybyronsociety.org/works/downloads/hebrew_melodies.pdf
http://www.oldandinteresting.com/antique-irons-smoothers-mangles.aspx
http://www.suzanneburdon.com/blog/2017/5/13/mary-shelley-and-motherhood
http://www.thedqtimes.com/pages/castpages/other/Victorian%20Life/victorianlifdollorigin.htm
https://beatriceknight.com/all-things-regency/regency-color-compendium/
https://byronsmuse.wordpress.com/tag/claire-clairmont/
https://canceratlas.cancer.org/history-cancer/19th-century/
https://candicehern.com/regencyworld/carriage-dress-november-1816/
https://en.wikipedia.org/wiki/Germ_theory_of_disease
https://eurohistorymed.weebly.com/1800s.html
https://fashionhistory.fitnyc.edu/1810-1819/
https://findoes.etoncollege.com/percy-bysshe-shelley/
https://frankensteindiaries.com/did-mary-shelley-and-jane-austen-ever-meet/
https://herreputationforaccomplishment.wordpress.com/2015/05/06/anatomy-of-a-regency-letter/
https://janeaustens.house
https://janelark.blog/2012/11/12/my-scandalous-woman-today-is-claire-jane-clairmont-byrons-mistress-and-mary-shelleys-who-wrote-frankenstein-stepsister/
https://jasnasw.com/2019/09/29/recap-of-jane-austen-meets-mary-shelley/
https://knarf.english.upenn.edu/Indexes/timeline.html#1810
https://knarf.english.upenn.edu/People/lewis.html
http://www.katetattersall.com/early-victorian-era-make-up/
https://learninglab.si.edu/collections/cosmetics-and-hair-for-women-in-the-1800s/jt0XFbuc078Tuzh8#r/209735
https://navigator.health.org.uk/theme/apothecaries-act-1815#:~:text=The%20 1815%20Apothecaries%20Act%20gave,been%20a%20lack%20of%20 standardisation

https://pastnow.wordpress.com/2016/03/30
march-30-1816-byrons-a-sketch-from-private-life/
https://petercochran.files.wordpress.com/2009/02/06-london-1815-18163.pdf
https://regencygentleman.wordpress.com/2015/01/09/the-top-hat/
https://regencyredingote.wordpress.com/2009/09/11/the-quill-the-regency-pen
(special thanks Kathryn Kane, *Kalligraph*)
https://regencyredingote.wordpress.com/2014/08/22/
fireplaces-during-regency-summers/
https://reginajeffers.blog/2025/02/14/cost-of-items-during-the-regency-period/
https://robertgreenbergmusic.com/mozart-clementi-duel/
https://rth.org.uk/regency-period/family-life/servants
https://shannondonnelly.com/2013/09/30/the-regency-meal-or-food-glorious-food/
https://shannonselin.com/2021/12/how-did-people-shop-early 1800s
https://susannaives.com/wordpress/2017/10/nursing-your-regency-infant/
https://susannaives.com/wordpress/
tidbits-on-mid-victorian-era-menstrual-hygiene/#
https://theshelleyconference.com/2021/09/02/
shelley200-interview-professor-nora-crook/
https://via.library.depaul.edu/cgi/viewcontent.cgi?article=1274&context=etd
https://victorianvocabulary.weebly.com/glossary-of-victorian-slang.
html#:~:text=Moucher%2C%20Moocher%3A%20A%20rural%20vagrant
https://www.themorgan.org/sites/default/files/pdf/education/
FrankensteinFamilyBios.pdf
https://victorianweb.org/previctorian/letters/rates.html
https://www.amdigital.co.uk/insights/blog/
byron-and-hobhouse-in-mediterranean-europe
https://www.aroid.eu/european-aroids/dracunculus/
https://www.ashmolean.org/press/new-ashmolean-story-gallery-press-release
https://www.bournemouthecho.co.uk/
news/15803922.200-years-frankenstein-mary-shelleys-bournemouth-links/#
https://www.britannica.com/topic/Childe-Harolds-Pilgrimage
https://www.britannica.com/topic/history-of-Europe/Health-and-sickness
https://www.britannica.com/topic/history-of-Europe/The-age-of-revolution
https://www.britishmuseum.org/about-us/british-museum-story/history
https://www.carnegiehall.org/Explore/Articles/2021/04/30/
Beethoven-A-Brief-History
https://www.davidcastleton.net/byron-polidori-vampire-villa-diodati-vampyre/
https://www.electricscotland.com/culture/features/singasang/dark_lochnagar.
htm
https://www.georgette-heyer.com/slang.html
https://www.geriwalton.com/the-postman/
https://www.historicalclimatology.com/features/
bread-or-blood-climate-insecurity-in-east-anglia-in-1816,

https://www.history.com/this-day-in-history/lord-byron-swims-the-hellespont
https://www.kristenkoster.com/a-primer-on-regency-era-currency/#:~:text=Terms%20for%20Regency%20era%20currency,%2C%20to%20Quids%20 (squids)
https://www.kristenkoster.com/a-regency-era-carriage-primer/
https://www.literarytraveler.com/articles/lord-byrons-castle-chillon/
https://www.louisebooyens.com/post/regency-interiors
https://www.mackinacparks.com/wp-content/uploads/2014/01/Games.pdf
https://www.metmuseum.org/art/collection/search/435888
https://www.nytimes.com/2023/11/09/world/europe/french-love-letters-18th-century.html
https://www.penguin.co.uk/articles/2022/08/geneva-holiday-frankenstein-mary-shelley#
https://www.plannedparenthood.org/files/2613/9611/6275/History_of_BC_Methods.pdf
https://www.plutobooks.com/blog/a-philosophical-view-of-reform-the-politics-of-percy-bysshe-shelley/#:~:text=As%20a%20boy%2C%20Shelley%20was,to%20vote%20on%20the%20question
https://www.romtext.org.uk/frankenstein-and-fantasmagoriana-stories-7-8-la-chambre/
https://www.taylorfrancis.com/chapters/edit/10.4324/9781315846507-15/constantia-percy-bysshe-shelley, https://www.thecarriagefoundation.org.uk
https://www.ucl.ac.uk/news/2005/aug/hand-other-woman-shelleys-life
https://www.uv.es/~fores/msaron1.html#:~:text=Her%20first%20child%2C%20Clara%2C%20was,day%20that%20the%20baby%20died
https://www.waldwissen.net/en/forest-ecology/forest-plants/shrubs-and-herbs/the-stinging-nettle
https://www.waterdatabase.com/lakes/lake-geneva/
https://www.wattpad.com/333536348-reading-the-regency-the-postal-system/page/2
https://www.wildlifetrusts.org/extinct-british-wildlife
https://www.worldjewishcongress.org/en/about/communities/ch#:~:text=During%20the%2017th%20century%2C%20
"I Love Not Woman the Less, but Man More" by Judith Shulevitz (*New York Times*)
"The Image of Greece in *Childe Harold's Pilgrimage* and *Don Juan*" by Stephen Minta (*Byron's Poetry*)
In Defense of Harriet Shelley by Mark Twain
In Search of Mary Shelley by Fiona Sampson
"Infanticide and Abortion in Nineteenth-Century Britain" by R. Sauer (*Population Studies*)
"The Influence of Switzerland on the Life and Writing of Edward Gibbon" by Brian Norman (*Voltaire Foundation*)
"Intertextual Abolitionists" by Jake Spangler

"Jane Austen's Lifelong Health Problems and Final Illness" by A. Upfal (*Medical Humanities*)
"John Steinbeck and the Missing *Kamatz* in *East of Eden*" by Daniel Levin (*Steinbeck Review*)
Journal of a West India Proprietor by Matthew Gregory Lewis
The Journals of Claire Clairmont, edited by Marion Kingston Stocking
The Journals of Mary Shelley by Mary Shelley, edited by Paula R. Feldman and Diana Scott-Kilvert
Lady Byron Vindicated by Harriet Beecher Stowe
"Lake Geneva as Shelley and Byron Knew It" by Tony Perrottet (*New York Times*)
Letters and Journals of Lord Byron by Thomas Moore
Lexicon Balatronicum by Francis Grose
The Life and Letters of Mary Wollstonecraft Shelley by Florence A. Thomas Marshall
The Life of Percy Bysshe Shelley by Thomas Medwin
"'Like a Fanciful Kind of Half Being'" by Martina Reuter (*Hypatia*)
"Locks of Beethoven's Hair Offer New Clues to the Mystery of His Deafness" by Gina Kolata (*New York Times*)
"The London Beer Flood of 1814" by Ben Johnson (*Historic UK*)
Lord Byron: The Complete Poetical Works, edited by Jerome J. McGann and Barry Weller
"Lord Byron Letter to Lady Byron, February 8, 1816," edited by Marilee Hanson
"Lord Byron Letters to Percy Bysshe Shelley, 26 April 1821," edited by Marilee Hanson
"Lord Byron's Darkest Summer" by Nina Martyris (*Lapham's Quarterly*)
"Lord Byron's Deformed Foot" by J. V. Hirschmann (*The Byron Journal*)
"Louise Duvillard of Geneva, the Shelleys' Nursemaid" by Emily W. Sunstein (*Keats-Shelley Journal*)
Mary Shelley: A Biography by Muriel Spark
"Mary Shelley: From a Scandalous Affair to the Creation of a Monster" by Lauren Corba (*Books Tell You Why*)
"Mary Shelley's Concealing 'To—': (Re)Addressing Poems" by Nora Crook (*The Wordsworth Circle*)
"Medical Dissertation on Nostalgia" by Johannes Hofer, translated by Carolyn Kiser Anspach
The Mirror of the Graces by A Lady of Distinction
Monthly Agricultural Reports in *The Observer* from 1816
"Mothering Monsters" by Anne Mellor (public lecture)
"My Hideous Progeny" by Mary Poovey (PMLA)
"Naughty by Nature" by Remy Melina (*LIVE SCIENCE*)
The New Family Receipt-Book, printed by Squire and Warwick
"Night-Time Logic" by Sara Cutaia (*Chicago Review of Books*)
Nineteenth-Century Literary Criticism, edited by Russel Whitaker

Obstetrics by Charles Meigs
"On the Very Scary Rise of the First Literary Vampire" by Nick Groom (*Lit Hub*)
Oregon Jerusalem Historical Society post, October 2015
Papers of Dodson and Pulman, Solicitors of Taunton and Vicki Parslow Stafford and Mary Jane's daughter for transcriptions of originals held by the Somerset Record Office
"Percy Bysshe Shelley" by Graham Henderson (Wordsworth.org)
A Philosophical Enquiry into the Origin of Our Ideas of the Sublime and Beautiful by Edmund Burke
"A Philosophical View of Reform" in *Percy Bysshe Shelley* by Jacqueline Mulhallen
"Pride and Prejudice and FEMINISM" by Sarah Lorraine (Frock Flicks)
"Reader, I shagged him" by Tanya Gold (*The Guardian*)
"Regency Swimwear" by Sarah Murden (All Things Georgian)
https://rth.org.uk
"Review of Fiona Sampson's *In Search of Mary Shelley*" by Rachel Cooke (*The Guardian*)
"A Revolution in Horror Literature" by E. Kaçmaz and H. Ş. Yavuz (*Journal of Language and Literature Studies*)
Romantic Climates, edited by Anne Collett and Olivia Murphy
"Secret Museums" by B. Pietras (*CNF Quarterly*)
"The Secret Power of Menopause" by Liza Mundy (*The Atlantic*)
"'She Walks in Beauty' and the Theory of the Sublime" by Howard Needler (*The Byron Journal*)
"Shelley and Claire Again" by John Harrington Smith (*Studies in Philology*)
"Shelley and Claire Clairmont" by Edith Wyatt (*The North American Review*)
"Shelley and Claire Clairmont" by John Harrington Smith (*PMLA*)
"Shelley Himself in Petticoats" by Stephen Hancock (*Romanticism on the Net*)
Shelley: The Pursuit by Richard Holmes
Shelley's Ghost by Stephen Hebron and Elizabeth Denlinger
Shelley's Poetry and Prose by Percy Bysshe Shelley, edited by Donald H. Reiman and Sharon B. Powers
Simpson's Chelsea, Pimlico, Brompton, and Knightsbridge Directory, and Court Guide Including List of Vestry, Parish Officers, Post Office Intelligence, Chelsea Charities, &c. &c (1863 London) by Anonymous
"The Siren's Call" by Nick Owchar (*Los Angeles Times*)
So Late into the Night, edited by Leslie A. Marchand
The Social and Political Philosophy of Mary Wollstonecraft, edited by Sandrine Bergès and Alan Coffee
"Songs and Stanzas, Stanzas and Songs," in *Byron's Poetry* by Peter Cochran
"Stop Multitasking. No, Really" by Oliver Burkeman (*New York Times*)
"Switzerland in the 19th Century" (Eidgenössisches Departement für auswärtige Angelegenheiten)

Tell Me Everything by Erika Krouse
"These Curious-Looking Plants Have an Addictive Appeal" by Margaret Roach (*New York Times*)
The Times of London digital archive, various dates in May of 1816
"'Truth of Soul's Life' or 'Distorted Optics'?" by Patrick H. Vincent (*The Keats-Shelley Review*)
"The Turncoat's True Character" by Duncan Wu (*The Guardian*)
"Undying Dread" by Franz Lidz (*New York Times*)
The United States Practical Receipt Book by A Practical Chemist
"The Universe Is a Haunted House" by Daniel Pietersen (*Sublime Horror*)
Victorian Parlor Games by Patrick Beaver
A Vindication of the Rights of Woman by Mary Wollstonecraft
"The Voynich Manuscript, Dr Johannes Hartlieb and the Encipherment of Women's Secrets" by Keagan Brewer and Michelle L. Lewis (*Social History of Medicine*)
"Was Lord Byron England's 1st Vampire?" by David Castleton (davidcastleton.net)
"We Shall be Monsters" by Jeff J. S. Black (public lecture)
"The Wholesome Revival of Byron" by Paul Elmore More (*The Atlantic Monthly*)
"Winter Foraging in Cold Climates" by Ashley Adamant (*Practical Self Reliance*)
Women's Silence, Men's Violence by Anna Clark
The Works of Lord Byron, Letters and Journals by Lord Byron
The works of Mary Shelley, Byron, Shelley, Coleridge, Wordsworth, and Keats
"World's First Travel Guide Goes on Display in London" by Julia Buckley (*CNN*)
The Young Man's Best Companion and Guide to Useful Knowledge by John Dougall
Young Romantics by Daisy Hay

WITH GRATITUDE

TO GUILLERMO DEL TORO and Chuck Hogan, whose op-ed "Why Vampires Never Die" in *The New York Times* on July 30, 2009, immediately inspired this novel.

To my late agent, Esmond Harmsworth—who loved this book and supported me so much during the writing of it. The world is a lesser place without you in it. I will be forever grateful for your kindness, wit, and literary gifts. I am gutted that you are not here to share a tray of sardines.

To everyone at Aevitas, especially Jen Gates. Here's to our storied beginning. To Godine for being the publishing house I always dreamed of—David, thank you. Celia, so many miles of thanks. Beth and Virginia, thank you. Natalie Sousa, thank you.

To all of the indie bookstores and libraries that support me. To Boston College Library for resources and space.

Writing is mainly solitary, and I'm thankful for early readers and my writing community and those who have helped in immeasurable ways: Rick Franklin and Little Guy, Adam Strauss, Heather Swain, Josie Hughes, Pie-Boy (bestie and book supporter), Barbara Strauss, Peter Strauss, Heather Swain, Owen Egerton, Maria Pinto, Walter Smelt, Heather Swain, Dawn Tripp, Zach Dodes, Dan Vonnegut, Lisa Borders, Erin McHugh, Barry and Gretchen Mazur, Lulu Davis, Joan Kwon Glass, Brendan Halpin, Jonathan Wilson, Mary Cotton, Elizabeth Lane, Angela Buchdahl, Mary Ann Buckley, Ben Shattuck, Rae Titcomb, Nick Petrulakis, Wendy Dodson, Nick Petrulakis, Desmond Hall, Jeffrey Lyle, Karen Grotberg, Steven Dunn and the Tinned Fish

Group, Stephen Naron at Yale for Yiddish help. To Nancy Bauer for philosophy expertise. Hooter Von Binken, Annie Hartnett, Marilyn Naron, Josie Naron, David Kudan, Heather Swain, Tania Rodriguez, David Lindsay-Abaire, Esther Choo, Laura Fischman, Jamie Forbes, Lisa Baker, Tarim Chung, Laurie Gwen Shapiro, Heather Swain; Asa Strauss and Ashley Clarkson for the fairy tale conversation; Jessica Shattuck, Claire Messud, Taylor Fogelquist, Ted Franklin and Dorian Lightbown, JC Smith, Deirdre Coleman, Daisy Hay; James Connolly (JFC)—forever gratitude for my foundation; Susan Church, Kristin Knuuttila, Elizabeth Silverman, David Yannetti, and again and always, Heather Swain.

This book is partly about siblings, and I am so grateful for mine—Jon and Nick.

To my mom, who cannot read this but who is woven into the pages.

Most and Forever—to A, N, S, E, A. You have my heart.

BOOK GROUP DISCUSSION QUESTIONS

1. "All love stories are ghost stories waiting to happen." What does Emily Franklin mean by this?

2. Who was the greatest love of Claire's life?

3. Claire says she has a voice in her head that can be critical and yet that voice isn't hers—who is yours?

4. What does Byron mean when he asks Claire to "say the thing"? In what ways does Claire resist and then ultimately do that?

5. Betrayal is part of the novel. In what ways is Claire betrayed—and by whom?

6. What themes in the novel are relevant today?

7. Who are the monsters in this story?

8. Can we separate the creators from their creations? That is, can we appreciate art made by people who mistreat others? What does this mean for you personally?

9. Claire calls herself an Ordinary Girl. What does this mean?

10. Discuss the idea of "being born into comparison." If you have siblings, does this resonate for you?

11. Siblings can be our fiercest defenders and closest friends and can also wound us easily. How does Mary treat Claire? Does this change in the course of the book?

12. Is Claire's view of Mary correct?

13. What is your view of Shelley reading Claire's journal in the coppice?

14. Who do you think was the father of Claire's child?

15. Who do you think sent Claire the journal?

16. If you received a journal from one year of your life, which year would you most like—or find challenging—to read back on?

NOTE ON THE TYPE

The text of *Love & Other Monsters* has been set in Garamond Premier. It is the creation of Robert Slimbach based upon designs and cuts of the original work of Claude Garamond he viewed in Antwerp, Belgium, in 1994. He worked extensively on the family. It was released by Adobe in 2005.

Claude Garamond's own roman letters were designed in his own Paris foundry. Modeled upon the roman of Aldus Manutius, it became the standard by the end of the eighteenth century. Garamond's cuts are still holding strong today.

Book design and composition by Brooke Koven